THE OTHER SIDE

THE OTHER SIDE

MARK LEICHLITER

LEVEL BEST BOOKS

First published by Level Best Books 2021

Author Photo Credit: Shawna Benson Photography

First edition

ISBN: 978-1-953789-52-5

Cover art by LEVEL BEST DESIGNS

This book was professionally typeset on Reedsy.
Find out more at reedsy.com

For Patti, always;
and in loving memory of my father
Albert W. Leichliter

All this might be easier if
there wasn't a song
still lifting us above it,
if wind didn't trouble

my mind like water.
I half expect to see you
fill the autumn air
like breath–

—KEVIN YOUNG, "REDEMPTION SONG"

Praise for THE OTHER SIDE

"*The Other Side* is a haunting procedural propelled by a smartly-developed cast of characters and rich descriptions of unforgettable landscapes. When Detective Steve Wendell tries to find a missing teen-ager, he must navigate the small, tourist-ridden towns of Northwest Montana to discover what happened to her while proving he's a resourceful and conscientious hero with a heart. You won't want to miss this perfect blend of atmosphere, mystery, and a protagonist you won't forget."

— Christine Carbo, award-winning, best-selling author of the Glacier Mystery Series

"A chilling story, surprising twists…everything you'd want in a great crime novel."

— Catherine McKenzie, bestselling author of *The Good Liar* and *Hidden*

"Sink into a gripping police procedural with solitary, cerebral Detective Steve Wendell as he struggles to find missing seventeen-year-old Brittany Rogers in the uncompromising wilds and beauty of Montana's Flathead Lake. Could she have fled the boredom of her small-town life? Or did she fall prey to a twisted human predator? As her father stokes resentments and burrows into conspiracy theories, Brittany's mother loses more than her daughter. Captivating characters and a landscape that simultaneously entices and menaces lure the reader into a page-turning novel of suspense and discovery."

— Deborah Turrell Atkinson, author of the Storm Kayama suspense series and *Feathers in the Soul: A Guide for Families Struggling with a Child's Addiction*

"The Other Side is a taut and thrilling tale. Mark Leichliter knows Montana as well as he knows his characters' dark and hidden hearts.Steve Wendell is a masterful creation—a dogged and honest man who can't forget the faces of the victims he serves.I couldn't turn the pages fast enough."

— Alyson Hagy, author of *Boleto* and *Scribe*

"Wow. Bravo to Mark Leichliter on his outstanding debut. *The Other Side* has more twists and turns than an alley in Venice, and detective Steve Wendell—committed, unrelenting, true to himself and his job—is exactly the man to uncover the devastating truth hidden below the waters of Montana's Flathead Lake."

— Peter W. J. Hayes, Silver Falchion and Derringer Nominated author of the Vic Lenoski mysteries.

"Small town secrets and hidden lives turn deadly in Mark Leichliter's *The Other Side*. Richly drawn characters and vivid settings are reminiscent of Gillian Flynn's *Sharp Objects* and will pull the reader into an intricately plotted thrill ride."

— James L'Etoile, author of *At What Cost, Bury the Past,* and *Black Label*

"Mark Leichliter's writing is strong and lyrical without calling attention to itself, brave and at the same time showing an admirable amount of restraint. He creates characters who captivate the reader. They surprise us, but in a way that ultimately feels right, inevitable."

— Barry Kitterman, author of *From the San Joaquin*, Fiction Editor of *Zone 3*

"Mark Leichliter's writing is clean, crisp, entertaining at all times. His characters fascinate, the plot charges ahead, he makes the reader think without hammering a point of view into your head. He is a writer to be savored."

— Tim Sandlin, author of *Rowdy in Paris* and *Jimi Hendrix Turns Eighty*

"Mark Leichliter is an accomplished novelist who portrays the breadth of human experience with intelligence and grace. His deeply affecting prose immerses readers in the lives of the lovelorn, the seeking, and the lost. His remarkable fictional worlds, diffuse with mystery, address the larger questions of life with beauty and sensitivity."

— Marcelle Heath, author of *Is That All There Is?* (forthcoming from Awst Press 2022)

Prologue

The girl stepped up on the lowest rung of the elaborate driveway gate, grasped two wrought iron bars, and thrust her head into the space between. Short like her mother, she struggled to see beyond the screening trees and the long, curving stone wall, making out only glimpses of the copper-accented roof and two of the three stone chimneys rising from the lakeside estate.

"Get down," Kristen hissed. "Somebody will see you."

"What if they do?" the girl said, gazing down the private road that curled through a deliberate, domesticated Montana forest. "Can you imagine?"

"Imagine what?"

"Living like this," she said. She released one hand and swung around to face her friend. "It's like something out of a movie. Think about the parties they must throw. House band, valet service, five-star catering. We're talkin' off the hook."

"Like you're going to be invited somewhere with valet service."

"Well, when I do, don't expect me to bring you."

"Unless you start turning in your homework, the only way you'll ever see the inside of this place is as part of a catering crew," Kristen said. "Minimum wage, tacky uniforms."

"Thanks, mom. I guess we can't all spend Saturday nights doing calculus. Don't be jealous because I want to live a little." She looked down the length of the stone wall. "Can't see shit."

"You can see it from the lake, you know. If you would get on a boat, that is. I've been by it like a thousand times."

"Big deal. You've seen it from a boat. I want to go inside. I'll bet this is where Johnny Depp lives."

"You're a moron. I mean, do you really see Johnny Depp living in Montana? If he did, it's not here. Look. The initials are right here as big as your face," Kristen said, pointing at wrought iron scrollwork welded within a circle where the two halves of the gate met. "Just another rich asshole."

"Yeah, well, I still want to see inside. See how the other half lives."

Both girls, seniors at Flathead High School in Kalispell, lived less than a mile away on the other side of Highway 93. Neither had her own car, and walking along the lake together was something they had done since middle school.

"Stop daydreaming. Let's get coffee before it rains." Kristen turned back.

Reluctantly, the girl released her hold on the gate and jumped down. "Hold up," she said to Kristen, who turned and stopped, her arms folded and her head lowered in annoyance. It was a stance regularly assumed, the head-tilt a near-constant for her height. "Spot me a smoke," the girl said, ignoring Kristen's glare. Over the last year, smoking had grown as much an excuse for their walks as talking, a habit both hid from their parents.

"You owe me, you know. Like you don't always owe me. I even bought your movie ticket last time we went."

"When did you and I go to a movie, dude? Like in middle school or something."

Kristen reddened. "Last Christmas. And I paid for your lunch just two weeks ago."

"I'll catch you for the smokes Monday when we're in town. Mom's off. She said I can take her car. We can do lunch and we'll be even."

The girls smoked as they walked, their exhaled breath joining with the mist that drifted off Flathead Lake, creeping up the steep, forested slope and curling among the trees. The pavement, sporadically wet where trees did not shelter the road, harbored mats of pine needles clotted in small puddles remaining from the previous day.

* * *

"Was there anything unusual about that day?" the police asked Kristen after her friend was reported missing. "You may have been one of the last people to see her before she disappeared. The smallest thing could help. Something you did that day. Something you talked about."

"Anything unusual?" No, she thought. Just Britany being classic Britany, bumming smokes and dreaming about people who knew places far beyond this one. "The only thing unusual that's ever happened to us," she wanted to tell him, "is you telling me that Britany has disappeared."

I

Part One

Chapter One

For the first time in two days, Sheila Rodgers was alone. With quiet, she might think, might solve the riddle of her daughter's absence. Yet she hadn't a moment's quiet before her younger sister called with accusations that Sheila was overreacting. Her sister's reprimands echoed those of her husband, who grumbled that Britany was "pissing right in our faces. Off God knows where playing adult."

"The police should be forming search parties," Sheila had pleaded with him. "They should be using helicopters and dogs."

"Stop it," he had replied. "She lied to us, and now she knows her lies are gonna come home to roost. When she drags her butt home, she's got questions to answer."

"Tom," Sheila pleaded. "We have no idea where she is. Anything could have happened."

"She's testing us, is all. Now she's afraid to own up to it. You've been too soft on her."

Her husband's voice had sounded again in her head as her sister said, "So she's not your perfect angel, Sheila. You and I both have some stories we'd rather Mom didn't know. I'm sure she went to a party or something, had a few drinks. She'll be home any time now, embarrassed for a hard lesson learned. Don't make a mountain out of a—"

Sheila had touched "end call" while her sister was in mid-sentence and then immediately dialed Britany's phone, praying her sister and husband would be right. She'd gladly let them throw her "overreaction" in her face if it meant Britany was okay. Britany's recorded greeting on her voicemail still sounded as Sheila dropped the phone on the couch. She followed the phone's path, slumping like a marionette cut from its strings.

* * *

The previous day she had called her daughter's phone every fifteen minutes for over five hours. Each time the call went straight to voicemail as it had done now. When she'd made the first call, she left an angry message demanding to know why her daughter wasn't awake. "I explicitly said you could spend the night at Kristen's so long as you were back here ready for church this morning. You're going to make us late," she'd said. Now she fantasized about hacking into Britany's mailbox to erase the shrill timbre of her anger. When she dialed a second time, her anger had only accelerated, so much so she hadn't left a message but instead redialed and hung up twice more in a span of a minute. When she tried again ten minutes later, she'd opted for guilt over anger and left a message that said, "Okay, sleepyhead, I'm really disappointed that you're missing church. Get yourself home as soon as you get this. I want both bathrooms spotless. Gram is coming over."

They had returned home from church and a trip to the grocery store to an empty house and dirty bathrooms with a houseful of relatives due in time for the Seahawks' kickoff. Sheila's anger shifted full throttle into worry. Tom's foul mood only accelerated. He thumped clean pans into cabinets and slammed the doors. "Where the hell is she?" he shouted when Sheila hung up from her first, unanswered call to Kristen's mom. "I thought she was spending the night over there. What kind of funny farm are they runnin' that they don't know who sleeps under their roof?"

While Tom stomped out to the garage where she knew he would sneak a cigarette—a sure sign of his stress—Sheila had begun a flurry of calls, first to the homes of, what she soon realized, were mostly childhood friends rather than current ones—numbers that had remained in her contacts unused for years. She thought she and Tom were engaged parents, aware of their children's whereabouts, but she was embarrassed to realize that she only had a handful of phone numbers for Britany's friends, and this included no more than an ancient landline for Kristen Schneider. Instead, her phone contacts were filled with parents with whom they ride-shared for Tommy's hockey team. The few numbers she had yielded no information. One sleepy sounding friend said, "Gosh, Mrs. Rodgers, I haven't really talked to Britany in months other than at school." She called Dairy Queen, where Britany worked, and reached a shift manager who could offer no better than "Sorry, Mrs. Rodgers, Brit's not scheduled to work until Friday."

Tom emerged from the garage and said he was going to look for Britany. "What are you doing?" Sheila implored when he picked up his keys from the ceramic bowl Britany had made in sixth grade. "You're not looking for the dog. She's isn't wandering around in back yards."

"Got to do something."

"Tom, we need help from the police. They know how to handle these things."

"I know how to take care of my own. I might just go by and give Kristen's dad a piece of my mind."

"Tom. Please."

Tom ignored her. When he returned a half hour later, Sheila saw the panic in his eyes. She begged him once again to call the sherriff's department. This time he relented.

They had forgotten that two of Sheila's three sisters, their husbands and children, and Sheila's mom were coming to watch the game. That she'd failed to phone any of them among her calls searching for Britany did not occur to Sheila until she heard her oldest sister, their mother in tow, sing "hello" as she passed through the front door. Sheila, wiping tears, ducked into the kitchen. She dabbed at her eyes with a paper towel and heard her sister explain from the living room as they shed coats, "Mom and I wanted to see if you need help with dinner. Brad and the kids are coming in a bit."

Sheila looked at her mother, frail after two months of chemotherapy. She looked like she might shatter if she fell.

Her mother, without greeting, asked, "Why is your face all red?"

"It's nothing," Sheila said. "PMS. Tom," she shouted into the next room, "why don't you get mom settled by the fire. I'll fix snacks." Her sister was close at her heels, and as soon as their mother had passed out of hearing, touched Sheila's retreating elbow. "What's wrong?"

The tears sprang anew. "Britany's gone."

"What do you mean, gone?"

"She was supposed to be at a friend's house last night, and never came home this morning." The words rushed out of her. "She was never at Kristen's. No one's seen her. I don't know what to do." Her tears flowed freely now. "I don't know where she is."

"There's some logical explanation." Megan stepped forward and gathered Sheila into a hug. She pulled Sheila's hair back from her face as she had done since they were children. "Just breathe a minute. It's probably car trouble."

Sheila pulled out of the embrace. "She doesn't have the car. She's supposed to be three blocks away. She's not answering her phone. Something has happened to her." Sheila began to sob.

Megan picked up a pad and pen she found near the phone. "Write down everyone you've called. Then we'll make a list of all her friends and any place she may have gone. We'll think it through."

With trembling hands, Sheila accepted the pen from her sister. "We've already called the police."

"That's great," Megan said. "The more help, the quicker we'll find out what's going on."

An automaton, Sheila followed her sister's orders. She had barely started on the list when she heard a commotion as the rest of the family arrived. Jessica, their youngest sister, was lost in a battle with her kids. Sheila's mind shifted to forming a plan for how they might keep the news from their mother. She'd already been through enough in the past months—chemo and radiation and physical therapy, the loss of appetite, the exhaustion, the financial worries.

Sheila couldn't face her mother. As if reading her mind, Meagan said, "No need to upset Mom, sis. This is all going to be some mix-up, a funny story we'll tell around holiday dinner tables for the rest of Britany's life about how you had to call the police when she'd just been suckered into a snipe hunt."

Sheila listened to her sister, but her voice sounded like it was deep underwater. Her thoughts sprang from one to the next, and she couldn't keep up. The doorbell rang. Accustomed to family who had no need to announce their presence, everyone turned at the sound. Sheila dropped the notepad and stepped into the living room just as Tom opened the door. The sight of the uniform triggered a gasp from Sheila, and she reached for the kitchen doorjamb.

The deputy saw the look on Sheila's face and said to the room, "Sorry, folks." Jessica looked from the deputy to her sister and nearly shouted, "What's going on?" When no one responded, she demanded again, looking directly at Sheila. "Sis, what's happening?"

The deputy looked at Tom, who held the door for him. "You reported your daughter missing?" Everyone in the room with the exception of Sheila seemed to step toward the two men who filled the narrow entryway. An imposing presence despite a boyish face, the deputy made the room seem to shrink.

Tom Rodgers wasn't a small guy, but he hadn't seen the inside of a gym since his high school football days. Just then his brother-in-law arrived at the open front door. A warden for Montana Fish, Wildlife, and Parks, standing six foot five, Brad stepped into the narrow foyer and stopped, his two adolescent children stuck on the porch behind him. Sheila backed toward the kitchen, her retreat stopped by her mother's raspy voice. "Someone explain to me why my granddaughter is missing." Her voice, commanding despite its rasp, sliced through the commotion.

Sheila's mother appeared someone she no longer recognized, her cheekbones nearly penetrating the thin skin of her face, her lips pulled back to reveal her teeth . "Mom, Britany didn't come home this morning."

Her mother straightened her shoulders and stood taller. "Then this young man has a job to do. All of you, get out of his way. Come into the other room so he can speak with Sheila and Tom in private." She turned back out of the room, and the others dutifully followed.

* * *

Sheila looked at the phone beside her on the couch. The house was silent. For the first time since calling the police, she was alone. No one drilling her with questions. Remembering how her mother took command when she wanted to disappear brought fresh tears. Had that only been a day ago? She hadn't slept. Hadn't eaten more than a few grapes and some crackers from the plate Megan brought. Her mind was filled with spiderwebs, cotton balls, lake fog. She wished she had inherited her mother's strength. The woman continued to surprise her. After the deputy left, her mother had entered the kitchen and, without a word, gathered Sheila in a hug and whispered in her ear. "We'll find her. Don't you doubt it." She turned to the others in the room, their faces a swarm of withheld questions. "Someone take me home and bring the kids. The rest of you get to work finding my granddaughter."

Now, having again heard her daughter's recorded phone greeting, she wanted her mother. Wanted some portion of her strength. Her certainty. That morning Tom had said that "normalcy" was the best medicine while they waited for Britany's return, so he opted for work and insisted that Tommy be sent to school. She'd argued with him, shouting so loudly she imagined the neighbors would hear. "For God's sake, Tom. Our daughter's picture is on the morning news." She pointed to the television. An annoying teen band had replaced the local news. Tears dripped off her chin. "Normalcy," she hissed. "What are the police doing? A deputy who is practically a child asks us ten questions? Why aren't they ringing every doorbell in the valley?"

"I'm just sayin' that there's a logical explanation," Tom said. "You made me call the cops. Now let them do their job. I'm sure they're doing things we can't see."

"The neighbors brought us flowers this morning. Flowers," she said. Her eyes drifted out the window. "What does that mean?"

"You're letting your imagination run away with you," Tom said. "We need something to occupy our minds." His voice trailed off. "I'm going to work. She's gonna be back before dinner."

Sheila had watched him walk out the door to the garage and had wanted to throw something at his back. Then her thoughts had been interrupted by Megan. She'd forgotten her sister had spent the night.

"I'm headed out," Megan said. "We've got a meeting at the church to distribute flyers with Britany's picture. You sure you're going to be okay here on your own? Wouldn't you rather help us?"

Sheila nodded. She couldn't explain that while alone she wouldn't have to listen to others tell her to stop thinking through the scenarios forming in her mind. Alone, she'd find the clarity to figure out exactly where Britany was. Instead she said, "Somebody needs to be here if she comes home."

Sheila wanted to call Britany's phone again if only to hear her voicemail greeting: "Hey, it's Brit. You know what to do." She missed the old outgoing message, the one Britany had recorded with excitement when they'd first given her the phone at fourteen, a message that ended in a fit of giggles among a roomful of girls.

She looked out the window. Rain had moved in overnight, and the sky was gray and close. Where was her baby girl, she wondered, shivering as if she had stepped into the October cold. "Where are you?" she asked of the empty room.

Chapter Two

Britany Rodgers existed only as a name and a photograph to Steve Wendell. That was one of many frustrating things about a missing person case. There was the sobbing mom and the incredulous father and the hysterical high school friends, but trying to put a person to the name was a long, backward trip without a map.

Who was this girl? He looked at the photograph. Though posed in the style of senior pictures, there was no getting around the youthful life force that sparkled within her eyes, so strong the camera could not dilute it. "This is the one Britany is leaning towards," her mother said as she cut the proof out of a sheet of a dozen poses. "But she can never make up her mind about anything. We'll be lucky if we haven't missed the yearbook deadline." Fresh tears appeared in Sheila's eyes. Wendell patted her hand that lay on the kitchen counter atop the scissors, the sort of gesture that would make his colleagues cringe. "Don't get close to victims or their families" was the repeated warning from a grizzled state trooper while he prepared for his detective's exam. "Keep enough distance that you don't blur your perspective."

Wendell looked at the photo of Britany and then at the contact sheet from which it had been removed. The page of photographs, now missing the pose he held in his hands, lay on the granite kitchen countertop. He thought the granite that showed through the hole looked cold and uncompromising, like lake water in winter.

* * *

When Wendell first met Sheila, she was bookended on the family couch by Britany's two aunts at her modest home in Lakeside. He requested that Sheila speak with him in the kitchen to ask some of the more intimate questions about Britany's life. He started with the party-line on missing persons: "There's about 650,000 people reported missing in the US every year," he told her. "Of those, less than 2,000 prove to be connected to actual disappearances." He emphasized that the overwhelming majority of teens had run away.

"Why on earth would Britany run away?" she asked.

"That's what I need you to help me ascertain."

"Would it change how you try to find her?"

Wendell respected the logic of her inquiry, but he felt an accusation behind the question. He sidestepped. "Ma'am, finding her is our only goal." Then he returned to the comfort of questions rather than tell this mother how different his role would be if evidence of a crime emerged. Nearly twenty-four hours passed before he'd been assigned the case. Wendell considered the potential distances covered, the potential leads grown cold.

Sheila reported that none of Britany's clothes or personal items were missing. Britany had no medical conditions. She did not own a car. Her mother was adamant that there was no boyfriend.

"We'll need to take possession of her laptop."

"She doesn't own one."

"A desktop or a tablet?"

Sheila shook her head. "Tom doesn't think the kids need such things. They use mine for schoolwork."

Wendell could not recall the last time he'd encountered a seventeen-year-old who didn't possess technology superior to his own. "Phone?"

"She has it with her."

"We've tried to trace her social media presence and came up empty."

"Tom hates that stuff. He doesn't let the kids have accounts."

Wendell scratched his head with his pen. There'd be some layers on this case, he knew. Some hard digging. He wondered if his superiors would give him a shovel.

Chapter Three

Sheila Rodgers described Kristen Schneider as Britany's closest friend. As Wendell waited for Kristen at the end of Flathead High School's volleyball practice, he wondered where he might be on the case tomorrow, knee-deep in a criminal investigation or in search of another missing teen with her picture stapled on telephone poles?

He watched Britany's friend practice spikes. Kristen lacked natural grace but achieved good velocity. She tried, Wendell surmised, to make up with power what she lacked in finesse. He didn't know the sport outside the occasional picnic variety, so he applied what he knew from tennis. Wendell tried to remember seventeen. Mostly it seemed a time that emphasized embarrassing moments with girls when he hadn't known what to say. Otherwise, he remembered a vague feeling of wanting something the future might offer. Typical, he thought as he assessed himself—a kid from a small Montana town who spent a lot of time imagining life elsewhere. What was seventeen like for this girl he was about to interview, he wondered. What was it like for her friend who had disappeared?

When the team moved to a blocking drill, Kristen struggled with timing, something he'd seen in rebounders on the basketball court. He studied everything he encountered, like the way a group of three girls seated on the bleachers—injuries, he wondered, seeing no crutches or ice, academic suspensions, perhaps—tried to mask when they looked his way. The way one braided another's hair. The way the remaining girl stole expectant glances at the door. Was Britany like her, waiting for someone?

A blow on the coach's whistle ended practice and was accompanied with a shout: "Where do we play from, ladies?" The girls, in unison, roared: "From the heart!" and all clapped their hands once in perfect rhythm. The assistant coach with whom he'd first spoken, an attractive history teacher, called Kristen's name and then walked her over to Wendell.

Kristen Schneider was six feet tall and the kind of lean that made for pointy cheekbones and an angular nose. She had straight brown hair that reached beyond her shoulder blades even when pulled up in a ponytail. She offered the sort of politeness that suggested parental expectations of good manners. She wore a t-shirt that read: "Our game is as tight as our spandex."

"Big match coming up?" Wendell asked.

"Bozeman."

"They any good?"

"Middle of the pack," she said. "But then so are we," she added with a frown.

Her teammates milled around the bleachers among scattered gym bags and eyed them with interest. "Maybe we could slip down to the other end," he said and stepped away.

Kristen looked toward her teammates. "I don't have long. My mom is supposed to give me a ride." She tapped the toe of her right shoe against the gym floor.

"It will only take a minute. Just routine." He was struck by how young she looked. She had a pretty face though it was interrupted by acne. "We can meet your mom if you like. Whatever makes you the most comfortable." He took another step away. This time she followed.

"I already talked to somebody," she said.

Wendell sat down in the first row. "That was one of our patrol officers. I want to make sure we don't miss any important details."

Kristen remained standing. "I'm sorry, but I don't think I'm any help. I'd give anything to know where she's at."

"I need help to make that happen."

She sat down but looked blankly across the gym floor.

"You two are best friends?"

"We've known each other since kindergarten."

"So you probably know her as well as anyone."

"I guess," she said, shrugging.

"She'd tell you things? Stuff she might not tell anyone else?"

"I suppose," she said, now looking at him. "Not that there's anything to tell."

"Does she have a boyfriend?"

"No."

"No one she'd want to get away to go see? Someone in college? No beaus from out-of-town volleyball trips?"

"Britany doesn't play volleyball." Kristen chuckled. "She's a total clod."

"How does she spend her time?"

"Music mostly. She plays guitar and sings."

"Oh, yeah? She any good?"

"She's really good."

"That must be a different crowd." Wendell looked around the gym. Most of the girls had left. Two played basketball with a volleyball at the far end of the gym. "You know her other friends?"

Kristen shrugged again.

"Her mom said she works at Dairy Queen."

"Yeah. She's saving up to buy a car."

"Does she have friends from work?"

"She doesn't talk about work. I don't really know."

"I thought you two were close."

Kristen reddened. He could not tell the source. "We don't get to spend a lot of time together anymore."

"I get it," he said, thinking people change, people move on. "Is she the sort of person who lets stress get to her?"

"Britany? Hardly. Stuff rolls off her."

"Your principal told me you are in International Baccalaureate. But they tell me Britany's not an I.B. compatriot."

"She thinks we're dorks."

"You're not in the same classes, so when do you see her?"

"We go to lunch when we can. We drive together on days one of us has a car."

"Must be a drag, having to rely on your parents and friends for rides."

"It blows. But what are you going to do?"

"Who does Britany ride with on days she doesn't drive?"

"Different people. Our friend Brandon a lot of the time. Most days, she hangs around town and waits for her mom to get off work."

"Do you know where she goes on those days?"

"How do I know? I'm not her babysitter." The tone accompanying her answer seemed out of character. "Look, my mom is probably here."

Wendell wrote down Brandon's name in his notebook. "Humor me with conjecture."

"Lots of kids go to the coffeehouse."

"Down the street? Bridger Coffee?"

She nodded and then stood. "I've got to go."

"I'll walk you out," he said. "About Saturday. Did she seem at all different to you? Nervous or distracted?"

"No."

"And you walked along the lake and then got coffee at Flathead Roasting like you told the deputy?"

"Yeah."

"Did you see anyone there you knew?"

"No."

"You told the deputy this was around 3:00. Did you talk about her plans for the rest of weekend?"

"No."

"And then the two of you walked back to your house?"

"No," she said. She tilted her head and looked at the floor. "I had homework. She stayed. I left."

"What was she wearing?"

"I told the deputy."

"I'm sorry, but I need you to tell me again. Little things can help. The more specific you can be, the better."

"Jeans. Luckys. Her favorite pair. They have flower-shaped stitching on the butt. A purple Patagonia jacket. Light purple, like lavender."

"This is helpful, Kristen. Any other details?"

"I've told you everything I know." Kristen looked exasperated.

"I understand these questions are frustrating. But I'm at a loss. Right now, you are the last person to see her before we lose track of her."

"I really wish I could help."

"Why'd she tell her mom that she was spending the night at your house?"

Kristen stopped abruptly. "What?"

"Why'd she tell her mom she would be with you Saturday night?"

"I don't know. Nobody told me that."

"Kind of sounds like she had a plan, doesn't it? Did Britany ask to stay with you?"

"No."

"Did she ask you to cover for her?"

"No."

"Kristen, nobody is in trouble here."

"I don't know why she would tell her mom that."

"But she does stay with you at times."

"She has since we were kids."

"Has she ever asked you to cover for her?"

"No. Never."

"Is it possible she's used you as cover without you knowing it?"

The question appeared to catch Kristen off guard, and she paused. "I suppose. I'm sure she's lied to her parents before. I couldn't blame her."

"Why do you say that?"

"They treat her like she's still a kid."

They reached the doors to the parking lot. Wendell held the door for her and watched closely as she passed him. "Would you cover for her if she asked?"

Kristen stopped again. They stood in the vestibule between two sets of doors.

"I would."

"Say you did. Say it was for a whole night. Where might she go?"

"I don't know."

"Kristen, you've known this girl almost all of your life. Speculate."

"Out with other friends," she said with anger. She absently stroked her ponytail, pulling it over her right shoulder. Wendell watched as she checked her attitude. "She likes to party sometimes."

"That's not your thing?"

Kristen shook her head.

"What are we talking here? Drinking? Drugs?"

"Just high school stuff. Somebody with beer. Maybe some weed."

"I need names, Kristen. I'm not asking you to rat anybody out."

She shook her head again. "I would if I could. We kind of go our own way anymore."

"You understand, right. If I'm going to find her, I need to know who she could be with. Who does she spend time with, Kristen?" Wendell asked, his voice now stern.

"They're just names she mentions. Names that don't mean anything to me. Boys. You know, guys she thinks are cute."

"Would Britany lie to her parents in order to spend time with these boys?"

Kristen shrugged.

"Do you know if Britany is sexually active?"

Kristen's face reddened. "She has, you know…" she paused. "She's not slutty or anything. There's been a couple of guys she's told me about."

"I need those names too, Kristen." She nodded, still red-faced. As she then recited two names, Wendell wrote them in his notepad. "And friends she might party with, those names?" Kristen provided three more names, all boys.

"Those are the people I know," Kristen said.

"Is there anyone new she has talked about recently? A boy she's interested in?"

"Like a week ago. Maybe more. She kept going on about this guy she'd met. Joshua. Or Jacob. Some name that started with a 'J'. Not from school. Couldn't stop talking about how cute he was. How interesting he was. I haven't heard her say anything about him since. She's like that."

"Like what?"

"Into whatever she's into at the moment. This guy was all she could talk about for a couple of days and then nothing. Like she forgot him."

"Did she say where they met?"

"I don't remember."

"You understand that protecting her would actually only hurt her right now?"

"I don't know anything. I promise."

Wendell retrieved a business card. "Promise me you'll call if you think of anything that might help. Even if it seems unimportant."

"Okay."

Wendell watched Kristen approach an idling red Subaru Forester. He guessed it was ten years old though not a ding marred the paint. She opened the back door and threw her backpack and gym bag in the backseat before getting in the front. Her mother looked at him. She was entirely ordinary looking, he thought, exactly the woman you would expect to have a teenage daughter and drive a practical car, a woman who attended volleyball games and parent-teacher conferences and bought Girl Scout cookies every year.

Across the street, a man raked leaves to the curb. Patchy clouds obscured the tops of the Swan Range. An ordinary scene on an ordinary fall day, he thought. Ordinary. Like the girl he searched for. Where did one look when an ordinary girl suddenly disappeared?

Chapter Four

Tom Rodgers looked into the direct glare of lights slanting through the tangle of the big rig's engine. He could not see who spoke to him. Laboring below a rig in an under-engine bay, he toiled within shadows. Newer shops had runway lights filling the perimeter of the workstation, but Pete Garolin, the owner of PG Diesel Service, was quicker to invest in people than technology. Annoyed at the disturbance, Tom moved to see who spoke to him and struck his head on the manifold. "For fuck's sake," he shouted and flung a wrench into a corner of the pit. "Wha'da ya want?" He rubbed his bald head against the pain.

"That's going to leave a mark," said Garolin. Pete's head appeared behind the truck's right tire. "I heard the cops came by while I was at lunch," Pete said. "Something I need to know about?"

Tom grumbled. His head hurt, and his shoulders ached from working above his head.

"Come up," Pete said. "Let's get a cup of joe."

Tom grumbled again but ascended the metal stairs behind the rig. "You rob a bank?" his boss teased. "For Christ's sake," Pete said as he opened the door to the breakroom. "Who brought fish for lunch? We'll have to pump it full of diesel to get the smell back." He stepped to the coffee pot and poured two cups. Tom sat heavily onto one of the red vinyl chairs that ringed a worn table. Pete placed a cup before him and gathered a loose spread of grease-marked newspapers into a stack. "Might as well change my name to Mariá the way you guys make me pick up after you." He sat down across from Tom. "What gives? You pledgin' to the peace officer's fund?"

"It's Britany." Dark half-moons appeared below Tom's eyes. He sprawled beyond the chair's framework.

"A little MIP action? Happens to the best of them."

"She's missing."

"Missing?"

Tom's voice quivered almost imperceptibly. "She told us she was staying at a friend's Saturday night. We haven't seen her since."

"Jesus, Tom. I'm sorry. You have no idea where she is?"

Tom reddened.

"Sorry, man. Of course, you don't." Pete looked like he didn't know what to do with his hands. He picked up his coffee and raised it to his lips but didn't drink, then he set it back on the table and looked at his longtime employee. "Is there something we can do? Isn't there a search? I'll close the shop. Gather the guys and join in. Shit, this crew knows the woods."

"There's no search."

"What do you mean, no search? What the hell are the cops doing?"

"They said they don't know where to start."

"They could at least start at her friend's, right? Find a trail."

"She was never at her friend's."

"You shouldn't be here. You should be with Sheila."

"Then what? Sit on my hands?"

"Your wife needs you."

"I don't know how to help her."

"Go home, Tom."

"I've got that suspension half torn down."

"We've got you covered. Go home."

Tom didn't move, though the look on his face softened as if something within him had melted. He cleared his throat. "How could I not know where my baby girl is?"

Chapter Five

The field of vision and pace afoot offered perspective that Steve Wendell valued, so he left his vehicle at Volunteer Park and walked the length of the public dock. October, with kids in school and the weather changing, the park was empty. Most of the private slips at docks up and down the shore were vacant, their boats transported to winter storage. He heard the muffled growl of a chainsaw—winter preparation of a different sort.

From the pier, he followed Lakeside Boulevard, the route Kristin Schneider had described taking with Britany on Saturday afternoon. Kayaks and canoes rested against trees or on racks near fire-pits among scatterings of lawn furniture and overturned fishing skiffs. Signs reminded passers-by to clean up after their dogs.

He'd driven this road as a patrol deputy, but he didn't feel he knew Lakeside well. Situated near the southern end of departmental jurisdiction, the sherriff's department didn't get a lot of calls here. The town was loaded with tourists during the summer but nearly as quiet as the hand-painted plywood snowmen with which civic organizers lined the highway in the winter. Wendell lived fifteen miles away on the other side of the lake near Bigfork. On clear days he could see the sunrise reflect off windows in Lakeside homes during his morning run.

He'd known Lakeside more intimately during his days on patrol, though despite having no local police, it wasn't a place patrolled with regularity. In a county of more than 5,200 square miles, limited resources meant there were portions of shifts with only four patrol deputies on duty. Which helped explain why the closest thing to a cop in Lakeside was a retired police car with a uniformed dummy propped in the driver's seat to slow speeders.

The truth was Wendell didn't have a long service record because, despite being forty-eight, he had only been with the department for seven years. He held the distinction as the oldest graduate in Montana Law Enforcement Academy history.

Fifteen years older than his classmates, he'd entered the Academy knowing he would be treated as a misfit. He had an advantage in the classroom because he was not a stranger to law enforcement, spending the previous fourteen years as a probation and parole officer, but his instructors voiced skepticism if he could meet the physical demands. An avid back-country skier and climber, he had no doubt he was fit for forty, but could he compete with guys at the prime of their physical lives? He responded as he had to everything in his life: he outworked and outsmarted his classmates.

Over his years with probation and parole, he'd experienced just enough adrenaline-fueled moments to make him crave more. And having endured the frustrations of inept bureaucracy, he wanted the rush of chasing down bad guys rather than babysitting them. His probation years were a meticulous drag through the sludge of bureaucracy working with offenders doomed to repeat decisions that guaranteed a return to prison. There were exceptions, of course, and the exceptions got him through the day and maybe, he guessed, through the first years of his career, but the norms he grew to expect weighed him down: the cycles of poverty and absent education, the omnipresence of addiction, the ready turn to violence borne of frustration. He craved skin-prickling, black-tunneled silence that accompanied alertness in the face of immediate threat.

Wendell didn't have the other responsibilities—no spouse, no children, no debt—that made life-change difficult, and at forty, he resigned his position and submitted his Academy application.

He hadn't been prepared for how monotonous a patrol day in semi-rural Montana often was—innocuous repetition interrupted by moments of prickled alertness. The job consisted of infinite miles on icy roads, repeat calls to addresses for which the domestic dispute call code was unnecessary, and far too many accident scenes. He learned how far the contents of a vehicle could spread in a rollover, and he could identify addicts by their shoulder-slumped, erratic walk—like lesser scavengers approaching a carcass. Though there were unpredictable calls and moments where he felt he accomplished meaningful police work, he tired of being unable to pursue an arrest because the overcrowded jail didn't have bed space. He saw superiors place stability of career over justice, witnessed prosecutors flock to the cases they found compelling while accepting plea deals on cases into which police had poured manpower. After five years on patrol, he signed up to take the detective's exam.

In truth, he was never well-suited for patrol. His mind was slow and ponderous, complexly analytical. Decisions as a deputy required swiftness followed by total commitment. Good deputies knew how to look authoritative in uniform and to be accepted as a friend when out. Colleagues regarded him as affable but aloof—a loner in a team environment. Wendell wasn't interested in invitations for fishing trips. He had a small but close circle of good friends that did not include people from the department. His interests and habits stood out. He read constantly and owned a vehicle that featured gas mileage over payload, chose solo sports over softball teams. Such traits, combined with the cardinal sin that he did not hunt, made him an outlier.

And what would his colleagues think of his methodology now, he thought, as he wasted precious time walking the route a missing girl might have taken? He looked at his watch. Time was always an enemy in an investigation. He stopped walking. The water came close to the road. Under cloudy October skies, it looked cold and unforgiving. Wendell shivered involuntarily. Anxiety rose within him when he looked within the foreign world of the lake. He lifted his gaze and looked across the lakes' expanse to the far shore and the rise of the Mission and Swan Ranges.

How had Britany seen her hometown?

Wendell had been involved in only a handful of investigations in Lakeside. The one that stuck with him was an assault case with roots in domestic violence—an altercation between a woman's husband and the man with whom she was having an affair, an out-of-work concrete finisher named Lee Jeffries. Jeffries had, years before, been assigned to Wendell as a probationer. He pled down on an abuse charge involving a different woman. A year after his probation ended, Jeffries was accused of statutory rape for what he claimed was a mutually consensual relationship with a sixteen-year-old. Those charges were eventually dropped because no witnesses would testify.

The assault case bogged down, first when the wife recanted her statements, then other witnesses—an assortment of friends on both sides—couldn't keep their stories straight. Convinced the case would escalate, Wendell was proven right, and a deputy was injured responding to a bar owner's 911 call while trying to keep peace among tribal drunks.

Wendell didn't want Jeffries's case to taint how he saw the community. If the bad apples turned a place to vinegar, every neighborhood would be contaminated. But the case helped Wendell see beyond the picturesque bays and the narrow lanes edging the lakeshore, beyond too the modular homes sandwiched between the thin strip of town and the road that climbed Blacktail Mountain. Lakeside existed in the intersection between part-time residents in big summer places with postcard views and blue-collar workers who frequented shoebox-sized casinos tacked onto convenience stores. Could a girl slip into the gap between those two worlds? Could she have attempted to run away from one to the other? He knew that if this case proved more tragic than a runaway teen or a bit of childish disobedience, Jeffries, as one of five registered violent offenders in Lakeside, would be high on his list to interview.

Wendell surprised himself to discover he had, amidst his ruminations, covered another half mile, oblivious to his surroundings. If scenic Lakeside could harbor Jeffries, what else might it hide? What might he have failed to notice within Britany's seemingly ordinary family?

While he walked and pondered, he knew the department continued to work through its protocols. It had been aggressive to get Britany's face before the public. He'd been pleasantly surprised at the level of department commitment and knew that the fact Tom and Sheila looked like most of the people in the Flathead valley—family-focused, working-class, conservative—had worked in her favor. Had Britany been another Native American missing teen, the resources would have been far sparser.

Wendell needed to determine whether Britany had any reason to run, towards something—friends, romantic partners, addiction—or away from something—bullying, pregnancy, abuse. He believed people might take unpredictable actions or react in what appeared irrational ways, but if viewed analytically, there were nearly always logical roots. The public wanted search parties that made good television backdrops for live reportage. Wendell knew meticulous pursuit of facts behind the scenes solved cases.

The road curved and then curved back on itself, climbed a steep hill, and passed through a tall forest. Long driveways descended to houses on the lakeshore. The woods were so thick that Wendell could see only rooflines, though it wasn't hard to imagine the spectacular views the homes beneath those roofs showcased.

Wendell's wandering mind did not help Britany Rodgers. If she needed help. He held out hope she did not. The job, however, prepared him for the likelihood that hope was misplaced. Even as he would prepare a face cemented in hope when speaking with Britany's family, his best service to them was to explore the unthinkable.

Time to get back to employing a different kind of legwork. Still, he played the game he employed on tough running days and, eyeing a power pole some fifty yards ahead, told himself that he would walk just that much further. Where its thin shadow slanted across the road, a discarded cigarette lighter lay at the road edge, crushed by a passing tire. His mind drifted to spying the cigarette pack visible in Kristen Schneider's volleyball bag. Nearby, in the brush alongside the road, were strewn two empty Bud Light bottles and a Monster can. Trash carelessly discarded. He hoped that someone had not discarded Britany with the same callousness. The job taught him that people were capable of unimaginable things. "Where are you?" he asked of the trees and sky and road.

Chapter Six

Parking in front the Rodgers's house, Wendell recognized Tom's big GMC from when he interviewed him at work. Tom had insisted that they leave the shop to talk, and they had spoken while leaning against the bed of the truck. Tom behaved like he was the victim of an embarrassing prank.

The house, a simple ranch style, was well-maintained with a neat yard and pine trees trimmed up high to let in light. Wendell had put off this meeting and stopped at Flathead Roasting, the coffeehouse where Kristen Schneider had left Britany after their walk, and at Dairy Queen, where Britany worked.

The Dairy Queen owner offered no insights. Wendell was dismayed to see how little he knew about his employees. Of those present, one was a middle-aged woman, and the other two appeared not likely to have graduated high school. He had a hard time imagining the Britany who stared so intently out of her senior picture spent time off with coworkers.

Wendell put on a stoic face. Experience told him that you didn't have to tell bereft parents, even those who had never suffered previous interactions with law enforcement, that their case held no daydreamy answers. Without real leads, he did the best he could to, as his father had liked to say, "Make your own luck."

The Rodgers's house felt post-funeral. Sheila played a DVD of Britany singing and playing guitar at a school talent contest. Britany's face appeared frozen on the television screen when Sheila stopped the video while she and Tom answered Wendell's questions. Britany's voice filled the room, clear and pure but airy, exerting control over a falsetto. Her smile exposed a sweet dimple and crinkle lines at the corners of her eyes. Before the first chorus was complete, Sheila left the room in tears. Tom looked steadfastly out the window. Wendell lasted another thirty seconds before he said, "She has a beautiful voice." He cleared his throat. "I need to search Britany's room."

Her room appeared what one would expect of a seventeen-year-old, loaded with items sentimental to a teenager—concert ticket stubs, leftover redemption coupons from last summer's carnival, photos of friends. There were hand-painted ceramic bowls of the color-your-own variety overflowing with mall-store earrings, and three best-friends-forever bracelets gathered dust atop a dresser. One desk drawer held a trove of holdovers from adolescence: horsemanship ribbons, an oversized plastic ring, handmade beaded necklaces. Elsewhere he encountered old phone cases and guitar picks. A stuffed giraffe occupied a dusty chair. Another drawer revealed faded t-shirts from soccer teams and family vacations.

In the top drawer of her nightstand, Wendell found a notebook filled with song lyrics. The classic ninety-nine-cent composition book, its only variance from the traditional was a green mottled cover rather than black and white. He thumbed through the book pages weighty with ink and filled in equal measure with lyrics, chords, and snippets of musical lines. Circled in flowery loops of ballpoint ink about two thirds down the first page and written at an angle were the lines:

You can't see where you don't want to look.
You can't feel what you aren't willing to touch.
I can't be what I don't believe.

When he asked Tom if he could take the notebook and copy its pages, Tom asked, "What is it, like a diary or something?"

"It's her music."

"Music," Tom said dismissively. "I wonder when she's going to get off that horse."

Chapter Seven

"Most of the calls are expected," Detective Stacey Knudson said. "There's the deluge from mom, several from dad. Two calls on Saturday to the Schneider girl. A few others—all local. There's one number that will get your attention. 415 area code. San Francisco."

"Yeah?"

"Straight to voicemail. Young man's voice. No name given, just a generic 'call me.'"

"A boyfriend mom and dad don't know about?" Wendell pondered.

"I don't know what he is, but I've got a name for you," she said. "Joshua Bianconi. I'm running him through NCIC now," Knudson said. "In the meanwhile, she's a teenage girl. There's quite a long list of calls."

"Of course," Wendell said. "Let's get at it." He took Knudson's list. He was pleased that she assisted him. Knudson was a detailed and meticulous officer, unruffled at time spent deconstructing video footage and combing through interview transcripts. He worried about her relative inexperience in the field but was glad to have her investigative skills as support. While he hadn't worked with her often, he appreciated her directness and dry humor. Most colleagues did not share his appreciation. Whether they held her gender or her directness against her, he wasn't sure.

A minute later, Knudson said, "Bianconi is eighteen. Served probation for vandalism. Two minor-in-possession charges. Pled out of an intent-to-deliver charge. Possession of a controlled substance. A real prince. Listed address is with mom and dad in California."

Wendell raised an eyebrow. "What's the Montana connection?"

Knudson shook her head. "Don't know. I've got numbers on the parents and his probation officer."

"Give me the suit," Wendell said, taking Knudson's neatly printed notes. "I can still talk his language."

He suffered through while the probation officer droned on about his desire to fish Western Montana. He'd taken his family to Glacier National Park two years before. Wendell suggested that he could show the man some Montana rivers without confessing that he didn't fish.

"Bianconi," the probation officer said. "Rich little puke. Got himself kicked out of two of the best private schools in the city. Got me in hot water."

"How so?"

"He suckered me into pulling strings and reduce his time if he rehabbed. Truth is, I don't think he had a habit. He played it up so I could get him in treatment. His father chewed me out for claiming his kid was a junkie. After that, he chewed on my boss for a while."

"So, Joshua Bianconi doesn't make your list of favorite clients."

"Nah, I think the kid's all right. Just doesn't know what to do with himself. He's smart, you know. But sideways. I mean, the type of kid who tests off the charts but still flunks out of every class. He's a year behind in school. Always throws in with the wrong sorts. Really, I kind of feel sorry for him."

"Sorry? How?"

"I may have been a C student in Psych, but I think he needs some boundaries and to be reminded that people care what happens to him."

"It may be nothing," Wendell said. "His number came up in the phone record on a case with a missing teen."

"He's a handsome kid," the probation officer said. "I doubt there's a shortage of girls."

"What's his capacity for violence?"

"His second expulsion was for assaulting a teacher. Claimed it was overblown. The teacher refused to press charges."

"Do you know of any reason there would be a Montana connection? Any reason a local girl would have his number?"

"He's in school in Montana. We petitioned for a special provision to let him attend school out of state."

"Where?"

"Let me grab his file. I remember it was some kind of alternative school. Pricey, as I recall. Hang on a sec."

When the California probation officer came back on the line, he said, "Like I remembered. An alternative school. My notes show his grades are good. I'm reading the most recent semester report from the school: 'Faculty and staff think he's made an excellent transition, demonstrates substantially increased levels of maturity and improved decision making, and is beginning to live up to his academic potential.' Peak Preparatory Academy. Kalispell, MT. Is that close to you?"

"Spitting distance." Wendell wrote the name of the school and showed Knudson.

"The notes indicate he found a good fit there."

"Probably nothing," Wendell said. "Out romancing the local population. Thanks for the information."

"Sure thing. Maybe I'll take you up on your offer to go fishing."

"Absolutely," Wendell politely lied.

When he turned back to Knudson, she already had the school website up. "I'll have you prepped," she said. "You'll know more than you ever wanted to about alternative schools for troubled teens."

Wendell shared what he'd learned.

"Smacked a teacher around," Knudson said. "Makes you wonder if he could hurt a girl too?"

"One step at a time," Wendell warned.

* * *

The director of Peak Preparatory, Dr. Murray Kragor, had left for the day, but agreed to meet Wendell at the school. When Wendell stepped out of the station, he was taken aback to see that the sun had set. The loss of time was one of the hazards of the job. In moments like this, as he turned onto the dark streets surrounding the sherriff's office where squat houses had curtains closed on the night and beyond the curtains, in the lights of kitchens and dining rooms, people lived the normal patterns of their lives, Wendell knew it was a good thing he remained single; his work hours and obsessive habits would certainly condemn a relationship. How many cop marriages had he seen fall apart? Still, he looked at the lit windows as he switched on the radio for distraction and pointed the car west.

Once he hit the foothills on the edge of Kalispell, the darkness was interrupted only by the lit houses spread on acreages that climbed up and down ridgelines and raised swells like a lower configuration of stars. He turned off the highway and navigated a dark warren of forest roads. Knudson called and provided a briefing. "Residential boarding school. They target kids failing in traditional schools. It's the whole gamut you'd expect: ADHD, depression, run-ins with authority figures, chemical dependencies. But they focus on kids who are academically gifted. The clinical staff and faculty are impressive. I'll tell you though, Wendell," Knudson said, "you know that pricey Gonzaga piece a paper you've got hidden in your file cabinet? Chump change compared to this place."

At the campus entrance, he was met by a staff member in an idling side-by-side. The man carried the big key ring and the oversize flashlight of a security guard but wore a Carhartt jacket. He escorted Wendell into a brightly lit building that looked like an upscale mountain resort. An enormous rock fireplace rose up through two floors of vaulted ceiling and log beams. Ten teenaged boys sprawled on comfortable couches arranged in clusters.

Kragor proved enthusiastic and infectious. He met Wendell with a thunderous "Welcome to Peak Prep." He ushered him to his office, which was a no-nonsense affair with framed inspirational posters scattered among photos of kids gathered around campfires and engaged in rock climbing, snow-shoeing, and canoeing. "Let's get right down to business, shall we," Kragor said. "I've called a meeting with Joshua and several members of his team."

"His team?"

"His residential counselor, his team counselor, one peer team member with whom he is close. A lot of what we do is rebuild student-to-adult and peer-to-peer relationships. To speak to one's actions in a group setting among people you trust is central to building relationships. We're more than a school acting in place of parental guardianship. We prepare our students to reenter a world beyond this campus."

"So 'preparatory' is way more than college prep."

"We're academically rigorous. Our graduates are certainly prepared for the college classroom, but they come from experiences and act upon behaviors that require us to ready them for the day to day living, not just the classroom. We encourage our students to assume ownership of their minds and bodies, as we expect them to take ownership of their actions and behaviors. You said that Joshua was identified as owning a cell phone connected with a case."

"Two outgoing calls were placed to a number registered to Joshua from the phone of a girl who has been missing since Saturday night."

"The girl who has been in the news."

"Yes, Britany Rodgers. We're following up on anyone who had contact."

"I should imagine so."

Wendell pushed ahead. "You're a bit remote." He motioned to the action shots on the wall. "Are your students out in the community with regularity? I'm curious how Joshua and Britany might know one another."

"Joshua has been quite successful at Peak. He's reached the final phase in his action plan and has earned greater autonomy. Students like Joshua are carefully guided towards independent actions, including privileges to participate in off-campus activities. This semester, Joshua has become involved in two community service projects. We place a premium on students learning empathy. He would have interacted with others his age while fulfilling his service contract."

Wendell started to ask for specifics about where Joshua had volunteered but was interrupted. "The presence of cell phone calls is troubling," the doctor said. "Our students are not allowed to possess phones. All contact with families is done on school phones and via school computers in a monitored setting. Our network is fire-walled. We know who our students communicate with."

"Are you saying that it is impossible Joshua received these calls?"

"Nothing is impossible. Despite the measures we take, this is a school, not a prison. Our mission is to educate. Something is amiss here, but I'm not the sort to judge until I have the facts in hand."

Overstuffed furniture formed a circle. Everyone in the room, including the two teenage boys present, rose and greeted Wendell with a handshake. One boy was heavier set; bushy hair framed a round face. The other was slender, somewhat androgynous in appearance, with dark hair styled in a complicated cut that resulted in the left side raising and then curling like the edge of an ocean wave. Both wore loafers without socks.

Dr. Kragor introduced the boy with the complicated hairstyle as Joshua Bianconi.

"Dr. Kragor speaks highly of you," Wendell said. Wendell watched to see if either a glimpse of pride or one of irritated bemusement registered on the boy's face. He displayed no reaction. It struck Wendell that speaking with the police was hardly a new experience for the boy. "I'm following up on two calls made to your phone this past Saturday in conjunction with a case I'm investigating."

"I don't have a phone," Joshua replied. He looked Wendell square in the eye.

"The cell record has calls made to a number registered with your name." Wendell opened his notebook and read the number aloud.

"That's my number," Joshua said, "but the phone is at my parents'. We're not allowed to have phones."

"Any idea who in Montana might be trying to contact you?"

Joshua shrugged again. "It would have to be somebody from the school. They're the only people I know."

"You don't know anyone else in the *whole* state?" Wendell said, trying for humor.

"My probation officer."

"Does the name Britany Rodgers mean anything?"

"No. Should it?"

Wendell observed his body language and the movement of his eyes. He reached into a portfolio and retrieved Britany's photograph. "Do you recognize this girl?"

"Oh, yeah, I do," Bianconi said. Wendell could not decide if it was a reaction of simple recognition or if Joshua, placed in the presence of a police officer, had started to work around a newly visible trap. "We met on a trail project I volunteered for a couple of weeks ago."

"Tell me more."

"We planted trees. She was there with a group from her school. Drama club or something. We hung out most of the day. She's cool."

"Funny you didn't recognize her name."

"She told me her name was Lindsey."

"You hit it off with Lindsey?"

"She was super chill. Some people look at you like you're a convict when you tell them where you go to school. She was different."

"Have you seen her since?"

Joshua glanced at Dr. Kragor briefly. Perhaps he wasn't so accomplished a liar after all. "Once," he said. "Last week."

"Just the two of you?"

"Nah, with a bunch of her friends. At a coffee shop. She told me to come by. I don't think she quite got it that Peak isn't like other schools where I can leave when classes are over."

"How did you get to town?"

"My brother was here."

"From California?"

"Oregon. He's in college."

"Does he visit often?"

"He's been here a few times. The school held a retreat for families last week. He's the one person I can count on to do the family therapy thing."

"Part of your brotherly bonding involved a visit to a local coffee shop."

"Yeah, you busted me."

"When was this?"

"Thursday."

"Where else did the two of you go?"

"Oh, you know, the usual. Caught up with our dealer. Robbed a liquor store."

Wendell, unfazed by the sarcasm, thought, this is the real kid, this boy who wants to give the finger to authority. Wendell heard Dr. Kragor clear his throat but maintained rigid eye contact with Joshua. "You said you went to the coffee shop specifically to see this girl in the photo?"

"Yeah, well, I was hoping."

"Not interested in the girls here?"

"She seemed different."

"Different. How?"

Joshua appeared thoughtful. "Not jaded."

Wendell nodded. "Then what?"

"Nothing. We talked."

"Was your brother with you?"

Joshua nodded.

"What name did you say she gave you?" Wendell asked, feigning.

"Lindsey."

"Did you and Lindsey sneak off for some alone time?"

"Actually, my brother hung out with her most of the time. I got to talking with one of her friends, this girl named Jaqueline. We're into a lot of the same music. Lindsey kind of checked out. She's more into Country and Pop. Not my thing."

"Let me get this straight. You go out of the way to see Lindsey, and you end up with Jaqueline."

Joshua shrugged.

"Have you seen either of them since?"

"How would I?"

"No double dates with your brother?"

"He left the next day."

"Your brother can verify all you've told me?"

"Yeah. Why the third degree?"

"Your Lindsey, Britany Rodgers, has been missing since Saturday."

"Missing?"

"No contact with anyone who knows her."

"Oh, man. You think she's run away or something?"

"Would that surprise you?"

"I only met the girl twice, so how would I know? But yeah, I mean she was, I don't know, upbeat, you know?"

"What'd you talk about?"

"You know, about her family and stuff. School. Music."

"Yet, apparently, you don't share the same taste in music. You moved on to her friend."

"It wasn't like that. I really liked her. We had fun on the trail. But Jaqueline," he paused for a moment, "she was really cool and into some of the same things as me."

"Did talking to Jaqueline make Britany mad?"

"No. I mean there was a whole group of us at one big table. She and my brother got along, which was awesome. He's shy around girls. Other people came by. I happened to be next to Jaqueline. We got along. Like I said, she's more my type."

Wendell let his stare do the work.

"Yeah, Jaqueline is hot. I didn't pay a lot of attention to anybody else."

"So, you didn't notice how Britany reacted."

"Look, it's not like I know either of them. Jaqueline was cool. It seemed, you know, there was more of a chance I'd like where things might go with her. I'm just being honest. I mean, they both seem nice, but then I don't really know them, now do I? I mean, obviously, I don't know this Britany chick at all. Apparently, she lied to me about her name, so who knows if anything she told me is true. And that's the last I saw of Jaqueline. The last I saw of either of them."

"I'm trying to figure out why Britany Rodgers would call your phone twice on the same day she ended up missing."

"I don't know how she would have my number, man."

"Don't pull my leg, Joshua."

"Why would I give her my number? I told you, I don't have my phone."

Wendell thought Joshua looked genuinely confused but pressed on. "You have to admit, this feels convenient. You're not in possession of your phone. A near stranger employs the means to find your phone number on her own."

"I don't know what to tell you. Talk to my parents."

"You can imagine what her parents are feeling. Their daughter hasn't been seen in over forty-eight hours. If you did know anything, it would go a long way to alleviate a whole lot of fears."

"She seems like a really nice girl. I'd tell you if I knew anything."

Wendell ended the interview by rising. "Thanks for your time, everybody," he said, taking in each face again. A look passed between the two boys, but Wendell did not register any clear meaning in it.

He walked out with Dr. Kragor. Once outside, Kragor said, "We're very strict about our phone policy. Just the same, I'll instruct the faculty and staff to be extra vigilant. If there is a clandestine phone on this campus, we'll find it." He looked up into the night sky. The stars, except to the east, were mostly obscured by clouds. "What were your impressions, if I may ask?"

"Something's hinky," Wendell said. "I just don't know what. Then again, the job kind of teaches you not to accept things at face value. You?"

Kragor remained looking at the sky. "Joshua has come a long way, yet he remains capable of many things, including deceit. Still, I'm inclined to believe he was being truthful tonight."

Wendell looked to where Kragor continued to watch the sky. He took a deep breath of the cool night air. "There's a storm moving in."

Kragor merely nodded in agreement.

"Do you have children?" Wendell asked.

"Yes. Two daughters. They attend the same school as the Rodgers girl."

"Do they know her?"

"Apparently only by name and face. And you, Detective Wendell, do you have children?"

"No. Never got around to it," Wendell said and started for his car.

"It would be hard, I suppose, in your line of work. Please know I will assist in any way possible to help you."

Wendell nodded and wished him a good night. "Go home to your family," he said even as he pictured his own tidy but empty Bigfork house.

Chapter Eight

Wendell returned to an empty office. He left the lights off and worked by his desk lamp. Knudson had left Britany Rodgers's cell phone log on his desk, meticulously identifying every call for the last six weeks. When Wendell called her and made plans for a breakfast brainstorm, he heard her children's voices in the background.

"Go home sometime tonight, Wendell. Okay?"

He called Bianconi's parents. Both numbers went to voicemail. Wendell thought best while moving, so he walked downtown for something to eat. The night was cool. He walked the circle around the county courthouse and up Main Street. October was his favorite month in the Flathead, the air crisp and filled with wood smoke as the temperatures dropped, the tourists thinned, and on a Monday evening in October, downtown was quiet.

He passed the windows of Bridger Coffee Company, the blinds pulled shut, the old exposed brick walls visible through the glass door. He peered within at the wooden tables and wondered which one was Britany's favorite. If Bianconi had spoken the truth, why had Britany given him a different name? What was she hiding?

As he crossed the street and neared Thai Terrace, he smelled the hot spices rise from their kitchen. He'd not eaten since breakfast. The restaurant, the red neon tubing of its window sign casting a glow onto the sidewalk, appeared empty.

"Is the kitchen still open," he inquired of the owner, who greeted him at the hostess stand.

"Yes, yes, of course. Just slow." She smiled. "Always slow on Monday."

"It's late. I don't want to put you out."

"Whole kitchen ready for you. You eat late tonight."

Wendell shrugged. "Work kept me," he said.

"You work too much. Need vacation. We close soon. All of November. Take long vacation."

"Back to Thailand?"

"Yes, yes. See mother. She no come here anymore."

"I'm jealous. Maybe you can pack me in your suitcase."

"Big suitcase," she said with exaggeration while miming dragging a heavy object.

Wendell ordered without the menu, Gaeng Khae and green curry shrimp with a side of sticky rice.

The food came quickly. He checked his watch—9:30 PM—the precious hours passing. If he were in California, he would camp on the Bianconi's doorstep for lack of any better lead.

***

He had been home for a little over ten minutes when Jan Bianconi called. Her voice was frantic.

"Detective Wendell, has something happened to Joshua?"

"No, ma'am. I certainly didn't intend to panic you."

"He hasn't done something, has he?"

"Not that we are aware of," Wendell said. He thought her question demonstrated something about Joshua's past. "He is a material witness."

"A witness?"

"Of sorts."

"I was frantic when I saw the area code. And then when I heard you were with the sheriff's department, well, my panic spun into overdrive. I was at a dinner party. My phone was with my things in the cloakroom." She spoke fast. "He's done so well there. This past summer, when he was home, he was another person, someone actually pleasant to be with. Tell me he hasn't ruined that."

"Mrs. Bianconi," he interrupted. "I called regarding Joshua's phone."

"His phone?"

"Yes. He indicated that his phone is with you."

"The school doesn't allow phones. It was a point of great contention for Joshua. At first, we also thought the policy was extreme. But over time, we have learned to trust that the school knows what's best."

"Are you in possession of the phone?"

"Yes. They've proven that they understand these things better than we do."

"These things, ma'am?"

"They know how to reach difficult children. We're pleased with the results at Peak. I'm certain that whatever you are calling about will prove an error."

"All I really need is a copy of his phone bill."

"My husband manages such things."

"Then may I please speak with him?"

"I'm afraid he is away on a business trip in Japan. He won't be back until Thursday."

"This is an urgent matter, Mrs. Bianconi."

"I don't like to trouble him when he's involved in important business."

"This is extremely time-sensitive. It's no more complicated than accessing your account records online."

"My husband handles all the finances. Don't ask me."

"You don't have access to your account?"

"I haven't touched a computer since college."

"Would you ask your husband to call me as soon as possible? Save us the hassle of a court order for the cell provider."

"Yes, of course."

"Is it true that Joshua's brother visited him this past week?"

"Yes. Jacob attended a family event at the school. He's such a good role model for his brother."

"I'd like to speak with Jacob. Can you give me his phone number?"

"Why on earth do you need to speak with Jacob?"

"He spent time with Joshua this past week."

"Joshua *has* done something, hasn't he?"

"Speaking with Jacob can help clarify a few things. I would greatly appreciate your cooperation."

"Yes, yes, of course, I wish to cooperate," she said.

Upon ending the call, Wendell tried Jacob. The call went to voicemail. Such tiny hurdles when so much was at stake. He knew he would not be able to sleep, so he changed into gym attire and went a few rounds on a heavy bag until bathed in sweat. Later that night, he heard raindrops on the metal roof, and despite the cool October night, he opened his bedroom window an inch to hear the rain as it filtered through the forest limbs. Once asleep, he dreamed of water, the vastness of a dark, underwater world, and he startled himself awake as if gasping for air.

Chapter Nine

The fire in the woodstove had burned to coals. Mist swirled among the pines surrounding Wendell's house. He checked his phone. 5:30 a.m. Time enough for a soggy run before meeting Knudson.

An ancient collection of pine needles gathered on the path mostly kept his feet out of the mud. The single-track snaked through the forest to the county road where an ATV trail had eroded a path five yards off the road edge. A mile along the road was required before he accessed a single-track that ascended through woods on abandoned logging company roads. The forest closed in on him, an ambiance he found comforting rather than claustrophobic. Fog swirled around tree trunks. Usually, he found mental clarity in the gloom, but today, focus proved elusive. The rain returned—minutes of drizzle interrupted by steady showers. The run was a slog, his shoes weighted by accumulated mud. He knew that when the sun arrived, lacy clouds would ascend the mountains, hang on ridges and spill down treed flanks.

He arrived early for breakfast. The parking lot at the Jewel Basin Café was full. He spent time at the counter over coffee while waiting for Knudson. Bill Remarr, an officer for Montana Fish, Game, and Parks, elbowed up beside him, raising his oversized mug to the girl at the counter. "Hey, Steve," Remarr said. His bushy mustache masked the movement of his mouth. "Hell of a thing, this Rodgers girl."

"Keeping me awake."

"You think there's something sideways?"

"I don't honestly know, Bill."

"You know the girl's uncle is one of ours?"

"Yep."

"I put an extra man on that side of the lake. We're watching the parks extra close, especially West Shore. I know the Forest Service is running all the fire roads over on that side too."

"I appreciate it."

"Say the word, and every man I can spare will help."

"I know it."

Wendell saw Knudson enter the restaurant, and at the same moment, the waitress waved him over to a table. "My partner's here," he said. "Wanna join us?"

Remarr turned and saw Knudson, who waved. "Nah, I already ate. One more for the road," he said. "Might be you want to drag this one out a bit given that pretty face of your partner."

Wendell ignored the remark. "I'm glad for the help. We're pretty slammed."

"Sounds familiar. We're spread about as thin as I've ever seen."

"Seems like we've had this conversation before," Wendell said.

"Amen to that," Remarr agreed, sliding onto the stool Wendell vacated. "Good luck. Hope your girl shows up quick."

Wendell joined Knudson at a table set against a window that faced east into the Swan Mountains, though mostly the view offered streams of mist that drooped like the tentacles of jellyfish. "Morning," he offered.

"You sleep?"

"Some."

"Anything new?" she asked.

"Talked to Bianconi's mom. Claims the phone has to go through the husband."

"Hopefully, we do better with Bianconi's phone than with Britany's. I can't believe we're stuck with triangulation. Last known position—Lakeside. Thanks for nothing."

Wendell nodded. "They're all longshots. Herberts wants a meeting right after morning brief."

"Where do you want to start?"

"Backwards mostly," he said. "Bianconi claims Britany used an alias with him. Some of her friends have indicated that there are other sides to her, other friends they don't know. I'll re-interview kids from Flathead. Talk with this other girl Bianconi chatted with. I want to catch the afterschool crowd at Bridger Coffee. She spends time there."

"She's not the only one," Knudson joked.

"I've probably seen her," he said, frowning, "but she'd look like all her friends to me."

Knudson nodded. "Sometimes when I'm waiting to pick up the kids, I look at strangers and wonder if one day they'll be part of something I'm investigating. I can't turn it off."

"Industry hazard," Wendell said.

"You're going to be in hormone hell today, aren't you, all those little pimple-faced darlings."

"And next I aim to start through the usual misfits and miscreants in the immediate Lakeside area."

"What do you want me on?" Knudson asked.

"Herberts will invest manpower on a search. I guess we'd better focus on where they should start."

Knudson shrugged. "It's the kind of thing the public wants."

Wendell nodded while looking out the window.

"What are we really doing while they go for a walk in the woods?"

"For starters, can you follow up on Lakeside patrol calls. I don't care if it's a lost dog. Review deputy write-ups. We also need to slog through the security footage we requested. I've hit the Saturday afternoon/evening tapes, but we need to work that backwards and forwards. Can you acquire ATM film from the two banks? That would really be a longshot, but you never know. There's a big RV park on the highway and that big condo complex. Will you check if they have any security cameras?"

"I'm on it."

"Can you also get me anything available on Bianconi's brother? I'll get you the details. I've got a call into him, but this family seems to live for voicemail."

"Okey-dokey."

"We've followed the script, right? What should we be doing that we're not?" he asked.

"You talked about her song lyrics. You sure this isn't suicide?"

"It's not impossible. She sees herself as a loner even though she's surrounded by friends," he said. "But no one reports awareness of depression. Everybody says she's upbeat. Easy going. I'm hung up on Bianconi saying she used an alias. What's that about? But then I'm hung up on Bianconi too."

"Understandably so," she said. "I want to go deeper on open missing person's cases and reported runaways too. But I don't think we can rule out a random disappearance. Some creep passing through grabs her."

"You're right," he sighed. He looked across the table at her. "That one scares me the most, the possibility this is something entirely random. Get in a car and you're gone."

"It's early. There's a thousand explanations."

"You think she'll show up at lunch today, tell her friends she just had to go see the ocean?"

"Stranger things have happened."

"I'm uncomfortable around strange things," Wendell said.

"Let's order. I'm starving."

Wendell didn't need a menu. He was a man of firm—some would say, inflexible—habits. Breakfast: two eggs, sunny-side up, wheat toast, link sausage. Knudson, on the other hand, couldn't make up her mind. But before the waitress arrived, his phone rang. "Maybe this is something." He rose and took the call outside.

"Detective Wendell," a deep voice on the phone said. "Stan Bianconi. My wife said it's something regarding Joshua."

Wendell relayed his need to gain access to Joshua's phone records and location.

"Really? I'm in Japan. You want to talk about a phone?"

"Your wife insists she doesn't have access to the phone account."

"My wife thinks phones magically appear, along with Mercedes and diamonds."

"Your cooperation can help an ongoing investigation."

"Josh doesn't have the phone."

"That's what I've been told, sir. But we have incoming calls to that number that are of great interest to us."

"No, you don't understand. I gave that phone to his brother. He was supposed to have it changed to his number."

"Jacob?"

"Yeah. Apparently, Jake had an incident. Took the old porcelain swim would be my guess. I was happy the kid wanted to save me the cost of a replacement. If it was Josh in the same boat, he'd buy the most expensive phone he could get his hands on."

"So, Jacob is in possession of the phone that is assigned to Joshua's number?"

"I'm sure he changed it over the same day I gave it to him. You know how kids are with their phones. It's like their brains are directly wired to them."

"When was this?"

"Before I left. Maybe ten days ago. He was headed out to one of the kumbaya deals the school puts on." Stan Bianconi became suddenly silent.

"Mr. Bianconi, are you still there?"

"Yeah, yeah, I am," he said, with a grumpy edge to his voice.

"Your cell provider would have sent you confirmation of a change to your account."

Bianconi ignored the statement. "What's Josh got himself mixed up in this time?"

"He's simply had involvement with someone we are trying to locate."

"Shit."

"Sir?"

"The little shit has got his brother to bring him his phone. Jake is about as book smart as they come, but he's shit for brains when it comes to common sense. He's always been gullible when it comes to his brother. It would be so like Josh to drag Jake into something. He wouldn't have any trouble at all convincing his brother. He'd tell him they've granted him new privileges. Tell him he'd use it to talk with us more. Jake would fall for it hook, line, and sinker." His voice had lost the edge of anger now, and he sounded sad. Bianconi sighed. "What do you need me to do?"

"I need the last two months of call records. Time is of the essence on this matter."

"Please keep me in the loop," Bianconi said. "He's a pain in the ass, but I love my son. I don't want to believe he's mixed up in something."

***

"I bet dad's right about the whereabouts of the phone," Knudson said. "I'll go through the call record as soon as we get it."

"I might need leverage on Jacob too. Test how mutual the brotherly soft-heartedness is."

The waitress arrived with their food. Wendell registered momentary surprise.

"The waitress knew your order by heart. You're either predictable, a good tipper, or a closeted flirt."

"Where do you put your money?"

"I'll stick with predictable, but I've been surprised before."

***

Eric Herberts appeared the studio model for the standard-issue cop—shaved head, a thick mustache still dark despite his fifty-seven years, a muscular upper-body that stretched the collars and short sleeves of his shirts but stretched their waists too. A former Marine, he projected a general attitude that suggested men like him were the last line of defense against a society that had lost its way.

Wendell was embarrassed that he had nothing to share. A detective without a lead was a thorn in the paw of his supervisor.

"Okay, so you're on prep school," Herberts said, pacing behind his desk.

Knudson took the only chair, and Wendell leaned on a file cabinet that was cluttered with two half-full coffee cups and a pipe stand that Herberts probably hadn't touched since he occupied the office. "What's the story? Past violence?"

"There was one altercation with a teacher, but the teacher dropped charges. The school expelled him. He's got a full sheet, all drug and alcohol related, and property crime. A kid who has a past of getting in over his head."

"Beat the shit out of a teacher," Knudson said. "He's not just in over his head, he's swimming with sharks."

"So, that's your primary," Herberts said.

"Yep."

"What are your other lines?"

"The family looks clean. Hard-working. Homebodies. Friends and neighbors suggest the parents seem to have good relationships with the kids. Always in attendance at the kids' activities. Active in their church. Dad has one prior fifteen years ago on an assault charge. A bar fight. Sounds like it may have been wrong place, wrong time. Pled out and paid out. No time."

Herberts grunted.

"The sisters-in-law like to talk. They say dad got big into church after the assault thing. According to them, before that he was a drinker. We'll dig deeper. Britany's peers suggest mom and dad are over-protective. If she's a runner, we need to know why."

"What else?"

"I think we may not know the girl who shows up in senior pictures and school playbills. And, if Bianconi is telling the truth, she gave him a fake name. If the Bianconi thing doesn't go anywhere, we go back to the usual on this one. Without a suspect, learn the victim inside and out."

"Victim," Herberts said. "At present, this is still a missing person's case. Check yourself, Detective."

Wendell winced.

"Let's dot the Is and cross the Ts. Roger me on that?"

"Yes, sir."

"Don't miss something while you look the other way."

Wendell nodded.

Herberts cleared his throat. “I’m going to turn it over to the flyboys and jungle rats. You two keep on the case. Where does the search team start? What did the phone GPS show?”

“GPS was turned off,” Knudson said.

“Turned off?”

“Dad is a bit of a conspiracy theorist,” Wendell offered. “Convinced the NSA is listening. He’s turned off location services on all their phones. Ironic, right?”

“So, we’ve only got triangulation,” Knudson said. “Wi-Fi when she was at a local coffeehouse and cell towers put her last call in Lakeside, but we can’t pinpoint.”

“Any suggestions for ground zero?” Herberts asked.

“I don’t think you have any choice but depart from the house.”

“The family will think it’s exactly what they want, right up until they’ve got news crews on their lawn and whackos with Tarot cards,” Herberts said. “We’re getting public pressure like a case of the runs. A county commissioner who knows somebody that knows somebody. This goes top priority.”

Chapter Ten

As he exited the station, Wendell saw Tom Rodgers pacing a circuit between a bench and a flagpole. His hands were thrust into his pockets, which made his shoulders hunch forward.

"Tom?"

Rodgers's head shot up at Wendell's voice. Dark circles shadowed his eyes. "You got something to ask me, then ask me," Rodgers barked. "Don't go snoopin' around to my neighbors and my family."

"Why don't we go inside and talk."

"I don't know what kind of bullshit you're pullin'. You should be out looking for my daughter instead of asking questions about me."

"I have to know Britany's life to find her," Wendell said. "We have to understand if there is any reason she might have left. I know it is uncomfortable, but the family is one of the places we have to start."

"My mother-in-law, my brother-in-law. My frickin' boss?"

"How about we get some coffee."

"Sittin' on my ass drinkin' coffee isn't my way. Shouldn't you go house to house? Why aren't you crawlin' up the ass of the Schneiders? That's supposedly where she was."

"Tom, we've talked to the Schneider family. There's no evidence she was ever there Saturday night. We're forming a search party. The officers involved are experts. I'm doing everything I can to provide them the most productive starting point."

"By harassing people who know me?"

"My focus is to determine if Britany had reason to go away on her own. Second to that, I have to try to find other people who might have information."

"You don't think Sheila and I know a damn thing about our own daughter. You think we don't have any control over what goes on inside our house."

"Tom, my only interest is to find Britany. The more I know about her, the better likelihood I have of success. I don't wish to be insensitive to what you and your family are going through—"

"You've got no idea what we're going through."

"You're right, Tom. I don't. Britany's not my child," Wendell said.

"Don't look that way to me. You're tyin' to find somebody to blame. Lookin' to accuse me of something sick."

Wendell sized up the man before him. "No one is accusing you. But we have to eliminate avenues of investigation. You have to understand, Tom, in many similar cases, there are patterns of abuse, and either the child flees to escape, or the abuse has escalated. It happens with enough frequency that we have to rule it out."

"I've never laid a hand on my kids," Tom nearly shouted. His face turned red.

Wendell pressed on. "I know what it looks like when we investigate a family, but it's something we must do. I don't expect you to understand why it is so critical, but I have to rule out every possible explanation. If we have a case of a runaway, we have to understand if there is anything that would cause the child to leave. And we have to know if the child was involved in something that might give her reason to leave, like an abusive boyfriend. I have to look at anyone with whom Britany has contact."

"It's a sick business."

Wendell said nothing but thought that Tom Rodgers had no idea the kind of sickness of which people were capable. He hoped he had no cause to find out. "I will follow every lead, speak to anyone and everyone who might shed any light on what might explain her whereabouts, anything at all to find her. It's not my intent, but I may irritate you in the process. If it helps me get your daughter home, that's worth it in my book."

"Okay, okay."

"We covered this before, but sometimes you remember new details. Has anything changed at home recently that you've not told us about?"

Tom shook his head.

"People tell me you used to drink."

"I *used* to drink. I've been sober for seven years."

"That still going okay? You're under tremendous stress."

"I'm on top of it. I may have been a weak man once, but God has made me strong."

"Church is important to you."

"God is important to me. He came to me when I was down. I'm not proud of some of the things I've done, but God forgave me. I changed."

"Seven years sober. Good for you. That's a tough road."

"Nothing at all compared to what our Savior suffered," Tom said.

"You have a prior arrest for assault."

"I spent time in bars when I should have been home with my family. Got caught up in business I shouldn't have. I let myself get in a fight that didn't concern me."

"Is that when you cleaned up?"

"It is. That's not a phone call I was ever going to make to my wife again. Spent the night in jail. Beat up. Sicker than a dog. But my wife helped me reach out to Jesus." Tom looked embarrassed.

"Any evidence Britany has experimented with drinking?"

Tom shook his head.

"Is church a big part of her life too?"

"She goes with us. I haven't asked her what it means to her." Tom stared at his feet. "You talked about phone calls she made. What's that about?"

"I am actively pursuing that information."

"What kind of calls?"

"Ones that don't fit her usual patterns. That's what we look for. We need you and Sheila to look for the slightest things that seem off-kilter. I need to know what she likes and what she dislikes, what she's afraid of, who she turns to for advice. All of it. The smallest clue could start us down the right path." Wendell zipped up his jacket against the cold. "About the phone,

Tom. You have location services turned off. Is there something specific that prompted that?"

"I don't like the idea of the government digging around my private life. It's the same reason I don't let the kids use Facebook."

"I've asked this before, but it's important. Has Britany ever had guys call her she doesn't want anything to do with? Has she mentioned guys from out of state?"

"Is there something about Britany I don't know?" Tom's shoulders remained hunched forward, though he'd removed his hands from his pockets.

"We've spoken to one person Britany spent time with recently. He claims she gave him a different name."

"Lindsey," Tom said.

"You know about that?"

"It's something I taught the kids to do with strangers."

"To protect them?"

"Yeah."

"Does the name have any significance?"

Tom grunted. "Just another name we had picked out when she was born. I used to tease her that I'd trade her in for a Lindsey." His eyes shifted focus. "Who's this guy?"

"Someone her age."

"I want to talk to him," Tom demanded.

"Absolutely not. You have to let us do our job, Tom."

"You keep saying she's run away. You treat her like she's one of those hippies you see backpacking through here. That's not who my daughter is." He straightened his shoulders and stepped toward Wendell. His hands were curled into fists though they remained at his sides.

Wendell chose his words carefully, walking a line between direct and cold-hearted. "We need to hope that Britany has chosen, for whatever reason, to depart on her own accord. The alternative would suggest she is the victim of an abduction. That's an entirely different set of consequences."

"The other…" Tom stammered. "If she's been taken—"

"Tom, if that's the road we have to go down, I'll tell you so. We don't know anything yet."

* * *

Wendell sat in his car for several minutes. He reached for Britany's growing portfolio. It opened to the pages copied from Britany's notebook. Her penmanship flourished with loops and swirls, and her Is were topped with flowers or hearts, the pages dense with ink. Wendell returned to the lyrics of a song Britany had titled "Like a Small Boat..." There were two lines at the start of the chorus that lodged inside his head:

There's an ocean divide
separating me from the other side

Chapter Eleven

"Should he have legal counsel?" Kragor asked.

"He's not under arrest. I have questions to revisit."

"And new evidence he's likely to possess a phone against school policy."

"If his dad's theory holds true." Wendell could not decide if the look of disappointment on Dr. Kragor's face stemmed from the failure of his school to combat contraband or from a belief that Joshua had backslid.

"We'll conduct a thorough search of his room."

"Do you think I can have a space that's a bit more private? And perhaps we can forgo the team?"

"I want his lead counselor present. For both his sake and ours. Joshua may legally be an adult, but the school bears responsibility."

"That's fine."

* * *

Joshua entered the room with an affected walk learned from hip-hop videos. But he'd lost the emo coiffure and now his hairstyle belonged in an Ivy League fraternity. Wendell wondered what sort of chameleon he faced. He was accompanied by a bearded counselor.

"You pulled me out of a biology test."

"Then you should be thanking me," Wendell said.

"I told you last night I don't know this girl."

"If you provide me your phone, I'm sure we can clear this up and be done with it."

"Open your ears, man. I don't have a phone."

"Treat the detective with respect," the counselor said quietly.

"He needs to respect me."

"I spoke with your father."

"So?"

"I'm sure you're not the only one here who wants access to your phone."

"What did my dad tell you?"

Wendell pushed limits and linked the only facts in his possession with conjecture, a currency in which Joshua had long trafficked. "Britany called you twice on Saturday, once at 4:53 when you talked for nineteen minutes and again at 5:36. And the thing is, that second call represents the last known contact with her. So, you can kind of see why cooperating is in your best interest."

"I don't know what my old man told you, but I don't have a phone."

"The first call. That's setting up a date?"

"What?"

"And the second call, what's that? You were running late? Whose car did you borrow?"

"I don't know what you're talking about."

"When did your brother get here?"

"My brother?"

"Did he give you the phone right away? Or once you were off campus?"

"This is bullshit, man!"

"Josh," the counselor intoned.

"This guy is bullying me." Josh slumped in his chair. "Jake didn't give me anything."

"The hard questions will come harder if we can't get through the easy ones."

"I don't know what you're talking about."

"How'd you convince your brother to bring your phone?"

"Don't listen to my old man."

"What other presents did he bring you? Some Oregon dope?"

"I don't think this is a fair line of questioning, detective," the counselor said.

Wendell did not remove his eyes from Joshua's but said, "I have a missing seventeen-year-old, and Josh talked to her the day she disappeared. I think these are reasonable questions."

Joshua covered his face with his hands. "I don't know what you're accusing me of. I don't know anything."

"Let's go back to the phone."

"I. Don't. Have. A. Phone," he shouted. Then he lowered his voice and took a deep breath. "I swear. You can search my room," he said, exasperated. The irritability could be a default position but made Wendell wonder.

"This girl magically calls your phone number. Randomly. Out of all the numbers in the world."

The anger shifted and his eyes threatened tears. "Jake had some weed. We smoked together. That's it." Joshua turned to his counselor. He opened his hands on the top of the table. "I'm sorry, Kevin. I know I fucked up."

"Josh, I appreciate you being honest," Wendell said. "Your brother brings you some weed. He brings you your phone. Did Britany want to party?"

"No, no, no," Joshua chanted. "I smoked with my brother. But that's it, man. I swear. I don't know about the rest. I don't know anything about this girl."

"Then why did Britany call your number?"

"You say Jake had my phone. You'll have to ask him."

"If something happened with Britany, you'd want to help, right?"

"I don't know anything about her."

"This all goes a lot easier if you cooperate. Otherwise, not only does it get harder on you, it gets hard on other people too. Cops showing up at your brother's room. That can't look good, right? Doesn't seem fair if the worst he's done is bring you a phone or shared a joint. But the campus cops might find more than a joint when they show up."

"What are you trying to do to me?"

"I'm trying to find a young girl. This girl," Wendell said, placing Britany's picture on the table.

"I told you. I don't know anything. You can give me a lie detector test. Whatever it takes for you to believe me."

Wendell paused and stared at Joshua. The boy looked like a boy, and he looked spent. Wendell cleared his throat in a practiced gesture. "You'd better get back to that biology test."

Joshua didn't move.

"Something to add?"

"No, sir," he mumbled.

"Josh, wait in the hall a minute, please. I'll walk you back," the counselor said. Joshua rose and complied, shutting the door behind him.

Wendell raised his hand. "No statements about the appropriateness of my line of questioning. I'm not going to apologize if I rattled the boy."

"No, I get it. The stakes are high. A lot of these kids will test you. When they first arrive, some of them act like thugs. Josh was that way. I've worked with him for a year and a half. He's changed. I think he's telling the truth."

Wendell looked from the counselor to the picture of Britany lying on the table. He nodded without a word.

* * *

A slow, steady rain had arrived, and the raindrops felt cold against Wendell's face as he walked to the car. He watched the rain bead on the windshield. He thought about the search party that would form elsewhere in the rain. Wendell dialed Jacob Bianconi's number, which went immediately to voicemail. Then he dialed Knudson.

"Get anywhere?"

"He's sitting on his hands." Wendell sighed.

"I've read his sheet. He sounds familiar with lying," she said. "I've followed up on Lakeside calls. One was an alarm reported by a caretaker on Sunday, but when the deputy arrived, the caretaker claimed it had been a system malfunction. The other was reported as an animal collision, but the caller was a bit of a whack job, and it wasn't clear if she was talking about a pet or what. The deputy found blood on the road and a headlight ring. I've got messages in to both deputies."

"Let's make sure we can rule out a hit-and-run," Wendell said. He appreciated Knudson's steadiness. She was experienced rooting in the brush but still green on the firing line.

"I've reviewed the security footage we have zippo."

"Anything on Bianconi's brother?"

"No record on our end of the world, so I did some surfing. So far, it seems that for everything Joshua's done wrong, his brother has done right. He was captain of his high school robotics team, and they won state, which, I suppose in California is a big deal. Model U.N. He computerized the lights for the school's musical theater company. The full geek quotient. High test scores, lots of college acceptances. Scholarship at Willamette."

"All while his brother is off being a little juvenile delinquent. It must really chafe Joshua's ass to have an older brother who casts a long shadow."

"Seems like it happens that way all the time," Knudson said. "Only he's not an older brother. They're the same age."

"Twins?" Wendell said. "Identical or fraternal?"

"Identical. A regular angel on one shoulder, devil on the other."

"Oh, shit," Wendell said. "It's been right in front of my face. Joshua was expelled from two different schools. He's a year behind." Wendell slapped his palm on the steering wheel. "Shit," he said again. "Stacey, call the Willamette Campus Police. Tell them to find Jacob Bianconi."

Chapter Twelve

Tom Rodgers stopped. Something that didn't belong, a bright purple object, emerged out of the rain-filtered gloom among thickets of brush.

During the meeting prior to the start of the search, he'd felt ashamed that he didn't know what his daughter had been wearing. He could tell the assembled volunteers her height by indicating where the top of her head hit him when she hugged him, though he'd be hard-pressed to tell precisely when the last time she hugged him had been—and yet he couldn't put a number to her height, no more than he could tell you what earrings she wore Saturday or what color she'd painted her nails. All things Sheila knew. But now he saw the lavender coat clearly in his mind, remembered the day when she'd begged him to buy it, promising to pay half. The beginning of last school year, the jacket a need manufactured before a trip to Bozeman and Missoula to look at colleges. Her desire to look like she belonged on campus. He'd argued, "If you have to change your clothes to fit in, then why would you want to?" Seeing her disappointment, he changed his tone, "Purple?" When she tried on the coat, he saw how happy it made her. The color fit her boisterous laugh and bright personality.

All weekend long as they toured campuses, he felt his camouflage jacket marked him rather than hid him. He'd stayed quiet as they took Britany to nice dinners and bought her sweatshirts in school colors. He'd tramped along at the back of campus tour groups. The names of the departments meant nothing to him. He had trouble hearing the student guide at MSU, an Asian girl who told all the right jokes for the kids but were lost on him.

On the way home, he eyed Britany in the rearview mirror. She wore the lavender Patagonia coat atop a maroon University of Montana sweatshirt. He said, "We'll see, Brit. I still think it would make more sense to get your first two years under your belt where you could live at home for free."

Part of him wanted to race toward the purple object tangled among the bushes. Another wanted to turn to the nearest searcher and ask him to check. He'd heard little of the directions the sheriff had covered prior to entering the forest near his home, something about grids and search logs, but then that's how it had been for days, his attention constantly switched from one thing to the next with long periods where he'd enter the feeling of fighting off sleep.

Rain dripped off his baseball cap. The forest was suspended in twilight. There were instructions about narrowing the distance between searchers because of the weather and emphasis on safety. The warnings stuck with him only because they felt foolish when they should all be focused on the unspeakable harm his daughter had surely suffered if she was out in these woods.

He took a deep breath. His eyes remained fixed upon the purple object while he moved mechanically forward. His glasses steamed over. Was that a log or rock, shadow or denim extending from the humped purple shape? He reached up to wipe away the moisture and tripped, his feet tangled in the limbs of a downed pine. Its trunk slammed into his ribs, and branches snapped under his weight. His glasses went flying. He groaned at the impact. Arms outstretched in a failed effort to arrest his fall, his left hand extended toward the purple object. He crawled forward, raking along the tree trunk, and gathered an empty dog food bag into his hands. The sullen rain pattered against the waxed material.

He heard branches break as searchers from each flank rushed to his aid. "You okay, man?" shouted the man who was first to arrive. He was perhaps twenty-five. A full dark beard disguised a thin face. A pair of boots appeared in Tom's peripheral vision as he looked up into this young face, and then he heard from somewhere beyond his peripheral vision, the familiar voice of Pete Garolin, say, "Tom, what happened, brother? You okay?"

Tom held up the bag.

"Jesus," Pete said. "You're lucky you didn't impale yourself." Pete stomped on a branch poking up from a nearby log, which broke with a snap. "You hurt?"

Tom shook his head and moved into an awkward seated position. Pain in his ribs had taken his breath away. "My glasses," he croaked. "Help me find my glasses." He shoved the empty dog food bag away, hating this weakness and hating too the sympathy encountered in the men's eyes.

Chapter Thirteen

Most of the seats at Glacier Park International Airport's five gates were empty. Mud season—no summer tourists mounted Glacier backpacking expeditions and too early for ski traffic. As Wendell waited for his flight to board, he spoke by phone with Chuck Burell, Willamette's Campus Safety Director. Wendell learned that Burell had retired after a career with the Marion County Sheriff's Department, then fashioned a second career and a post-retirement income. "Campuses are complicated places from a policing standpoint," Burell said. "My security officers are well-trained, but with this kind of request, I walk the point." About his contact with Bianconi, he said, "He's covering something up. Denied he'd been to Montana."

Kragor had verified Jacob's participation in group workshops. Why lie? "I hope you didn't send him skittering into the underbrush," Wendell said.

"Held my cards close. With kids like Bianconi, so long as we remind them that anything and everything can block the release of transcripts, we're usually okay."

Burell's assured tone offered Wendell no comfort.

* * *

He passed the flight focused on his notes, which included a thick folder of questionnaires from canvasing they'd completed. He dug deeper into Knudson's typed notes about Tom and Sheila Rodgers. And he wasted time he didn't have staring into a grainy photograph Knudson had printed from a security tape. In it, Britany Rodgers sat in a comfortable leather chair, looking vaguely in the direction of the camera. Knudson had dropped the photograph in Wendell's lap while he worked his way through a stack of police reports from the Lakeside area. "It's not much, but we've got a clean timeline," Knudson had said. "You know the Lakeside Centerplace building?" Knudson pointed to the photo of Britany.

Wendell nodded.

"Security goldmine. They have a lobby that's open to the public and a card-access gym upstairs, which explains all the cameras. 4:42 p.m. Saturday. I've got the footage all cued up."

Wendell followed her to her desk, eager as a puppy.

Knudson started the video. "She enters the building at 4:19. Hangs in the lobby the whole time. A couple of phone calls to friends, which the phone record corroborates, including this one," she said, fast-forwarding the tape. "4:53. She's on the phone for nineteen minutes. That's our first call to Bianconi's phone."

Wendell had watched with fascination as Britany talked on the phone, laughing and smiling, gathering her hair in her hand and bringing the heft of it over one shoulder.

"She makes another call at 5:36. Bianconi again. It's less than a minute. Then she gets up and we only get her in glimpses near the front windows. I've got her from a different camera on the corner of the building walking outside at 5:41."

"Tell me you've got who she's waiting for."

"I wish. We've got nothing past the doorways and sidewalks. If she's meeting someone, he apparently doesn't leave his car."

"Of course not."

"The call to chat. Set up a date? A call back to see if he's close. This looks like an appointment with Joshua Bianconi to me," Knudson said.

"Or some Bianconi," Wendell agreed.

As Wendell stared at the photo, Britany remained stubborn in her silence.

In the final minutes of the flight, Wendell turned back to the pages from Britany's journal. There was a long song about fireworks that left Wendell wondering if the lyrics were a metaphor for sexual awakening. Another about horses at a rodeo. Nearly all the lyrics were readable either as superficial narratives or as metaphors with no clear point of entrance. They were interrupted by occasional lines that showed both poetic ability and possible psychological significance, like a line in the song about fireworks that described their refection over a lake as: "a swimming trail of colored glass shards." Britany's friends and most of her teachers dismissed her as ordinary, but was that a fair statement about anyone?

Britany had received honorable mention in a state poetry competition for a poem that appeared in her notebook titled "Like a Small Boat." It was filled with images of troubled water, storms, and rocky shores. What storms did she face that no one else knew about, he wondered as the pilot came on the intercom to ask the stewardesses to prepare the cabin for landing.

* * *

He reached the Willamette campus shortly after 7:00 p.m. "I appreciate the personal touch," Wendell said upon meeting Burell.

"You could have a lot riding on it," Burell said.

"Or I could be barking up the wrong tree."

"Wouldn't be police work if you didn't have that. Most kids are done with dinner. We might catch him at his dorm."

The men walked past sculpted ponds on sidewalks lit by decorative light posts. They talked about similarities in their pasts patrolling large, rural counties. "This is a tough beat," Wendell said as they crossed a groomed lawn and past red-brick academic buildings.

"Not exactly meth labs and grow plots," Burell agreed. He card-swiped them into a side door of Matthews Hall, and they were immediately met with a swirl of noise. They took a back stair to the second floor. Bianconi's door was partially open, that neighborly, moving party of college communal living. Through the open door, Wendell saw the back of what could have been Joshua Bianconi's head. Expensive headphones encircled his neck. At the sharp rap of Burell's knuckles on the door, Jacob Bianconi swiveled in his chair. He stood up quickly.

Burell, a squat, broad-shouldered man, pushed into the room. The entry was narrow, blocking the vision of much of the room. Wendell, against all logic, tried to imagine that when he stepped inside he would find Britany Rodgers reclined in a bean bag chair.

"Jacob," Burell said as he strode to the center of the room, "this is Detective Wendell of the Flathead County Sheriff's Department in Montana. He has some questions for you. I know I can count on you to be fully cooperative." Wendell thought Burell took the whole *in loco parentis* thing a bit too literally.

Wendell watched the color drain from Jacob's face. He'd clearly not shared his brother's encounters with authorities. If Joshua was a chameleon, accommodating and manipulating his environment, Jacob was a Gila monster, incapable of moving fast enough to keep pace with the sun. Wendell took in the unmade bunk beds, a pile of laundry that spilled out of an open closet, a poster of a woman sprawled topless across the hood of a Ferrari, a shelf of textbooks heavy on physics and astronomy and fronted by a row of shot glasses. A quarter-full bottle of tequila served as a bookend.

Wendell made a show of removing the lanyard that held his detective badge from under his dress shirt. He seized a chair from the desk on the opposite side of the room, unzipped his portfolio, and opened the three-ring binder into which he organized his notes. "Let's chat about what brought you to Montana last week."

Jacob's eyes shifted nervously to Burell, who leaned against the closet. He made no attempt to revert to the lie he had told Burell. "I went to see my brother," he mumbled.

"I'm afraid you're going to have to speak up," Wendell said. "I have a hearing impairment," he lied.

"To see my brother," Jacob repeated.

"Joshua?"

Jacob nodded.

"Tell me about him. Why he is in Montana."

"He goes to boarding school there."

"You two are twins, right? Yet you're in college. How'd that happen?"

"Josh had some problems in the past."

"What sort of problems?"

"He just...he and our old school...school really isn't his thing."

"But it's your thing."

"Me? I love school."

"Whereas Josh got himself expelled."

Jacob nodded.

"From a couple of schools."

Jacob nodded again.

"Tell me more."

"He hung out with the wrong people. They got him into stuff he shouldn't have. One thing kinda led to another."

"Including run-ins with the likes of me?" Wendell smiled.

"Yeah."

"So, Mom and Dad shipped him off to get him out of their hair."

"It's not like that. It's a therapeutic school. They help him with his..." Jacob stumbled, searching for a word "...issues." He began to play idly with a pen, spinning it in circles atop his closed laptop.

"What are Josh's issues? Drugs, beating up teachers? Lying?" Wendell emphasized this last word. Jacob did not respond. His attention focused on the twirling pen. "Does he lie to you?"

Jacob shrugged. The gesture made him appear adolescent.

"Are you two close?"

Another shrug.

"He shares things with you?" The question received no response. "I mean, come on, who can you gritch to about your parents if not your brother?"

This received a hesitant smile.

"You went to Montana to see your brother. Show him your support."

"The school reaches out to families. Last spring, I went on a climbing trip with him they sponsored. It's pretty cool. They had a workshop last week."

"What was the workshop about?"

"Rebuilding trust."

"Successful?"

"Huh?"

"You two have rekindled a trusting relationship?"

"Yeah, I guess," Jacob said. He stopped the spinning pen. "We get along better than we have in a long time."

"Seems to me he still uses you."

"Huh?"

"Hasn't he used you before? To settle things with Mom and Dad?"

The boy didn't answer.

"He's never asked you to lie for him?"

"Yeah. But he's changed."

"Did he ask you to bring him his cellphone?"

Jacob didn't respond, but Wendell saw him react at the mention of the phone. "It appears you both struggle to manage your cell phones."

"I don't know what you mean."

"I've left you several messages."

"Oh, sorry. I broke my phone."

"You told Mr. Burell that you lost it."

"I meant that it's not working."

"Was that why you asked your dad to use your brother's phone?"

"Sorry, what?"

"Your brother's phone. The one you picked up last time you were home."

"Oh, yeah." Jacob keenly focused on some point of fascination with his shoe. He shifted from staring at his feet to picking at a small hole in the knee of his pants. "I haven't gotten around to getting it switched over to my number."

"So, you're using your brother's phone number?"

"No, well, I mean yes," Jacob said. "But just for stuff I had to take care of. I meant to get to the store today."

"Because your dad was under the impression you'd probably taken the phone to your brother, even though it's against school policy."

"I wouldn't do anything that would get Josh in trouble."

"That's the thing, see," Wendell said, "I'm trying to help your brother. I hoped you could help me."

"What's are you talking about?"

Wendell opened the folder he'd placed on Jake's desk. Britany's graduation photo stared out from it, the kind of photo she or her family would see years from now and think how young she looked. "Did you meet this girl when you were in Kalispell?" He pushed the folder closer to Jacob.

Jacob flinched. "Yeah," he said. "Josh knew her. We bumped into her in a coffee shop."

"*Bumped* into her."

"Josh had met her before. He hoped she might be there."

"Your brother said you and this girl hit it off."

"Yeah, I guess."

"I thought your brother went there looking specifically for her."

"I don't think Josh really knew her."

"What's her name?"

"Josh introduced her as Lindsey."

"That's an odd way to put it. He *introduced* her as Lindsey."

"That's the name she'd given him. But her friends at the table called her Britany."

"Why do you think your brother lied about her name?"

"He didn't. She lied to him."

"She's the liar," Wendell said flatly. Jacob did not respond. "Your brother has a history of telling lies to save himself. Lying to authorities. Lots and lots of lies to your parents, right? To you."

"She admitted it later. She was embarrassed about it." Jacob flicked his hair out of his eyes. The action made him look so much like his brother Wendell felt transported inside Peak Academy. "What's going on?" Jacob asked. "Why are you here?"

Wendell tapped the photo with his index finger. "This girl," he said. "This girl you met in the coffeehouse is named Britany. Britany Rodgers. She's seventeen. She's missing."

"Missing?" Jacob sat forward in his chair with such sudden movement that Wendell saw Burell shift his stance. "What do you mean?"

"I don't think there are a lot of alternative definitions for the word. She didn't come home Saturday night. And I am prepared to scour every inch of the planet to find her. Including flying to Oregon to see you."

Wendell saw fear in Jacob's eyes.

"Which brings me to Joshua's phone. The one you're using. Which makes sense after all, when I review the calls." Wendell removed a stapled sheath of pages from beneath Britany's photo, which crept an inch closer to Jacob when disturbed by the movement. "There's this Oregon number that seems awfully popular. Makes me wonder where a call might lead." Wendell leaned forward in his chair. He let a moment of silence do its work. "But it's two calls to a Montana phone that have me curious."

Jacob pushed back in his seat.

Wendell watched him. "I wonder if you don't need a little break. Should we step outside a minute and let you have a smoke?"

"I don't smoke," Jacob said weakly.

"Why do you have a lighter?" Wendell asked, leaning forward and picking up a cigarette lighter from the desk. He laid it back down next to an ashtray. "This wouldn't prove to be a roach?" he said, pointing to the ashtray.

"It's my roommate's."

"I'd hate to waste even more of Mr. Burell's time. Following up on probable cause to search for illicit substances. Charging minors in possession." Wendell pointed to the tequila bottle on the bookshelf. "That would mean involvement with the Salem PD."

Burell looked squarely at Jacob. "I prefer to respect student privacy. But I am duty bound to act on criminal activity."

"Do I need a lawyer or something?"

"You certainly have that right," Wendell said. "Of course, it's up to Chief Burell whether he feels it necessary to search this room. University property and all that. Which would make for kind of a bum rap for the old roomie." Wendell reached forward and spun the cigarette lighter, copying the distracted fidgeting Jacob exhibited with the pen. "The thing is, I just want to find Britany." He tapped the photo again. "My interests are a lot more urgent."

"Has something happened to her?"

"You tell me."

"I don't know anything."

"I think you do."

"I don't. I swear." Panic labored Jacob's voice.

"Let's go backwards. You arrived Wednesday. Then a trip into town with your brother on Thursday."

Jacob nodded.

"The two of you smoke a couple of bowls and wind up at a coffeehouse where you meet Britany Rodgers."

Jacob visibly flinched.

"How is it you ended up with Britany instead of your brother?"

"There was a whole group of kids. There's this blond Josh was into."

Wendell consulted his binder. He inserted his finger at a tab, turned a page, and said, "Jaqueline."

"Yeah."

"But Josh is there to see Britany."

"He was, but Jaqueline is exactly Josh's type."

"So he pawns you off onto Britany."

"It wasn't like that."

"Enlighten me."

"We were all just talking. Joking about the music on the Sirius station or whatever. The guy behind the counter. His mustache."

"But Josh wanted time with Jaqueline. How'd you pull that off?"

Jacob looked embarrassed. "Josh was dressed all hipster and shit. We went to the restroom, and I took his hat and coat. Most people can't tell us apart. He said Britany was into him. He said it gave me a way in." Jacob's cheeks flushed. "I'm not like Josh. It takes me time to get to know people."

"You posed as your brother."

"Yeah. I mean, it wasn't like I was pretended to be him, other than by name."

"Which got you alone with Brittany."

"We weren't alone. There was a whole group."

"But she had your attention."

"Yeah."

"And you gave her your phone number when you left. Or rather Joshua's phone number."

Jacob nodded. Wendell looked at Britany's photo. He pictured the surveillance video of her at the Lakeside Centerplace. The appearance of waiting to meet someone. "This may be that point where you want to think about having legal representation, Jacob."

Jacob's head snapped up. "Did something happen to her?"

"I'm obligated to inform you that anything you say that's incriminating can be used against you."

"I didn't do anything."

Wendell looked to where Burell remained standing in the doorway. "You don't wish legal counsel?"

"I didn't do anything."

"Okay, Jacob. Tell me what you do know. You gave her your brother's phone number. Did you make plans to see each other?"

Jacob shifted in his seat. He nodded.

"I need you to speak up."

"Yes," he said.

"Tell me."

"She said she'd call me Saturday, and we'd go to dinner."

"I thought you told your brother you were leaving Friday."

"I figured I could drive back Sunday," Jake said. He picked up the pen, removed the cap, put it back on. "Britany is missing?"

Wendell ignored the question. "You figured you'd get lucky."

Jacob shrugged. "I guess. I don't know. I liked her."

"Tell me about this date."

"She called me Saturday afternoon. I'd about given up. We talked a while. It felt easy like it had at the coffee shop. She gave me directions to pick her up."

"In Lakeside."

"Yeah."

"Okay, so?"

"We went to dinner at a brewpub. It was like a block away."

"Okay, you come to Montana. Meet a pretty girl. The night's going well."

"Yeah."

"All the while, you're pretending to be Josh."

"She'd only met Josh one other time. I was just being myself."

"Yet you and Joshua aren't exactly the same people."

"It was obvious Josh had told her some stuff. Some girls like Josh's edge. That he seems he's all badass. She gave me grief about not ordering beer. Said she was sure I had a fake I.D. But it was just teasing. I was able to be myself."

"What'd you talk about?"

"Lots of stuff. About how she was over high school. How sick she was of shallow people. We both hate it that people don't want to talk about real stuff."

"Real stuff?"

"People want to talk about their drama. Bullshit over friends. Meaningless crap. We talked about, I don't know, issues. We talked a lot about how different we are from our parents. She seemed more mature than most high school girls."

As Wendell continued to lead him, Jacob told about how they had driven a few blocks to a park on the lakeshore and flirted while they took in the pretty view. Josh said, "She asked me if I had a blanket."

Wendell raised his eyebrows, shifting into the role of an indecent fan to keep him talking. "You did, didn't you? A regular boy scout."

"I did." Jacob chanced a half-smirk.

"So, you've got a girl and a blanket and a dark night by a lake…"

"We went out to the end of the pier. We were alone."

"A regular romance."

"Mostly we talked."

"Talked. You don't kiss and tell?"

"It wasn't like that."

"How was it?"

"She's nice. It felt like more than a hook-up."

"What happened that it stopped being great?"

"Nothing."

Jacob explained that Britany had a flask in her purse with a little Fireball whiskey in it and how she tried to get him to go buy more. He looked nervously at Burell. "I had some weed, though. We smoked a joint. I wish I wouldn't have."

Wendell's ears perked. "Why is that?"

"It didn't seem like Britany's regular thing."

"It would seem that may have been to your advantage."

"She got all hyper. I mean, that's kind of how she is. But the weed amped her up. She got goofy. Said we should skinny-dip. She even lifted her shirt and flashed me. I mean, just her bra, but still..."

Wendell felt suddenly let down. "Keep going," he said.

"All of a sudden, she said she was cold. She said she wanted to skip."

"Skip?"

"Skip. Like little kids. It was a whole topic for her."

"Skipping was."

"Nah. How we don't do the things we did when we were little kids because we think people will judge us."

"Okay. Where exactly did you go skipping?"

Jacob painted a picture of them on a road alongside the lake. He told how she talked about how boring her family was. How controlling they could be. He explained that when he saw how she became kind of down talking about her family, they shared another joint. Wendell watched Jacob closely.

"Then I made the mistake of telling her that the woods reminded me of a Tim Burton movie. She gave me shit about being a city boy. The next thing I know, she runs off into the trees."

Wendell leaned forward. "Did you follow her?"

"Yeah, but I didn't run like she did. I couldn't see."

Wendell could feel the story build again. He wanted to hold his breath, something he'd felt before in interrogation rooms.

"I slipped. I fell to one knee, and when I started to get up, she jumped out from behind a boulder, growling like a bear. Like it was the funniest thing ever."

"A regular old bit of slapstick," Wendell said, not hiding the disappointment in his voice. That's it, he thought. Two stoned kids. "You're off playing in the woods. Then what?"

"We were up on a point. You could see the whole lake. I laid the blanket out on this big rock. We kissed for a while. We laid there and looked at the stars. I wanted to...well, you know, but she wanted to talk. Said I was a good listener," he said. "She talked a lot about how she wanted to see somewhere different." Jacob paused. Wendell grew impatient. The kid had become quite a talker. A nervous tick, Wendell wondered. Jacob suddenly looked up at him, making eye contact for one of the first times in the interview, and asked in a rush, "Do you think that's it? That Britany just ran away?"

"Why don't you finish your story?"

Jacob looked nervous. "I liked talking to her. She's sweet. But she kept leading me on. We'd get so far, but then she'd push me away. We fooled around. I, I," he stuttered. "I was, you know, like hard, and I kind of rolled her on top of me, and I knew she could feel it. Her shirt was open and I was, uh, you know...she was kind of grinding on me." Josh paused. "Then she'd stop."

"Go on, Josh," Wendell encouraged.

"Well, she was all over the place, right? One second she told me she wanted to get back to the car. The next she asked me if I had a hotel room. I didn't want to be an asshole, but I tried to convince her to keep going."

"Tell me what happened, Josh."

"Nothing happened," he said, a tinge of anger in his voice. "I tried to slide my hand down, you know," he said, reddening. "But she pushed my hand away and stood up. Said she was ready to leave. Looked all pissed. She picked up the blanket."

Jake paused, and Wendell let his stare bore into him. "But when we got to the road, she acted like nothing had happened," Jake continued. "We were across from a place with a closed metal gate. There was a speaker, an intercom thing, and a code pad, and she started to fuck around with it. All giggly and shit. She said she'd heard there were parties at this house." He frowned. "I couldn't figure her out. Two seconds before, she froze me out. I thought she was cool, but she was turning into a sloppy high school girl."

Impatient, Wendell interrupted him. "You were hoping she'd be a different sort of sloppy. What happened, Jacob? She didn't give you what you wanted, so you decided to take it?"

"No way. I'd never do something like that. I was just really frustrated. The next thing I know, she climbed between the bars to the other side."

"She climbed through the gate?"

"Yeah, I mean, the bars were far apart. You could walk right through. Like just the thought of it is what's supposed to keep you out. I yelled at her to get out. She walked up to the gate and said, 'See, it's not even real.' She told me to follow her. 'Let's go see how the other half lives,' she said. I told her that she was being stupid. I mean, there were 'No Trespassing' signs. She started daring me. Tried to see how far she could push me. She started to back away. When I refused to follow her, she told me to fuck off. She said, 'I thought you were different.' Then she walked away through the trees. It was so dark, I lost sight of her."

"What did you do?"

"I figured she was waiting to see if I'd follow. I called and called her name. I knew she wasn't supposed to be inside that gate. I waited for like ten minutes. Finally, I decided I didn't need her shit. I left."

"You left?"

"Yeah. I told you, she jerked me around all night."

"You left her there."

"Well, she lives in that town, right? She knows people."

"Let me get this straight," Wendell said. "You get an underage girl drunk, feed her some joints, think she's going to put out, and when she doesn't, you abandon her."

"It wasn't like that."

"What was it like?"

"I thought she was cool."

"Sounds like you thought she was easy."

"No. I liked her."

"What a load of crap. What really happened?"

"I told you."

"Were you angry?"

"No, just frustrated. Girls do this kind of shit all the time. Act like they want one thing and then they want another. I swear. I left. That's it."

"You left a girl to wander around in the woods. Why didn't you try to phone her?"

"I left my phone in the car. By the time I got back, it had been like another twenty minutes. By then, I felt bad. I mean, obviously, she would have been pissed. The last thing she'd want would be to talk to me."

"Seeing how you abandoned her and all."

"I mean, yeah, okay, I left. That was uncool. I figured she'd called a friend or found a party."

Wendell sat back in his chair and then rubbed his face with his hands. "You're telling me this girl, this girl who never comes home, you left to wander around in the dark inside someone's fence?"

"I feel really bad about it. I've wanted to call her a hundred times since."

"But conveniently you didn't."

"The whole thing…pretending to be Josh, using his phone…it was stupid. I turned off the phone, and I've never turned it back on."

Wendell cupped his hands in front of him, palms pressed together and fingers touching his chin as if in an attitude of prayer. He watched Jacob silently. The boy looked scared, but Wendell could not identify the source of the fear. Did its wellspring form in what had been revealed or what remained hidden?

At last, Wendell said, "Can't you see how ridiculous this story looks?"

Jacob nodded. "I know, I know. I told you everything. I didn't know she was missing."

"Then why didn't you return my phone calls?"

"I thought you were calling about something else. After your first message, I turned off my phone."

"Why'd you think I called?"

"I told you. Josh and I got high while we were together. If they tested him, that could get him kicked out of school."

"You don't really think I'm going to call you because the school wanted your brother to piss in a cup."

Jacob shook his head. Tears appeared. He wiped them away with the back of his hand. "I sold some to one of his friends at school," he said, his voice trembling. He paused and sniffled. When he spoke next, his voice was barely audible. "I took Josh's phone from home because I . . . ," he stammered, "I met this dude here. There are kids looking, you know, looking to score." He looked at Wendell and then at Burrell. "I know it was wrong." More tears came. "When you called, I assumed the dude at Josh's school got caught. I was scared. I don't ever do anything like this."

"You just make up stories about dumping dates in the woods."

Over the next twenty minutes, Wendell tried every means to pursue Jacob's story. He returned to facts and sometimes cited them wrong on purpose, and Jacob corrected him every time. He tried to push the pursuit of intent to distribute and impose greater fear. He told Jacob to produce the phones, and Jacob removed two identical phones from a backpack. He tried to get Jacob to empathize with what Britany may have experienced after he abandoned her, which produced new tears. Jacob's story never changed. As hard as he tried to find a more sinister mask for Jacob than the one worn by posing as his brother, it simply didn't seem a part of his make-up.

When Wendell and Burrell walked back across campus, Wendell said, "Sorry to tie up your evening."

"That's the job," Burrell said, shrugging. "You worked him about every way I've seen a suspect worked. If he's telling the truth, where's that leave you?"

"Precisely nowhere," Wendell said.

Chapter Fourteen

An inversion had settled into the Flathead Valley like a giant had pressed an enormous cotton ball to the valley floor. As the plane descended into the clouds, Wendell thought of those who searched a wet forest. Absent an inversion, the forest would be electrified with light, the last of the aspen leaves competing with the turning of the tamarack, confetti of fallen leaves, and needles softening its floor. Today the forest would remain dark and close, and in the damp press of moisture, the ascent of ridges would seem more difficult and the descent into ravines more sinister, desperation closer at hand and grief lurking in soundless hollows.

Wendell's mood fit the weather. He knew better than to expect the threads that bound a case to unravel easily. The sunrise that had accompanied his Portland departure offered evidence that another day distanced him from Britany Rodgers.

Wendell had called Knudson before departing.

"He left her?" Knudson nearly shouted into the phone. "I'd like to give him a pointy heel in the nut sack."

He ignored her and asked, "Remember that alarm call you said you'd found in the patrol reports from Lakeside?"

"Yes," she replied. "I hope to catch the deputy at shift change."

"Do you remember if that was right on the lake?"

"I think so."

"Let's see if we have a connection. How about the report of an animal collision?"

"A deputy returned to the location and found a dear carcass fifty yards off the road. Still bloated."

"Okay. Let me know about the other."

"Will do. Anything else?"

"Keep following your nose."

"My nose wants to go up the street to the bakery," Knudson joked.

* * *

Herberts's reaction had been blunt: "You put a lot of faith that this prick isn't lying."

Wendell did not disagree. "The search turn up anything?"

"Zippo."

"How about the tip line?"

"Every Nancy Drew and Miss Marple in the Northwest, alongside every UFO hunter. You've got a lifetime of follow-up. Get me something."

On the flights, Wendell had returned to his notes and mapped next actions. He spent the layover in Seattle studying property ownership maps along Flathead Lake. Tired and dispirited, as he exited the Glacier airport terminal, he made one more phone call, this time to schedule a little therapy.

* * *

Steven Wendell liked the space between science and craft, between the certainty of chemical reaction and the evasive dexterity required by the tactile. Like kneading dough where the lessons of touch were as important as the activation of yeast. It might take two dozen tries to make the needed adjustments to perfect a recipe. In cooking, like policework, abject failure always remained a possibility—doughs that failed to rise, sauces that broke—but most improvements along the way were so subtle that only other devoted cooks would notice. Investigations proceeded in a similar manner. Cases required distinct balances, and every case included, usually multiple, failed approaches. Wendell worked most comfortably alone. Cooking, however, did not offer gratification when preparing a meal for one.

Because he was a good cook and good company, his friends readily accepted dinner invitations. They never knew what to expect. He found pleasure unlocking unfamiliar flavors and mastering novel techniques. When work consumed him, or when loneliness crept in, he planned a dinner party. To see a friend's delight at a good meal, to share good conversation reenergized him. The yin to his ordinary go-it-alone yang.

His favorite person to cook for always remained a party of one—Lorena Stroblova. She not only ate with more enthusiasm than anyone he knew, somehow consuming volumes despite her petite figure, she made the act of eating entertaining and nearly erotic. Revealing her mother's Spanish origin, Lorena was boisterous, bold, opinionated, and alluring. She inherited her mother's dark hair and almond eyes and her Czech father's fair complexion and his temper. She commanded every room she entered yet seldom revealed anything she didn't want others to know. Men were entranced by her beauty and mystery. Wendell proved no exception. Their relationship was the most unconventional in Wendell's life.

They had met when he was forty and she thirty-two. Their first encounter was accidental—literally. He had been in the awkward silence of the "driving to the movie after dinner" phase of a blind date when Lorena side-swiped him in the theater parking lot. He was enchanted even as she moved from cursing him energetically in Czech to tear-laden apologies in English.

What he knew of Lorena's past was limited to what she told him. Wendell long ago vowed he would never use the information available to him outside of work. They had known one another for eight years, so piecemeal, he knew enough to imagine more. He knew she spent her twenties exploited by men who trafficked on her good looks and temporary visa status. She'd first travelled to the U.S. on an H-2B visa and worked two summers in Yellowstone. After a year back in Czechoslovakia, she managed a student visa for a year in Bozeman, though in reality, she passed much of the year in California, accompanying a man only to be abandoned by him. Among his charms, the man had freed himself from loan sharks by pedaling her as a nude model. Once back in Bozeman, she married a man twenty years her senior, a man, from what Wendell could deduce, who acknowledged she only needed him for a path towards permanent immigration. Even if the marriage was a farce, the two remained married, though they'd not lived within five hours of one another in over ten years.

Wendell had focused his education in psychology and spent his career with daily exposure to criminals, so he saw enough repeated patterns to suspect Lorena had been abused. Those suspicions only enhanced the respect he held for her nearly brazen self-confidence. The woman he knew was outspoken and charming. She built an extremely successful business as a trendsetter in home décor among the valley's wealthy. Lorena readily admitted that she had reached a place in her life where she used men for her own purposes. They had, after all, more frequently used her.

What Wendell learned of Lorena's life offered him a pointed reminder that he was a party to adultery. Their "mutual mental health sessions" involvement, as Lorena liked to reference their arrangement, had transacted quickly after two awkward attempts at more traditional dates. Driving her home after the second date, she was characteristically blunt: "I am attracted to you," she said, "and I could use a good lay, but I've had enough of relationships." He had come to appreciate the rigidity of their arrangement. If he were honest, he was scared of anything more. He'd not been involved in a meaningful romance since he was twenty-four. And he knew himself well enough to worry that his obsessiveness and his devoted work habits would doom any serious relationship.

From the beginning, their sexual relationship, while passionate and intimate, was a practical matter. Neither allowed room for emotional connection greater than friendship, even if it was a friendship both valued. To make this possible, they permitted no observation of birthdays or holidays and no token exchanges of favors—no emergency faucet repairs or complimentary haircuts—no accompanying the other to social events, and no talk of other relationships. They both accepted a silent pact: an invitation to share a meal acknowledged a desire for intercourse.

But the meals and the conversation that accompanied them were as important to Wendell as the sex. Their tête-à-têtes were full and engaging, earnest, in their own way as intimate as the other pleasure they exchanged.

They talked about ideas, books, current events. He tried not to overstep the restrictions they placed on their relationship, but Lorena was one of the only people with whom he shared his own past.

This night, however, Wendell sought Lorena's company with a greater sense of urgency than normal, need that bordered on self-preservation, and Lorena, uncharacteristically, had returned the focus of the conversation to the personal almost immediately. "You seem distracted," she said. "Work?"

He nodded as he took a bite of linguine alle vongole.

"This missing girl?"

"Yeah," he said. "I'm sorry if I seem distracted."

"Don't apologize. There's no purpose in it. Why does this case have you so…so tangled up?"

"I'm not a step closer to knowing where she is."

"That's not unusual, is it?"

"No, but usually there's a starting point."

"You will solve it. You are good at your job."

Wendell did not reply. It felt a case that, day by day, receded further as new cases arose. There was a risk that it was terrain he would return to only because he had failed.

"There's more," Lorena said.

"Pardon?"

"Something bothers you about this case. Something you don't like to talk about."

Wendell thought before he answered. Sometimes he felt Lorena could see within him what he could not. "It's just," he said at last, "all the people on this case—the parents," he corrected, "they're my age."

"Yes?"

"It's got me thinking."

"Umm."

"If my life had been different, if I had kids, they'd be the age of this girl. It's strange to think about."

"Strange, yes. But you don't have children, so there's no purpose to wonder such."

"You're right," he said distantly.

"There's more," she said.

"What?"

"Don't pretend I'm stupid. I hear it in your voice."

Wendell marveled at her. "I think half the people I've interviewed for this case are lying. But I can't tell. You'd see right through the bullshit."

"Now you're changing the subject," she said. "Talk or don't. I don't care. But don't start to talk and then lie to me."

"I'm not lying."

"You are, what's the word?" She paused a moment. "You use it sometimes when you talk about suspects…withholding. It is the same, no?"

Wendell smiled. "Another kind of lying. Absolutely. You've withheld plenty from me."

"That is my prerogative."

"Yes, it is."

"And yours as well," she said. "But don't look like you want to tell me something and then stop. It's teasing, which is really just being a bully."

Wendell fingered the ribbing at her sleeve. "You're right on all counts," he said. "Looking for this girl has me glancing backwards. I wonder how my life might have played differently. One turn here, a chance encounter there. An accident. It could have been an entirely different life."

"This girl's disappearance is hardly in the realm of the placidly philosophical," Lorena said.

Wendell nodded. "I've told you about Michelle, the woman I dated in my twenties."

"Dated, ha. The one you were supposed to marry. The engagement that never finalized. Yes, I know about Michelle."

"We lived together for over two years. Did I tell you that?"

"Alluded, Mr. Detective. Told, no."

"During the first year, she got pregnant."

"She got pregnant. Spoken like a man. No, you impregnated her. Aren't you the one always saying that facts matter?"

"True," he said. "She said she wasn't ready to be a mother. She was still in college. She had aspirations for a career."

"What about you?"

"I was terrified. I had no idea what I was doing with my life. I had an undergraduate Psychology degree and no prospects. How would I go to grad school with a family? Plus, I didn't think I'd be much of a parent."

"And are you? You've never said a word about a child."

"Michelle miscarried."

"Oh, Steven, I'm so sorry."

"It was like a switch flipped. She went from thinking a baby was going to ruin her world to devastated."

"And you?"

"Honestly, I think I was relieved." He paused, swallowing. "I still feel guilty for that."

"We can only feel what we feel," Lorena said. "I think in the circumstances, your relief is natural."

"I didn't succeed in hiding my feelings from Michelle. We'd drifted apart long before. I could feel it but not admit it. After the miscarriage, things fractured. We were never the sort to argue, but there was a coldness between us. Subjects we avoided. More and more time apart."

"But you think it's your fault that she returned your ring."

"Probably."

"Why do men always think the world revolves around them? Can't you accept that she decided you weren't the right man?"

"Ouch," Wendell said.

"Oh, stop," Lorena said. "You loved her. Love wasn't enough. Baby or no baby. It happens. I don't know why people are obsessed with handing out blame. Wouldn't it have all been worse if you married, the baby lived, and then you broke up anyway? Wouldn't three people be hurt instead of two?"

"You're right," he said.

"Of course, I am right."

Wendell resumed eating.

"Don't think me harsh," Lorena said.

They ate for a while in silence.

"This case," Lorena said. "You think that the worst has happened."

Wendell looked at her without answering.

"You want to talk about it?"

"What would be the point?"

"Okay. We don't talk. I'll do the dishes. Then I'll make you forget for a while."

Chapter Fifteen

The deputy who had responded to a Lakeside call on Sunday from a caretaker reporting a home alarm only had four months on the job. Sensing his nervousness, Knudson spoke in the praiseful tone she used with her eight-year-old. "He said he wanted to drop it," the deputy said of the complainant. "He told me he reviewed the alarm codes and dismissed it as a false trigger. I didn't have any reason not to believe him."

"No reason you would," Knudson had said. She tried to bolster his confidence. "Your paperwork is spot-on. Detailed."

"So why the review?" he asked.

"We're looking for connections to other cases," she said. "Tell me about this guy."

"He's not who I'd pay to watch my place."

"How's that?"

"Didn't seem put together. More like a guy you'd pay to mow your lawn."

"Did he seem nervous?"

"No. Apologized for calling it in."

***

On the drive to Lakeside, Knudson filled Wendell in on Greg Evans, the caretaker from the deputy's report. "Two DUIs spread over six years, a bankruptcy. Divorced. Not so much as a parking ticket after 2007."

"The owners?"

"From California. Heidi Tomlinson. Her husband died three years ago. I found an article about the house in an architectural magazine. Took years to build. Imported Italian tile. Repurposed beams from a Cathedral. Tons of rock from Oklahoma. The husband died before he set foot in the finished house."

"Oh, man. Poor guy."

"Poor wife."

"How'd they make the money?"

"He designed medical devices. Some kind of genius. Made his first million while he was still in his twenties. Primary residence is Newport Beach. An apartment in NYC."

Evans was waiting for them at the gate. He had a long, thin nose and dark, deeply inset eyes, a spotty beard, and dark hair dominated by a cowlick near the crown. His heavy leather work boots thumped onto the stamped concrete as he stepped off the Gator. Evans was content to conduct the interview leaning on the Gator like they were co-workers on smoke break. While they talked, Wendell eyed the initials that formed a symbol in the decorative iron gate that blocked the long driveway.

"I don't know what the fuss is about," Evans said. "Like I told the deputy, it was a false alarm. Probably a bird into a window or a deer knocking a tree branch against the glass. I'm of a mind to thin them out. I sure hate to cause you trouble."

"We've had a number of break-ins in the area," Wendell lied. "You're sure your cameras didn't catch anything?"

"I've checked all the footage. I should have done it before I called."

"Mind if we have a look just the same?" Knudson asked.

"I cleared the cache. Nothin' there, like I said. Honestly, the alarm system is beefy—enough that we get lots of false triggers—but the security cameras aren't much. Mostly for show. One in the front and one in the back, plus one in the great room. It's all overkill. It's Montana."

"You must get looky-loos," Wendell said. He approached the gate.

"People buy in Montana because it's quiet. The owner is from California. I guess she's used to alarms and whatnot."

"So, it's just you and the deer."

"Pretty much."

"What do you do besides provide security?"

"Maintenance. That's a full-time job," he said. "The house is 10,000 square feet, and I've got five acres to look after." He spoke with pride.

"Care to show us around?"

"I'm behind as it is," Evans said, looking towards the lake. "Today I've got to get the boats prepped for winter. That rain we had the last couple of days, there's more of that coming."

Knudson chimed in. "Aw, can't you take pity on a couple of poor cops? Show us the secret doors, the hidden passages, the dungeon." She grinned.

"I suppose I could spare a few minutes."

"Just a quick lay of the land, then we'll be out of your hair," Wendell said.

"I'll give you the nickel tour. You won't see anything like this place. Took 'em years to build. Everything, right down to the drawer pulls, is custom."

Evans climbed back into his Gator and triggered the gate with a remote. They followed him down an immaculately paved road that curved through well-spaced pines and past a cherry orchard. The cherry trees were pruned with precision, and the forest looked like a golf course. Near the house, the forest gave way to a vast lawn that tumbled down the hillside in tiers of stone planters and a picturesque view of the lake and the Swan Range on its other side, which now sported a fresh coat of snow. Wendell took in the perfection of the grounds. "Maybe there's more to this guy than meets the eye." The house belonged on a magazine cover, a sprawling construction of stone that Wendell assumed would get the real estate tag of "modern western." He whistled his approval as Knudson pulled the car under a massive porte-cochere that rose from large log posts and was crosshatched with timber beams. They heard the fall of water from a pond settled into the landscape near the front walkway.

"Where's the bellhop?" Wendell joked.

Wendell spotted a security camera mounted inside the portico roof at its apex. "You say that's the only one on the front of the house?" he asked, pointing.

"Yep. We get you there and again from inside as you come in the front door."

Evans opened the massive wooden front door and ushered them into a space vaulted thirty feet high with beams crisscrossing the span. A wall of stone harbored a fireplace that looked big enough to step within rose near the center of the room. Every window offered a travel poster view. "This thing came out of a convent or some such," Evans said, closing the front door. "Weighs like 500 lbs. but closes as quiet as a coffin lid."

"Is the family home?" Knudson asked.

"No, they're hardly ever here. A mom and her adult daughter. Seven bedrooms and ten bathrooms. Mr. Tomlinson died before it was finished. I don't think Mrs. Tomlinson likes coming here. Mostly it's the daughter who uses it."

"How old is she?" Wendell asked.

"Early twenties, I guess. She's some kind of professional pool player. Didn't even know there was such a thing until I met her. I've seen her play on TV a couple of times."

"What's her name?"

"Annie."

"And the mom?"

"Heidi."

"Were either of them here Saturday night?"

Evans scratched the cowlick. "Annie was here a couple of days end of last week. She does that, in and out. You never know when or who she's going to bring with her. Sometimes it's a whole group, and mercy what a mess I have to clean up. I don't think that's what Mr. Tomlinson had in mind when he built this place. They wanted grandkids, not pool parties and Jell-O shots."

"Saturday night…the false alarm," Wendell prompted.

"I can't recall which day she left," Evans said. "Maybe Saturday. Maybe Sunday. It's not like she talks to me. Now Heidi, she always calls and lets me know. I pick her up at the airport even though they keep a car there."

"Did Annie have guests with her?" Wendell asked.

"Yeah, two fellas. Hangers-on. Came to eat Mrs. Tomlinson's groceries and drink her booze. They treated me like I was a piece of the furniture."

"Had you seen them before?" Knudson asked.

"Nah. Course half the fellas she brings here look the same to me. You never know. One time she musta had fifteen people with her. Next time it's just a girlfriend. Doesn't even give me a head's up to have the fridge stocked."

"You called our department on Sunday," Wendell said.

"I guess that's right. One day is the same as the next to me."

"Could Annie or her friends have triggered the alarm?"

"It's entirely possible," he said. "I only know they weren't here when I called it in 'cause I walked the place after seeing the alarm panel. I guess that was Sunday. They musta cleared out early."

"Where were you Saturday night?"

"Home. Trying to sleep. They were playing music real loud."

"Where's home?"

"I've got an apartment above the garage."

"So, I'm confused," Wendell said. "You're here on the grounds but don't respond to the alarm. If you don't monitor it, why isn't it directed to the security company?"

Evans looked sheepish. "It's set to notify me and not the alarm company. When we first started up the system, everything went through them, so we were always getting calls, and if we didn't respond right away, they called you guys. It was a pain. A deputy told me we'd had so many false alarms he wouldn't respond anymore. We had the company reset the system so that as long as I'm on the grounds it notifies me. Comes through my phone. Only sometimes I don't notice it right away. Or sometimes my phone is dead. I'm bad about remembering to charge it. The other night, I forgot to plug it in when I went to bed. I didn't notice the alarm until the next morning."

"Kind of defeats the purpose, don't you think?"

"It's bad on my part, I know," Evans said.

"Do you have a security room?" Knudson asked.

"Right over here." He walked them across the great room. Their footsteps sounded loud in the big house. A sweeping staircase rose opposite the fireplace, and at its base, on the backside, Evans opened a panel that appeared nothing more than wainscoting but slid into a recess to reveal a closet-sized room filled with electronics. A laptop lay closed upon a counter. One wall was filled with the glass cutouts of a sophisticated alarm panel.

"This is mighty impressive," Knudson said. "Have you ever had a break-in?"

"No."

"Trespassers?"

"Nope."

"But false alarms are part of the norm?"

"Used to be worse. Took them a while to get some of the bugs out. Come winter, unless the family flies in for a ski weekend, a lot of the time, I'm the only person in the place. I mean, I still inspect everything if I get an alarm. Check all the window sensors. The security cameras."

"There's no other help?" Wendell asked.

"I've got a man who works part-time for the summer season. Whenever the family is here, there's a woman who comes in and cleans every day. She's got a sister that helps out sometimes. She cleans twice a week the rest of the time."

"So, you follow up on an alarm. When you don't find anything, what do you do?"

"Clear the code."

"What was different that you called the Sheriff's Department on Sunday?"

"Most of the time it's just me, so I kinda know what's what. This time, I kept comin' across their messes, you know? Annie and her friends. Beer bottles and full ashtrays. Broken glass out by the hot tub. Food by the fire pit. Wet towels on the dock. It pisses me off, ya know? I'm not their maid. But if I don't clean up after them, it's not gonna happen. They'd walk right by. When I saw them earlier that night, they were already pretty well badgered. Actin' like fools. I don't know what they may have gotten into, so I figured it was better to CYA."

"Cover from Mrs. Tomlinson."

"Yeah. I mean, she can't expect me to discipline her kid, right? But by the same token, I can't call the cops on 'em when they're on their own property. I figured, if something was trashed or they'd tried to break into the wine cellar, I'd better have cover."

"But you didn't let our deputy onto the property."

"I'd cooled down. Plus, they'd cleared out, so I had time to check the sensors. Other than needing to clean up after them, I couldn't find nothin'. I figured they'd probably triggered an alarm by accident. No need to waste more of your man's time."

"You mentioned the wine cellar," Knudson said.

"Yep. Mr. Tomlinson was like a kid in a candy store when it came to wine."

"The daughter doesn't have access?" she asked.

"No. Her mom knows how she is. She turns a blind eye to most of it. But she knows well enough not to give her access to that cellar. There's bottles in there that would cost you a month's pay."

"But you have a key," Knudson asked.

"Yes, ma'am."

"Mrs. Tomlinson clearly puts her trust in you," Knudson said.

"Yes, ma'am. I'd do anything for her."

"How long have you worked for her?"

"Three years. Her husband hired me, but since he passed, Heidi has come to depend on me. I make sure I take care of the place to her standards."

"You say you found wet towels at the dock," Wendell said.

"Yes, sir. That's how they are. Expect somebody else to pick up after them. They left food out by the fire pit. Can't believe every raccoon, deer, and chipmunk on the West Shore didn't come have a bite."

"Didn't it seem odd? Wet towels in October by the lake?"

"They were pretty well lubricated when I saw them, and that was still early. Maybe they thought it would be fun to go skinny-dipping in 50-degree water."

"Did you hear anything? More people arriving?"

"No, but I had the TV on." Evans hitched his pants up. "Look, I don't want to bring trouble on Annie. I get irritated when I've got to pick up after her, but then when it comes down to it, that's part of what I get paid to do."

"Do you think we could finish the nickel tour?" Knudson asked. "Only time I'd get to see a place like this is on TV."

"Or as a crime scene," Wendell added, which made Evans glance at him.

"You've got to show us this wine cellar," Knudson said. "The detective here is quite the connoisseur."

"That right?" Evans asked.

"I've been known to open a bottle."

"I'm no connoisseur," Evans said, "but I can tell good wine from bad. Not like this here." He led them through a dining room and then down a set of stairs hidden behind a wall of built-in china cabinets. The staircase was paneled in rich, dark wood that glowed under the low light emitted from wrought iron sconces.

"I told you there'd be a dungeon," Knudson joked.

At the bottom of the stairs they reached a foyer placed before a door where there were two leather recliners and a lamp fashioned from moose antlers. "In case selecting the wine exhausts you," Wendell joked.

Evans extended a retractable key chain from his belt and unlocked the door. The moment the lock turned, muted lights clicked on inside the cellar.

"It's not a dungeon," Knudson said, "it's the secret laboratory." Evans appeared pleased as if the wine collection was his creation.

"Looks like your boss watched over his collection," Wendell said, pointing to a camera mounted above the two chairs.

"Oh, yeah, I forgot about that one," Evans said.

After admiring some of the labels, Wendell asked if Evans would show them around outside. As they stepped onto a vast stone patio, both the detectives stopped, stunned by the view. "I see this lake every day of my life," Knudson said, "and it still gets me. Who wouldn't want to wake up to this?"

"It's a special property, ma'am," Evans said.

"I see the fences don't extend the full depth of the property," Wendell said.

"I think they just wanted to screen the property from the road."

Another huge house loomed to the north, separated by forest and rock outcroppings. A small, run-down log cabin was barely visible to the south.

The proximity of shack and mansion offered one of Wendell's favorite anomalies about Flathead Lake. He rooted for the shacks and fishing cottages—leftovers from another age—to hold out against developers. This cabin was set in thick pine and its roof, blanketed with moss and fallen pine needles, slumped towards the middle. "Do the Tomlinsons get along with their neighbors?"

"Aren't around to know them. The Wards there," he said, nodding to the old cabin, "like to give me a hard time. Complain about anything they can."

"Do the Tomlinsons give them cause to complain?"

"Well, I'm surprised the old man didn't bitch about the music the other night. Otherwise, it's just sour oats."

"How so?"

"Some see this place as rubbing people's noses in the money. The Wards, they never owned this land, but back in the day, they treated it like it was theirs. Poached on it. Dumped their junk on it. This house reminds them what they don't have."

"But they've got the same view," Knudson said.

"Ain't it the truth? Fact is, ole Ward sits on property worth a couple of million. Never spent a penny on it. Dates back to his grand pap. Those who didn't work for a thing are always the ones who complain the loudest."

They reached the docks. Nestled into a rock outcropping stood a boathouse that matched the architectural finishes of the house. A large deck extended from its southern side. Near the water, a rack emptied of its kayaks cast a thin shadow. Two boats—a twenty-four foot open-bow speedboat and a twenty-nine-foot pontoon—perched on their shore stations at a dock extending from the boathouse. Near the entrance to the dock, a small peninsula of groomed land jutted into the water. A stone fireplace rose from the jetty, ringed by rock benches. The boathouse had a storeroom for kayaks and stand-up paddle boards in iron racks alongside life jackets and paddles hanging on pegs. There was a large, tiled restroom with showers and a separate room above the boat bays filled with comfortable recliners, a stocked bar, and video arcade games. "They know how to do it with style," Knudson said.

"Mrs. Tomlinson has a sister with two girls. They're as apt to be here come summer as anybody."

They stood at a wall of windows over the water.

"That's where you cleaned up their little food orgy," Wendell asked, pointing to the stone fireplace.

"Yep."

"These men with Annie, she didn't introduce you?"

"Not hardly."

"You said you didn't like the look of them. Why's that?"

"They're weren't the types of people I'm used to being around."

"What type is that?"

"Well, you know, gays."

"You spent part of the evening with Annie and her friends?"

"No, no, not at all. I just saw them. When I told Annie I was turning in. They acted like I was something on the bottom of their shoe."

"Where was this?"

"By the spa. Pain in the ass to keep the pH right."

"And then you went to your apartment?"

"Yep. Don't know how early they cleared out, but they were long gone the next morning."

"Did that strike you as strange?"

"Everything about them strikes me as strange."

Evans walked the detectives to the spa and then onto another, larger patio above it adjacent the great room. Wendell noted one more security camera near the center of the house. He asked about it and about the sensors that triggered the alarm.

"The sensors are your standard burglar alarm stuff, on ground floor windows and all the doors. It's the window sensors give us problems."

They circled the house and returned to the driveway. They thanked him for his cooperation. As the car climbed the curving road, Wendell asked Knudson, "What'd you think?"

"His story was all over the place. 'I called it in, but I knew it was a false alarm. These people bother the shit out of me, but I can't remember when they were here.'"

Wendell nodded.

"What are you thinking?" Knudson asked.

"I'm not."

"Yes, you are."

He frowned. "Some of the most unrelated things, the food left out by the fireplace, the broken glass, the wet towels, they're so specific," he said.

"And?"

"And nothing most likely. Did you get a load of those monitor screens in the security closet?" Wendell asked.

"Yeah, six of them, but he says there's only three cameras on the property. Then he suddenly recalls there's a fourth by the wine cellar once you point it out," she said.

"Makes you wonder what else he conveniently forgot. I suspect Evans has something he'd just as soon hide, but I'd be surprised if it's what we're looking for."

"Like he's dipping into more than his salary?"

"Dipping in one fashion or the other. Don't know. He seems awfully fond of his boss."

"What if this *is* the place Bianconi was talking about?" Knudson asked. "Lonely caretaker. A girl wanders in from the woods. Maybe he's more aggressive in his security than he lets on. A shoot-first, ask questions later kind of guy."

"You know the mantra: explore every possibility. Let's run it up the flagpole," Wendell said. "Stop once you're through the gate. Let's get a picture to share with our Oregon dope dealer."

The gate automatic opened as they approached it. Wendell scanned his surroundings after he took a picture framing the wrought iron initials at the gate's center. "I walked along here the other day," he said. "Didn't get quite this far."

"Out for a stroll?"

"Thinking."

"Yeah?"

"Let's make sure Britany doesn't have friends nearby. Somebody who hasn't shown up on our list. Longshot," he said. "You've read all of the statements we've taken so far. All of my notes?"

"Yep."

"I walked here the other day because of what Kristen Schneider told me. About how they'd walked along the lake that afternoon. Remember?"

"Yeah."

"And then our boy Jacob tells us about their late-night saunter. Same basic route, right?" He exhaled sharply. "Longshot, like I said, but let's make certain that Britany didn't have a reason for coming here. Let's meet some of the neighbors. Make certain she doesn't know Evans. Then I've got one more Lakeside highlight I want to share."

"Another mansion tour?"

"Not exactly."

Chapter Sixteen

Most of the neighbors had departed to winter homes. The Wards, whose narrow, rutted road imposed a closed gate halfway to the water, did not respond to their knocks. They followed the sound of a chainsaw and found Jerimiah Ward at the back of a trailer adapted from an old pickup bed. He threatened them for ignoring the no trespassing signs and said, "Ya think I got nothin' better to do than stare into people's windows?" Then he offered a laundry list of complaints about "rich assholes who buy up Montana."

They rang two dozen more doorbells in the area immediately surrounding the Tomlinson estate before a check-in with the Rodgers. Sheila and Tom appeared to have aged in the days since Britany had disappeared, the wrinkles around their eyes deeper, their skin sallow. Wendell knew anything other than sudden news of Britany's return held no meaning for them. As they rose to leave, Sheila stopped them with a statement phrased as a question: "You think something awful has happened to Britany, don't you?"

Wendell knew that no matter how much he wished to reassure these bereft parents, there was only room for truth. "Sheila, with each day that passes, the odds shift. You have to prepare yourselves for the possibility of an unfavorable outcome."

"Unfavorable outcome," Tom huffed. "That's a handy way of saying she's dead."

"Tom!" Sheila said.

"Tom, I can't tell you what we will discover," Wendell said calmly. "I can only promise you that we will find out the truth. Until I have evidence otherwise, I operate under the principle that she's still alive."

"We won't quit on her," Knudson said.

"Looks to me," Tom said, "that you're right where you were five days ago."

"That's not fair," Sheila said.

"Nothing is fair," Tom said. He rose from the couch and strode across the room. The front door slammed on his exit.

"I'm sorry," Shelia said quietly.

"No need to apologize," Wendell said.

"He gets impatient."

"Totally understandable."

"Have you got someone to talk with?" Knudson asked. "I know the department has offered resources. I hope you've put them to use."

"I have my family and my church."

"Lean on them," Knudson said.

Sheila looked at her with eyes full of tears. She turned to Wendell. "You'll tell me the truth, no matter what?"

"I will."

"I don't want people trying to protect me."

"I keep my promises," Wendell said.

"Tom said that you've asked our neighbors questions about us. Talked to our friends."

"We have. I can't risk missing anything."

"Tom doesn't get it, but I understand. He takes things personally. It's his nature. You wouldn't be doing your job if you didn't consider the worst in people."

The comment struck Wendell. He didn't like the implications of what the comment said about him. But she was right, if he didn't envisage what people were capable of, he would fail Britany. He wanted to argue that there could be a vast difference between imagining the worst things people were capable of doing and seeing people as inherently bad. Wendell could tell there was more she wanted to say. "Sheila," Wendell said softly. He let her name hang in the room.

Sheila looked at a framed photo of Britany on an end table. "Will you pray with me?" she asked.

Wendell could not explain the complex mix of instinctual reactions he had to her request. While he wished to be respectful of other's beliefs, religion held no capital for him. The Methodism of his parents, while earnestly faithful if docile, held no meaning for him. It had been a church of printed congregational responses to the pulpit, first and second verse hymns, and heartfelt if unimpassioned sermons. Still, even this placid church teaching of his youth strayed from the natural bearings of his mind, which demanded logic and evidence. When he first encountered the scientific method in junior high, it felt such a natural means of testing and verifying ideas that he applied its principles against things outside of science, including church teachings, as he studied for confirmation to appease his mother. He could not locate the evidence he required within the calls for faith the church demanded. Still, the sincerity of other's beliefs was easier to encounter on bumper stickers that advertised a driver's religious view than a grieving mother who asked him to join her in prayer.

Knudson saved him. "Of course." She gathered Sheila's hands in her own.

Wendell settled for silent contemplation while the women prayed. The prayer brought Sheila comfort. That was not insignificant in Wendell's mind.

When they departed, they passed Tom trudging up the hill. Wendell raised his fingers from where he rested his arm on the car windowsill as they passed. Knudson turned to Wendell. "We're making friends wherever we go today."

"If you thought Tom's reception was cold, just wait. Take a right when you hit the highway."

* * *

They pulled into a sparsely graveled drive beside a doublewide with a plywood lean-to loosely nailed near its entrance, and a canvas awning stretched over a hoodless, rusted Chrysler Crossfire, a snowmobile, and a stack of slumped cardboard boxes. A wooden porch sagged before the dented front door of the trailer. A pickup with tall rails was loaded with split firewood beside a large pile near a hydraulic log splitter.

"On your toes. We're about to visit one Lee Jeffries. Doesn't like cops and has a particular dislike for me."

"A blast from the past?"

"Funny how criminals always blame you for their jail time. I was his PO back in the day. Then when I first came on the job, I caught him on an assault case. It kind of blew up, got a bunch of other people involved and some hurt, including one of our own. A colossal shit-storm. Jeffries walked away from the original charges, but he remained convinced I had it in for him."

"Are we looking at him for this?"

"He's a hard case, but I doubt it. He's the sort who has a history of wrong place, wrong time. Throw in poor decision-making skills, and anything's possible. We've got to look. If Britany was his wife or girlfriend, it'd be another story. But he might be useful. Who better to catch bad guys than a bad guy?"

They were met at the door by a version of Lee Jeffries that had aged considerably since the last time Wendell had seen him. Jeffries continued to wear his hair long. Today it was loose rather than in the ponytail to which Wendell was accustomed, but there was less of it than in the past, and where he used to be all sharp edges and lean muscle, he'd grown a small paunch.

"Well, well, my favorite dick-wad," Jeffries greeted them. "And his lovely wife."

"This is Detective Knudson."

"Sure it is. I wondered when you'd show up."

"I bet you put coffee on."

"I don't expect you'll stay long."

"So, you not only knew that I'd come, you know what I'll ask you."

"You want to ask me if I snatched this Rodgers chick. Make sure I don't got her chained up in the bedroom."

"Do you?" Wendell asked.

"Funny guy," Jeffries said, his eyes on Knudson.

"You won't mind then if we have a look around."

"I think we can talk right here."

"Do you know Britany Rodgers?"

"No," he said flatly. "I know her old man. We know some of the same people. I never set eyes on his girl."

"That so? When's the last time you saw Tom?"

"I think the last time I saw him was at a meeting. Years ago."

"No offense, but it doesn't look like you've quite been staying current with your meetings."

"Like I said. A ways back."

"I'm sorry to hear that."

"I bet you are."

"No, I really am. Booze gets in the way of a lot of things," Wendell said.

"Lubricates a lot of others."

"Were you two close?"

"Close? Nah. Drank together a few times. My understanding is he cut that shit out entirely. Found Jesus and all that."

"He convert you?"

"We were bar buddies, nothin' more. Tom's a good man. Had my back once when it counted."

"How's that?"

"You ought to know, Mr. Detective. Bunch of good boys got themselves in a bar fight on my account."

Wendell well-remembered the number of assault charges filed in the brawl that spilled out of a Lakeside bar that had started with Jeffries. But he didn't know Tom had been among them. "Must have been closer than you let on if the man was willing to go to jail on your behalf."

"In my experience, fights kinda come your way. Ain't necessarily more than that."

"Can you account for your whereabouts Saturday night?"

"I was at the bar."

"I suppose you have friends who will back you up on that."

"You know it."

"How late?"

"'Til close."

"Then?"

"Home."

"Alone?"

"Brought a date home."

"She stay the night?'

"She did."

"And she'll stand by her man."

"Her name's Valerie, and yeah, she'll stand by me cause it's the truth."

"You know we will follow up."

"I've got you a whole list of phone numbers, Wendell."

"You really are prepared."

"Surprised it took you this long. Tells me you're runnin' on empty."

"I've got to say, I'm not sure how to react, what with you being the sudden model of cooperation and all. Valerie must really have you by the ball sack."

"I've still got mine."

"Now there's a glimpse of the Jeffries I know and love."

"Bite me. Or maybe your lady friend would like a taste."

"Charming," Knudson said.

"There's a word Jeffries has never heard," Wendell said.

"Don't you have anything better to do than come here and jerk me around?"

"We do, in fact."

"Then why are you here?"

"Because you know people."

"You're thinking ole Lee would snitch."

"That's not what I'm asking."

"I'm no snitch."

"You can hear what people talk about."

"Ironic, ain't it?"

"What's that?"

"You'd think the cops would know people. Protect and serve and all that."

"You make a fair point."

"Come again?"

"We could serve people better if we knew them better. And we'd be more likely to know if a girl like Britany Rodgers has reason to run off."

"What kind of game are you playing now?" Jeffries asked.

"No game. It's just got to go both ways. When we get a call from a neighbor that somebody is beating his wife, we get told by the husband to mind our own business. We get a call about a missing teenager, and we're told we aren't doing our job."

"Your side is never going to look at me and think of anything but another way to put my ass in jail."

"Our job," Wendell said, looking at Knudson rather than Jeffries, "is to protect people who need protection and to help people when they need help."

"I ain't lookin' for either."

"No, but I am," Wendell said.

Jeffries eyed him suspiciously. "You're seriously askin' for help?"

"I am."

"Well, I'll be a monkey's uncle. Can't tell if you're stupid or desperate."

"You can think whatever suits you."

"Stupid it is." Jefferies made a show of retrieving a pack of cigarettes from his shirt pocket. He removed one and tapped it on the face of the pack.

"Okay then," Wendell said, "I don't really give a rat's ass because I've got a girl missing."

"What is it you want?"

"Any talk floating around?"

"Plenty of talk."

"What sort?"

"Just talk. Some say she's got a boyfriend in Canada. Others say she put her thumb out and hitched it for greener pastures."

"What do you say?"

"Me. I say there's all sorts of strange folk everywhere you go in this life."

Wendell watched Knudson. "What sort of strange folk?"

"Shit, Wendell. You the one that used to be parole. There's every kind of evil in prison. You know that. If some of them go in aren't fifty ways of fucked up, they are when they come out." He lit the cigarette and drew in, his already thin cheeks dimpling.

"Do you have reason to believe that Britany encountered someone who would harm her?"

"The only thing I know is people are lookin' at their own kids differently."

"How do you mean?"

"The people I know, they're working people. Tryin' to get by. Something like this here happens and nobody knows why, people get scared for their own kids."

"Are scared people taking action we should know about?"

"Like oiling their rifles?"

"If that's how it goes."

"That's how it goes."

"And how goes it for you, Jeffries? What are you doing for work?"

"Firewood. Handyman work where I can. Got one buddy hires me on his landscaping crew summers. Another brings me on his concrete crew when he can, which ain't often. Hard to get work after you've done time."

"Your friends look out for you."

"Those that can do."

"There's something to be said for that."

"This a regular ole bull session now, Steve-O?" He gathered a clump of mucous in a wet suck and spit it onto the ground next to the steps. "You ain't one of my friends."

"Is Greg Evans one of your friends?"

"Who?"

"Caretaker for the Tomlinson place on the lake."

"Don't ring a bell."

"Next to Jerimiah Wards."

"I know the place. I helped clear timber off that site."

"The caretaker. Greg Evans."

"Skinny little peckerwood? Got a grin like he just pulled out of your momma?"

Wendell nodded.

"He's a sack of shit. Back in the day, me and a buddy were contracting. Just getting our start, you know. Ole Evans somehow always knew our bid. Underbid us even if he was too busy to take it. He had a pretty big outfit back then. Ran it into the ground. Any rate, he didn't need to worry himself with the size of jobs we bid. Did it cause he likes to piss in people's faces."

"Know anything about this gig he's got now?"

"Old fart work. No more than a beck and call man. Seen him around town. Hardware store, that sort of thing."

"Do you know the woman he works for, Heidi Tomlinson?"

"Nah. That's how it is. Unless you do work for them, don't know 'em. Even if you do, you're getting let in and paid by the likes of Evans."

"Too good to consort with the hired help?" Wendell wanted to keep Jefferies talking. He didn't know that he had any actual information, but there was truth to police not knowing a community. They had so few dealings in a town like Lakeside that it was easy to fall out of touch, despite an inordinate number of petty criminals and general trouble-makers among the town's population. That was the old Lakeside natives still talked about. "Hillbillies" Herberts called them. That profile of the place hadn't been true for a long time, and yet there remained truth in it, though Wendell supposed you could find the likes of Jefferies anywhere. And while you'd have to strain through all the shit Jeffries dumped, there might be useful insight.

"You're part of a service they buy," Jeffries said. "Hard part is they are particular and peculiar. They got these visions in their heads. More often than not, halfway through, they change their mind. Don't question costs until it's some little thing you never even give a thought. That's where their eye goes."

"So, you hire somebody like Evans to take care of your place, and so long as the place looks the way you want it," Wendell said, "you don't really care if it's Evans or the next guy."

"Yeah, sure. Evans is a perfect fit, 'yes, sir this, yes, ma'am that.' Takes his sweet time and probably pockets the change from the hardware store to boot."

"Is he the sort who would try to get his lady boss in the sack?" Knudson asked.

"Rumor's always had it that he likes 'em young."

Wendell saw Knudson shift her eyes from where she'd been looking past Jeffries within the darkened house to his face. "How young?" he asked.

"Maybe ten years ago, supposedly he knocked up a teenager. Paid to get rid of it. Story was she wasn't his first."

"You sure on that?"

"Just tellin' what I heard."

"Because you had a bit of that in your past too. Statutory rape charges, as I recall."

"Mutual consent," Jefferies sneered. "You'll remember that charge was dropped."

"How convenient."

"Hey, a man can't control who's attracted to him."

"He sure as hell can control whether he puts his dick in a minor," Wendell snapped.

"Yeah, well, ancient history. Besides, that was a unique situation. That was a love story."

"What became of your true love?"

"She moved on," Jeffries said.

"You keep any young company these days?"

"I'm clean as a whistle. You guys haven't had a sniff of me in years."

"Okay, Mr. Clean. How about Evans? Are there still rumors about him?"

"Don't really know. People like to talk about the young guns, not the old farts. His time has passed. You go into any bar, and there's still hangers-on takin' up space, same as they have forever. Same stool. They're like the wallpaper now. People don't pay them mind. Not when there's young chicks dancin' to the juke box and young guns pickin' fights. Time's passed for guys like Evans."

"And you? Has time passed you by?'

"I mind my own business."

"Keeping it straight and narrow," Wendell said.

Jeffries ignored him and stepped back within the threshold. "Sounds like you're grasping at straws."

"I prefer to think of it as rattling the woodwork. Overturning the turds. That sort of thing."

"Yeah, well, chasing turds is right up your alley."

"About that list of friends who can testify to your whereabouts Saturday… " Wendell said.

"You're a predictable fuck, you know that, Wendell."

"Apparently we both are."

Jeffries grunted.

"Maybe we've got more in common than we would have thought," Wendell said.

"You and me are nothing alike."

"Maybe we've misunderstood each other," Wendell said.

"I think we understand each other just fine. Cops and robbers, just like kids. You stick to your side, I'll stick to mine. You got what you came here for," he said, handing him an inky piece of notebook page of phone numbers. "You rattled my cage. Time to mosey on. Though you can leave the little woman if you want."

"Dream on, little man," Knudson said.

"Stay out of trouble, Jeffries," Wendell said.

"Trouble? Me? I'm a model citizen."

Chapter Seventeen

"Love the little romance," Knudson teased as they drove back to Kalispell. "He's quite the catch." Knudson laughed and then turned serious. "You think there's any truth to what he said about Evans and teenagers?"

"Lee Jeffries isn't exactly a trustworthy source," Wendell said. "When things blew up with him, it started a kind of ground war. Jeffries was sleeping with another guy's wife. Guy finds out, beats the shit out of him. Jeffries fights back. Another day in the life, right? But the real mess started between guys who defended Jeffries and guys behind the other guy. Every Tom, Dick, and Harry in the Lower Valley came out of the woodwork. Territorial shit. For all I know, Evans could have been in the other camp, and Jeffries is blowing smoke."

"But now we know that Tom Rodgers is in his camp. That's the assault Tom pled on before he got sober, isn't it?"

"Seems likely."

"Which makes it more likely Jeffries knows Britany."

"Absolutely. And it rekindles our awareness that Tom can be pushed to violence."

"That stuff with Jeffries and the statutory rape business, that was real?" Knudson asked.

"Yep. I was his PO. This dad brings charges, right? Says Jeffries is sleeping with his teenage daughter. The girl, she swears she's in love with him. Wants to marry him. Refuses to testify. Eventually her old man drops the charges. I think Jeffries was twenty-nine or so."

"And that's why we made our little visit."

"Kind of a 'tick the box' situation what with his past."

"Do you think Jeffries has moved from opportunist to predator?"

"Maybe," Wendell said, sighing. "Or someone like him."

"We could ask all the same questions about Evans," Knudson said.

"Yep. And more questions for Tom. Or we could be nowhere at all," Wendell said.

They drove for several minutes in silence, then Wendell laughed.

"What's so funny?"

"It's not funny, really. More pathetic. People like to talk to Jeffries. I was thinking that he probably has more friends than I do. Friends who would do anything for him."

"Aw," Knudson intoned, "That makes me sad."

"Seriously. Remember what he said, that he would know more than we would. He's right, you know. If we get a pulse on a place, it's through guys like him. The view from the gutter. Most of the time it's all we've got. We're not talking to pastors and counselors at the Boy's Club or teachers. We need to be talking to grandmothers walking loops around the park. Until we are, the truth is, guys like Jefferies know more than we do."

"Because the rats talk to the rats?"

"Yeah, but also because the rats really do like the rats."

"And he has more friends than you do," Knudson said, offering him a big smile. Wendell had come to love her smile and tolerate her sarcastic humor.

"That's right."

"Poor Wendell."

"Don't you forget it."

"I had no idea you were trapped in such angst," she teased.

"Drive the car, Detective."

Knudson looked suddenly somber. "We work too damn much to have friends. So we get stuck hanging with the likes of each other. And we know how *that* goes."

Wendell eyed her. He wondered if the comment was a reference to the law enforcement pairing of her marriage or something else. He reached in his coat pocket and removed a pack of gum. He offered her a piece. Rather than ask the question on his mind, he said, "Pathetic, aren't we?"

Knudson laughed. She nodded in acceptance of the gum, which Wendell unwrapped for her like they were a married couple. "We really are." She leaned over and snatched the gum from him with her teeth. Then she changed lanes quickly to avoid a semi entering the four-lane highway from a crossroad. "Jesus," she said. "Moron. Where's a cop when you need one?"

"You've got the power, sister. You want me to light him up?"

"Nah. We've got a girl to find."

"That we do."

After a minute of silence, Knudson looked at Wendell. "Do you ever get lonely?" she asked.

Wendell fidgeted with the portfolio in his lap.

"I do," she said. "I mean, I'm married to a cop, right, and still Joe doesn't like to talk about work, which I get. It's not healthy. If we did, it would probably turn into bitching about administrators, you know. We'd compare which shop has more bureaucratic bull. And we don't need to bring the job home to the boys," she said. "But sometimes with Joe, there's not a lot else to talk about besides work or the kids."

Wendell watched her closely. He saw her check the side mirror and a look cross her face like she was about to say something and then changed her mind. "Don't listen to me," she said. "I don't know that I could name two friends I like to spend time with. Nor could I tell you the last interesting conversation outside the walls of the office I've had. Cause, baby, I'm telling you, Cub Scout moms and the sidelines of soccer games don't count.

"But inside those walls," she whistled. "Whew, that's a whole different set of landmines. I think Joe forgets that I'm one of two women in the department with rank. Guys look at me differently, even ones I've served with for years. When it comes down to it, they still see me as a girl. A lot of them, even though I know most would never say it in earshot, think that I got my shield because I filled a quota. Others think I whored it out to get the promotion. I say screw them. I mean it's not like I'm going to get asked to join the department basketball team."

"You want to be on the basketball team?"

"No," she laughed. Then her expression changed. "No, I just feel like an outsider."

"I'm not exactly the first guy on the invite list to the department picnic," Wendell said.

"I know. I think you get what I'm saying."

"And you think I'm lonely."

"You're single. You don't appear to date. I watch. You go your own way around the department. You've got the highest clearance rate of any detective in the squad and unless he knows it's the hard puzzle case nobody else has the smarts to solve, Herberts still throws you scraps."

"Like a missing seventeen-year-old," Wendell said.

"Why do you think you got me for help?"

"You're a good detective. You think your way through a case. I'd take you over anyone."

"I'm not fishing for a compliment. I've got tits, so I get why I'm the pariah. If I had a dick, maybe people would listen to me."

"I listen to you."

"I know. That's still taking some getting used to. But you. You've got a dick. A pretty nice one from what I have imagined." She laughed, then laughed more loudly still when she saw Wendell squirm. "God, it's fun to bait you."

The two made eye contact, and she smiled at him. "So why doesn't your lovely dick get you a pass? What'd you do to piss off Herberts?"

Wendell happily addressed the second question while taking a wide berth of her bait. "I don't fit the mold," he said. "Herberts likes me fine on the day he presents monthly statistics to the brass. But he won't invite me over for a steak afterwards."

"Because you have an opinion, including one about his statistics."

"Yeah, but also because I'm not part of his tribe."

"Tribe?"

"I've still got hair. Haven't reached for the chrome dome razor."

Knudson laughed. "And no mustache."

"A look I could definitely rock, I must say."

She laughed again. "Now I'm doomed for the rest of the day picturing you bald."

"You'd lose me in the crowd."

"That's the truth," she said. They had reached the southern edge of Kalispell and the businesses that lined the highway. "The bald, cheesy mustache tribe."

"Don't ever tell a Montana man that his facial hair is cheesy."

"Amen, brother," Knudson chuckled. "But seriously," she said, as she eased into an intersection to make a left turn, "when you say *tribe*, what does that mean?"

Wendell heard the seriousness behind the question and knew that it had taken something for her to mention the second-class citizenry she felt no matter the innuendo and teasing that accompanied it. "You know there's good police in this department," he said. She nodded. "Most of them, in fact. But there's the stereotype too. The guys who measure one another by how many times their body weight they can bench press. They hold it against you if you can't cite QB stats from memory on Monday morning. The hurrah boys." He exhaled a long breath and spoke softly, "The guys who think because they enforce the law, they are the law. That's the tribe I speak of."

Knudson nodded again.

"Of course, I'm a liar too," he said, his voice rising. "The biggest reason I became a cop is to drive fast and shoot straight."

Stacey laughed, but Wendell saw her contemplative expression that followed as she pulled into the station lot.

"I see the way they watch your ass when you're walking away," Wendell said, "and how they try to play sly when they're making off-color jokes as they watch your reaction."

"Please tell me you still watch my ass, too," she said. "I may want an equal voice, but I work hard for this ass."

Wendell didn't respond to her even while he was aware of his own hypocrisy. "I don't think suggesting something is native to a culture makes it right," he said instead. "I see them fall over themselves to get lake shifts in summer bikini season. I hear the bitterness and the mockery when they call the tech guys geeks and robots. I get it, but I don't have to like it. We make our choices, and I choose to distance myself from the department when I'm off the job."

Knutson turned serious. "People respect you, Steve. You know that, right? They know you outsmart them. They just don't see the same patterns they've built to keep themselves sane, the wives and kids, the booze, the comradery."

"I know," he said. "And I know you don't get that pass either. You're supposed to be one of the guys at work and then still go home and be Suzy Homemaker."

"Don't forget seductress," she said. "Horny housewife."

"Lonely and horny," he said. "What a combination."

"More often than you'd care to know," she said.

Worrying that he'd risen to her bait, Wendell said, "We've got rich California housewives to call," as he exited the car.

Knudson jogged a few steps to catch him. As they crossed the parking lot, she said, "Tell me if I'm overstepping, but were you married and it didn't work, or are you still the prize catch?"

"The latter," he said.

"On purpose?"

"I was engaged once, in a time long, long ago."

"What happened?"

"Life," he said.

"You know there's guys who think you must be gay."

"Would it matter if I was? Would I be a different cop?"

Wendell used a key card to swipe them into the station. Before he opened the door, he rapped on the department insignia centered on its glass twice with his knuckle, something he'd done every time he'd walked through that door for eight years.

"For luck?" Knudson asked.

"To remember principle."

Chapter Eighteen

Heidi Tomlinson proved the epitome of courtesy. "Yes, yes, by all means," she said. "Whatever you need. Search the property. Anything that might help. I can't imagine what her poor parents must be going through."

Greg Evans, by contrast, complained about "people tromping through the property and making more work." Wendell reminded him that the woman who signed his paycheck assured them he'd be cooperative.

Heidi Tomlinson appeared unsurprised to learn that her daughter had been present at the house over the past weekend. "Annie loves the Montana house. She uses it more than I ever do. But I can't keep up with that one. She practically lives on the road."

"Do you know where she might be now?" Wendell asked.

"I haven't talked to her for at least a week. I know she has a tournament this weekend in Connecticut. She's mostly in New York when she isn't travelling."

His call to Annie Tomlinson went to voicemail. "Want to give me odds on a return call?" Wendell asked Knudson.

"Unless we offer her a photoshoot or an endorsement contract, I'd say slim to none, Knudson replied, spinning her computer monitor for Wendell to see. The screen featured a raven-haired beauty who leaned across the maroon velvet of a billiards table, face set in rigid concentration and dark, intensely focused eyes. She wore black harem pants and a deep-cut black silk blouse that revealed cleavage accented by a large pendant necklace. Long gold earrings tipped in rubies nearly touched the table's surface as she sighted the length of the cue. An elaborate snake tattoo encircled her arm. "Apparently, she's taken the nine-ball world by storm over the past two years. Sponsors are lining up out the door. The nickname they've tagged her with is 'The Stone Princess.' Hence all the jewelry, I presume. Though I don't know how you can notice anything but her tits."

"Industry hazard, I suppose," Wendell said. "Let's make certain she knows we're serious about contact. Agents, tournament directors, whoever we can call to ensure a response."

"Okay."

"I want you to lead the re-interview with Evans. He's hiding something. I'd like you to have a visit with the security company too. Find out exactly how their system works."

* * *

Wendell requested the most senior members of search and rescue for the Tomlinson property. Meanwhile, the general search in the forest near the Rodgers's home continued fruitlessly, and the number of volunteers diminished with each day. "It may be another dead end," he told the team assembled before the gate to the Tomlinson property, "but I want you to treat the entire property like a crime scene. Even you think it's trash, tag it and bag it." Mist clung to the lake surface and drifted in dreamy vapor trails. Next, Wendell addressed the techs. "We've got the owner's cooperation. Be respectful but thorough. If we had to do this under a warrant, we probably wouldn't be doing it at all."

As they descended to the house, Knudson shared her findings. "Two guys I talked to shared the rumor about Evans dating a girl ten years ago, but one says she was in her twenties, the other swears she was in high school. Nothing concrete."

"Concrete is overrated. I go for porous and insubstantial."

Knudson chuckled and continued. "The security system is as he described. The installers said that they wouldn't recommend customers erasing their digital files as often as Evans does. They admitted that they sold the

Tomlinsons a package they didn't really need." She paused. "A year after they installed the system, Evans came back and purchased two more cameras. Battery-powered and wireless but compatible with the software. He paid for them on a credit card where the rest had been direct billed. He's the account holder on the card, not Tomlinson."

* * *

Greg Evans met them at the massive front door.

"I'd like everything unlocked and open," Wendell said.

"Already is," Evans said. "And the cleaning ladies are here. So is Rodriquez, my summer help. Pulled him off a framing job to be here, so you're costing the man money."

"We appreciate your cooperation," Wendell said. "I'd like you to walk one of our techs through your security system."

"I don't know what you're looking for," Evans said.

Wendell ignored him. "We'll start with your apartment. Then we'll do the main house and talk with the other employees."

"That's my personal property."

"You'll never know we were there," Wendell said. "It's not like you're conducting criminal activities."

"No," Evans said, a bit too quickly for Wendell's taste.

Evans's apartment above the garage was spacious, with hickory kitchen cabinets, granite countertops, and a nice view of the lake. It was sparsely furnished and clean. Too clean, Wendell thought, as he observed the slept-in look of Evans's clothes. A single recliner faced a big screen TV. Wendell whistled when they first entered the apartment. "Looks like I'm in the wrong line of work."

"Mrs. Tomlinson treats me well."

"I'd say so. These digs on top of a paycheck. You're doing okay."

Evans shrugged. "Can't complain."

"She puts a lot of trust in you."

"I've never given her any reason not to."

Wendell ran his hand across a clean, empty granite counter. "Do any entertaining?"

"Pardon?"

"Friends? Dates? Or is it just you?"

"I stick to myself."

"Must get lonely. Big house. The family hardly ever around."

"I like it quiet."

A closed laptop was placed before a stool. Wendell rapped his index knuckle on its surface twice. "Is this the unit you monitor the security cameras with?"

"No, that's back at the house. This is mine."

The single bedroom appeared as recently cleaned as the rest of the apartment, its walk-in closet more spacious than Evans's few belongings required.

"Does the housekeeper clean here too?" Knudson asked.

"No."

"Wow," she said. "I need you to come ride herd on my kids."

Wendell laughed, then said, "Maybe you can show her the ropes. Detective Knudson's going to be your partner today."

"Maybe we'll discuss cleaning products," Knudson said.

Wendell stopped in the doorway. "Where do you keep your personal vehicle?"

"There's a garage on the backside of the boathouse. I park it in there with the equipment."

"Why don't you show the detective."

Wendell found the housekeeper, Esmerelda Santiago, and her sister, Rosa, seated at a small table before a bay window in a nook off the kitchen. He learned that Esmerelda worked Mondays and Thursdays and daily when Mrs. Tomlinson was in town. Rosa worked whenever the extended family was present and one day a month for help with deep cleaning. Both women stood when Wendell approached. Esmerelda offered him coffee, which he greedily accepted.

"This place is vast. How do you keep up?" he asked.

"The dust comes even when there are no people," Esmerelda said. Her large smile revealed two gold crowns and the surprise of a dimple.

"My house is where dust goes to make babies," Wendell said. Both women smiled uncertainly at the remark.

"And if you're ever missing a sock, you'll find it under my dryer," he said and received the laughs he was looking for.

"Socks are always in search of their lost spouses," Esmerelda said. "Like Honduran wives." She laughed.

The three joked some more. Wendell suggested they were all in the business of cleaning up other's people's messes. Then he turned to business, asking Esmerelda when she'd last worked.

"Monday," she said. "Always on Mondays. That's my big day, especially after the family has been here."

"Have they been here recently?" Wendell asked.

"Yes. Miss Annie and two of her men friends. They arrived while I was working on Thursday."

"Were they still here Monday?"

"No. Just their messes. Those men, they were filthy. Like pigs. Their room take me two hours to clean. I thought the gay men were supposed to be clean, like that funny man used to say on his TV show, Mr. Seinfeld." She made a motion like pushing a vacuum cleaner. "Vroom, vroom," she said, laughing.

Wendell joined her in laughter. "Tell me about Annie's friends."

"They did not speak to me."

"Had you seen them before?"

"No. Never. Ms. Annie, she bring lots of different friends when she visit. Never the same people."

"Do you get along?"

"Oh, yes. She nice to me. She's a good person. She just needs to grow up more. I think she still misses her father."

"Were they close?"

"I did not know him. He died just after he hire me. So sad. Everybody says Ms. Annie is just like him. Like all the same things. Her mom say she is tomboy."

"And her mom? What's she like?"

"She's very nice lady. Quiet. She don't come here much. I think this house make her sad."

"Do you and Mr. Evans get along?"

"Mr. Greg? He do his job. I do my job. I clean."

"Do you clean his apartment?"

"No, no. I work for Mrs. Tomlinson. He do his own."

"Did anything seem unusual when you came to work on Monday?"

"Towels."

"Towels?"

"Lots of towels missing. More than what I find in the trash."

"You found towels in the trash?"

"Yes. Stained. Wine maybe. Blood. I don't know. They just throw them away. If they treat them right away, they would be fine. But now the stain is set. I am not going to dig through the trash to try and wash their towels. Such a waste."

"How many towels? You said you thought the stains were blood? A lot? A little?"

"I don't know. I don't dig in trash. They are not my towels. Mrs. Tomlinson, she buy expensive towels. Thick, soft ones."

"Was there anything else strange, besides the towels?"

"There was broken glass in the other trash can. I think maybe that explain the stain. And there was the mess those boys left behind. Drinks spilled on the carpet in their room. Ashes. They burned a hole in the comforter. Bottles everywhere. Disgusting. I don't like those boys. I don't know why Miss Annie is friends with such people."

"You refer to them as boys. How old were they?"

"I don't know. Like Miss Annie, I guess. Twenty? Twenty-five? I cannot tell. My own children are older. I have grandbabies now."

"Do you know when the garbage is picked up?"

"Mr. Greg takes care of it."

"Can you show me the room where they stayed? Annie's as well."

Esmerelda led Wendell up the grand staircase, which opened onto a large lofted area with views overlooking the main patio. Long hallways stretched from opposite sides. They took the left hall and walked nearly its length before she showed him into a bedroom that was larger than his living room and featured a king-sized bed and a separate seating area. The room was at the front of the house, and looking out the window, Wendell saw glimpses of the yellow rain gear worn by the search and rescue team.

"I show you," she said. "Cigarette burn." She held up the comforter from a corner of the bed. "We will probably have to replace. But you won't find any stains on the carpet. I scrub and scrub, but I get everything out."

"Stains?"

"From where they spill alcohol. Maybe coffee too. But now you never know," she said with pride. "They treat Mrs. Tomlinson's home like a cheap motel."

"Did you find blood stains?"

"I don't think so."

Wendell examined the room, though it was as clean and neat as a suite at the Four Seasons.

Next was Annie's room, a suite that featured a living room arrangement. It had more personal touches than the guest room, including a picture of her parents on the nightstand and another on the wall of Annie as a child literally standing on her father's feet at a pool table. A walk-in closet dwarfed the number of outfits suspended from one of its many closet rods.

"How often is Annie here?"

"Oh, once every few weeks. More in the summer. You never know when she will come."

"And her mom?"

"Almost never. It's best when Annie's aunt is here. Then the whole family come. Her aunt brings her kids. Then it is like a house should be."

"How old are the aunt's children?"

"One is in high school. She will graduate this year. The other is younger."

"Do they have friends over when they are here? Neighbors? Friends of friends?"

"Sometimes they bring friends with them from where they live."

"Anyone local?"

"I don't think so."

Wendell removed the photograph of Britany from the file he carried. "Have you ever seen this girl?"

Esmerelda retrieved a pair of glasses from a chain around her neck. "Only on the TV," she said. "So sad. It breaks my heart." Esmerelda paused. "Is that why you are here? You are looking for her?"

"We're in hopes we might uncover information that could lead us to her."

"In this house?"

"Yes."

Esmerelda made the sign of the cross. "Ay, Dios."

"It is important you tell me about anything even the slightest bit out of the ordinary."

"Like the towels and the comforter?"

"Yes."

Esmerelda concentrated for a long while in silence. "I can think of nothing else." She removed the glasses, tucking them away again within her blouse and folding her arms tightly. "I get shivers," she said, "thinking what if that poor, lost girl was here."

He found Peter Martin, a department lab technician, admiring the fireplace. Martin was lanky and slope-shouldered. Some of the patrol officers poked fun at Martin, but Wendell found him smart and thorough. "Hey, Pete," he said. "Like our new digs?"

"Bet the monthly electricity bill is more than our entire forensics budget."

"Care to put some of that budget to work?"

"Sure thing."

"I'll show you their security room. You can assess the system."

"No problem."

"If there were additional elements to the system than what we've been told about, more cameras, for example, do you have a way to detect them?"

"Hidden microphones almost certainly. Cameras and such, most likely. There's only so many places you hide a camera."

“Good. I want you thinking about that as you survey the house.”

* * *

“Never distrust the Wendell instincts,” Martin said a half hour later.

Wendell followed Martin back to the suite belonging to Annie Tomlinson. A stepstool was set up underneath a smoke detector, which hung from its electrical wires. “I don’t think you require a security camera focused on a bed. Somebody’s a creeper,” Martin said.

“Son of a bitch.”

“High-end camera. Remote capture. Based on the angle, you’ve got a view of most that side of the room, all the way into the bathroom door, the bed for sure.”

“Check all the other bedrooms for similar setups.”

“Rodger that.”

“Put this back together for now. Same as you found it.”

“Not tipping your hand.”

“Not yet.”

Wendell checked in with the leader of the search team, who reported that they had found nothing. He then called Knudson’s cell. “Where are you?”

“In the boathouse garage. Getting the full tour.”

“Can you duck out on your buddy and talk?”

“Sure.” She came back on the line a minute later. “What’s up?”

Wendell told her what they’d found. “I’ll have Martin pull all the details to compare against the purchase order you found at the security company. Keep him comfortable. Let him believe we’re ready to move on.”

“You don’t want to take it downtown?”

“Not yet. Mrs. Tomlinson’s given us permission, but let’s take care of business, get a search warrant, make sure we have full access to his apartment, seize his computer, swab him. We’ll move on the warrant immediately, get in here with a full team the second we have approval. Have you gotten anywhere?”

“Not really, but we’ve got a signal 13P,” she said, warning Wendell that

Evans was the sort who wouldn't hesitate to eavesdrop on the call.

"Okay," he replied. "I'll come find you in a bit."

He went back upstairs and found Martin again, who was perched on a stool shining a light at the smoke detector in the guest room where Esmerelda said Annie Tomlinson's friends had stayed. Martin stepped down off the ladder. "Anything?" Wendell asked.

"Not this one," Martin said. "And not in three of the other rooms. But there's one room at the end of the hall that's hot. Exact set-up as the other one."

"Show me."

Martin walked him to a room on the opposite side of the hall, all the way to the end. He shined a red-beamed pen light at a dark window of the smoke detector unit and Wendell saw the light reflect off the camera lens hidden there. "Totally inconspicuous," Martin said. "The system downstairs is definitely set up to manage more remote cameras, but I didn't see any evidence of these on that end."

Wendell nodded. He heard the sound of a vacuum and followed it until he found Esmerelda using an upholstery tool on the blinds. He asked her to accompany him to the room where Martin had found the second camera. "This room," he motioned, "Does it have any special use?"

"Especial?"

"Do either of the Tomlinsons use it?"

"No, no. It the girl's room."

"The girls?"

"Mrs. Nancy's girls. Mrs. Tomlinson's nieces. They always stay here. Always this room ever since they first come here. We call it the girl's room."

"The teenagers you told me about earlier."

"Yes. They could have their own rooms, but they always stay together."

"You said the one is in high school? A senior."

"Yes, they are not really girls anymore. Grace will turn eighteen next summer. Marcy is two years younger. Fifteen but a birthday coming soon. They make the house a happy place when they are here."

"Lots of work for you with teenagers in the house."

"I take them any day. Very nice children in that family."

Wendell thanked her again.

"This room? Is there something wrong with it?"

"No, no. Nothing wrong."

"The girl you look for. You find anything that help you?"

"I don't know yet."

"I hope you find her."

"So do I, Esmerelda."

* * *

Wendell found Knudson and Evans on the back patio. "Careful, she's going to want to move in."

Evans ignored him. "Your search team find anything of that girl?"

"Pretty tough with the rain. There is something I want to ask you about."

Wendell saw Evans stiffen. "The maid said she saw stained towels in the garbage this week. She says you always take care of the trash. Ring a bell?"

"I don't dig through the trash."

"What day do they pick it up?"

"I take it to the green box site myself."

"When did you do that?"

"On Monday. I always take the trash in on Monday."

"But you didn't notice anything. Esmerelda said they were stained, maybe blood."

"I dump the trash. I don't comb through it. I don't have a clue what bloody towels would be about. Maybe Annie's friends. I did find broken glass but didn't notice any blood."

"The first time we talked, you said you'd picked up towels by the dock after the weekend. Did those have blood stains?"

"No. Just towels left out in the weather along with their mess. They apparently made S'mores out at the fire pit."

"You said you found broken glass."

"By the spa. A wine glass."

"You and Esmerelda don't talk?"

"As long as she does her job, there's nothing to talk about. I've got too much work to do to ride herd."

"Must be odd, being the only person in a big place like this for days at a time."

"Nah, there's always work to be done. Speaking of which, if you're done with me, I've got to get back."

"Yes, of course. Thanks again for your time. We'll get out of your hair as soon as search and rescue are done."

They watched Evans walk away towards the boathouse, pulling a hood up on his rain jacket as he stepped out from the protection of the patio cover.

Wendell told Knudson about the second camera Martin found. "In the room where the teenage nieces stay."

"Shit."

"At the least, we've got a voyeur getting his jollies. Beyond that, we've got work to do."

"Do you think we have an abduction on our hands? Cameras. Bloody towels. Teenage girls. Shit, shit, shit."

"I only know that I want to start in that room with a full forensics team. Let's go to the car and type up this affidavit. See if Herberts can't get the DA to camp in the judge's courtroom. We'll phone in to see if we can't get help from the state lab the second we have a warrant."

"Let's find out what this prick is really up to," Knudson said.

Wendell released a long breath. "We may not like what we find."

Chapter Nineteen

A regular stream of personnel in matching blue raincoats emblazoned with the words SHERIFF or STATE CRIME LAB on their backs, underscored by their various units—FORENSICS, CRIME SCENE INVESTIGATION—tramped through the Tomlinson front door. They left a muddy puddle behind on the stone floor of the entryway. Evans sat on the fireplace hearth. He continued to deny any knowledge of Britany Rodgers or about the cameras.

"Cooperation is all we ask for," Wendell said. "Clear the air on these cameras, and maybe we can clear the air on all of it."

"I've been cooperating," Evans said.

Wendell chanced giving him another out. "I get that Annie brings trouble. Does having a way to keep track of her...is that an insurance policy should you ever need evidence for Mom?" Evans refused his bait. The two continued in this fashion for another minute, and then Wendell stood and feigned exasperation and strode to the other side of the room. He signaled for Knudson to join him. "I'm tag-teaming to you," he said. He had seen something in Evans open when she asked the questions. Knudson looked at Wendell warily. "Give him an ally. You're going to have to help him say what he doesn't want to say."

Knudson joined Evans on the hearth and perched next to him as if ready to spring to her feet. Wendell paced on the opposite side of the room. Knudson recognized that Wendell had dramatized his exasperation, for Wendell seldom ruffled. She wanted to show him that she could contribute more. Despite her relative inexperience at interviews, she took a deep breath and leaned closer to Evans. She whispered, "Nobody could really blame you for spying. I bet she teases you. The type who would put on a show if she knew you were watching." She paused, waited, and then tried to set the hook. "I know I'd watch."

Wendell observed from a distance as Evans looked up from his feet. He said nothing, but Knudson knew she had his attention. "I bet she's a total bitch to work for though, huh?" she said. "I mean, you can see it in her face. She likes eyes on her, right? Has to be the focus. I bet there's no pleasing her." Knudson paused and gave him room. "Wanting this, wanting that. Last-minute requests. Clean up her messes. A bitch, right?"

"She's all right," Evans offered half-heartedly.

"Still," Knudson said, "that good looking, that…what's the right word for her…a temptress. I'd watch her too."

"You like women?" Evans asked quietly.

"Let's put it this way: I like certain activities with certain women, but only if there's a man in the mix," she lied. "Spices things up in interesting ways, but it's really all about the man. Double the pleasure, all that."

Evans grunted as a response. Knudson pushed the strategy further. "Can't let such a thing get around the department, you know," she whispered. Knudson felt uncomfortable with her strategy even in the midst of employing it, but she could see a change in Evans' body language, and she watched as his legs parted wider and felt the slight pressure of his left thigh against hers. She suppressed a shiver. "Either I'd be out of a job or invited into every married dick's bedroom. But this one," she said. "Young, famous. A pool player. There's something about a beautiful woman and a stick, you know?" She paused. "What's she like?"

"I don't know."

"I've seen videos of her at tournaments. Total tease, right? Is she that way around the house?"

Evans nodded. He looked to where Wendell stood near the kitchen. "Walks around in her bra and panties. Skimpy bikinis." Evans looked at her. "She's like you," he said, conspiratorially.

"Like me? How?"

"Men and women. Sometimes at the same time."

"Now you're just taking advantage."

"No, it's true."

"How do you know?"

"I've seen her."

"You have?"

He nodded.

"It's not fair to play to me like that."

"I'm not."

She pretended to look around the room. "Man, I'd love to see." She renewed her charade and then leaned in. "How?" she whispered, "does she know you're watching?"

Evans looked nervous, glanced again towards Wendell.

"The cameras," she said. "I get it."

Evans offered no response, but she felt ever so slightly more pressure where their thighs touched.

"Very sly. You get to watch. Makes it even hotter."

A faint smile appeared on Evan's lips.

"I still don't know if I should believe you. What if you're thinking, I got a cop on the line, I'll show her."

"I've seen her."

"If only you had videos." She paused briefly. "You don't, do you."

"Maybe."

"Would you show me? I mean," she said, "after the boys and the gear are gone. Maybe I could come back. Off the clock."

"Maybe we could work something out." Evans grinned. Knudson remembered how Jeffries had described his smile as belonging to "someone who'd just pulled out of your mother," and while she found Jeffries's analogy disgusting, it felt accurate. She swallowed and held her course.

"The cameras I get. I don't blame you," she said. "But the rest of this...the girl..."

"I don't know anything about that," he declared defiantly.

"Because I don't see that. I mean...the cameras...that's just watching pretty girls."

Evans didn't comment.

"But this other. Was she here? Did you see her on the cameras? Did Annie take a little dip in those waters?"

"I told you. I don't know her. I know this house. I know what goes on in it."

"I've seen that."

"I've got no reason to lie about seeing that girl. If I knew she'd been here, I'd help you."

"But you lied about the cameras."

"I didn't say anything about any cameras."

"I say no big deal. Give me a woman who doesn't close her curtains at night and show me a man who won't look. But there are others who will hold that against you. These tech boys, they'll turn up video on your computer—"

"I'm not going to lose my job."

"If there's trace material, even fragmented files, they'll find it, no problem. And if there's footage of the nieces on your computer, well, that's child pornography, and that's a whole different ball game. No tolerance there. I might not be able to protect you."

"I haven't done anything wrong."

"There's different ways to see that. We're only here because we're interested in this girl. You cooperate, and the other stuff goes away."

"I can't tell you what I don't know."

"I may have an easy time fantasizing about some free-play with our Stone Princess, but there's others who have an easier time imagining all kinds of horrible things they think you did to Britany. They'll picture it in their heads, and then you're already ninety percent of the way to guilty."

"I don't know any more ways I can tell you that I've never seen that girl."

"Because with your camera expertise and all, you'd have video, right?"

"She wasn't here."

"Of her undressing."

"Dammit. Listen to me."

"Maybe she drinks too much. The clothes come off."

"I don't know what kind of shit you're pullin'."

"Or maybe you kidnapped her, tied her up where you could spy and get your rocks off. But something went wrong. She wouldn't cooperate." Knudson paused. "Or maybe you couldn't get it up, and you got frustrated, tried to clean up your mess with those bloody towels the maid found in the garbage—"

Evans sprang to his feet. "I've never seen her!" he shouted. "Don't you get it?" Wendell arrived at Knudson's side nearly instantaneously, and all other sound in the room seemed siphoned up the chimney. Evan's mouth was tight with rage.

"Sit your ass down," Wendell commanded.

Evans complied but whined, "Your partner is trying to frame me."

"I thought you didn't know anything," Wendell sneered.

"I don't."

"Then go back to shutting up."

Knudson rose from the hearth. "Don't move a muscle," Wendell warned Evans.

The two walked to the sunroom. Rain streaked the glass. "He hasn't said it yet, not in a way we can use, but it's there. We push him hard enough with the evidence from the cameras," Knudson said, "and he'll cop to it. I'm sure of it. But I can't get him to budge on Britany. Not even a little."

"How'd you get him as far as you did?"

"Like you said, I gave him an ally."

Wendell remained silent for a moment, looked at her. He wanted to say something but resisted.

"I'll need a shower after this," she said. "He's a perv. I don't know beyond that. I'm no criminal psychologist. That's your turf."

"Let's take him back to the shop. Present the cameras, the receipts, let him sit behind locked doors, and see if that doesn't take him to the next step. Maybe his computer will reveal what he won't. Meanwhile, I asked forensics to start with the niece's room." Wendell paused, looked out the window into the rain towards the lake. "We're creeping up on bad news on this one," he said.

"We've known that for a while," Knudson said.

Wendell didn't respond. "She's out there somewhere."

"We'll figure it out, even if it's uphill against the wind and the rain." She sighed.

"If there was evidence out there, it's been degraded since day one. Erased," he said.

"If Evans does know anything, we've got enough on him that we'll uncover it with time."

"We ran out of time days ago," Wendell said. "We just haven't said the words. This is a murder investigation now."

"A murder investigation without a body."

"We set the bar high."

"Didn't we, though?" She looked closely at Wendell, saw the tiredness in his eyes, the wrinkles in his clothes. She wondered if he'd slept. She followed his gaze to where he stared at the lake, the water grey with weather and capped with sizable waves from wind out of the south. She placed her hand on his arm. "At least we're not out there today."

"She may be."

Knudson didn't respond.

"You were in the boathouse with Evans before."

Knudson nodded.

"The boats," he said. "They've got covers? Do I remember that right?"

"They do. He's a clean freak. You should see this truck. Early '80s, but it looks like it belongs on a showroom floor. Fastidious, maybe so much so we won't pull anything off his computer."

"But if there was trace evidence on a boat, it might be preserved under a cover, even if it was out in the weather until yesterday. I'll get the team to work both boats, his truck, anything he touches," Wendell said. "Meanwhile, we do the job, same as always—make contact with Annie, locate her friends. We'll get Evans downtown. Bring in the cameras and go a few rounds."

"Oh, joy. More time with my perverted friend."

* * *

As Wendell placed him in a marked cruiser, Evans protested and looked to Knudson to save him but received only an "I told you so" shrug and a head-tilt towards her partner.

"Are you arresting me?" Evans asked. "Do I need a lawyer?'

"We're detaining you for questioning."

On the ride in, Wendell tried Annie Tomlinson's cell number again. "I've got her manager's number back at the shop," he grumbled. "I swear, every damn witness in this case is a poster child for witness protection. Can't someone answer their phone?"

The cameras the techs removed from the two bedrooms, "bagged and tagged," lay on Wendell's lap. The team retrieved two laptops, and the crime scene group was sweeping the house for prints and bodily fluids.

Once back at the department, they let Evans stew. Wendell called Heidi Tomlinson, who claimed little knowledge about the security system and had no idea why there would be a camera in any of the bedrooms.

Wendell called Annie Tomlinson's agent, who said, "Don't take it personally, Detective. Annie never answers her phone, but she does eventually return calls if you leave her enough messages."

"This is time-sensitive," Wendell said. "Any chance you could help me out and get word to her to call me immediately."

"Not likely. She's somewhere between New York and Frankfurt as we speak."

"Frankfurt?"

"Headed to appearances in Montenegro, the Czech Republic, and Bulgaria."

"I thought she was scheduled to play in Connecticut."

"She was. The tournament director is pissed. But a lot of these Eastern European organizations have been trying to book her for ages."

"Why so last minute?"

"Last minute? No, this is classic. Annie makes everybody else scramble because she's had a sudden whim."

"This is critical. It's a part of an ongoing criminal investigation."

"Involving Annie?" Wendell heard the public relations panic in his voice.

"Involving her house."

"In Montana, you said."

"Yes. She was just here. She travelled with two men. You don't by chance know those men or how I could get in touch with them?"

"I can barely keep on top of her business life."

"I really must talk to her."

"I'll make certain she gets in touch."

"It's imperative that she does." Wendell hung up and rubbed his face.

Knudson turned to him. "Trouble?"

"Just another missing witness."

"Annie?"

"She's jetted off to Europe. Christ. No Annie. We don't know the identities of her friends. Let's talk with flight services and get a passenger manifest."

"Maybe the only person we actually need is right down the hall."

* * *

They laid out the cameras side by side with the invoice for their purchase on the table of the examination room and tag-teamed Evans for half an hour. "I find it interesting that we have your signature, as big as day, purchasing two cameras and paying for them with your personal credit card," Wendell said, "and when we find the cameras, they're hidden in the only two rooms inhabited by young women."

Evans stammered and backtracked. Finally, Wendell left the room to observe over the video feed. Knudson returned to an approach similar to what she'd applied at the house. Evans eyed her suspiciously and then looked at the camera installed near the door of the room. Knudson followed his line of sight and said, "See, we're little more than voyeurs ourselves recording our own brand of porn." She turned back to Evans. "Our real interest isn't in cameras, *unless* they reveal an interaction with Britany Rodgers."

"I've told you a thousand times. I've never met this girl," Evans said. "I swear on my mother's grave."

"How do I know you didn't hate your mother?"

"Listen, stop jackin' me around."

"It looks bad on the surface, right? An underage girl disappears, and suddenly we stumble across your hobby."

"I've got nothing to do with that girl. I've told you every way I know how."

Wendell was proud of the textbook way that Knudson drilled the redundancy. He wanted to hear her continue to place Britany's name in every question. "If come clean about all the rest," Knudson continued, "it would make it a whole lot easier to trust you."

Evans appeared to think for a moment. "I can't afford to lose this job."

"We both know that ship has sailed. We're talking about the woman's daughter and her nieces. Let's talk more about Britany Rodgers."

"You set me up."

"Right. This is all an involved sting operation."

"But you think I'm responsible for this girl's disappearance."

"Lying about these cameras only makes you someone we can't trust. Tell the truth about one thing helps us accept that you are telling the truth about another."

"If I admitted to knowing about the cameras, then what would happen?"

"Assuming we find no evidence of a connection to Britany, I can't really foresee anybody on our end wasting time on a prosecution. We've got bigger fish to fry."

"Here it comes," Wendell said aloud as he watched over the video feed.

Wendell's cell phone rang. He answered with annoyance, barking "Wendell" into the receiver. Lonny Berenger, the man in charge of the State Crime Lab working the Tomlinson house said, "I think you better get back down here. We've got blood. Trace amounts."

"Where?"

"Inside one of the boats. We've only got traces in a couple of crevices. And a little spot under a seat. Has the look of somebody who cleaned."

"I'll be there in fifteen."

"Wendell, don't get a speeding ticket on the way down. Could be from fishing for all we know."

"Good work, Lonny."

As Wendell ended the call, he heard Knudson over the video monitor say, "Write it out. Same as you just told me." He watched as she pushed a pad of yellow legal paper towards Evans.

Wendell heard Evans say, "I don't write much. Never liked it."

"You'll do fine," Knudson said.

* * *

Wendell seldom had reason to run lights and siren and had no legitimate reason to do so now. He felt the engine downshift as he passed an F350. He gave vehicles room, thumbed the siren in quick blips as needed. How many times had he responded to accidents in this stretch of 93? Open vision, straight road, turn lanes—he could never figure out why it remained so deadly. One friend joked about Montanans and four-lane roads: "All that asphalt confuses them."

Driving fast relaxed Wendell. The rain had moved off, and the road was already dry except where an abundance of truck traffic beyond the road's planned capacity had worn grooved hollows.

He wondered, *what had they really uncovered?* He pictured the faces he had encountered in these last rapid days. The face, like the days, threatened to bleed one into the next: The Rodgers, seated on their couch, eyes turned elsewhere; Kristen Schneider, forehead wrinkled in concentration; the identical faces of the Bianconi brothers, dark eyes hidden behind sweeps of hair. He recalled a framed photograph of the Tomlinsons, the daughter, Annie, at fourteen or fifteen already demonstrated the sharp-featured beauty that contrasted with her jowly father. He remembered the look of fear in Esmerelda's eyes when summoned to the niece's room and the prideful look in Evans's as he showed them around the Tomlinson house, his fingers touching things—tables and lamps and picture frames. These faces arrived unsummoned. One did not. He tried and tried to picture Britany Rodgers's, but it was as if she was always in motion, her back turned towards him.

An eighteen-wheeler suddenly lurched out from a side road in front of him. Wendell hit the siren, slammed on the brakes, and turned the car into a skid, not so hard as to roll but hard enough to bring the back end around and eat up some road in the left emergency strip. Then there was the widening expanse of the turn lane and the intersection, and he straightened the car but continued to brake, smelled smoke from the tires, and heard their protest. The semi staggered to a stop. Wendell came off the brakes and back fast onto the accelerator. The car shot around the front of the truck. He inhaled deeply. His stomach fluttered. But instead of the road ahead he had a vision of Lee Jeffries' leering grin as he waved from the wooden porch outside his trailer saying, "Good luck turd hunting."

* * *

Crime scene personnel were scattered among the stone patios and at the shoreline. The bay shone bright and clear but beyond, out near the middle of the lake, a hazy band of clouds lingered low on the water, and the far shore remained hidden.

He found Berenger in the boathouse. "Nice digs," Berenger said by way of greeting. Berenger wasn't easing towards retirement. Instead, he reveled in mastering new investigative techniques. The round glasses and unruly—if thinning—hair reminded Wendell of a favorite college professor.

"Talk to me," Wendell said.

"I'll show you what we've got downstairs." They walked until they stood on a wooden dock between two boats. Berenger stopped alongside the speed boat. "We've got prints aplenty in all the expected places—steering wheel, throttle, tie-downs, cover-snaps. Right here." He pointed to the floor behind the passenger seat opposite the wheel, "is where we've got blood remnants. There's a service hatch that has a groove near the seal that collected it. Hard to notice. Not much, but it's there. And there's a spot the size of a dime on the underside of the seat."

"The underside? Spatter?"

"Possibly. Or residual off something on the floorboards. We could be chasing a lake trout. Samples are already headed to the shop. We'll know when we know."

"Nothing on this case can come soon enough."

"I prioritized the bloodwork and the prints from the boat. It'll take more time to work through all of the prints we lifted inside the house."

"Tell me what you see, Lonny."

Berenger bent down and stared into the boat for a minute. "What bothers me most is that the whole scene looks clean. Too clean."

"Like somebody tried to clean it on purpose?"

"Exactly. There was effort. Because there's nothing else, no footprints, no dust. But then again, the whole place is immaculate. Ordered. So, the fact we found anything seems out of sorts too." Berenger stood and scratched his head.

"What if the cleaning happens in the dark? By flashlight. Until just the other day, the boats were on their shore stations."

"That would make sense. But then if you're trying to cover something up, why not come back in the daylight and check your work?"

"If something happened here," Wendell queried, "and the cleaning is imperfect, wouldn't you expect more mistakes, more spatter?"

"Not if what we have is only a method of transport after the commission of a crime that happened somewhere else."

Wendell looked out the open doors above the water. He was silent for a long time. "I thought boathouses weren't allowed on Flathead," he said.

"This one is grandfathered," Berenger said. "I remember this place as a kid. Ages before there were big houses on the lake. Used to be a cabin built onto a boathouse. Course you wouldn't recognize it now."

"Imagine what those old-timers would think."

"There's a lot they wouldn't recognize, including me."

Wendell nodded. He looked down into the water, which was so clear he could see the individual, colorful stones on the lake floor. "We have a witness who claims she saw bloody towels in the trash. You find anything?"

"You could outfit a health club with the towels they've got," Berenger said. "All laundered and stocked onto shelves. Nothing to offer evidence."

"Okay." Wendell looked out into the lake once more.

Berenger followed his eye. "We don't know that it's her blood, Steve."

"I know." Wendell turned and took in the shadows near the boathouse ceiling. "You found nothing in the bedroom. Not so much as a hair?"

"I should hire this housekeeper," Berenger said. "Diddly squat."

"And the caretaker's apartment?"

"He could be married to the housekeeper. Sorry, man."

* * *

A gentle mist returned. Wendell paused under a covered deck and called Knudson.

"He lawyer up yet?" he asked.

"Surprisingly, no."

"Whatcha got?"

"He's copped to the cameras, though he claims he placed them for security. Protection, he says. Admitting to the cameras is as far as he goes. You?" Knudson asked.

"Blood. In one of the boats. Not much, but we've got blood." Wendell said. "Let him stew, why don't you? We'll all go another round when I get back."

* * *

As Wendell crossed the parking lot outside the department, his phone rang. He was surprised to see that the caller was Lorena. There was something serious in her voice. They'd barely moved beyond pleasantries when she said, "We need to talk."

"Sure," Wendell said, mildly off-balance.

"Not on the phone."

"Okay. When?"

"Tonight?"

"Honestly, Lorena, this case is blowing up. The next couple of days are probably shot for me."

"This is the missing girl?"

"Yes."

"Then that is where you are needed."

"Lorena, what is it? Is everything okay?"

"We'll talk when you finish the case."

"Lorena."

"It is nothing. Call me when you are able."

Wendell returned his phone to his pocket. Part of what worked in their arrangement was the absence of drama. They shared no commitment, and that, because it was by mutual agreement, decreased the complications. At least the emotional ones, he thought. What might make her so serious? Had they crossed some threshold he had failed to notice? Was she in some trouble to which he was not privy? He stopped abruptly. Could she be pregnant? He looked up at the building that housed the department offices, shook his head, and said silently, "Get your head in the game, Steve."

Chapter Twenty

After Wendell read Evans's written statement, he said, "Let's have another go at him. See if he's consistent."

When they entered the interview room, the first thing Wendell did was throw the statement down on the table and say, "What a load of manure."

"Whatdaya mean," Evans stammered. "I told you everything. Wrote it down just like she said."

Wendell nitpicked every aspect of the statement. When Evans showed no signs of budging, Wendell relented, "Okay, say you're just another pervert. Walk us through Saturday night again."

Evans repeated his account of the night in detail, then shrugged.

"That's it?"

"That's it. Watched *Saturday Night Live* until I fell asleep."

"Surely you checked the tapes from your little project in Annie's room."

Evans nodded meekly.

"And?"

"Annie never slept in her room that night."

"Did you find that odd?"

"Not really. Sometimes I find blankets where she has slept in the theater. Even when her mom's here, they'll go in there and start a movie and fall asleep."

"Walk me through the next morning."

"Sunday's are supposed to be my day off. I slept in. When I got up, I found all their messes."

"Tell me about that again."

"Bottles and glasses out by the pool. A broken glass at the spa. Towels on the dock. Trash and food and more bottles out by the fire pit. Shit, there were whole bars of chocolate and a bag of marshmallows half full of dirt and ash. Nothing compared to the kitchen, though. When Mrs. Tomlinson's not in town, the housekeeper does weekly cleaning, so the dishes, all of it, that was up to me."

"And Annie and her friends, they're still asleep?"

"They were long gone."

"Did you see them?"

"The sound of the garage door is what woke me up."

"You said you found wet towels by the dock. Was there rain that night?"

"No. When I walked up to the apartment, I remember how clear the sky was. Full of stars. Everything was dry that morning."

"Sprinkler system?"

"Nah, I always blow it out the first of October."

"The broken glass at the hot tub. Were there bloody towels there like someone had hurt themselves?"

"Not that I found."

"And the bloody towels in the trash?"

"That's Esmerelda's thing. If she says she saw them, then I trust her, but I didn't see them."

"Have you spent any time on the boats lately?"

"I'd never take one of the boats out. Not my place."

"Have you been on the boats at all?"

"Spent a day winterizing them. That's about all of them I ever see—get them ready for the season and put them put back up for the winter."

Wendell's questions continued for another ten minutes, then he returned to Britany. Evans never budged.

"Look, I've answered the same questions from you a million times, and I'm done. Are you arresting me?" Evans asked at last.

"I think we're done here," Wendell said. Evans's face did not hide his surprise. "Let me see about a ride home."

As soon as they closed the door to the interview room, Knudson stopped Wendell. "You're not releasing him, are you?"

"What do we actually have? Cameras we know he purchased."

"We have a written statement."

"And no meaningful corroborating evidence. A confession does us no good if we can't offer evidence that a crime was committed."

"I had to do things to get that confession."

"What things, Stacey?" Wendell said, alarmed.

"Nothing. I mean, I just took him places that were uncomfortable."

"You didn't use a line of questioning that can come back and bite us, did you?"

"No."

"Okay, then," Wendell said. "We don't get any shortcuts."

"He violated those women's privacy."

"I'm not a fan of releasing him. We've still got police work to do."

"But now we have evidence of blood."

"We *may* have evidence of blood. And at present, no direct connection to Evans."

"This is bullshit, Steve," she said hotly.

"Yes, it is. But we have to follow the rules if we want to make things stick."

"What if we kick him loose and he destroys other evidence?"

They were interrupted by the sounds of shouted obscenities and a commotion from the front lobby. Wendell heard his name interspersed among a slew of profanity. When they reached the main counter, they found Tom Rodgers restrained by two deputies. "I want to see that son of a bitch," Rodgers yelled, pointing with his chin at Wendell. Then he shrugged violently out of the grip of one of the deputies and dragged the other behind him.

Wendell saw the deputy Tom had shrugged aside reach towards his utility belt, apparently undecided whether to go for his big flashlight handle or his taser. "Gentlemen, I don't think there is any need to restrain Mr. Rodgers," Wendell said. "He's here to have a conversation. Isn't that right, Tom?"

Tom appeared momentarily confused by the lack of confrontation. He looked at the deputy, who still had hold of his arm.

Wendell's attention was focused on the other deputy whose hand had settled on his taser. "Stand down, deputy." The deputy looked up, and his face, already flushed, reddened more.

Rodgers pulled his arm away and pointed a thick finger in the air. "You're a lying piece of shit, Wendell."

"What have I lied to you about, Tom?"

"I've heard you arrested somebody."

"We've made no arrests."

"That's not what I've heard. And you've pulled people off the search."

"Why don't you come on back, and I'll fill you in on exactly where we're at."

"People are saying that you've got a crime scene."

"What people, Tom?"

"Your people. Other cops."

"I'm sorry I haven't checked in with you and Sheila today. Come on back, and we'll bring you up to speed."

"I shouldn't have to beg for information."

"You're right. We should keep you better informed."

Wendell ushered Tom through the door and turned him down a corridor to a conference room in the opposite direction of the interview room that housed Evans.

Tom refused to sit down, so Wendell remained standing as well. Knudson entered with a cup of coffee, which Tom waved off angrily.

"The truth is, Tom, even though it's been a busy day on Britany's case, we don't actually have anything concrete to report. Otherwise, I would have called. There's nothing meaningful yet."

"You'd rather keep us in the dark."

"Quite the opposite. We need you involved."

"Why'd you pull men off the search?"

"We chose some of the best qualified men from search and rescue for a second location. We're entirely focused on Britany's case."

"It feels like we're the last to know anything."

"We received a lead that expanded the search."

"Where?"

"We're not at a point in the investigation where there's a benefit to release specifics."

"I'm not a fucking reporter."

"Tom, we need your cooperation. If you make contact with people we are interviewing, we might lose the opportunity to gain information that could help us find Britany."

"Because you don't want the parents involved. The last thing you want is our help."

"It's not like that at all, Tom," Knudson said. "We have proven procedures to maintain the integrity of the investigation."

"Easier to keep us on the firing line."

"Something else has you upset, Tom. What is it?" Wendell asked.

"You don't want us involved in your investigation, and we don't need you involved in our concerns. I'll handle it."

"Handle what? You've asked for honesty from us, Tom. We need it from you."

"You're not the one who has dead babies showing up on your front steps," Tom fumed.

"Dead babies?" Knudson asked with alarm.

"A doll. One of those that looks real. You, know, life-sized. Cut apart. Right on our fuckin' doorstep for my wife to find."

"Was there a message with it?" Wendell asked.

Tom nodded. "Said our daughter had disappeared to make up for the sins of women who had abortions."

"Did the note directly reference Britany?"

"Not by name."

"Do you have it?"

"I didn't want Sheila to see. I threw it out."

Wendell wanted to explode at Tom with irritation but retained his cool. "Tom, this is exactly the kind of thing you need to call us about. When did this happen?"

"This morning."

"It's in your trash at home right now?"

"Yeah. I put it in a bag so Sheila wouldn't see."

Wendell exhaled. "We need that evidence. We've got to follow you home."

"Evidence," Tom said, exasperated. "A bunch of kooks try to get my goat right when my family is down on its knees. Freaks. Like I'm some sort of liberal baby killer."

"You're probably right, Tom. It's likely someone trying to grab a piece of the spotlight to publicize their cause. But we absolutely have to follow up. It could be something else."

Rodgers's face suddenly drained of color.

"We need to investigate every possibility, Tom."

"I don't want Sheila to know anything about this."

"I'll have a crime technician meet us at the house. We've got to make sure no news of this leaks."

"You don't really think…" Tom's voice trailed off. He looked away from the two detectives.

"Tom, you're probably right, and it's a misguided protester. Like the way the Westboro Baptists show up at military funerals to grandstand for publicity. But you understand, don't you, that for Britany's sake, we can't afford not to pursue this until we know for certain."

Tom nodded.

"Have you received anything else disturbing?"

"We've had a couple of nasty letters. Sick stuff. I've always been the one to go to the P.O. Box, so I open everything before Sheila sees it. Mostly it's cards offering prayers, even a couple of letters from other parents who have been through the same thing. You've seen the house. The whole yard is lined with flowers and balloons. Those are the normal people, the good people."

"Have any of the offensive letters talked about abortion?"

"No."

"Have any threatened you or your family?"

"One said that we had it coming."

"This is all in keeping with much of what we warned you and Sheila to expect from the start. Have you been passing these letters along to someone in the department?"

"They made me mad. It's easier to throw them away."

"You understand why we need to see them, don't you?"

Tom nodded.

"How many letters, Tom?"

"Only a handful."

"Any claims of responsibility?"

"No. I'm not stupid. I would have brought those to you."

They remained standing, which made the questions feel more awkward to Wendell. He understood that for Tom to display his fear through anger offered him a means to focus his emotion. Wendell made a quick, instinctual assessment of the room, the relative position and distance each had naturally established. He took one casual step back and looked specifically to see that the restraint snap was fastened on Knudson's service revolver. His own weapon was locked in his desk, his ritual when in the office. He made eye contact with Knudson, but she did not register any specific acknowledgement of it. "Tom," he said, turning back to Rodgers, "I know we've asked you and your family a lot of difficult questions. It's not something we enjoy. I need to return to a few of those questions again."

"Are you kidding me?"

Wendell ignored the response. "You've stated before that to your knowledge Britany doesn't have a boyfriend and is not sexually active. Does that remain your belief?"

"You're one son of a bitch," Rodgers said, raising one fist.

Wendell watched the fist in his periphery but did not break eye contact. "I don't want to add to your frustrations, Tom, but the truth is that some of Britany's friends believe otherwise." Wendell's tone was measured. "I'm not suggesting they're right. We just need to know with confidence we've pursued all angles of inquiry."

"Is this how you get your rocks off, Wendell?"

"We told you about the boy from Oregon she spent time with the night she disappeared. Obviously, that came as a surprise. Is it possible Britany has kept other parts of her life secret?"

Tom dropped his arms to his side. He looked like he had been punched. "I know my little girl," he said quietly.

Wendell didn't reply but gently rolled a chair near Tom. Then he grabbed another and sat down. Tom followed suit and sat heavily as if his knees had given out.

"There must be boys she talks about? Familiar names you've stopped hearing? Any past break-ups?"

"I don't know." His voice deflated.

"Has she ever had a conflict with someone who is likely to be active in the pro-life movement? A fallout with anyone from your church, an argument in school?"

"Britany gets along with everybody."

"Have you or Sheila ever had such run-ins? People with whom you have been politically active?"

"We stick to ourselves. We don't bother anybody. I've got my beliefs, but I don't go spoutin' off about them."

"If Britany was sexually active and she found herself pregnant, would she consider an abortion?"

Rodgers reddened again and stiffened his grip on the chair's arms. "Britany would never do that. She's had an accident is what's happened," Tom said. "She's hurt and can't get to us. That's why we haven't heard from her."

"Tom," Wendell said calmly. "I'll drive you home. We'll collect this evidence and get it out of your home."

He then turned to Knudson. "Stacey, why don't you complete that release and then swing by the Rodgers and pick me up." Wendell rose from his seat. He wondered for a moment if he might need to help the big man up, but Tom Rodgers stood slowly and shuffled towards the conference room door.

* * *

The men drove in silence. Wendell knew he had pushed Tom into uncomfortable terrain and did not wish to poke at an open wound. Yet, it wasn't as if they could exactly turn the conversation to football. Tom's big truck felt cumbersome and unwieldy. Wendell felt the rumble of its diesel exhaust system as they climbed the gap near Somers. His phone had rung five minutes before, and he'd checked to see if the call was important. The call was from his friend, Joel Estes, so he let it go to voicemail. As he slowed for the forty-five-mile-an-hour zone near Somers and the beaches, he ventured what he hoped would be a neutral question. "What was Britany like when she was little?"

"We did everything together," Tom said. "Fish. Hunt. Ride. She lived to ride. When she was little, we spent every spare minute on horseback."

"I didn't realize you own horses."

"Sold 'em a couple of years back. Sheila never wanted much part in it, and I can't ride anymore without it getting to my back. Hate to know what I spent on those animals—boarding, feed, vets, shoes. It's a shame, though. Britany was born to ride."

"What changed?"

"I don't know. Kids grow up, I guess."

"Have you two remained close?"

"Too busy for her old man these days."

"Teenage girls," Wendell said.

"You have kids?" Tom asked.

"No."

"It's the only good thing I've done in my life."

Wendell wanted to say how much he looked forward to meeting Britany, but then he thought about the blood in the Tomlinson boat. Instead, he said, "Everybody we've interviewed has commented on how kind Britany is. I'd say you've done right."

"She's a charmer. Lord knows she can get anything out of me she ever wanted." Rodgers grew silent. When Wendell looked at him, he saw that Tom's head was turned away to the passenger window, and he saw a small tremor ripple the muscles across the big man's back.

Chapter Twenty-One

When Wendell finished briefing Sheila, he met the evidence technician in the driveway. There he briefly glimpsed the doll parts left on the Rodgers's porch. He phoned Knudson, who was still en route, and told her to pick him up at the Centerplace building. He used the walk to think. Wood smoke rose from the chimneys of nearby houses. The rain had returned. Wendell didn't mind. In the rain, sound softened, and objects grew muted, which encouraged focus. That was what he needed now—closer awareness. If they were to build a case against Evans, they would need every shred of evidence possible and could make no mistakes.

He passed now along streets that were paved and wound among a pretty wood where the pines were well-spaced and native grasses grew in the open spaces. Housing lots had been surveyed but no homes built; the wooden survey markers sported faded ribbons. The pavement shined black in the rain and led nowhere. At the bottom of a hill, a sign advertising the development lay half-hidden in weeds, weathered and encrusted with bird droppings. Two splintered posts rose above it. Wendell wondered if this is the route that Britany would have taken home had she not gotten in Jacob Bianconi's car. "And then where, Britany?" Wendell asked the indifferent rain. "Where did you go?"

Wendell stopped. The rain dripped out of his hair and off his nose. He closed his eyes and tried to imagine Britany walking the opposite direction up this empty street, but all he could see was her father, the quiver of his shoulders that revealed his silent sobs, and Wendell thought of the children he had always wanted and never had, the family he had so often longed for. In the late fall, when the rains came and mist clung in the low places like spider webs and he knew a long winter awaited, he felt the absence the keenest. Yet he knew the thought of the ones lost because they had never been present was a much gentler pain than the loss that wracked Tom Rodgers. Wendell opened his eyes and walked on.

At the Centerplace, Wendell stood before the warmth of the gas fireplace. He stared at the chair where the security tapes revealed Britany sat on the night she disappeared. She inhabited the leather chair as if at home in her living room—one leg draped over a chair arm, her long hair swept over her left shoulder. There was a moment in the security footage, just as the screen on her phone lit up, and she looked at it before placing the phone to her ear, when she smiled. Something about the smile had plagued Wendell. Not because it was out of place. He had registered the smile originally simply because it told him that the caller had brought her pleasure rather than fear or annoyance. But now, he recognized what he had seen in the smile: a charming young woman aware she had the power to make others do what she asked.

He shifted his gaze and looked outside into the grey day. He thought momentarily of Lorena and her earlier call. He heard again the tone with which she had said, "We need to talk," and wondered what she wished to talk about.

Then he remembered the call from Joel Estes he had let go to voicemail. He checked his phone and heard Joel's relaxed voice inviting him to dinner. "Thought you might like some company. You know, come hang out with the good guys for a change." Joel was a fireman, and his fiancé, Christine, a paramedic. "You're down in our neck of the woods anyhow, so swing by and have a bite. It's stew. We'll keep it warm. Any time that works."

As he tucked his phone away in his jacket pocket, he saw headlights swing in a U-turn as Knudson pulled to the curb precisely where he imagined Jacob Bianconi had parked when he collected Britany.

"You got our friend delivered without dispatching any vigilante justice," Wendell said as he got in the car.

Knudson frowned. She drove in silence for a time, then said, "We can at least go to the Tomlinsons. They can force our hand and bring charges."

"Our priority has to be linking Evans to Britany. I've got an off-duty parked on the Tomlinson gate. If Evans wants to leave without being followed, he'll have to sneak out on foot or take to the water. We need a day or two. Let the techs do their job. We get the evidence. We use it for leverage, create a chain that gets us to Britany. That's all that matters."

"I'll let you tell that to the mothers whose daughters this perv spied on."

"If it gets us the opportunity to tell Sheila what has happened to her daughter, then I'll gladly tell her I delayed justice to get answers."

"Spoken by someone who is not a parent."

Wendell brushed the heat of her voice aside. "We tell them today, we tell them tomorrow, it's not going change what Evans has done. Right now, we've got to keep our eyes on the ball."

Knudson changed lanes aggressively. "Christ, what is it with guys and sports metaphors?"

Wendell understood her anger. "Stacey, we've got holes to fill."

"I know, I know."

"Tell me, how is it three people present on the property don't know Britany's there? Annie shows up on Thursday, and that's when Evans chooses to go on the hunt? It doesn't make sense. He's a voyeur, right? He minimizes risk. He isn't even physically present. Is this the guy who snatches a girl and then brings her where there are witnesses?"

"What about the abortion thing? What if that's real and there's somebody we don't know about?" Knudson asked.

"There's nothing in her notebook to suggest it. She's underage, so she would have to have parental consent."

"Or go outside the system."

"There's that," he agreed.

"You saw the doll?"

Wendell nodded.

"God, there's some sick people in this world."

"Some desperate ones, too," Wendell said. "Evans is smarter than he appears. Could he plant this doll in an attempt to throw us off his scent?"

"Smart enough we can't find evidence connecting him to Britany but not smart enough to remove the cameras? I don't know."

Wendell nodded. "Say he acted on impulse and then has to clean up after himself. Nothing pre-meditated. Could this be part of his attempt to clean up?"

"Get us looking elsewhere?"

"Maybe."

"Is it me," Knudson said, "or is it convenient that it's always Tom who shows up to bitch at us. Tom who finds the doll. Who controls the mail, the phones. Controls what his wife sees. Where his kids go."

"It's convenient that the doll will have his fingerprints all over it. You make a fair point."

"How much do you want to bet those are the only fingerprints we lift off it?"

"When I drove him home, that was a man who was entirely broken."

"Guilt? Say he lost his temper? We know he has one." Knudson sighed heavily. "What about Bianconi? His story seems bullshit. He's pissed that she's a tease. Something happens out in the woods. He's a smarty-pants. He concocts a diversion? Wants us chasing down rabbit holes."

"We've had eyes on him. We've got no evidence of a second trip to Montana."

"He's got money. Easy enough to hire someone to drop off a package."

"True."

"What about the opposite? Let's say his bullshit story is true?" Knudson asked. "She wanders onto the property on her own? Wrong place, wrong time. Encounters Evans. An opportunity drops into his lap."

"If this is him..." Wendell paused for a moment. "If this goes where we fear it is about to go, we've got to discover an explanation for why he accelerates from a voyeur to an active and violent participant. We need to look for some kind of accelerant."

Knudson appeared reluctant to speak. "Earlier, back at the house when we first confronted him, I played along to get him talking. Pretended I shared his interest in Annie. Suggested I could be interested in him. That got him. The idea that a cop could play into his fantasies excited him. That's the closest he came to telling me more."

"You got in the deep water, didn't you?" Wendell asked.

Knudson reddened. "I did." She paused. "Do you think that's part of it?"

"I don't follow."

"Maybe he got in over his head too. Maybe a woman took him somewhere he didn't know he was ready to go. Something that threw him off his game and got him out from behind the camera."

"It's worth exploring. We need to talk to women from his past. Continue to explore these rumors he had a relationship with a teenager. And we've got to talk to Annie Tomlinson. An independent, sexualized young woman to whom he has access. What's that do to a guy like Evans? Does he crave more than what a camera gives him?"

"Promise me something."

"What?"

"Even if we can't connect him to Britany, we still charge him for what he's done."

***

Tired but curious, Wendell pursued the easiest avenue into Evans's past. He quickly learned that his mother was deceased. Pursuing a name mentioned in the mother's obituary, Wendell discovered that her sister resided in Kalispell. Greg Evans's aunt lived in a senior apartment complex five blocks from headquarters. To have a conversation a walk away sounded more pleasant than chasing down prostitutes and middle-aged bar regulars.

Delores Stimpson used a walker. Her rounded shoulders rolled inward as she shuffled along, but she appeared alert. She offered to make Wendell tea and turned down the volume on the pennant-race game on TV. She took her seat in a recliner and pointed Wendell towards a small couch, its age masked by two afghans.

"Greg's not in trouble, is he?"

"Would it surprise you if he were?"

"Trouble has always followed him. Never knew him to look for it. Not like his father. I always felt sorry for Greg in that regard."

"Why is that?"

"He didn't get a fair shake. My sister and his dad were terrible parents. They could be mean when they were drunk. I found him on my doorstep more than a few times."

"Were they abusive?"

"I had my suspicions. His dad wasn't in the picture much. His momma, well, I guess it depends on where you draw the line between being strict with a child—spankings or a switch, that sort of thing. She hadn't wanted a kid no more than you want rain on your wedding day. Didn't always know how to handle one."

"Are you and Greg close?"

Delores grew intent on some aspect of the game and leaned closer to the TV. When she leaned back, she said, "Close? Not really. I tried to do right by him. Made sure he got a good dinner. I already had two of my own to look after by the time Lila had Greg."

"Does he visit?"

"Nah. Greg's the lonesome sort. He came and saw me a couple of years ago on my birthday. That was nice. Back when he was still married, he came around on holidays. Course I can't say I was surprised when the marriage didn't last."

"Why do you say that?"

"Never saw him as the marrying type. Never comfortable around people. Women in particular. That woman he married...she was a gruff one. Ordered him around. Treated him more like he was her child than her husband." Delores jumped back in her chair, her attention on the game again. "About time," she said to the TV. "I was beginning to think there wasn't a man on this team capable of hitting the ball.

"Always wished Greg would find a passion. A sport. Music. No self-confidence. A boy can't go anywhere without it. Now my Allen, he had it in spades. Lettered in baseball and football every year of high school. Greg was different. Tinkered with things. Always some broke-down appliance opened up. Never did much in school. I blame the parents."

"You said his dad wasn't around."

"Disappeared," she snorted. "Walked out when Greg was little, maybe five or six. Went back to Washington. Turns out he'd been stepping out on Lila from the get-go. Had kids with another woman. All girls on that side. Wild ones. The stories I've heard about those girls." She grunted. "A lot of good that did you," she said suddenly, directing her comment to the TV. "Get a man on base and then the next batter flies out."

She turned back to Wendell abruptly. "You know, Greg went to live with his dad for a time in middle school. Stayed most of a year. He was never the same after."

"How so?"

"Came back timid. Like a dog that's been close to guns." Rather than looking at the TV, Delores looked out the window of her apartment, where a colorful maple dominated the view.

"Do you know what happened?"

"Hard to know. A whole family of strangers, half-sisters or no. A woman he didn't know. A dad nothing but trouble. I begged Lila not to send him, but she'd taken up with another man and was determined to drink herself into her grave. So off Greg went." She looked out the window in silence for a time. "Who knows what Greg was exposed to."

"Where's his father now?"

"Long dead," she said flatly. "Years ago. Car accident. Drunk."

"You said that trouble has followed Greg. Does that include trouble with the police?"

"Not to my knowledge. Bosses who let him go. Money troubles. That wife. But it all comes back to his beginnings. Always does. He'd be a different man if he had different parents."

As he closed the door on her apartment, Wendell heard the volume on the TV go up. The sun had made a brief return, and he walked back to the office on uneven sidewalks raised by tree roots though a thick duff of fallen leaves.

Chapter Twenty-Two

Wendell arrived at Joel and Christina's with a mix and match six pack of European beers he'd put together from a specialty shop. It was after 8:30 when he rang their bell. He heard Joel shout "It's open!" from the back of the house. Wendell found them curled together on the couch before the TV, Christina in yoga pants and a silk camisole and Joel in omnipresent sweatpants and t shirt. Wendell immediately regretted intruding. He opened the refrigerator to deposit the beer when Joel looked over the back of the couch and said, "Hey, hey now. How about we walk one of those soldiers over here."

"Christina?"

"No thanks."

Wendell grabbed a Scotch ale for Joel and removed the cap with a bottle opener shaped like a trout. "Sorry to interrupt your evening."

Joel didn't respond, just took a swig of the ale and smiled with satisfaction.

"Joel made stew, Stevie," Christina said. "I kept it warm for you. There's fresh bread on the counter." She was the only person he had ever known who called him "Stevie" and the only one he would never admonish. "You're not interrupting anything. It's shit for weather."

"What are you watching?" Wendell asked.

"You don't want to know," Christina said.

"It's something Christie found. Right up your alley. Dark murder stuff full of troubled coppers. It's set in Norway."

"Denmark," Christina corrected. "And it might just be a little too up your alley. Get some stew." Christina turned off the television and rose from the couch, extending a hand to Joel. He promptly pulled her back onto the couch, which resulted in a giggling scream.

"What's the good word?" Joel asked.

Wendell retrieved a bowl from the cupboard. "This case may be about to go in a whole new direction."

"We'd heard they pulled some of Marston's crew off the main search," Joel said.

"So much for keeping things quiet."

"You know better than that," Christina said. "Firemen can't keep their mouths shut. I heard about it at the gym." She was barefoot and obviously braless, and Wendell felt all the more that he had intruded. He looked away.

"The fact you wanted to keep it quiet can't be good." Joel took another swig of beer.

"I don't know anything definite," Wendell said. He sat down at a granite bar. Against his protests, Christina cut him a thick slice of bread. "But no, I don't think it's going to be good."

"Have a beer."

"My night may not be over."

"Stick around, at least. You haven't taken your jacket off."

Wendell looked down at himself, embarrassed. His coat was beaded with rain. He looked at the floor and saw that he had dripped water everywhere he had walked. "Oh shit, I'm sorry guys. Show me where I can find a mop."

"Don't worry about it," Cristina said. "I think I'm going to have some tea. I'll make you a cup."

"I'm fine."

"It wasn't a question," she said. "And you're going to have seconds. This is probably the first meal you've had since breakfast. Or did you have breakfast?"

Wendell shrugged. She still held the knife she'd used to cut the bread and pointed it at him with a hand on her hip.

Joel sat down at the counter. The three talked about their upcoming wedding. All assiduously avoided more talk of work.

When Wendell's phone rang, he looked at the screen, motioned something meant to be an apology, grabbed his coat off the chair back, and walked out onto the back deck.

The rain had picked up, and despite remaining under the house eaves, the wind blew raindrops in on him. He held the phone with his left hand and tried to maneuver into his coat with his right.

"Wendell, I've got lab results for you. We've got a positive blood match to Britany Rodgers."

"Okay." Wendell managed to get his arm into the jacket sleeve. The coat hung off his shoulders and over his back, so he turned his back into the rain, which left him facing the window. Christina reached into the cabinet where she kept their Tupperware. Joel had retrieved a mop.

"Sorry, man."

"Yep."

"We've got three sets of prints from the boat. Greg Evans and his assistant, Eddie Rodriguez. The third we don't have on file."

"Thanks, Lonny. Maybe Mr. Clean isn't so clean after all."

"He missed the blood, but it was evident the main cabin was cleaned. Not so much as a print anywhere near the blood residue."

"Where'd you find the prints?"

"For Rodriguez, strictly around the engine housing. Evans had prints there as well and, on the wheel, the throttle, and the cover."

"The third set?"

"Only on the underside of the cover."

Wendell replaced his phone in his pocket. He inhaled deeply and turned back into the rain. Three dim lights from boat docks on the other side of the bay offered the only illumination along the shore. They appeared to shimmer because of the rain, and the effect made them hover like lonely stars against the dark outline of trees. He heard the water below, small waves reaching for the gravel shore then receding back into the darkness. He looked down onto the water, but it steadfastly refused to reveal its secrets.

Chapter Twenty-Three

He made one stop on the way back to the office. Christina's tea had done little to revive him. How he wished he could curl up on their couch and fall asleep. He decided to take a risk on Dairy Queen having coffee. The smarter bet would have been next door at the convenience store, but Wendell could never pass up an opportunity to work.

He was waited on by a girl who looked so much like Britany Rodgers, his heart raced. Her nametag identified her as "Tina."

"Is it too late for coffee?"

"I need to brew a fresh pot," Tina said. "If you don't mind waiting."

"Not at all."

"It's pretty fast."

As Tina filled a coffee filter, Wendell identified himself as a police officer and asked her if she often worked with Britany.

Tina nodded.

"I've got to say, you look so much like her you really threw me for a loop."

"We get that all the time."

"I bet. You two could be sisters. You must go to school with her too."

Tina looked embarrassed. "I don't go to school anymore," she said.

"I really just came in for coffee," Wendell said. "But your coworkers haven't been any help. Do you mind if I ask you a couple of questions?"

"I don't know if I can be much help. I don't know her very well."

"I suppose you two get twins jokes."

"We confuse the customers. It's pretty funny but it can be embarrassing. One time a guy thought I was Britany and asked me for a date. Turns out it was somebody I used to go to school with, and he didn't recognize me."

"You should have accepted, and he wouldn't have been any the wiser."

"Until he met my five-month-old."

"Would have been worth it just to see the look on his face."

Tina laughed. "I've sworn off boys."

"Wise move," he smiled. "Boy or girl?"

"Girl. Her name's Brittani too. Spelled differently. It's one of the things we joke about. I'm sorry the coffee's not faster."

"No problem."

"Do you think you're going to find her?" Tina asked quietly.

"Not for lack of trying. Maybe you can help."

"I'll try."

"Did she talk about a boyfriend?"

"We don't talk about stuff like that."

"Do you know who she hangs around with?"

"Not with people from work, so I don't really know."

"How about customers? Anybody around more than they should be?"

"Not that I know of."

"I want to show you a picture. Maybe it's one of those customers you two have confused in the past. Let me run to the car." Wendell returned with a manila envelope. He removed a photograph of Greg Evans. "This guy come in here?"

Tina shook her head. "I don't think so. Unless they're regulars, people look alike to me."

"That's okay."

"I'm sorry I can't help."

"If you haven't seen him, you haven't seen him."

"We get a lot of flirty old men. I guess they're harmless. The really old ones, the grandpa types, some of them are pretty cute. Old people love their ice cream. Course they're not flirting, just being nice. Britany has all of them wrapped around her finger."

"What about the not-so-grandpa types?"

"Britany probably gets more of the late-night drunks since she works weekends. They can be a different story. She probably smiles her way through it."

"That's what everyone says about her."

"That's Britany. I wish I got to work with her more. She's always a blast. You never know what she'll do. A few weeks ago, we were closing together, and she started singing and dancing with a mop, and there were still customers here."

Wendell laughed. "I've heard recordings of her singing. You should charge admission."

"That's the truth. Everybody loves her. She's so nice to people, sometimes I worry about her."

"Worry, why?"

"She just seems naïve. I was the same way. She gets caught up in things, ya know?"

"How do you mean?"

"Like a few weeks ago, we worked the same shift. Some guys were in, maybe college age. Trying to be suave. They invited us to a party. Britany played along. She even wrote down the address. That kind of thing can get a girl in trouble."

"Did she go to the party?"

"I don't know. Didn't see her until this last week when we worked the same shift. I'd forgotten about it by then."

"When was that?"

"Friday night," she said.

"Anything unusual happen?"

"No."

"No impromptu Dairy Queen Karaoke?"

"No," Tina laughed. "We ran out of Pumpkin Spice blizzard mix, which irritated some crazy lady, but Britany smoothed that over. Made her something not on the menu. Then about closing time, she had a long conversation with a customer about her tattoo. You'd have thought they were best buds."

"A regular?"

"Not that I know. Afterwards, Britany wouldn't shut up about how much she liked her outfit. That's Britany for you. They even took a selfie together."

"The customer took a picture with Britany?" Wendell asked. He imagined that somewhere there was a stranger with a picture of Britany on her phone twenty-four hours before she disappeared.

"I'm sure the whole idea was Britany's. That's how she is. One time after work, she came through the drive-through, and I waited on her, and she filmed the whole thing on her phone. Knowing Britany, she's probably got a hundred selfies on her phone with people she doesn't know."

"They took the picture on Britany's phone?"

Tina nodded.

How desperately Wendell wished he had that phone in his possession.

"The guys you talked about…do you remember if they took a picture with her too?"

"I don't think so."

"You said those guys invited her to a party. Is Britany the sort who would really go?"

Tina reddened suddenly. "What do I know? I got pregnant at seventeen."

"Maybe you're the best person she could listen to."

"Hardly."

"What do you think? Would she?"

"Maybe. I worry she does things without thinking. Stuff we all do. I look at her and see how I used to be." She looked around. The only other employee, a man in his mid-twenties, mopped the floor near the drive-up window. "I mean, look at me," she whispered. "Is this my life forever? Working fast food in Lakeside, Montana?" She poured Wendell's coffee.

"You could take classes at the college."

"I didn't even finish high school."

"So, you complete your GED."

"But I've got the baby."

"There's always a way." Wendell paid for his coffee and left a two-dollar tip in the jar.

"I don't know where I'd find the money."

"There are scholarships."

"I don't know."

"You want a different life for your daughter, right?"

"Yes."

"Then you've got to make change happen." Wendell reached in his coat pocket and retrieved a card. "Call me, and I'll put you in touch with a counselor at the college I know. She could get you started."

"You'd do that? You don't even know me."

"I would."

"I'll think about it."

"You've still got your life ahead of you, Tina," he said. Wendell turned to leave and then turned back. "You said she wrote down the address the guys gave her. Did she put it in her phone too?"

"No, she wrote it on her arm."

Of course, Wendell thought as he stepped out the door. Where else would she write down an address?

* * *

The coffee had cleared a few of the cobwebs, and he felt numb. He risked becoming mesmerized by the steady monotony of the windshield wipers. In the morning, he would need to tell the Rodgers of the fate that had likely befallen their daughter.

His phone rang just before 2:00 a.m., awakening him from a troubling dream, and he fumbled the phone twice before getting it to his ear. "Detective Wendell?" asked an unfamiliar female voice. The glow of the phone offered the only source of light in the room. Wendell heard his name a second time and managed a groggy "Speaking."

"It's Annie Tomlinson. I'm so sorry. I just realized the time difference when you answered. I'll call back later."

"No, no. I need to speak with you," he said, abruptly alert.

"I'm terribly sorry. I'm so jet-lagged I didn't think about the time difference."

Wendell sat up in bed and turned on a lamp. "I'm glad you called. I've been trying to reach you for several days."

"I'm in Budapest. I had a message at my hotel to call you."

"We were told you were scheduled to play a tournament in Connecticut."

"I was, but this was too good an opportunity to pass up. My manager said you called about the Montana house. A break-in or something?"

"Not a break-in," Wendell said and retrieved pen and paper from the nightstand.

"Oh, thank goodness."

"The property is fine. An ongoing investigation places a missing person on the property."

"A missing person?"

"You were at the house last weekend, is that correct?"

Wendell had a hard time hearing her answer and wondered if they'd lost the connection. He repeated the question.

"Yes. We left Sunday morning."

"Who accompanied you?"

"Just a couple of friends. What's this all about?" Annie asked.

"Can you tell me about your relationship with your caretaker, Mr. Evans?"

"Relationship? My mother manages the house."

"You saw him while you were here?"

"Of course."

"Was there anyone else on the property? Any local friends?"

"I don't know anybody in Montana."

"Did Mr. Evans have a guest?"

"Not that I saw."

"Did you notice anything unusual?"

"Unusual how?"

"Anything out of the ordinary. People who shouldn't be at your house? Odd behavior by Mr. Evans?"

"No," she said, confused. "You said someone is missing? Is it someone I know?"

"That's part of what I'm trying to ascertain. Do you know a girl named

Britany Rodgers? She's local. Seventeen years old."

"No. Should I?"

"We're pursuing evidence that places her on your property."

"What sort of evidence?"

"I'm not at liberty to say. The investigation is ongoing. There is, however, something else you need to know."

"Yes," she said.

"I wish we could speak in person. It involves you."

"Involves me?" she said, shock registering in her voice.

"When will you be returning to the U.S.?"

"What is it?" she asked in a rush.

"Over the course of our investigation, we have gathered evidence that Greg Evans installed a camera in your room. It's likely he has been watching you."

"Excuse me. Did you say he watches me?"

"We are filing criminal charges against him."

"Watching me? That's disgusting. He spies on me, like when I'm undressing?"

"Likely so, ma'am. I'm sorry to have to tell you this by phone. I know it is troubling."

"He has tapes of me?"

"We're trying to determine that."

There was a long silence. Wendell again feared that he had lost the connection. "Ms. Tomlinson?"

"I'm still here. You're sure about this?"

"Yes, ma'am."

"Is that the only camera? Has he been spying all over the house?"

"We found only one other that wasn't part of the house security system."

"Where?"

"In a guest room."

"I can't believe this. It's so, so disgusting. What kind of person would do that?" She paused. "He's always given me the creeps. I guess now I know why."

"I'd really like an official statement from you, Ms. Tomlinson. Can we meet when you return?"

"I've made numerous commitments here."

"When might you be back?"

"Not until Christmas."

"I would appreciate the opportunity to sit down with you on your return. Your cooperation can help us guarantee prosecution."

"Of course. Whatever I can do to make sure he goes to jail. Detective?"

"Yes."

"Do you think he's involved with this missing person? What did you say his name was?"

"Britany Rodgers. We're investigating every possibility."

"Oh, my God."

"We'll appreciate any help you can provide, Ms. Tomlinson."

"Yes, of course."

"I'm glad you called. Can I have a number where I might reach you again should the need arise?"

"You can go through my agent again. He'll get a message to me."

"And can I have the names and phone numbers for the friends who travelled with you this weekend?" After gathering the information from her, Wendell said, "I'm sorry to have brought you disturbing news."

"Yes, well, I'm just glad you caught him. I want you to lock him up."

"We'll do our best. I look forward to meeting you once you're back. Best of luck in your tournaments."

Wendell was unable to return to sleep. After a half hour, he arose, started a fire, and grabbed the Tolstoy novel he'd been neglecting. Lorena had given him grief when she had seen the novel on his nightstand. "As if you don't already live in darkness, you must read about it too."

"You don't care for him?"

"My father loved him. He made me read all the Russians. I left him behind with the past," she said.

Wendell's mind drifted as he tried to read. He returned to work, shifting through the neatly typed notes. He reviewed the information they'd gathered from the doll left on the Rodgers' doorstep. He returned to the interview notes with the Bianconi brothers. After reading them, he felt he'd driven long distances to find a cul-de-sac. That left them with Evans. Wendell had no doubt they possessed ample evidence for the judge to grant an arrest warrant, yet without recovery of more evidence, the case remained too thin to appease a prosecutor. He needed to marshal the details and inconsistencies necessary to move Evans to confession. Evans claimed no knowledge of Britany. Perhaps he simply held out for the lesser charge. At some level, Wendell wondered if Evans hadn't wanted to confess to his involvement with the cameras. It made a kind of psychological sense that if the act of voyeurism had lost the satisfaction he craved, he might wish to share what fed his fantasies. Wouldn't any crime that involved Britany be an extension of sexual depravity? Perhaps the way forward with Evans was not to focus first on Britany's whereabouts or her final fate but on the psychological needs that initiated action. He consulted a couple of old psychology texts from grad school and then spent two hours reading journal articles about voyeurism online.

It remained full dark when he departed for his run, donning a reflective jacket and a headlamp. Though his preference was for single-track, to run two hours before sunrise in the late fall in bear country tempted fate, so he chose a course that took him along backroads and through the village of Bigfork and then up the road into Wayfarers State Park. Overlooking Flathead Lake, the park was a frequent destination for romantics seeking sunsets. Had he been chasing a sunrise, he needed to be on the other side of the lake, comfortably ensconced on Joel and Christina's deck or one of the Tomlinsons' many terraced patios. But he would be at work before the sun rose, and he remained uncertain what he chased.

Chapter Twenty-Four

"Christ, Wendell, you've had us put resources all over Blacktail Mountain, then a wild goose chase down at the shore, and now you want a water search?" Undersheriff Ben Marston barked his objections from the back of the briefing room. "It's frickin' October. Do you know what the water temperature is? You think it's nothing to put my guys at that kind of risk?"

Wendell didn't remind Marston that the grid search on Blacktail was never his idea. Instead, he turned to his usual tactic for the easily agitated Marston—flattery. "I know it's asking a lot, but I wouldn't ask if your team wasn't so well trained."

"It sure as shit is asking a lot," Marston barked. "Jesus, do you realize this lake is almost 200 square miles of surface area? At the end of October? We could have a storm system move in any day and shut us down until spring. You ever been out on that lake when the wind comes in?"

"I know the weather is not conducive..."

"Not conducive? Can't see the end of the dock, let alone the rock that's will tear a hole in your bow. You get me a twenty, and then we've still got to get a weather break. Otherwise, we might as well be looking for our balls at an orgy. Not to mention the bureaucracy nightmare. State agencies. Tribal permission. Migraine time."

Wendell had anticipated Marston's reaction. He was the guy you wanted in your corner when the bullets flew but was otherwise focused on adrenaline-pumps for "his guys"—bomb reports, armed stand-offs, high-profile drug raids. He oversaw SWAT as well as Search & Rescue, but his resources, and his heart, belonged always to SWAT, evidenced by his fatigue-style uniform and the military flattop he'd sported since leaving the Marine Corps twenty-five years ago. And Wendell did know that he asked for a lot. Despite the clarity of the lake, it was deep—369 feet at its deepest point—and if someone truly wanted a body to disappear, it wouldn't be hard. He knew some of the lake's history, like the forty-six years it had taken to find the remains of a Navy pilot who had ejected over the lake in 1960. And that took side-scanning radar, recovery experts, and a cadaver dog. But if Britany was dead, without a body, they had yet another hurdle to successful prosecution of Evans.

He'd still take Marston's complaints over what awaited him: notifying the Rodgers that their daughter was probably dead. That and a day locked in the company of Greg Evans without putting his head through a wall.

He'd made good on his promise to Knudson that she could put the handcuffs on Evans's wrists. "I'm sending a uniform with you to make sure you don't shove a nightstick up his ass," he'd said to Knudson when he handed her the warrant.

"You're not coming?"

Wendell shook his head. "I'm headed to the Rodgers."

"Do you want me to come with you?"

"No, I want Evans in custody. I'll take a victim's services counselor with me. You concentrate on a strategy that gets a confession. Help him imagine we've got more forensic evidence than we really do. Meanwhile, let him cool his heels." Wendell cleared his throat. "I know I don't have to tell you this, Stacey, but..."

"I know, I know," she said. "No mistakes. Make it stick."

"We're thin right now, Stacey. Razor-thin."

"I know."

"We can't let him know that we need his help."

"Why take the backseat? It's your investigation."

Wendell looked out the office window for a time before he answered. "I want you to have the satisfaction. Given what he is. Given what he's done." After a pause, said, "Sorry, that's bullshit. Honestly, I'm using you. You're bait. I need to watch how he responds to a woman who has power over him."

Wendell sat in his desk chair while Knudson perched atop the desk. He looked up, and she made eye contact and then smiled and said, "Not even a little stick?"

"I'm sure someone will take care of that once he's in prison."

"A girl can dream."

* * *

The day slogged forward, pierced by the depth of the despair that escaped in a wail from Sheila Rodgers. The knowledge that he'd only fueled their nightmares worsened the feelings with which he left their home. After breaking the news, he'd remained a mute witness near their fireplace while the victim's services counselor and Sheila's sister wrapped her in an embrace. Tom Rodgers had sat silently holding his wife's hand and then, once others moved to comfort his wife, removed himself to the garage. When Wendell pulled away from the curb, Tom stood in the open garage door. He stared vacantly into the street.

Evans, as Wendell feared, seized full advantage of his Miranda rights the moment he entered their custody. In his lawyer's presence, he backed away from any criminal intent with the cameras and now stated that he had placed them for additional security precautions.

"And the greatest security needs happen to be in the rooms inhabited by teenage girls and an attractive young woman," Knudson countered.

"They're the most vulnerable occupants of the house," Evans's lawyer said. "My client wished to provide them additional protection."

Evans remained steadfast in his denial of any contact with Britany. "I've never laid eyes on her," he said. "You're barking up the wrong tree." As for the presence of his fingerprints on the Tomlinson's boat, he said, "Of course, you're gonna find my fingerprints all over it 'cause we winterized it last week. You'll find them on the pontoon boat too."

"How convenient."

"You can't fault me for doing my job."

"I suppose scrubbing Britany Rodgers's blood out of the boat is just part of your job."

"I don't have a clue what you're talking about."

"Why is it we've found Britany's DNA on the Tomlinson's boat?"

Evans looked genuinely shocked. Watching from a video monitor, Wendell couldn't tell if the shock was surprise registered at not cleaning the crime scene thoroughly enough or at evidence of her presence. "I can't tell you," Evans said. "Neither boat's been used but maybe four days out of the whole summer. If you found something on that boat, I can't tell you how it got there."

The morning wore on. Wendell watched Knudson try every approach she could think of to get Evans to budge. When he called her out of the interview room after two hours, Knudson looked exhausted.

"Let's get him into a cell and let the iron do its job," Wendell told her. "In the meanwhile, we go back to police work. Evans isn't going anywhere. I'm going to try and scare up his ex. I'll dig deeper into his past. Maybe we can find precursors or a pattern of behavior. You focus on anybody who would call him a friend and anybody he ever worked with before."

"Got it."

"But first, get out of here for a while. Go and get some lunch or get your nails done. Be around somebody other than criminals for an hour."

"Because that's exactly the advice you're going to follow, right?" she said.

"I've got an errand to run. Something I've neglected."

* * *

Wendell had never been to Lorena's Whitefish store. The drive gave him a chance to think. He'd been stonewalled by criminals with regularity, but Evans was resolute in a manner that was uncommon. An ability to lie without appearing inconsistent was a rarity among those who found themselves in interrogation rooms. Both as a cop and as a probation officer, Wendell's experience taught him that he could usually hear an offender's lie.

To hear the truth was sometimes harder.

Lorena's shop paralleled her attire—sophisticated and understated. The sales clerk directed him to a cramped office at the back of the store. Lorena worked at a drafting table with her back to him. "So, this is where the genius happens," he said.

Startled, she turned around rapidly and then showed renewed surprise. "Steven," she said. "Why are you here?"

"I'm contemplating a design makeover. Do away with the whole aging bachelor scheme."

"Is something wrong?"

"You said we needed to talk."

"I did," she said, "but..." she paused.

"Am I interrupting?"

"No. It's fine."

"If this is a bad time, I can go. I needed to get out of the office."

"No, no. We can talk. Maybe we go down the street and get coffee."

While they walked, she asked him about the case.

"It is what you expected, is it not?" she said.

"It is."

"And now you must face it."

Lorena's matter-of-fact exchange with the world was one of the things he appreciated most about her.

"You think it cannot help her family, but it can."

They reached the coffeehouse, ordered, and found a table. "I've needed to talk with you," Lorena said, "I have been putting it off."

"You sounded so serious on the phone the other day."

"I'm getting married," she said without prelude, "and this will necessarily change our...our relationship."

"Married?" The word nearly sent Wendell out of his chair, yet he reacted to it outwardly the way he would to a suspect's confession. "That's out of blue. Besides, I thought you were still married, at least in name," he said, in reference to the man she had married in Bozeman years ago. It was a fact that stuck with Wendell, for it meant he had long been guilty of adultery.

"We filed the paperwork last spring. Officially, I have been divorced for six months. Of course, beyond legalities, we were never really married."

"And this future husband?"

"An architect. We have known each other a couple of years, professionally. As more than that, only recently. I didn't know he thought of me in that way."

"What way is that? As the marrying type?"

"Don't be difficult, Steven. You know what I mean."

"And now he is going to make an honest woman out of you."

"I wasn't looking for someone to marry."

Unintentional as he knew the comment was, he winced. But then, he reminded himself, he refused to consider marriage, had not wished for anything more than what they shared. And what was that? Friendship? A casual yet comfortable sexual partner? A respite in loneliness? "I hope he makes you happy."

"Why do you sound angry when you say that?"

"I'm not."

"Then what?"

"I don't know. I mean, we've never," he started the sentence but didn't know where to go with it.

"You mean a great deal to me," she said, saving him. "From the beginning, we both said we didn't want more, but your friendship is the most important of my life."

"Is that what this is, friendship?" he said, with more cruelty than he intended.

"It is for me," she said. "I thought so for you too."

"It is," he said. "I'm sorry. I didn't…I didn't know you were seeing someone else."

"There is much we do not talk about," she said.

"We agreed to that a long time ago."

"I've dated occasionally. You must have known that."

"That's not something I allow myself to think about." He knew that was an understatement. He'd been blindsided because he refused to consider

Lorena's life outside the time they spent together. What else had he missed, he wondered.

"I did not think you the type to fall prey to jealousy."

Wendell did not respond.

"Tell me you haven't dated too," Lorena said.

"I didn't know you were looking for something serious."

"I wasn't."

"Is this the guy you've waited for, Lorena?"

"He is a wonderful man. In different circumstances, he's someone you would like. I wish that you could be happy for me. I am thirty-eight years old. I do not want to be alone forever."

Again, the comment stung, even if that was not its intention.

She must have seen a look pass across his face, for she said, "I enjoy my time with you better than with any man I have ever known."

"Then why are your marrying someone else?"

"Because I am selfish. And I am also a realist, like you. I would want all of you. You can't give me that."

"What if I could?"

"Then you would be lying to yourself. That would only end up hurting me."

"I would never hurt you," he said.

"That's not quite right. You would never *want* to hurt me. There is a difference. You are already married to your job. You can't change who you are. And I wouldn't want to be the woman who asked you to."

"Some cop I am," Wendell said. "I never saw this coming." He rose from his chair. "I do wish you all the happiness in the world."

"Oh, Steven," she said, looking up at him. "Don't I at least get a kiss goodbye?" Tears welled in her eyes. She rose and hugged him with all the energy of her body, and he wanted to hold the embrace and melt into her. When he turned away from her, he waded through the crowd lined at the coffee counter, oblivious to its presence.

* * *

Knudson waited at his desk when he returned. "Wow, three-martini lunch," she quipped.

"What?" he snapped.

"You're supposed to look rested, refreshed, ready to do battle again. You look you've been through the ringer."

Wendell ignored her.

"I took your advice," she said, smiling.

"What advice is that?"

"I got my nails done." She placed her hands before him like a woman showing off a new engagement ring. The gesture struck him as a measure of femininity seldom present in the environment of the department offices. Her nails glistened, their red a contrast against her dark outfit.

"Good for you," he said. He gestured towards the interrogation room. "I'll take point this time."

* * *

Wendell grilled Evans methodically with no effect. Evans had the look of someone who had waited through endless lines at the DMV for the fourth or fifth time, only to be told he still didn't have the required paperwork. "Why me?" he whined. "You say this girl was at the house, why not look at Annie's friends? Who knows what they are about."

"Unlike you, they don't spy on girls."

At last, his lawyer tried to put a stop to it. "Your interrogation, detective, has become little more than harassment of my client. If you can't offer some firm evidence to corroborate your accusations, I'll file a petition to rescind the arrest warrant."

Wendell turned his attention to the lawyer. "You know," he said, "despite years in the system, I've always wondered how you do it. How do you defend someone when you know they have committed a crime?"

"You've crossed another line, detective," the lawyer said. "And now you are merely harassing me as well."

"Drop the woe is me act, Counselor. I've got a missing girl. Oh, hell," he said, "let's admit what we all know, this girl is dead. Your client killed her."

"Detective, that's quite enough. We're done here. If you don't put a stop to this, I am going to—"

"Going to what?" Wendell interrupted. He rose from his seat. His face reddened, and he slammed his palms into the table with a loud slap. He leaned menacingly towards Evans.

Knudson rose from her seat. The lawyer scooted back in his chair.

"Your lawyer has run out of ways to protect you, Greg," Wendell said. "Why don't you show him some tears. You want to cry to your momma? Oh, wait, your mother never protected you." Wendell shouted. He closed his fist and hit the table again. "Is that what you think about when you get your jollies off with these girls? How you'd like to smack your mom around? Get even?"

"Steve, stop it," Knudson said.

Evans cowered in his chair. One arm covered his head as if he had been struck. Wendell looked at him and saw at once the child in him who had been beaten. The man's body could not contain enough scar tissue to hide his child-self. Wendell saw his hands before him, still clenched in fists, and felt ashamed. The lawyer's voice sounded like it came from another room. He grew aware of pressure against his chest and looked down and saw Knudson's freshly painted nails standing bright against the dark fabric of his sport coat as she pushed him away.

II

Part Two

Chapter Twenty-Five

That winter was one of the wettest ever recorded in the Flathead Valley. One dreary, grey month elongated into the next. A long spell of bitter cold trapped the roads and trails in ridges of ice and imprisoned Wendell in the misery of the gym.

The forensics team completed work on Evans's laptop and produced fragments of video from the security cameras—seldom more than an isolated frame, but the images displayed naked scenes of Annie and of her cousins changing clothes. The lengthiest footage revealed Annie in a sexual encounter with another woman.

Wendell had voluntarily removed himself as the lead detective from the case, which brought some cooperation from Evans's attorney, but he continued to gather information that linked Evans to Britany's disappearance. Over the winter, Wendell put in the legwork that built a much clearer picture of Evan's past, one that solidified psychology that might forge interest in Britany Rodgers.

Sheila Rodgers sought him out only once over the winter. The sky held the look of twilight all day. Snowflakes drifted irregularly. There was grey in her hair that hadn't been visible before, and her shoulders slouched forward. They walked to Bridger Coffee. It was not until they were in the coffeehouse that Sheila used Britany's name, and he saw once again the rawness of her loss.

"Do you honestly think you will ever find out what happened to Britany?"

Wendell inhaled sharply. "Without additional evidence, I don't think Evans will tell us more. The cameras allow us to prosecute him—what is legally referred to as "surreptitious observations and recordation," but now that he's certain he's going to jail, the threat of it isn't really a motivator anymore. I'm focused on finding evidence that suggests he's done this before. If I can uncover anything, it not only helps me understand what motivates him, we might gain leverage that will get him talking."

"You still hope you can make this monster confess."

"Or evidence on another case we can prosecute. If I learn something more about his compulsions, I may learn somewhere new to look for physical evidence in Britany's case."

"You mean finding my daughter's body."

"Yes. Finding Britany's body is crucial. But I am also looking for evidence that can connect Evans to Britany. Her phone. Personal effects. Anyone he may have spoken to about her. I'm won't quit on you."

"But the sheriff's department has."

"They haven't. I promise. No one has forgotten Britany. Our office is full of good people who are relentless. I can guarantee you that I am."

"I appreciate you saying that."

"It's not talk, Sheila. I'll do everything in my power to bring you answers."

"I was in Walmart the other day," Sheila said. "Tommy had to go to the bathroom. I was waiting for him, and there on the wall is a whole display of missing children. Two dozen of them. Teenage girls. Little boys. A toddler. Some of them have been missing for years, so long that they have to post photos of what they assume they look like as an adult. Is that my Britany's fate, to forever have her picture thumbtacked on a corkboard in Walmart people ignore on their way to the restroom? I need to know what happened to her."

* * *

Wendell had spent his own money and his time off traveling to discover more about Evans. He had returned to Oregon and re-interviewed Jacob Bianconi. His story never faltered.

A trip to Chewelah, Washington had brought strange encounters with

Evans's half-sisters and their clannish extended family, most of whom lived in adjacent houses scattered on a timbered tract sporting two sagging barns, several outbuildings leaking accumulated junk, and rusted timber equipment. Wendell counted three generations, from Evans's half-sisters to their grandchildren. It was as if it was a family genetically inclined to produce female offspring, and when introduced to the teenage granddaughters of Cindy, Greg Evans's oldest half-sister, it required no imagination to see in their faces what she must have looked like forty years ago. The protruding bellies of an impending fourth-generation bulged from two of her granddaughters. The whole lot seemed entered in a contest to expose the most cleavage.

For a woman who had given birth to six children, the first when she was sixteen, Cindy remained thin and angular, and though her heyday had passed, one could see that she had once been attractive, a countenance she tried to maintain with make-up. The nearly continuous presence of a cigarette explained a deep rasp in her voice. Wendell learned immediately that she liked to talk. "Little Greggy," she rasped, "I remember when he came to live here. Don't think I've seen him but twice in all the years since. When daddy told us he had a kid with another woman, with another *wife* no less," she laughed, "and he was to live with us, we were beyond curious. Who was this kid from Montana, from this other *marriage*, when there were already three of us and daddy passed through only every few weeks? Left us to think that he liked that family more than this one. We built Greg up in our minds. We imagined this other life Daddy lived must be like something from TV while we were stuck here in hand-me-down clothes hoping our granddaddy would stop by with groceries.

"But then he shows up, this quiet punk scared of his own shadow, and daddy goes and gives him the lean-to while we're stacked three to a bedroom like cordwood. Mamma wouldn't hardly look at him. Daddy doted on him. When daddy was around, that is. Greg being here didn't seem to change none of Daddy's habits.

"I'll tell you one thing, Greg didn't fit. Shy when we were hell-raisers. Didn't stand a chance. This is a family where you gotta make yourself heard, or people are gonna forget you're there. We saw right off that we had the upper hand, and Greg, he was one of those kids who kind of, well, how do you put it? It's like he had a target on his back. Didn't help he was the only boy of course."

Wendell asked her to tell him more.

"Oh, mostly we just teased him. He was fun to embarrass. He wasn't used to girls, so it was easy to get him to squirm. Talk about our periods. Hang our bras all over the house. We'd threaten to shove a tampon up his nose." She laughed. "He'd probably only been here a week or so, and one morning before sunup I'm sitting on the toilet, and Greg stumbles into the bathroom all sleepy-eyed, a boner poked out of his pajamas. I never left that alone. All I had to do if he annoyed me after that was straighten my finger and put it down the waistband of my pants, and he'd run off.

"He had it comin' though. Always showed up where you didn't want him. One time I caught him watching my boyfriend and me. We'd snuck off to an outbuilding where we'd set up a nice little secret place. I was, well, shall we say, offering my boyfriend a little treat, and I look up and whose face is pressed against the window? That night I beat his ass. I might be a girl, but I was stronger than him. He threatened to tell Daddy what he saw, so I told him I would tell daddy that Greg was the one doing it to me. That shut him up."

"You said you beat him up. Do you mean that literally?"

"I got fists and nails and know how to use them."

"Did your father abuse him?"

"Daddy wasn't a talker when it came to disciplining his kids."

As much as Cindy liked to talk, one of her sisters, Mary, proved reluctant. Mary lived on the other side of the same property, below a ridge and on the far side of a wood. Her house proved charming, whereas the others looked neglected and haphazardly erected in the first place. It featured freshly painted window boxes and shutters in the style of a European mountain village. The kitchen where Mary spoke with Wendell contained original, glass-fronted cabinets, but the paint was clean and crisp, and the cabinets displayed china. She showed him to an uncluttered kitchen table and brought him coffee.

She was slow to respond to his questions, slow enough he wondered if she wished to hide something, but once he moved the conversation off of Greg Evans and onto the quaint house, she opened up and talked about her grandfather. The house used to be his. "He was one of this town's early mayors. Helped start the fire department. Sat on the school board. No one could figure out how my mother was my granddaddy's. We were a trial for him," she said. "This whole family is associated in people's minds with my mother and my daddy and all the stories that follow them around. Not with my granddaddy.

"Of course, I was no better than the rest, pregnant at nineteen. The first in my family to go to college—granddaddy's money and encouragement of course—and I had to drop out. My daughter's father stayed on less than a year. Unlike my sisters, I learned my lesson. Had no more dealings with men and learned granddaddy's business. He owned a distribution company—trucking, supplies, warehousing. Brought himself up from nothing. Never put on airs, like this little house. And look at us now. Lower than nothing."

"Looks to me like you've done a lot right," he said. He pointed to a photo montage that included faded shots of a young woman in cap and gown.

"I made certain my daughter got an education. She's in Seattle now. A lawyer. Two fine young boys."

"Your grandfather must have been proud."

"He passed long before he saw what she became. But I like to think he saw I was doing right. I think that's why he passed along this house to me. Boy, did that ever cause a row. Granddaddy was smart enough not to give anything to my momma. Sold the business. I still work for the man he sold to. All the money he gave to the Catholic Church. You want to see a riot, just make mention of that to my family."

Mary, three years younger than Cindy, painted a similar picture of Greg Evans as a shy, reclusive teen—a kid caught suddenly in an entirely unfamiliar and chaotic environment. "People love to tell stories on this family, and most of them were probably true," she said. "We were out of control. I don't know a lot about Greg's home life, but stepping into this bunch had to have been a shock. I'm part of this family, and I continue to be shocked by its behavior."

When Wendell asked her about Cindy's account of Greg's voyeurism, she said, "You clearly haven't heard the other side of that story. Cindy always baited him. I was only eleven that summer, but I thought I'd seen enough of my oldest sister that I couldn't be shocked. She proved me wrong. She'd lift her shirt up and flash him at the dinner table when momma had her back turned." Mary interrupted herself. "This is embarrassing to talk about. We sound like such a bunch of heathens." She cleared her throat and lowered her voice. "She did tell me something about Greg, though."

"What's that?"

"According to Cindy, and I remind you, you've got to consider the source, she said that at night she used to sneak into the little lean-to room where daddy put a couch for Greg, and she would give him blow jobs. She used to brag about it. Of course, I didn't really even know what she was talking about. I was eleven. I don't know if it was true, but I wouldn't put such a thing past Cindy. Not for one minute. I do remember though, toward the end of his time with us, that if he ever got mad at Cindy or he threatened to tattle to daddy, she'd say, all sing-song, 'I'll tell dad what we've been doing,' and that would shut him up every time."

* * *

What Wendell learned about Evans's history suggested difficulty in adulthood maintaining sexual normalcy. In his ex-wife, he encountered a tall, gruff woman who twice out-weighed Evans. She possessed unfocused anger at a world she believed had mistreated her and offered multiple remarks that painted her as someone convinced that the government had it out for her even in the "hoops" she had to jump through to maintain eligibility for her disability checks. She labeled Evans as "a weak, pathetic man" and claimed he never wanted to work hard enough to provide for them. She eagerly disclosed the name of the girl Evans turned after their divorce, labeling her a "doe-eyed slut. I should have whupped that man soon as I learned he took up with a teenager."

"A teenager?"

"The ink on the divorce papers wasn't dry before he moved her in with him. Don't know how long he'd been sneakin' out on me with her."

"How old was Greg when you divorced?"

"Just turned forty. Mid-life crisis. I'm glad we never had kids. Imagine having to explain that."

"Was he ever violent with you?"

"Greg, violent? No. For all his faults, he's a softy."

"Did he have any unusual sexual requests?"

"Sexual requests? How do you mean?"

"Role playing?"

"Eww. No."

"Did he ever force himself on you?"

"No. Sex with Greg was...boring. He was always a lot more concerned with him getting his than with my pleasure. But then that's just how men are in my experience."

* * *

Meeting Becky Simone nee Truesdale, the woman Evans's wife had labeled a "doe-eyed slut," her appearance defied the description. Becky, now mid-thirties, had a sweet, ready smile and an easy laugh. She was otherwise the sort of person you might encounter on the sidewalk, identify as a parent because of the accessories she carried, and not fully register that you had passed her. When Wendell told her the reason for his presence, she said, "I don't believe it for a second. Greg's not that kind of guy."

"Just what kind of guy is he?"

"Greg's a sweetheart. He came along when I needed him. My life wasn't going anywhere."

"How did you meet?"

"At work. I was waiting tables. He was a regular. Big tipper."

"How long were you together?"

"Almost five years."

"What happened to end it?" They spoke in Becky Simone's neat west-side Kalispell bungalow. The presence of children in the home was obvious—a soccer ball and cleats on the screen porch, bikes chained against a railing outside.

"We didn't fit anymore." She paused. "There was no *anymore* about it. We never really were a match. I wanted a family. Greg didn't. He said he was too old. We'd drifted apart."

"You two never married?"

"No. Might as well have been. I moved in right away. We did everything together. But more and more, he just wanted to stick around the house. He didn't like to go out, not even to dinner. I was only twenty-three when we split. I got bored easily."

"How did he handle the break-up?"

"Oh, I think he knew it was coming. Said he understood. He was so calm and accepting that it made me sad."

"He didn't exhibit any anger?"

"That's not Greg's way. He always treated me nice. Even when we split. I mean, he was way older than me, right, so everything we had was really his. But he was super generous. Told me to take anything I wanted. He even put down the deposit on my first apartment."

"You were still a teenager when you met. Didn't you find the age difference odd?"

"At first, I thought it was weird, but he was different from other guys. He took time to get to know me. Talked to me. Guys my age weren't like that."

"Is it possible he was interested in you specifically because you were young?"

"Oh, I knew what that was about. Older men wanting younger girls? Big shocker. Why would I mind, though? Older men treat you like you're a goddess. Young guys are after one thing, and then it's 'wham, bam, thank you ma'am.' Older guys buy you things."

"How would you describe your sex life with him?"

"I was eighteen. Horny all the time. It's mostly what I thought about. And Greg, he had an appetite, you might say. Sex was probably the main reason we were together. In truth, looking back now, I can see that we didn't have a lot in common beyond that."

"Did he like to watch you undress or masturbate?"

"These are awfully personal questions,"

"I'm sorry. I know this is awkward, but I'm trying to help prosecute someone we believe may be a sexual predator."

"Is it really necessary to talk about this stuff?"

"I need to know if there has been a pattern to Greg's past behavior."

"Oh," she said and paused. "He liked to watch me. You know," she said shyly. "And sometimes he took pictures. I didn't mind. Not that I'd let my husband do such a thing. But back then, well…that seems really stupid to me now."

"What did he do with the pictures?"

"I don't know. I never really thought about it."

"Did he ever try to hurt you or force you to do something you didn't want to do?"

"No. Never."

"Have you kept in touch?"

"We did in the first couple of years. Not since. Haven't really thought a lot about him for a long time if I'm honest. I met Brad six months after I moved out of Greg's place. I was a different person by then. I'd grown up. We got married. Started a family. Greg is ancient history."

"Do you think he is capable of violence?"

"Not the Greg I knew. Not in a million years. If anything, he's the opposite. Complacent. People push him, and he doesn't push back. You don't really think Greg has done the things you are accusing him of, do you?"

"That's what I'm hoping to find out."

"I can't imagine it," she said, and then she visibly shuddered. "If it is true," she paused, "that gives me the creeps. To think I was with somebody who could do such a thing. Like I didn't know him at all."

* * *

The more Wendell probed Evans's past, the more he discovered a psychology that might produce sexual perversion. But nothing pointed to violence, and he still had uncovered nothing that connected him to Britany. The trial on charges stemming from Evans's voyeurism was scheduled for the spring. And still, Wendell had to call in favors when the county attorney reminded him how much county jail bed space was at a premium.

"What if I've got a murderer on my hands, and he disappears after you refuse to charge him?"

"Steve, with the cameras and multiple victims, we can get you three counts. That will be a six-month sentence. If he's a good boy, he's out in three."

"It's three months I don't have now."

The prosecutor's last words were simply, "Bring me the evidence that gets us a prosecution on the Rodgers's case, and we'll file in a heartbeat." Then the prosecutor added, "Give us a murder case, Detective. We've spent a lot of man-hours on a guy who likes to take dirty pictures."

Experience taught Wendell that the demands on time alone made prosecutors turn towards some criminal offenses and away from others. It was necessarily a world of compromise and conflicting interests. But to understand the system and to like it were two different things. As he walked out of the County Attorney's office, he could not help but hold conflicting images in his mind: the childlike fear he had seen in Evan's face when he had lunged for him in an interview room and the hopelessness and defeat etched in Sheila Rodgers's slumped posture.

Chapter Twenty-Six

The winter had proceeded in an endless progression of dreary days and dead ends. There had been new cases, of course. Among them, Wendell was assigned to the beating death of a four-year-old in Evergreen, as mercilessly brutal a case as imaginable, albeit a straight-forward investigation with an immediate confession and ample corroborating evidence for the guilt of a twenty-two-year-old live-in boyfriend. The boy's twenty-year-old mother pleaded with Wendell: "Why would he do this?" Why indeed, Wendell wondered. What corrupted gene or cosmic cruelty made present such evil in our species? The murderer, a man-child himself, had, upon confession, simply said, "He wouldn't stop crying."

That the official files did not classify Britany Rodgers's case as a murder chided Wendell. In the statistical world, she remained a missing person. As if that explained her loss. As if that brought comfort to her family.

On a wintery night in mid-January, Wendell awoke abruptly with the shocked realization that he had failed to review a single element of the case that day. The realization felt similar to when, a few months after his father died, Wendell stopped seeing his face when he closed his eyes. He'd become so comforted by the fondness of memories that reached him each day thinking about his father that their abrupt departure left him mourning all over again. He rose from bed, walked to his desk, retrieved a photograph of Britany Rodgers from the case files, and taped it to his bathroom mirror.

As he looked at her picture, he wondered who this girl really was. What memories stalked her? He looked in the mirror, saw her face taped there but saw himself as well, the lives of strangers so oddly intertwined. When at last he turned away, he returned to his desk and retrieved the pages he had copied from her notebook. He searched within them for the girl he had never known. He fell asleep at his desk, the pages of song lyrics and musical notes scattered across its surface like an incomplete puzzle.

Stuck in the gym because of wintery weather, he drove to Kalispell at 5:15 each morning, completing his workout in time to devote an hour to Britany's case before he officially clocked in. He hadn't given up on evidence that would cement the case to Evans, but he had reopened his mind to other possibilities.

Just before Christmas, he'd interviewed Heidi Tomlinson. This interview marked the first time he'd been back in the house since they had arrested Evans. She appeared much as he had imagined her based on photos, phone conversations, and time spent in her home. Raven-haired like her daughter, sharp edges highlighted by attire that displayed an athletic build. Her clothes, like the furnishings in her home, were precisely coordinated—crisp and tailored. He thought of Lorena. Heidi Tomlinson was warm and unguarded, traits at odds with the angularity of her features and her deliberate style. She brushed aside his handshake and gave him a hug.

"I feel like such a fool," she said. "Trusting that man."

"Greg Evans is convincing," Wendell said. "He's may even believe in his own innocence."

"I brought him into this house. I made him responsible for our security," she said, "when really I provided him the tools to spy on my daughter and nieces. And me as well, I suppose."

"We have no evidence of that," Wendell said. "He's spoken of you with nothing but respect in our interviews."

"I suppose that's supposed to bring me comfort. Instead, it only makes me feel more violated." She rolled a section of a substantial gold necklace between her thumb and index finger absently. "Then I realize it could have been so much worse. Do you really think that Greg hurt that girl?"

"It's an ongoing investigation," he said, "so there's really not much I can share. I know you are full of questions, and it's your home and your family.

I can tell you that Evans denies involvement."

"Big deal."

"I don't take anything at face value, ma'am."

"I had the hardest time coming here this Christmas," she said. "I could only think about the crimes he committed in this house. If that girl was here, if… in my home." She looked beyond Wendell out the windows onto the lake. The water was gray and choppy. "But then I thought that Christmas in Montana had always been our tradition. It was for years even before we built the house. Denny was insistent that he wanted to be where it snowed. Did you know he had Montana roots? Grew up on a working ranch. Most people would never guess that. I came back this year because I knew that's what Denny would have wanted."

"It must be difficult."

"I look around this house, and I see him in every detail." Wendell watched her scan the big room. "I feel closer to him here than anywhere. Sometimes that's what brings me here, and sometimes it's what keeps me away." Her eyes settled on Wendell. Her eyes were chocolate brown. "You don't wear a wedding ring, Detective Wendell."

"No, ma'am."

"Divorced?"

"Never married."

"How on earth did that happen?"

"A job hazard, I guess, ma'am."

"Stop calling me ma'am. Call me Heidi." She paused. "I didn't mean to make you uncomfortable."

"My job requires me to ask the most personal questions conceivable. I guess turnabout's fair play."

"Never married, but you've lost someone you loved, haven't you?"

"I have," he said. Heidi Tomlinson held her eyes on him. He looked at her directly. He felt the cool detachment he sometimes saw in a suspect's eyes when questioned. "I was engaged once. More than twenty years ago."

The two fell silent before Wendell interrupted the awkward quiet. "Did you meet Greg Evans before your husband hired him?"

"You always have that," she said.

"Pardon?"

"You can always go back to work. Go back to asking questions."

"Old habits," he said.

"A man not accustomed to sharing. Denny was like that. Kept in most of what he felt." She cleared her throat and turned slightly on the couch. "My husband did all the hiring. I think Greg reminded him of men he knew growing up. Enough so that he recognized much of the world has passed by men without formal educations. I think Denny knew he could have easily been such a man."

"Was your husband generous by nature?"

"He could be. Maybe it was a way to assuage his guilt. He could be ruthless too. Competitive. A lot of people didn't like doing business with him. Ultimately, if the price wasn't right, and if he didn't think he could do the job, he never would have hired Greg."

"Did you have reservations with Greg?"

"Honestly, if you hadn't discovered what you have, I'd have no reason to believe Greg wasn't extremely capable at his job. He's meticulous, really."

"He's protective of you and of the house."

"Yes, but we didn't know for what reason, now did we? He used me."

"Most criminals are merely opportunistic. In my experience, when it comes to these kinds of offenses, I'm not sure people like Evans exert control over their behavior. Most have been victimized in the past. He may barely be conscious of what he was doing."

"His self-awareness, no more than his history, matters little to me."

"I understand that. He harmed people you love."

"I don't even know her name," Heidi Tomlinson said suddenly.

"Pardon?"

"The missing girl. I don't know her name. And now her life is entangled in mine."

"Britany."

"Britany," she repeated. "That poor, poor girl. She must be so lonely."

Wendell looked at her and saw that she stared vacantly out into the gray, winter-shrouded lake. She sat in a way that looked unnatural—as if she had grown up with parents who reprimanded her to mind her posture. *She must be so lonely.* He replayed the line in his head. It seemed an odd statement and yet it resonated with him as something he'd felt about Britany's final hours. As much as he wanted to give the Rodgers answers and closure, Heidi Tomlinson had spoken to what really drove him. Britany had to have felt so entirely alone, so terrified and helpless.

Heidi turned back to him. Her expression unchanged, still poised, rigid. "Your job must be lonely. Your thoughts focused on the dead. How do you manage?"

"It's work that suits me," he said.

"How did you get started?"

"If you don't mind, I'd like to focus on Evans," Wendell said.

"Oh, yes, I'm sorry. I forget myself sometimes. Perhaps I am projecting. I've been so lonely since Denny died," she said. "There are so many reminders of him in this house." She stopped as suddenly as she began. "There I go again. You came here as part of your investigation, not to hear me prattle on. There's something about your nature that makes me want to open up." She smiled, which altered the lines in her face in a way that made her appearance more youthful. "You've missed your calling," she said. "You should have been a priest."

"Having people want to tell me things comes in handy," he said.

"Is that a learned skill or innate?"

"People have always wanted to tell me things."

"It's because you listen," she said. "Which is rare. That and they can sense that you are kind. It's a lethal combination to have people pour out their hearts."

Wendell smiled.

"I don't have people I can talk to anymore," she said. "Others are surprised at that. They think I am surrounded by friends. Which, by all appearances, is true. But we don't really talk about anything that matters. And I have so much time on my hands. That's something they don't tell you about those of us who have money. Unless you are hot in the pursuit of making more money, you're bored a great deal of the time. You fill time with trivial things. When you are the awkward bird like me, and you despise pettiness, you end up alone a great deal. Denny always said that I needed a creative outlet."

"You and your daughter must be close," Wendell said to get her back on track. "You have her to talk with."

"You are not proving nearly as perceptive as I thought you were, detective. Since Denny's death, Annie and I hardly see one another. When we do, we might as well be barefoot and negotiating a room littered with broken glass."

"I'm sorry to hear that."

"Oh, it's no huge surprise. She was always a daddy's girl. We never saw eye to eye. Probably because we are too much alike."

"She looks a great deal like you."

"She did more than inherit my features. Stubborn as the day is long. Likes to get her way. A contrarian. She works so hard to stand out simply because she's so desperate to fit in. My daughter has—and this is difficult to admit—made choices I do not begin to understand, choices that I never could imagine my child making."

"What sort of choices?"

"Every sort, Detective. Even this silliness of billiards. She chose to play pool over an education."

"It appears that she has been quite successful."

"Oh, of course, she has. Annie is extremely talented—at pool and at most anything she puts her mind to. She's exceedingly bright, but she makes poor choices. Imagine choosing a career that takes one constantly into casinos. She parades around in gowns that look like lingerie. Giving away the shop, as my mother would have said…" Her voice trailed off.

"Who does she spend her time with?"

"Oh, who knows. It's a rag-tag bunch that always changes."

"Have you met the men she traveled with here in the fall?"

She shook her head.

"You said Annie was a daddy's girl. Did he get to see some of her success in billiards?"

"He taught her the game. No surprise. You've seen it, the snooker table. One here. One in every house we've ever owned. Snooker, of course. Not pool. That would be too easy. Chess disguised as pool. They were cut from the same cloth.

"Those two did everything together. Skiing, fishing, car racing for a time, if you can believe that. Hunting. You name it. They were fiercely competitive. She'd just begun to make it into the prize money at tournaments when Denny died. But, oh yes, he was proud. He was blind when it came to Annie. Denny saw what he wanted to see. He focused on the fact that the TV commentators took notice. Denny simply chose to ignore that the talk was as much about her ruthlessness. She's quick to demean opponents. That used to be unheard of in the billiards world. The media have given her a nickname—the "Stone Princess." If Denny heard such criticism, it didn't matter to him because he knew that you could not separate the two, the persona and the player. So, he dismissed the fact that she didn't come home as often and that when she did, the two of them didn't do the things they used to do. He counted the product endorsements and looked past the lies."

"The lies?"

"It's a terrible thing when you realize that your child lies to you. I'd become aware of it in high school. She'd say she was with a friend when she was meeting a boy. Covered up the evidence she had been drinking. Of course, the lies are bigger now, covering up the reality of a lifestyle she knows I would never approve of."

"When you say lifestyle, are you referring to her sexuality?" Wendell asked.

"Not at all. I saw that she was conflicted about her sexual preferences as a teenager. When she came out as bisexual, Denny viewed it as a phase. I've only wanted her to find love. Someone who cares for her. I really don't care what gender that someone is. But I don't know what Annie is looking for. It certainly isn't love. I don't accept that her sexuality gives her license to be promiscuous. Or why she thinks it is all right to make rash decisions and act as if there are never consequences. Of course, I am a parent; I find it impossible not to believe it is somehow my fault."

"Maybe she doesn't know how to process her grief over losing her father. Sometimes people push others away only because they are uncomfortable with themselves."

"Are you certain you aren't a psychologist rather than a policeman?"

"Work hazard," Wendell said. "Probably a dangerous one."

"Well, you are probably onto something. She certainly has pushed me away," she said. "I don't want to leave you with the impression that I don't love my daughter. I do, even if she frustrates me to no end. And I certainly wish to protect her from the likes of Greg Evans. Yet I haven't. I have failed her. Just another in a long series, I fear."

"We're all ultimately responsible for our own lives and our own choices."

"Is that what you would say to this missing girl?"

Wendell had no response.

They talked several more minutes. Wendell steered the conversation back to Evans. He asked about her nieces and about how her sister handled the news. When they finished, Heidi Tomlinson walked him to the immense front door; her heels struck the stone floor of the foyer. Before she opened the door, she asked Wendell, "The girl to whom you were engaged, may I ask what happened?"

Wendell was momentarily taken aback by the personal question. When he answered, he did so blindly. "I failed her."

"You never found anyone else?"

"I wasn't looking for her when I found her," he said.

Chapter Twenty-Seven

He finally had the opportunity to meet Annie Tomlinson a week later. They spoke by phone before Christmas, and she renewed her promise to meet with him upon her return from Europe. While she did not share her mother's strict posture, she inherited her dark features and prominent bone structure. Yet while her mother embodied practiced understatement, Annie wore bright red lipstick and emphasized her already large, dark eyes with smoky mascara. Where her mother deflected attention with questions, Annie sought it out. Despite January cold, when she removed her coat, she wore a sleeveless blouse. Wendell recognized a large diamond pendant visible in the cleavage revealed in its neckline from photos he had seen, as well as the large, colorful snake tattoo that curled up her left arm—gold, and patterned with intricate geometric bands of red and brown, it twined through a tangle of aqua and blue flowers that sprouted from bright green vines. When Annie stroked the ball, the snake appeared to slide along her cue, springing forward in attack.

Wendell observed the winks of his colleagues when the desk officer escorted her into the detective's bullpen. Whereas her mother might slip into a room from an unseen vantage point and then startle you with her presence, Annie moved across the bullpen as if an entourage followed in her wake. As she approached, she wiped the ink from her fingers after having provided prints as they'd required from all in the Tomlinson house.

"I'm sorry for the circumstance," Knudson said. "I'm a big fan."

"Do you play?" Annie responded.

"Occasionally."

"Are you any good?"

"Only if I've had a sufficient quantity of beer," Knudson joked.

"You have to make it vodka to keep your opponent guessing," Annie countered.

They had barely begun the formal interview when Annie said, "I want to see the tapes."

"I don't know if that's a good idea," Wendell said.

"Believe me, it's nothing I haven't seen before." Annie laughed. Her laugh was fuller than what one would expect from her slight figure. Like her mother, she was all sinew and muscle. She looked ready to sprint away.

"We've only got fragments recovered from his hard drive."

"The question is, when will I see myself on the Internet?"

"So far, we have no indication of any footage beyond what we have entered into evidence."

"You know what they say: 'There's no such thing as bad publicity.' It might be a career boost."

Wendell wondered if the attitude Annie projected was similar to the dark humor he'd heard at so many accident scenes, a coping mechanism for stress. "Probably not the images you would want your mother to see," he said. "Or your nieces."

"What's a matter? Not a flattering angle?" She laughed again and then said, "I'm serious. I want to see."

Wendell stood. "Let me get a laptop. Forensics has moved the files onto a secure server."

"Secure," she said. "So all the cops have seen me in my altogether, just not the fire department or the road crews."

Wendell stopped and turned back to her. "We'll set you up in an interview room so you can have privacy. I assure you that we've been very careful in protecting this evidence. We hold to strict professional standards."

"I'm sure you do," she said. "But you've seen the film. How do I look?"

Wendell turned away again, refusing to engage her. He wondered what motivated her aggressiveness. When he returned with a laptop, he led her to an interview room. "I do need to warn you, Ms. Tomlinson, the prosecution will want to show some of this footage at trial. It will greatly strengthen their case if a jury sees the extent of the personal invasion Evans committed."

"A picture is worth a thousand words and all that," she said.

"In this kind of case, absolutely."

"Righty-o. Let's get this show started."

Wendell opened the laptop. "Evans erased his files. This is what our forensics team salvaged, so you'll never see more than three or four seconds of continuous footage. He had this camera in place for well over a year, so there is still a lot of material," he said. "I'll step out."

"Not staying? You mean that you haven't familiarized yourself with the subject?"

Wendell ignored her. "Detective Knudson will stay with you."

"In case you haven't noticed, that's the way I like it," Annie said.

* * *

When Knudson approached him at his desk a few minutes later, he asked, "Still a comedy routine in there?"

"Actually, she was pretty stone-faced."

"Ah, the routine is reserved for me. Defense mechanism or personality disorder?" he asked.

"Maybe a little of both."

They returned to the interview room and took seats opposite Annie.

"At least he focused on my best side," Annie said.

"I'm sorry you had to see that," Wendell replied.

"He did this to my cousins? Watched them like this?" she asked, her face suddenly appeared stern.

"He did."

"I want to see him prosecuted."

Wendell was pleased to see the serious turn. "Did you ever have any inclination that Evans was observing you?"

"I always found him creepy," she said. "He just has this quality, you know? I don't know how to describe it. Like he's smirking at an insider joke."

"But he never approached you directly?"

"Never. I mean he might make it a point to find me and say hello after I'd first arrived for a visit. Otherwise, he only talked to me if he had questions about the house. He did seem to always find some project when I was out on the deck sunbathing. I'm used to people looking at me, so maybe I've grown immune."

"This is rather different than fans at a tournament," Wendell said.

"I know. It's weird to feel victimized even though I never even knew there was a crime."

"You were victimized."

"You said that the cameras were in my room and in the room where my cousins stay. Did he target us?"

"The psychiatrist who has evaluated him suggests that his voyeurism is sexually motivated. He has a clear bias towards young women."

"You haven't found any other cameras?"

"No. Not those beyond the house security system."

"And where are those? Don't they show anything that helps your case?"

"Honestly, the cameras in your home's actual security system assume criminals are polite enough to knock first. They would never provide the kind of material Evans was looking for."

"So those were the only other cameras he used. You're sure of that?"

"Do you have a reason to think we've missed something?"

"No. I'm just surprised. I would think a peeping Tom would spy everywhere he had the chance," she said. She swept her hair over one shoulder. "Plus, I worry about my mom. She can be naïve. Do you think any of us were in danger? You think he did something to this missing girl, right?"

"We continue to investigate that possibility."

"But you have evidence, don't you?"

"I'm afraid that's part of an ongoing investigation. We can't share details beyond the case directly involving you."

"Even if I am in danger?"

"Has he contacted you?" Knudson asked.

"No. But isn't it possible that he would try to get to me?"

"Evans does not have the means to make bail," Wendell said. "He will remain in custody until the completion of his trial. You have nothing to fear."

"Even if he is a kidnapper or a rapist?"

"Ms. Tomlinson, most criminals are merely opportunists. Evans found himself in a position of access in a setting where he had control. He was in the presence of victims who fed into a sexual proclivity. This isn't a criminal who will fly around the world to find you. With your help, we are going to win a prosecution and Greg Evans is going to remain in jail. You are not in danger."

"All right."

"The prosecutor will want you to testify."

"I'd like nothing better."

"That weekend you were here in October, do you remember seeing Evans?"

"I'm sure I must have."

"Do you recall anything out of the ordinary that weekend?" Knudson asked.

"No."

"Evans told us he was irritated with you. He said you and your friends left messes to clean up. Did he say anything to you?" Wendell asked.

"Not a word. But that's not a surprise."

"How's that?"

"He passive-aggressive. Nice to my face and then I hear about his complaints from my mom. I'm not sure she doesn't enjoy it."

"Evans claims he sought you out to say goodnight. He says you and your friends were in the hot tub," Knudson said.

"I really couldn't tell you. We were pretty drunk."

"Drunk enough to go for a swim in October?" asked Wendell.

Annie laughed. Wendell was again surprised by the volume and animation of her laughter. "Yeah, well, it's a game I've played ever since I was a kid. You jump in the freezing lake, and I mean all the way in, head and all, then you run back to the hot pool. Feels like your skin is on fire."

"Sounds like a recipe for a heart attack."

"Good for getting sober."

"I imagine. Your friends joined in?"

"I dared them into it. They're prissy Manhattan boys. Never swam in a lake before. Quite the virgin experience." She laughed again. "They claimed that their nut-sacks retracted into their throats." She laughed louder still. When she stopped, she asked, "How'd you know we'd gone swimming. Was Evans spying on us then too?"

Wendell forged on. "These friends," he paused, consulting his binder. "How well do you know Frank Busternese and Johnny Devonshire?"

"I've known them for over a year. We've partied together. We went to Johhny's parent's place in Sag Harbor last summer. We've all been guests at friend's weddings more than once."

"How did you meet them?"

"I met Johnny through a mutual friend. They're a package deal."

"They're models?"

"Johnny is. Frank is a designer."

"How is it you invited them to Montana?"

"We were at a party in Manhattan. We decided to continue the party. They thought the idea of Montana was adventurous. I think they were expecting horses and cowboys."

"How would you describe your relationship with them?"

"They're gay, detective. I was odd man out that night. If that's what you're hinting at."

"You would describe yourself as bisexual, am I correct?"

"You *have* watched the tapes." She smirked. "I thought I was supposed to help you prosecute Evans for violating my privacy, but right now, it feels like you're just as interested as he is."

"There may have been another crime committed here. It's my obligation to uncover anything that might help in all potential prosecutions."

"And that investigation includes my sex life," she said.

"I am afraid it does. You were targeted by Greg Evans. We need to make certain we understand why."

"You need to know how I get my rocks off in order to understand how he gets his rocks off?"

"In a manner of speaking. I have to cast a wide net."

"Hook me by the gills alongside all the other fish."

"You could say that."

"Because, detective, this could be misinterpreted as a kind of victimize the victim sort of thing." She looked directly at Wendell and held his eyes. "You know, determine if I had it coming. Was I asking for it? Is this how you approach rape cases?"

Wendell stiffened. "Nothing could be further from my intention, Ms. Tomlinson," he said. "I absolutely do not wish you to feel that way. In criminal investigations, information is power. In this case, I need to try and understand Evans's motivations. I certainly do not wish to be insensitive to you in the process."

"Because I didn't ask to have the starring role in somebody's little fantasy."

"I understand, Ms. Tomlinson. I would never think differently."

Knudson interrupted him. "Ms. Tomlinson, I can tell you there's no one I'd trust more to look out for a victim's interests than Detective Wendell."

Annie Tomlinson took in Knudson and nodded. Turning back to Wendell, she said, "So the more you know about why I became the object of his little jerk-fest, the more likely you are to understand if he's involved with this girl."

"Not to diminish the importance of your case, but yes, that's right."

"Then fire away, detective."

"I appreciate your understanding."

"Though it does seem the tapes speak for themselves."

Wendell ignored her last shot, though he did think she could offer Evans an expert course in passive-aggressive behavior. "Did one of your friends hurt himself that night?"

"What do you mean?"

"Any accidents? Cuts, falls, that sort of thing?"

"Not that I know of. Why?"

"Your maid found bloody towels in the trash."

"Nobody said anything to me," she said. She paused for a long moment and appeared to be thinking. "But that's huge for you, right? I mean, if Evans did something to that girl, it's going to match her blood."

"The garbage had already been removed by the time we started our investigation."

"So you don't even know if the girl was at the house?"

"There are details of that investigation I am not in a position to share. Suffice it to say, it is vital that we are able to place her on the scene if that was the case."

"I'm sorry I'm not much help."

"You can only tell me what you know. Do you remember anyone breaking a glass?"

"Not that I recall. That's not to say it didn't happen."

"Were there times during the weekend when your friends weren't with you?"

"I'm sure there must have been. I'm not a babysitter. Frank and Johnny are about as mellow as they come. And they certainly would have no interest in a teenage girl, not unless they wanted to talk fashion trends."

"Did any of you leave the property at all that night?"

"No."

"Did you or your friends take one of the boats out that night?"

"In the dark? In October? I may have been drunk that night, but I'd have to be past drunk to do something that stupid."

"Did anyone open a window or change any of the alarm settings, try to get in the wine cellar, anything that might trigger the alarm panel?"

"An alarm? What do you mean?"

"Evans made initial contact with our department because he had notification of an alarm that night."

"Wouldn't we have heard it?"

"It would have simply triggered a warning in the security system. With people present on the property, there would not have been an audible alarm. You wouldn't have any reason to know it had been triggered."

"I don't know a thing about the alarm system. That's the sort of thing I foolishly expected our caretaker to do. Maybe Frank or Johnny tried to open a window. I can't say."

"When did you last see Frank or Johnny that night?"

"I think we were in the kitchen. I remember them making sandwiches. I was drunk and tired and wanted to crash."

"I thought you said the swim sobered you up."

"I was exaggerating. In the same way that I could confess that swimming in general, and skinny-dipping in particular, makes me horny."

Wendell was adjusting to Annie's proclivity to attempt escalation with her snide remarks. "I'm curious, particularly if you'd all had something of a rough night, how it was that you chose to depart so early the next morning?"

"I got the call from the people who brought me to Eastern Europe. It all came together fast. I had a lot to do in New York if I was going to commit to them."

"Did you see Evans that morning?"

"No."

"Is it conceivable that Evans could have someone on the property without you knowing it?"

"I pretty much passed out at the end of the night. He could have had a marching band hidden in his apartment, and I wouldn't have known it."

"To your knowledge, have you ever had any contact with Britany Rodgers?"

"You've found me out. I spend all of my free time consorting with high school kids."

"We're looking for some reason she might have been drawn to the property."

"As opposed to being kidnapped by a sexual predator," Annie snapped. "Because the man who spied on me and on my teenage cousins, the man who has watched me undress...watched me have sex, couldn't possibly be interested in a teenage girl, now could he?" Annie sprang up from her seat. "That couldn't possibly have been me who disappeared, now could it? It couldn't have possibly been my little cousins raped, and God knows what."

"Ms. Tomlinson, I know this is disturbing. It may be even more disturbing once at trial when these images are shared with a full courtroom. The prosecutors will work to help prepare you for the emotion involved."

"Don't you worry about my emotions," Annie Tomlinson snapped. "Go do your job and find the evidence that will put this creep away." She marched out of the interview room.

* * *

Wendell grew quiet after Annie's departure. When he spoke, he said, "Meeting the daughter makes me wonder about the dad," Wendell said. "The mom is put together in every way. Poised. Maybe too poised."

"You never said a lot about that interview," Knudson said.

"She pesters you with questions, like if she asks you enough questions, she never has to answer any about herself."

"Like she's hiding something?"

"I don't know. Certainly, she is someone used to controlling what she wants you to see."

"And her bitchy daughter? How do you see Annie?" Knudson asked.

"Insecure. She overcompensates by projecting confidence and tries to disarm by provocation."

"Putting that Psych degree to full use, are we?"

"What was your take?" he asked.

"Me?" Knudson said, dramatically placing a hand to her heart. "I couldn't get past wondering where I could buy a set of knockers like those. Two kids and mine are shot."

If Knudson's intent had been to mimic Annie Tomlinson and disarm by provocation, she'd been infinitely more successful. Wendell was knocked into silence. If his partner could surprise him so, he wondered what else he had missed.

Knudson laughed. "I don't know how you made it through the interview, Wendell. I couldn't take my eyes off them, and I've got a pair of my own." She laughed again.

Wendell reddened.

"You're so easy to have fun with," Knudson said. "But seriously. Stone Princess is right. That girl is never going to let you hear anything she doesn't want you to hear, so maybe that nut didn't fall so far from the tree."

"We need her," Wendell said.

"She won't charm any jury," she said, "but maybe they'll side with her anger. Who is the ultimate victim if not the one who appears she could never be victimized?"

"We need every day of a sentence if we're ever going to prove a murder case," he said.

"We may have to take what we can get," Knudson said. The defeat underlying her words felt like a punch to Wendell. Idly he opened the case binder where Britany's photograph awaited him accusingly.

Chapter Twenty-Eight

In late February, an early-morning dog walker found a decomposing body alongside the Stillwater River near a Kalispell park. Kalispell PD detective Mike Depavich played pick-up basketball with Wendell on Friday nights throughout the winter, and they'd worked together on inter-agency cases in the past. He told Wendell on the phone, "It's probably a longshot, but I thought of your open case."

When Wendell arrived, Depavich met him near the main picnic shelter in Lawrence Park, where Kalispell PD had set up an incident command post. Between the perimeter formed by the Buffalo Hill golf course atop the steep surrounding terrain and the natural barrier of the Stillwater River, were it not for the playground equipment, the park offered forest isolation in the middle of the town. The terrain along the river was overgrown in thick trees, providing bedding grounds for deer and frequently serving as a squat for the homeless.

Depavich walked with Wendell. "The body is partially submerged. There's no way somebody drags her through this jungle and doesn't leave evidence."

"What about the guy who found her?" Wendell asked as he mentally measured distances from the woods to the nearest parking place.

"Dog nosed off into the trees and wouldn't come back."

"Frickin' cold to walk your dog."

"Dog doesn't care."

"I guess not."

"Sun was barely up when he found her."

"What a way to start your morning. Poor bastard."

"Ripped his jacket open, scratched his face when he came wheeling out of these trees."

"Sounds like it could be your guy."

"Accountant. Golden Retriever. Fifties. I don't see it. But then I've been wrong before."

"Haven't we all," Wendell agreed.

Walking was difficult, the trees thick and tangled and as many fallen as standing. There was enough snow to hide holes amid inter-laced branches, and Depavich tripped twice, stumbled, and cursed. They emerged alongside the river, which lazed in a dark channel through the ice. Twenty-five yards upstream, a cluster of crime scene technicians bent to their work inside a triangle of police tape.

"I only got a glimpse from a dozen yards," Depavich said. "Based on her size, the cut and color of her hair, the color of her jacket, I'd say teens or twenties. It would save me a world of hurt if she turned out to be your girl."

While they waited, the two men stamped their feet and talked about a shared acquaintance, a fireman who had recently appeared on a television reality show. Their breath hung in the air around them. When the crime scene team rolled the body onto its back, they approached without being summoned. Despite a corpse compromised by time, weather, water, and nature's processes for managing death, Wendell saw enough immediately to know this was not Britany. "Sorry, Mike," he said. "Looks like she's yours to work."

"Shit," Depavich whispered softly. "Fucker couldn't have dumped her in the county for you guys to find?"

Wendell patted Depavich on the shoulder and turned away. He felt a brief nearly parental relief and then recognized that his case remained as cold as his snow-filled boots.

* * *

In early March, the Flathead Valley received a ten-day flirtation with spring, and Wendell used it to convince Ben Marston that his search and rescue team would benefit from early season open water training. Marston agreed to put two boats on the water as an opportunity to train new personnel. He authorized two additional private boats captained by certified search and rescue non-department personnel that would concentrate along the shore where a body might be moved by tides. A Montana Fish, Wildlife, and Parks boat joined for oversight. They would stick to the waters within the Flathead County boundaries and begin the bureaucratic processes required to unite with the Lake County Sheriff's Department and the Confederated Salish and Kootenai Tribal Counsel for a summer search.

One of the private boats belonged to Joel Estes, and Wendell joined the search from it. He had not been on the water in more than twenty years. While he tried to fool himself, he could not deny the quickened heartbeat or the rush of sudden dizziness he experienced as he stepped onto the gently swaying vessel. He took two purposeful breaths to steady his mind and calm his nerves. Observing his friend, Joel inquired, "You able to find your sea legs?" Wendell nodded by way of reply. "But maybe you'll pass on the waterskiing?" Joel chuckled. Wendell had never shared the backstory for why he feared water, and Joel never asked.

Wendell appreciated that Joel had said nothing more, though he was embarrassed that his fear was so obvious. He worked in a culture where you didn't display vulnerability. "Do the job," they'd been taught in the Academy, "and try not to take the job home with you." How often had he attended the bloody aftermath of a suicide or encountered a decomposing body to be met by crass jokes and savage one-liners: "Going to have to update the dating profile; she's got new holes to plug." He recalled an accident scene where a man, working alone, had slipped and, as the official report read, "become entangled in" a log-splitter. The other deputy on the scene described the cause of death at what had clearly been a slow bleed-out more succinctly when he said, "Talk about your splitting headache." Wendell understood the psychology of such remarks, even if he wasn't a participant. His own coping mechanism was to see every scene as a puzzle: how the sun of a bright winter day, even in single-digit weather, heated the surface of the snow and made the man lose his footing; how the elastic loop on the man's gloves hooked on the machine as he tried to catch his fall and drew his upper body into the path of the splitter; how the cold and shock would have dulled the pain and slowed the rate of blood loss . . .. He didn't mind that his colleagues were frequently morbid or dismissive of emotion. Rarely interested in displays of machismo, he still didn't want others aware of his fear.

Yet the thought of being submerged in the alien world underwater filled him with dread. His mother, his brother, and Lorena—in addition to a few strangers who responded to an emergency call—were the only people who possessed knowledge of the accident that had landed him and his fiancé in the Flathead River when he was twenty-five. His mother and brother knew only the sparest details. Only Lorena had been his confidant. Only she heard him tell of the suffocating dark water that filled the submerged car or about the panic he experienced while he fought to remove their seatbelts while the car sank. Only she had heard about his mental battle between panic and logic once he realized that he had to wait for the pressure to equalize in order to open the door. Wendell tried to convey the experience of that anguished wait, though he left out the sound of Michelle's screams as he told his story. Lorena wrapped her arms around him without a word.

He had never looked at water the same way again. He had told no one, not even Lorena, about how he felt a shift between Michelle and him as they sat, wrapped in blankets, across from one another in the ambulance. He remembered watching the water drip from the ends of her long hair, remembered the small puddle that pooled on the shiny metal floor. She would not meet his eyes. Had he said something as he tried to calm her panic? Had the accident reinforced the anger she expressed earlier that night during an argument—one he regarded as silly and redundant—over the ever-increasing size of the wedding? Had she brought up the miscarriage she'd suffered the year before?

He'd been driving too fast for conditions, speed fueled by frustration. She was right to hold him responsible for the accident, but could she not also hold him accountable for saving them from the river?

At first, she postponed the wedding, then she stopped planning its details.

It felt to Wendell she slipped farther and farther away, as if the river current had wrapped around her after all and slowly carried her downstream. A month passed. Two. He knew he loved her but wondered if that was enough. Ten weeks after the accident, she asked him to meet her at a spot alongside the Whitefish River near where she worked. When they met, she motioned him to get in her car. Wet mascara stained her cheeks. "This isn't working," she said. "I don't feel like the same person anymore. Not since the miscarriage. Maybe before that." She curled a tangle of hair around her finger, a habit she had whenever she was nervous or pensive. "I think I've changed since the accident. Or maybe I need to change. I don't know. I want to go away. Go to school. Start something new." Wendell put up no arguments. He'd felt a divide for months.

When he had closed the passenger door and watched the silhouette of her head through the back window as she drove away, he felt as if he were again underwater. He turned around and looked at the water of a different river, seemingly hardly a river at all as it revealed itself here and again in a channel bubbling through clogged passages of ice and snow. He turned away from the water, and he honored her wishes. For years when he thought of her, he remembered only the panic on her face when they were trapped inside the car as the water rose.

To be present on Joel's boat brought the memories with Michelle back. Once on board and away from the dock, he took refuge in the maps spread on the small folding table they'd brought on board. He felt he owed something to Brittany to be present. By the end of four days, Wendell had to admit that the quiet found on the lake among duty-bound men and women was manageable, though the step from dock to boat each morning still kidnapped his breath.

The crew aboard the Sheriff's vessel had taken precise GPS readings on three locations of interest revealed by the side-scanning sonar. They would return in the summer to those locations with divers, but Joel was confident they would prove nothing more than submerged logs. The sonar unit was still new to the department, and the men needed more training from an experienced private crew that had run searches in western waters for years.

"Why are you so confident of failure?" Wendell asked.

"Because you are. I've seen the change," Joel said.

"What do you mean?"

"Four days on the water, and your entire demeanor has changed."

"Oh, yeah, you think you've created a new fishing buddy? Think again."

"The first day out," Joel said, "you looked at the water like it would capsize us. Today you look at it like it's hiding something, and you want to take it back."

"I think it *is* hiding something from me," Wendell said.

"Yeah, but there's more."

"And what is that?"

"You're frustrated."

"Of course, I am. I mean, what are the odds we're going to find her? Even if she's here."

"You *know* she's here."

"I don't know anything."

"Bullshit," Joel said. "But there's something else…you're frustrated with the search grids. You think we're looking in the wrong place."

Wendell looked at his friend. "Okay. Hear me out. I've got this guy pegged as careful, right? Precise. You should see the way he trims hedges. The way he cleans. Everything at right angles."

"Okay."

"He does this. Whatever is behind it. He's not going to *dump* her body; he'll dispose of it. Make sure it's never found. Won't he motor to a really deep part of the lake? Pick a place where the random fishermen won't hook her with a down-rigger? Won't he weigh the body, make sure it never resurfaces?"

"If what you say is true, we're not only looking in the wrong places, we'll never find her."

"Not if he doesn't tell us where to look."

The men looked out across the lake opposite the near shore. On the water, it was easier to recognize the true vastness of the lake and the rigors of the task before them. Easier to give into hopelessness.

On the fifth morning, winter fog returned, and the lake went grey. "We'd be searching for more bodies if we went out there now," Marston said. Although each of the previous four mornings had opened with a thick swell of uneasy dread, as he pulled out of the parking lot at the Eagle Bend dock, Wendell felt a gray depression settle in like the fog atop the water.

* * *

A week later, the day before Evans's trial, Wendell met one last time with the District Attorney to review his testimony. She assured him that they had a strong case and a good opportunity for a maximum sentence. "His lawyer will challenge you on a coerced initial confession. Just don't demonstrate any emotion whatsoever, and you'll be fine."

"Say he gets the maximum sentence, that's what, six months and a fine?"

"It's six months we don't have now. More with adding destruction of evidence."

She read the doubt on Wendell's face. "Look, Steve, I know it's not the conviction you want; bring me compelling evidence on the Rodgers's case, and we'll prosecute."

* * *

In one of those moments that left him wondering about the cosmic nature of what Wendell's grandfather used to sum up with the cliche, "When it rains, it pours," in the span of fifty minutes, Wendell learned three disparate facts: that the girl in Depavich's Lawrence Park case was a nineteen-year-old runaway known to Spokane police as a meth addict and occasional prostitute who had died of exposure; that, in a rare show of bureaucracy-busting success, all the agencies with supervision authority over the waters of Flathead Lake had not only agreed to begin a unified search commencing as near May fifteenth as weather permitted, Marston had secured the expert services of an Idaho water search firm equipped with side-scanning sonar for four days in early June, which doubled their search capacity; and that Greg Evans was found guilty after less than an hour of deliberation. Wendell was pleased but knew he'd gained no more than a few months of investigation time with Evans behind bars. With no new leads, he felt nearly as desperate as Depavich's teenage victim must have as she froze, craving for a hit of the drug that had brought her a death sentence from the first moment she'd tried it.

Chapter Twenty-Nine

On the day Greg Evans became a long-term resident of the Flathead County jail, Wendell travelled to the other end of the lake in Polson to meet with Martin White Crow. White Crow worked with youth alternative programs on the Flathead Reservation. He founded a prisoner reintroduction partnership after a long career with the Department of Corrections and still regularly volunteered time working with inmates. Wendell had turned to him for help many times in the past with Native American parolees. White Crow still frequented the prisons where he had worked as a counselor and he maintained friendships with prison staff. They met at White Crow's favorite ice cream shop.

"You haven't lost your sweet tooth," Wendell said, gripping White Crow's hand.

"I've lost a few of the others," White Crow laughed, "but apparently not the sweet one." The men caught up on mutual acquaintances, and White Crow made a production of tasting three different kinds of ice cream before settling on a double scoop cone of Moose Tracks and an order of French fries. Wendell opted for coffee.

Wendell asked about a former parolee he'd tried to keep tabs on over the years, a soft-hearted kid from Pablo who probably would never have wound up in the system if he hadn't been born to alcoholics.

"He works for the tribal council now, that kid. He runs an afterschool sports program down in St. Ignatius. We did all right on that one."

"We don't get many wins."

"Not enough." White Crow added salt to the fires and took another bite of ice cream. "But that's not what you wanted to talk about."

"No, it's not. I need help."

"What kind of help?"

"The kind that requires connections on the inside."

White Crow whistled around a spoonful of ice cream and leaned back on the legs of his parlor chair. "You are in the deep, dark water."

"I am," Wendell said. He provided a precis of the Evans prosecution and of the evidence connected to Britany Rodgers's disappearance.

"You think this girl is dead."

Wendell nodded.

"And you think this man killed her."

"It's where the evidence points."

"But you're not sure."

"I'm not," Wendell admitted. "Evans will never talk to me. He'll never talk to any cop again, most likely. Right now, absent him, I've got no evidence I know how to follow."

"He's not the sort of man who is prepared for the inside."

"Yes."

"This kind of man might try to improve his position with the hard cases."

"I think so."

"Or he might be a complete fool," White Crow said.

Wendell nodded.

"He might talk."

"He might talk."

White Crow unwrapped the paper from his cone with great care. He took a long time. He ate the final pieces in silence. "If this girl is out there," he said, nodding towards the window and to the lake, "she needs to come back to land. She needs to come home to her family."

"She does," Wendell said.

White Crow made a sound that was little more than a grunt. Then he said, "Eat some French fries. They only kill you slowly." He laughed and wiped his lips. He rose from the table. The legs of the chair screeched on the floor. "You come down and play ball sometime. Play with these kids. You see the good you done." White Crow turned and departed. Half a container of French fries remained splayed on the table. Wendell placed one in his mouth despite the fact that it was cold.

***

Two weeks passed before Martin White Crow called and said, "Your man is not talking."

Wendell had recently been assigned to a string of burglaries focused on high-end residences in remote parts of the valley. Pressure was high because several of the burglaries occurred in summer homes owned by former NFL players. Wendell had again drawn Knudson in the rotation as his floater.

"Lucky us," Knudson said as they drove a private road near Bigfork, "back in the land of Champaign dreams and security cameras."

"Don't remind me."

"I'm sorry I've been AWOL on the Rodgers's case," she said. "I know you're working it on your own time."

"No big deal," Wendell said.

"It is a big deal. Has Herbert's authorized any time?"

"They've sprung for a full water search. That's no small commitment of resources."

"They just like to use their toys."

"Needle. Haystack," Wendell said.

"It doesn't hurt that the Rodgers have stayed in front of the media. Is that you?"

"Mostly Sheila's sisters. They push her into the interviews," he said.

"Good for them. Different family and Britany's long forgotten."

"She already seems pretty forgotten."

"Guilty as charged," Knudson said.

"I didn't mean it that way. You worked the case beautifully."

"You don't lie worth a shit, you know that?"

"Don't, Stacey. I couldn't have asked for more from you. Some cases don't produce leads."

"I see you. I know you haven't stopped. I should be there with you."

"You've got a full caseload and a family. Let it go."

"Like you've done."

"Well," he shrugged. "I'm a misfit and a troubled bastard, right? What else am I supposed to do? Stalk the divorcee crowd at Ladies Night? Join a bible studies group?"

"Combine the two."

"That's my target demographic? A divorcee bible thumper?"

Knudson laughed. "You know, I've missed you," she said.

Wendell said nothing, though he would admit within the confines of his head that he'd missed her too. He hadn't deciphered which he missed more, her capable investigative skills or the sound of her laughter and the smell of her perfume. "Let's go catch some bad guys, shall we?"

As they pulled into the driveway of a massive log home, she said. "Will you let me cook for you one night this week?"

"Are you any good in the kitchen?"

"I make a mean box of mac n' cheese."

"Oh, yum."

"Seriously, would you come to dinner?"

"Socialize the beast, so he doesn't bite?"

"You got it."

"Sure."

"Great. Tomorrow night. I'll make the hubby cook. Bring the Rodgers's case files."

* * *

When Wendell met with Marston and other senior members of the Search and Rescue team in advance of their summer campaign, he had to admit he was pleasantly surprised at how studiously Marston appeared to listen to his briefing. Wendell had spent considerable time talking with friends of Evans that dated back twenty years. Evans had once been quite the fisherman. His old friends helped Wendell map parts of the lake they fished regularly.

Wendell again floated his theory about Evans as the sort of man who would make sure that a body deposited in the lake would not be found.

Marston took the map Wendell had created and overlaid it atop a depth chart of Flathead Lake and quickly shaded a fan-shaped search area originating at the Tomlinson dock. Atop this he laid in the spots they'd identified in the spring as ones in need of more scrutiny. He then consulted a complex map provided by the Flathead Lake Biological Station that showed circulation patterns, water temperatures, and myriad other biological measures. Marston appeared involved in some sort of calculations. Finally, he turned back to a clean map of the lake that only had a few depth markings in rings. On this he began to lightly shade an area atop the white map. He lifted his pencil and looked at his work. "We only get the Idaho side-scanner team for four days. I say that's our target area." He sighed heavily. "The lake is 197 square miles. The odds we're looking in the right place are against us." Marston took off his glasses and said, "We're shooting in the dark."

Wendell touched the shaded area of the map spread before Marston. "But it *was* dark, right? Evans would have been on the water at night."

Marston looked at Wendell like he was a teenager reporting for his first job.

"He's going to use the depths provided by the fish-finder. Add in some instinctual memory. But he's still got to navigate, right? So, what prominent lights are going to be visible across the shore? Dark water, October cold, a body he wants rid of…isn't he going to keep pretty well on a straight line? I've looked at the weather that night," Wendell said. "Quarter moon. High clouds. Shore lights should have been visible."

Marston snapped his fingers and stood up fast. "Somebody pull up a satellite map," he barked. "We'd look into Woods Bay across the lake. What in Wood's Bay is going to provide a prominent light?"

There was a flurry of activity. Men who passed a lot of time on the lake talked about visible landmarks. A young deputy brought up the satellite map. "Maybe the lodge there in Wood's Bay," the young deputy said, tapping the screen. It would be lit up at night."

Marston turned to Wendell. "Can you get me on the Tomlinson boat dock tonight?"

"Of course."

Marston laid his pencil on the map, the eraser lined up with the location of the Tomlinson dock and a point across the lake. "We've got a fishing trip to plan, boys," Marston said loudly and clapped Wendell on the back.

Chapter Thirty

Days before the Idaho search experts were scheduled to arrive, Wendell attended Flathead High School's graduation ceremony. Sheila appeared as fragile as a cancer patient. He had not seen her since March when he had attended her mother's funeral. When he approached her, Sheila greeted him with a hug and thanked him for attending. As they spoke, Tom turned to join her, saw Wendell, and stomped away.

The principal offered a tasteful tribute to Britany, and there was a chair left empty among the graduates where several classmates left flowers or trinkets.

Wendell encountered Kristen Schneider at the conclusion of the ceremony and congratulated her. She was among five graduates with a perfect GPA. She looked older to Wendell, which he attributed to her having cut her hair. "I heard them announce a whole string of scholarships with your name. Great job."

"Thanks."

"I take it your parents have accepted that you'll be out of state."

"Reluctantly. But after Britany and all, I think they saw maybe it was best I got away."

Wendell nodded.

"Do you know someone who is graduating?"

"No," he said. "I'm here for Britany."

"My dad said that you are searching the lake."

"We are."

"Did you know that she was afraid of boats?"

"No, I didn't."

"I can't stop thinking about that. If you're right, and she's...she's in the lake..." She did not finish the thought. "I'm sorry that, you know, back when this happened, that I wasn't any help."

"Kristin, there's nothing to apologize for. You did help. Your statement helped us locate where we think Britany may have been that night."

"I heard about that man you arrested. People say that's where Britany was. It doesn't make any sense." Kristen started to cry. "I'm sorry," she said. "I guess it's graduation. I keep thinking I'll look up, and she'll be here." Kristen looked suddenly defiant, though the tears continued. "Do you know the hardest part? It's admitting to myself that Britany had disappeared a long time ago. She'd moved on. We were still friends, at least on the surface, but she had a whole life that I wasn't a part of anymore."

Wendell didn't reply, but he wanted to say *get used to it, girl. Your whole life may be a series of others moving on.*

"It's ironic," she said. "I always thought I was the misfit and Britany was the one who belonged, but now I see that was never true. She worked so hard to try and stand out. She was always looking for something she was not."

When they parted, Wendell's mind wandered. He thought he'd heard echoes of what Kristen had expressed ever since he'd been assigned Britany's case. *Standing out in order to fit in.* But what was it she thought she'd fit into? He remembered a part of a lyric he encountered in her notebook:

> *I am the weed you missed*
> *in your sea of perfect grass.*

Wendell was on the back deck of a burglarized house on Stillwater Lake when Marston called. It was the third day the Idaho boat worked alongside the Flathead Sheriff's unit. "We're going to put divers in the water," Marston said. "They have what they have labeled 'objects of interest.' I thought you might want to be here just in case."

Shocked, Wendell asked, "How deep?"

"Almost 180 feet."

He and Knudson finished their interview in an expedited fashion and were on their way to Bigfork when they heard the radio call for the Medical Examiner to dispatch to the docks at Eagle Bend. He didn't have to ask Knudson to turn on their emergency lights. They reached the dock in Bigfork to find an empty slip. The Medical Examiner's van pulled in five minutes later, just as a Sheriff's Department boat came into sight. Marston handed Wendell the bowline. "We've got bones," he said.

"Bones?" Wendell asked.

Marston stepped off the boat onto the dock. "Some dispersal but not too heavy. We've plotted the entire site. I had the dive team bring up the skull so you would have teeth," he said to the M.E.

"Bones," Wendell said again. "You said bones, not body."

"Bones," Marston repeated. "Only partially visible in sediment."

"Is that possible?" Knudson asked. "It's only been nine months."

"We're talking freshwater," Dr. Gary Caldwell, the lead Medical Examiner, said. "Bodies degrade faster in freshwater than above ground though it would still be a surprise as there are far fewer scavengers. It's not impossible. The sedimentation is surprising, though if there was sufficient weight added to the body, it could disturb the sediment. Much like an anchor would."

"Any immediate evidence of something used to weigh the body down?" Wendell asked.

"Nothing apparent, but he could have used her clothes to hold weight. Rocks or something," Marston replied.

"Did you see remnants of clothing?"

"It's dark down there, and the sediment gets stirred up even when you're careful. It will take time."

Wendell frowned. The look did not escape Marston. "Look, we brought you remains. I don't have the math skills to calculate the odds against that."

The foursome climbed aboard the vessel, and Marston directed them into the pilothouse. He opened a heavy blue equipment chest. Dr. Caldwell donned protective gloves. A human skull lay on a foam insert within the case. Caldwell bent near but did not touch the skull. He looked from the skull to Wendell and back again. His look was not lost on Wendell.

"We can pull DNA from teeth and rule out your victim with total accuracy," Caldwell said, "but on first glance, given the presence of superciliary arches and evidence of a pronounced temporal line, I'd say this is male."

"We've got the wrong body?" Wendell said incredulously. "In the whole of this damn lake, we find a body, and it's the wrong one."

"Are you fucking kidding?" Knudson added.

"It won't take me much time at all to give you an answer who it's not," Caldwell said. "But it might take me nearly forever to tell you who it is."

"Jesus, Mary, and Joseph," Marston said. "You're pulling our legs."

"I'll be surprised if this proves a skull deposited nine months ago," Caldwell said. "I'm no expert in osteology, but based on a few factors I can see already, such as the prominent cheekbones and greater rounding in the orbital structure, this skull looks Asian or given our location, and what appear incisors that are deeply scooped, there is far greater likelihood this individual is Native American."

Wendell said. "How old?"

"I can't hazard a guess," Caldwell said. "I think we need to consult with a forensic anthropologist."

"Are you telling me that not only have we unearthed the wrong body, we've got a paleo Indian on our hands?"

"I won't attempt such conjecture. But I can say this skull assuredly does not belong to a seventeen-year-old girl."

Wendell squatted near the open case displaying its unlikely occupant. He dropped down onto a bench that circled the pilot cabin and pinched the bridge of his nose with his fingers.

"I'll be a son of a bitch," Marston said. "I wish we could play catch-and-release with this one. We're going to be so buried in paperwork that we will want to trade places with this fellow," he said, nodding at the skull. "Feds. State. Indian Affairs. Wounded heart rez lawyers. Glad it's your case."

"Nice, Marston. Wash your hands why don't you," Knudson said.

"It's not my case."

"I bet you'll be front and center when the news cameras come out," she said.

Marston's ears reddened.

Wendell dropped his hands to his knees. He looked at Marston. "Secure the site and map your findings, same as you would do if this had been Britany. Your guys will have their hands full. We've only got the Idaho team for another day, so they need to keep searching. Public Affairs gets to do their job and coordinate the press."

"You call the shots now?" Marston seethed.

"My case, remember. You want lead on this?"

"Fuck no." His large ears reddened more, bright against his grey flattop.

Wendell turned to Caldwell. "Get your anthropologist here. You've got someone in mind?" Caldwell nodded. Wendell continued, "Marston can coordinate with them."

"Great. Lose my guys to a bunch of bone-diggers."

"And the politicians and administrators can argue over all the nonsense," Wendell said.

Marston grumbled. Caldwell picked the skull up, turning it in the sunlight. Wendell rose and looked at the cabin's occupants. "Can we all agree to keep this as quiet as possible for this moment at least? Make the bosses earn their pay?"

"Quiet is all I know," Caldwell said.

"I've got work to do," Marston said. "I don't need reporters in the way."

"Good. Stacey," Wendell said. "I wonder if we don't have a window here."

"How do you mean?"

"Everybody and his brother have seen our vehicles, seen the boats. Now they've seen Caldwell's rig. There have been articles on the Idaho specialists in the paper. What if we let it slip that we've found remains? We've got some time, right? Time before we have to share what remains we've found."

Knudson finished his thought. "Time enough to make someone nervous that what we found can implicate him."

"Maybe he looks for a deal. At the very least, maybe he asks some questions to see how much we know," he said. Wendell looked to the two men. "We've got a seventeen-year-old murder victim, and we still don't have a body or her murderer," he said. "Will you guys keep a lid on it until we can't?"

"No skin off my nose," Marston said.

"And you'll keep the Idaho team working?"

"Invoice stays the same whether they work or sit."

Wendell smiled. "Your mug will look good holding up your buddy on the nightly news," he said. "Back in the day, he probably had the same haircut."

Chapter Thirty-One

Wendell steeled himself for another day on a boat.

While the remains Marston's team found meant nothing to Wendell's investigation, he felt responsible for their discovery. He didn't need to be present, but he was immensely curious. Curious enough to give up a day off.

Caldwell could not disguise his excitement. Wendell appreciated his geeky enthusiasm. Caldwell's motivations paralleled his own, which resided in academic intrigue mixed with childish wonder.

"It's a beautiful day to be on the lake," Caldwell said. "I do believe boating season is upon us." Caldwell wore a pair of shorts that should have been retired in 1970, which also seemed a probable date for the last time Caldwell's legs had seen the sun.

"I didn't take you for the boating type," Wendell said.

"I practically grew up on the Finger Lakes. My father was an enthusiast. Strictly motorized craft whereas I have an affinity for sailing." He wore a booney hat with a neck shade. "I keep a 3.65 meter single-handed at Somers. I'd be happy to take you out sometime."

"I prefer my recreation far from the water."

"You've no idea what you're missing. Being under sail is enchanting."

Wendell enjoyed Caldwell, even if he did sound like he belonged in an English novel. Partner him with an anthropologist for the day, and there ought to be amusement. "When's your bone-digger arrive?"

"More of a bone-analyzer, you might say. While I'm sure archeologists would be intrigued by these findings, Dr. Moore's expertise is in osteology.

Perhaps we'll bring an archeologist on board should the remains prove significant."

"I stand corrected."

"It's a common misconception. Dr. Moore phoned upon her departure. I expect her imminent arrival," he said. "You will be quite taken with her."

As if on cue, a Prius with a University of Montana logo pulled into the parking lot, and Caldwell waved excitedly at its occupant, an attractive brunette. Wendell guessed her age to be forty. She wore yoga pants and a halter top that showcased an athletic body. "Come," Caldwell said. "I'll introduce you."

"Veronica," Caldwell shouted, hurrying across the parking lot. "I appreciate that you were willing to drop everything."

"There was nothing to drop," the woman said. "I'd hoped for a project to busy my summer." Wendell was intrigued by an Australian accent. "Otherwise, I'd travel and spend money I haven't made."

"Let me complete introductions," Caldwell said. "Dr. Veronica Moore, University of New South Wales. Detective Steven Wendell, Flathead County Sheriff's Department."

"Detective?" Dr. Moore said. "Are we to investigate an ancient murder mystery?"

"A nine-month-old one," Wendell said. "Pretty ancient in my world. I'm only a tag-along today."

"The specimen was discovered while in search of a murder victim," Caldwell explained.

"Oh, my," Dr. Moore said. "I was merely trying to make a funny."

"You couldn't know," Wendell said. "I had no idea Missoula has a forensic anthropology department."

"Oh, it doesn't," she said. She laughed embarrassedly. "I mean, it's a fine anthropology department, but it is a master's level and undergraduate program of study, so our research capacity is not exactly, shall we say, strapping. I've reached the end of a year as a visiting scholar. I've become quite taken with Montana. I shall be reluctant to leave."

"And we will be saddened to have her depart," Caldwell said. "Though I know her colleagues in Australia will be pleased to have her back. Veronica has done remarkable work identifying aboriginal skeletal findings and has contributed greatly to our understanding of human migration. She's written some excellent papers on genetic distribution patterns."

"Well, I'm way out of my league," Wendell said.

"I am quite out of my comfortable surroundings as well. My knowledge of North American pre-history is bookwork at best."

"Oh, come now," Caldwell said. "We'll provide you an osteologist's dream."

"I'm anxious to see what you've found."

Wendell retrieved an equipment case from her car while she grabbed a daypack and a cooler. While Wendell followed the two to the Sheriff Department boat, he heard snippets of their conversation. Caldwell explained how they'd found the remains. They made quite an odd pairing, he thought, yet they stepped with similar buoyancy.

When Moore leapt aboard the boat and then turned to offer Caldwell a steady hand, he looked mildly embarrassed. Two search and rescue divers turned to see the new arrivals. "To whom must I ingratiate myself in order to join the dive team?" she asked.

"Good luck with that one," Wendell said.

"Lt. Marston leads the search team," Caldwell said. "He's rather protective of them."

"Damn straight I am," Marston bellowed as he emerged from the pilot-house. He stopped upon seeing Dr. Moore. "We're not on a sunbathing cruise."

Caldwell nearly tripped over a turnbuckle. "Lieutenant, this is Dr. Veronica Moore, a forensic anthropologist from the University of South Wales."

Moore strode forward, hand extended. "A pleasure, I'm certain. And what's the harm in a little sunbathing in the interest of science."

"Ma'am, you can have your science. We'll supply manual labor."

"But tell me you have followed all proper crime scene protocols just as if you were preserving evidence."

"Yes, ma'am. I'm a stickler for procedure. Without protocols, things fall into chaos."

"Marston's all about mitigating chaos," Wendell said.

"I'm who you call when the shit hits the fan," Marston boasted. "This here is a bit out of the ordinary, but it's good training for the boys."

"It's always good to work with professionals. I've been on some crime scenes where they had no clue how to preserve evidence, let alone secure an excavation site. What artifacts have you brought to the surface?"

"Only the skull, doctor. At the time, we assumed it was a crime scene with a victim that needed to be identified. I thought teeth would be our best bet."

"Excellent. We'll want to look for materials beyond the skeleton itself, other artifacts that can help with the accuracy of dating—the presence of hunting tools, that sort of thing—but the process itself is not significantly different from a traditional investigation."

"Let us bring you your boy. Then you can have at it however you see fit."

Moore assessed Marston and said, "Your team is an anthropologist's dream excavation group. But it's about more than bringing bones to the surface. There are countless bits of material that might look like no more than stones or detritus—all further complicated by darkness and sediment. For all those reasons, I'd like permission to join your divers."

"Ma'am, this is no swim with the pretty fish dive."

"I'm fully certified."

"This is a deep-water dive. We're talking nitrogen narcosis protocols. The whole shootin' match."

"I'm deepwater certified."

"This site is 180 feet. Almost double the depth PADI will certify for. We're not far from the edge where we would need hypoxic breathing gas. This is technical diving. We're risking lives here."

"And you serve as divemaster, so your people become your responsibility."

"My people are *always* my responsibility, ma'am."

"I absolutely respect that. But tell me you're don't love every minute of it," Moore said, charming Marston with a smile.

"I do enjoy a challenge."

"But you won't give me permission to join the dive."

"No, ma'am."

"Can we be done with the ma'am? Call me Veronica."

"Trust my boys under the water, Veronica. You can call the show. Tell us exactly the sorts of things you want us to look for, manage how we handle what we bring up, but you won't be probing the murky depths."

"Fair enough, Lieutenant" Dr. Moore said, though her disappointment was apparent. "Where have you got our friend stashed?"

Marston led them into the pilot cabin. A long table filled most of the cabin. Marston retrieved the equipment case that was secured under a bench seat. Dr. Moore took the case that Wendell had carried from her car from him, opened it, spread a thick cloth atop the table, and unzipped a rolled bag containing numerous small hand tools and measuring devices. She put on gloves and lifted the skull out of its case. She held it up in the light of the windows.

"Certainly male," she said. "There are evident superciliary arches, but more revealing is a pronounced temporal line. The sediment and cold water have offered remarkable preservation. The full jaw is intact, as are the teeth. None of the complications you get with the ways open-air remains are scattered by animals, excavations, and shifting earthwork. There is minimal mineralization."

She turned to Marston. "Dr. Caldwell said you saw what appeared a complete skeleton."

"All laid out like it's naptime."

"Uniform remains. We likely have a specimen In situ. There's absolutely no presence of remnant tissue or hair, so this guy's been here a long while. Yet, obviously, it was not overtaken by sediment deposits, or you would never have spotted him. So that may assist us in positing a time window. That's a rather uninformed opinion, mind you. But with this preservation, we have an excellent opportunity to properly date this specimen."

"But there's other bones too," one of the divers said. "Won't that screw things up?"

"Other bones," Moore asked. "Multiple remains?"

"I don't know. Big bones. Bigger than a human."

"How big?"

"Reminds me of when I've field-dressed an elk. Never killed a moose, but that kind of size, I'd say."

"Intriguing," Dr. Moore said. "That could help us a great deal. Are you filming the site?"

"Graphing it. Not filming," Marston said. He cleared his throat. "An underwater camera has been in my budget requests for years," he added.

"Well, you're filming now. I've brought my gear," Moore said. "Not my first sunbathing trip on the high seas."

* * *

Wendell was impressed with the efficiency with which Marston's crew worked. Not that he was surprised. Marston's territorialism irritated him, but he was extremely good at his job. But Wendell thought that Marston was a bit too ready to deploy his SWAT team in a valley that had seldom need of such tactics and took joy spending limited department funds on what he regarded as toys, like the second armored assault vehicle he'd convinced the department to buy. But then, of course, there would be no skeleton to bring to the surface if Marston hadn't worked the side-scanning sonar system into a past budget as well.

"I'll man it myself," Marston boasted. He examined Moore's camera. Moore began to transform the pilothouse into a makeshift laboratory. While the divers prepared their equipment and donned dry-suits, Moore, Caldwell, and Wendell cleared the center table and wrapped the entire surface with a thick, rubbery Visqueen. She then moved outside and spent time explaining how she wanted the divers to establish a central transect point and measure distances precise distances to each piece of material found.

"It's dark, and it's deep," Marston complained. "We'll have limited dive time and a decompression ascent. We can't fiddle-fart down there."

"I have every faith your team is capable of extreme efficiency. You wouldn't do a smash and grab on a recovery at a crime scene. You film and run the light. One of you takes stills. One measures. And one records."

She handed the deputy closest to her a magnetic board. "The measurements are recorded on an X/Y axis like this," she said, writing on the board. "I'll pull the measurements from the film and stills, you erase the board, and we go happily on. Every item gets a tag." She pulled a flexible cord from a dive bag and showed them where it had a number hard-stamped in the material. The tag gets filmed with the specimen and the measurement. It's not textbook, but as close as we can get for conditions. In and out."

"You make it sound so easy." Marston made no attempt to hide the dismissal in his voice. "Minus the 180', the dark, the cold, the restrictive gear."

"You wouldn't command tactical squads if you like what is easy."

"We're not scientists."

"Much better than scientists. I'll take you hurrah boys over grad students every day."

* * *

Once the divers were in the water, Moore removed the athletic halter to reveal a red bikini top and turned a chair on the aft deck towards the sun. "Waiting sucks," she said. "I wish we had a live video feed."

"Is it killing you not to be down there?" Wendell asked. Caldwell followed them outside and dawdled at the rail.

Moore shrugged. "The work is in the lab, but the fun is in the field. Not the way the movies paint it, mind you. Mostly it's grunge-work with little reward, but still, when something is unearthed, I want to be there. I just hope they don't screw this up."

"And only moments ago, you were such a convincing cheerleader."

"Cops can be great on a site. They follow directions. But they don't know what they're looking at, so you don't always get a lot of thinking beyond the edges, so to speak. No offense, detective."

"I suspect Detective Wendell shares your sentiments," Caldwell said. "In my experience, the best detectives tend to be contrarians within police society."

"No one ever accused me of being a great thinker," Wendell said.

"Modesty does not become you, detective."

"It's not modesty," Wendell said. "Police work is problem-solving. You're on the alert for what is out of place, and then try to find a reasonable explanation for why. That's largely a process of elimination. Your work must be similar. You take what you are presented with and try to discover what's missing."

"It's true," she said. "I want to know what the isotopic evidence tells me. I want to extract DNA, look for the vestiges of disease in tooth sockets, or diet in anomalies of bones. By contrast, whenever there's any kind of find, the public wants the narrative, not the facts. On a pre-history discovery, the media leaps to the missing link story. If it's an archaic find, they want murder as a cause of death. With a specimen like we have here if he proves to be old—and by the by, I'll stake my place in the lotto pool that he's not—because of the location, the coverage will be Siberian land bridge. People aren't happy without a story. They can't handle that sometimes people just get old and die—even if old is twenty-eight—or that he got taken out by an abscessed tooth or starved to death over a bad winter."

"If everybody died from untreated infections, I'd be out of a job," Caldwell said.

"If only," Wendell added.

"And what on earth would you do if you weren't a cop?" Caldwell asked.

"Exotic dancer," Wendell dead-panned.

"Seriously."

"I'd probably fall back on my degree and be a psychologist. I'm intrigued by why people behave the way they do."

"And you, Veronica," Caldwell asked. "What if not anthropology?"

"Something to support my travel addiction, a writer or photographer. Or better yet, a food critic. Then I can indulge two passions at once. Feed my wanderlust, so to speak," she said. Her laughter came easily, and her smile declared that she laughed with regularity. "Your turn, good doctor."

"Cabaret singer," Caldwell said without hesitation.

"You insisted we be serious," Wendell said. "What's good for the goose..."

"I am serious. All my life, I wanted a voice that could put me on Broadway. Short of that, a good, rollicking, irreverent cabaret show. A few bad limericks. A touching ballad. Keep a glass of wine in my hand through the whole performance."

"This I would have to see," Wendell said.

"Oh, you should hear my shower performances. My wife will testify that I have the song list worked out."

Moore burst into loud laughter. She raised her legs and rested them on the railing. "If only I had a beer," she said. "Blue skies, sun on my skin, a couple of entertaining blokes."

"Skeletons under your feet," Wendell added.

At Caldwell's probing, she spoke about her travels. She and Caldwell began to trade stories about trips they'd taken. They told of places that made Wendell feel like the family friend invited to a slideshow of vacation photos unable to join the conversation. He began to fidget with a bungee strap that had held one of the air tanks in place against the railing. It felt like the boat rocked more than usual, yet he didn't allow himself to look out onto the water to see if a passing boat had created a wake. Finally, he got up and returned to the pilothouse and added more tape that was not needed to the plastic that now coated the center table, then he returned to the open door of the cabin and watched Moore and Caldwell.

"You don't sit well, do you?" Moore said to Wendell.

"Ants in my pants my mother said."

"The poor boy doesn't understand the good life the water provides," Caldwell added.

"Childhood trauma?" Moore chided.

"Something like that."

Moore heard the serious edge to his voice. "Sorry. I was only teasing."

"I grew up on a farm," he said, as if that offered an explanation. He saw her puzzled facial reaction. "There was always something that needed to be done, and I had parents who were quick to point it out. No, I don't sit well."

"Hopefully, we see a bag full of bones rise, and we can put you to work." Then suddenly she started laughing.

"Care to share?" Wendell asked.

"I'm sorry," she said. A wide smile overtook her face. "I just heard what I said again in my head. Sometimes I marvel at what an absurd life I lead. I mean, can you imagine what someone would say if they learned, I was on a boat in Montana, hanging about in my togs while I waited for some poor bloke's bones to arrive? Death underfoot and all that."

"They don't know what they're missing," Wendell said.

"At least I work on bones. You two go after the freshies."

"Always a hit at the dinner party," Caldwell said, joining in her laughter, "when you refer to the recently deceased as 'freshies.'"

"I hope you don't find me offensive, detective. I know you've got a victim out there. Just having a poke."

"I've heard plenty worse."

"I've testified at my fair share of difficult cases. Outside perspective and all that," Moore said. "The demanding light of science. Tell me about this girl."

Wendell gave her the high points of the investigation. "And by the way," he added, "we want to keep this little expedition," he gestured around the boat, "as opaque as possible in the hopes that it perks our suspect's interest."

"Hope he goes fishing?"

"Something like that."

"My lips are sealed," she said. She made a girlish jester of zipping her lips, turning an imaginary key, and then stashing it inside her bikini top. "So, you've got blood evidence on the boat, outright denial by this stellar boy scout with the hidden cameras, and no shred to link your victim to him."

"Nice summary."

"There it is again," she said.

"There what is?"

"Our desperate human need for a narrative. You're missing evidence and the story alike. You need the evidence to make your case, but it's the missing story that won't let you sleep at night. You can't figure out how the girl got to the place that put her on the boat. We're all inclined to look for the story. But what if it's purely an accident? A flat tire that puts her at the wrong place?" Part of Wendell wanted to tell her that there was no car, explain the complexities that led him to the Tomlinson place at all, but he remained silent and let her carry on. "What if she's a two-pot screamer who gets lost in the woods?"

"Pardon?"

"What?"

"A two-pot screamer?" he asked.

"She can't tolerate her liquor."

"Oh," he said and then marveled at how close she was to Jacob Bianconi's story.

"You'd rather have a nice clean linkage—victim to perpetrator. Give him a reason to have her there and explain your blood. Some explanation, whatever it is, that the two are connected. It's natural. And solid police work. But what if her placement at your scene isn't because of him at all?"

"That's actually been a leading theory based on our interviews. That she really was simply drunk or high. That she's...how did you put it?"

"A two-pot screamer."

"There you go. She's incapacitated and runs into the wrong man, presents him an opportunity. I just don't have the evidence to link him conclusively."

"Given his other crimes, he would seem the logical sort to be your opportunist. But maybe the desire for narrative has fogged the evidence?"

"Come again?"

"Sometimes there's a story we want the evidence to prove. Take the locations where we most often find archaic remains—exposed riverbeds, collapsed caves, the occasional happenchance excavation—places we would not otherwise have the opportunity to look. We get this great gift of a suddenly exposed site with a treasure trove of materials. Layers of artifacts, predator species mixed in with prey. Everybody naturally dreams of intact groups in a mass burial or this perfect intersection of early humans and evidence of their food sources all neatly tied together. But then you dig through the evidence and find that it's a depository where floods wash in material and have done so for millennia, and it all gets churned up, and the nice, normal, identifiable sedimentary layers look like they've been run through a food processor. You date individual bones, and none of your narratives hold up. They've accumulated by accident. Individuals are unrelated, maybe even separated by a time gulf that defies the imagination."

"I've searched for other explanations, but I don't have evidence that leads me anywhere."

"It sounds like you don't necessarily have the evidence to support your current narrative either. The presence of his other crimes may be coincidental."

"You just defined the last nine months of my investigation in a single sentence."

"There may still be a narrative present, but it's not the narrative we thought we were ready to hear."

"How do you mean?"

"Okay, well, humor me. I only know my own field. There's an extremely famous find about five hours south of here on a ranch. Have you heard of the Anzick boy?"

"I think so. Something about a DNA record."

"Right. The first ancient Native American genome to be fully sequenced. It was a boy. Scientists labeled him as Anzick-1, the remains of a small child, a Paleo-Indian dating to something like 12,000 years BP…"

"Before present," Caldwell interrupted. "Before 1950 when radiocarbon dating became accepted."

"Exactly. And it's like 12,500 – 12,700 BP, to be more precise. The dating is that good. He's found with all kinds of Clovis points, like over a hundred tools made out of antlers and stone. And that fits with the narrative of the time, right, as Clovis sites opened up all over North America. There are actually two skeletons uncovered, but our boy predates his buddy by a couple of thousand years, so there's myth one busted. But this is 1968. It still seems to some researchers that Clovis points share similarity to spearheads found in Europe, and for a long time, this prompts some to look for European ancestors and thereby some mechanism of dispersal from Europe to the Americas. Now researchers follow the science they think they have before them, but you have to wonder if it isn't also informed, at least in the background, by the narrative that keeps Europe as the center for where our visions of modern humans developed."

"The old Eurocentric, white is right vision of the world," Wendell said.

Moore nodded. "Of course, this doesn't sit well with a lot of Native American thinkers, who don't necessarily want to share ancestral linkage with their oppressors. Besides, they already have origin myths that place them here as a chosen people."

"Another narrative," Wendell said.

"Right. But then the science comes along. Once we map out the sequence, not only do we have clear evidence that there is direct genetic linkage between our 12,000-year-old boy and modern Native Americans, we can trace this sequence to Asia."

"That supports the idea of a land bridge across the Bering Strait, right?" Wendell asked.

"The Beringia Hypothesis. Yes, quite right. Or perhaps some theories about peoples that migrated in coastal populations along the western shores of the Americas. It gets even more complicated because DNA analysis shows Anzick-1 is more related to indigenous people of South America than those north of glacial advancement, but that's another story altogether, one suggesting southern dispersal before eastern and likely multiple migrations rather than a single one. But that's beside the point."

"And the point is, when it comes to the likely death of a seventeen-year-old girl, exactly what again?" Wendell asked.

"That there seems logic on your side to link your peeping Tom to her death. That narrative seems natural. But its presence may cloud your vision from a different narrative."

"A polite way to say I'm barking up the wrong tree."

"Not necessarily. But it is a big forest you've got here," she said. Then she suddenly jumped to her feet and shouted, "Eureka! We've got bones." She pointed to an airbag that bobbed on the surface in a circle of bubbles. She turned back to Wendell. "Let's see what story these tell, shall we?"

* * *

The recovery team brought the remains on board in the span of two dives. Recreating the arrangement of those remains as they had appeared on the lake floor would take several days; in-depth analysis would require weeks. "Once you have initial confirmation that these remains are Native American, we must notify reservation authorities. You may not have weeks," Caldwell warned her. "It's fortuitous that we're not in tribal waters."

"I'm always in support of repatriation," Dr. Moore said. "but science has its place as well. Without science, we can't identify these remains as indigenous."

Wendell enjoyed the precise work of helping reassemble the skeleton. While Moore, Caldwell, and Wendell recreated the scene encountered below, Marston returned to his grid maps and redeployed the sonar unit. As dusk arrived and Marston piloted the boat to its slip at Eagle Bend, Moore hunkered over the tedious array of tiny bones forming the left hand while Wendell read measurements to her from the laptop screen. The deputies tried to convince Dr. Moore to join them for a post-expedition beer, but she begged off to continue working. "I promise that I'll buy a round once we're ready to move him off to the lab," she said. She then asked Marston to let her spend the night on the boat.

"It's secure, Doctor. It's a restricted access dock, and we can lock the pilothouse. It's Montana. I can probably find keys in half the cars."

"I'm superstitious, Lieutenant. I like to stay close to my work. I've got my camping gear. I'll be quite comfortable."

"There's no head on board."

"I'll sneak away later, get some dinner, use the facilities. I'll be just fine."

"Suit yourself," Marston said. As the other men loaded into their pickup trucks, Wendell told Dr. Moore that he would stay awhile if she'd allow.

"Oh, I was counting on it," she said. "And then I thought you'd take me to a nice dinner."

* * *

By the time they departed for dinner, several elements of the skeleton were arrayed on the table. As the deputy had described, two large bones, which Moore speculated were ungulate, straddled the space where they would have to reconstruct the man's ribs. The animal bones were below the spine and nearly buried in the sediment. "He's looking quite handsome," Dr. Moore said.

"Maybe he'll buy you dinner."

"I don't think he's reliable."

"Could be tough to find a place that would accept his currency," Wendell said.

"I guess it's up to you."

"His loss."

"Before we go, why don't you awe me with your analytical prowess and tell me what you see here. What's our narrative?"

"This sounds like a trick question," he said.

"No tricks. Deduction."

Wendell circled the table once. "Despite what you said earlier about accidental conclusions and misreading the evidence, I'd look for an explanation that places hunter and prey in the same place. We've got no primary river current to deposit material at this point in the lake. We're not near the shore. We're deep. So, I think boating accident. Weather. A canoe capsizes. Our guy isn't a swimmer. I suppose an outside shot could be a winter crossing. A fall through the ice, but I'd have to know the weather patterns were so different that the lake froze regularly because it's rare that it does now."

"I like it. Go on."

"The bones aren't dispersed, so something has weighed him down. Otherwise, he bobs around, sinks, and rises as the gases do their thing, and he falls apart over time. How does someone get an elk out of the backcountry, minus the ATV and pickup? Quarter it and carry it out. Maybe the guy gets sunk by the very thing he thought would keep him alive."

"What evidence would you need to support your theory?"

"Something to show that this was his prey, like, I don't know, the nick of a spearhead in a bone. What I'd really want would be material that's long gone. Parts of a canoe. Or ligature he used to strap the carcass on his back."

"By crikey, that's inspired," Dr. Moore said, clapping. "Well done. You're spot on in regards to evidence of tools. Can you imagine the labor and violence necessary to hunt and process a kill when all you've got are stone tools?"

"We really are in parallel universes," Wendell said.

"Perhaps we are," she agreed. "Let's get some dinner. But there's one thing I'll require."

"What's that."

"Once we step off that dock and turn the key in the gate, we don't get to talk about work—yours or mine—for the rest of the night."

"Agreed. No dead bodies."

* * *

Veronica, in the way of women that remained mysterious to Wendell, removed the tank-top, slipped a red floral pattern dress on over her bikini top and yoga pants, then removed the pants. "My hair must be a fright, but you'll have to take me as I am," she said, as she exchanged flip-flops for sandals.

Over dinner and wine, their conversation ranged over their personal lives, families, food, film, books, and hobbies. While the venues were in opposition—water vs. snow, ocean vs. mountain—they were both outdoor enthusiasts. Their tastes in literature and film were nearly identical. But as she began to speak about her travels, Wendell saw that her wanderlust was as central to her personality as was his knowledge of his home ground.

Dinner extended into an after-dinner drink and then coffee. As they talked, they watched the street flood with a crowd from the summer theater playhouse next door, and Wendell looked at his watch. He suddenly realized they were the only customers remaining and that, besides a manager and bartender who talked quietly as they totaled the night's receipts behind the bar, only their waiter remained. Wendell signaled him and apologized. "I hadn't even noticed," Wendell said. "I'm so sorry to make you hang around."

The waiter, twentyish and likely working a summer gig on college break, looked from Wendell to Moore and back again and offered an expression that seemed to say: *I get it, man.*

They joined the last of the theater crowd that lingered on the street. "This little town is charming," Veronica said.

The night was clear, and Wendell saw a visible shiver run the length of Veronica's body. She acknowledged the cold with a rapid stomp of her feet and an audible exhale. "You do keep it cold here, don't you? I guess you'll have to race me to your car." She grabbed his hand and ran down the sidewalk. She stopped running when they were a block from the car but did not let go of his hand. At the car, Wendell retrieved a coat he kept there in case of emergency and draped it over her shoulders. As they drove to the dock, Veronica remarked on the night sky. "It's enchanting," she said. "We have too much light pollution in Sydney. Of course, I'll still argue that I have the better sky."

"It's strange to think about, isn't it? That we've spent our lives looking at entirely different stars."

"Useful perspective," she said.

They entered the small parking lot near the dock. "Are you seriously going to sleep on the boat tonight?" he asked.

"I am."

"It's perfectly secure."

"Are you offering other accommodations?" she asked.

"I am."

"Can I raincheck? Once I've got him fully prepped and boxed up for transport to the lab, I'll sleep better. It's silly, I know, but I feel like I owe it to him."

"To spend the night with him," Wendell said.

"One of my charming eccentricities."

"Necrophilia?"

Veronica laughed and then turned serious. "I try never to forget. Before I take laser slices from teeth and open up joint sockets, I remind myself that the remains I work with were people with families and loved ones. A way to show respect."

"It's romantic."

"Stop."

"Should I be jealous?"

"Most certainly." Veronica got out of the car, and when Wendell started to do the same, she motioned for him to stay. She passed the front of the vehicle, the headlights momentarily illuminating her, and walked to his window. "Will you join us tomorrow?"

"I can't. The bad guys don't take days off."

"That's a shame. Can I cash in on that raincheck tomorrow night?"

"That's the beauty of a raincheck. I'll cook for you."

She leaned in the window and kissed him. Without a word, she stepped away towards the locked gate at the end of the dock. Just before she reached the gate, she turned and said, "I'm stealing your jacket. Don't expect to get it back."

Chapter Thirty-Two

The following day, Wendell made arrangements to meet Sheila Rodgers for coffee. He had offered to stop by Sheila's workplace to save her a trip and assured her that he did not have major news. "Just a check-in," he'd said. Tom had long ago refused to communicate with him. Tom's grief had taken him deeper inside a paranoid vision of officials, and he now saw the police as an embodiment of a government that controlled his freedom. The last time Wendell spoke with Sheila, she admitted that she didn't know if the marriage would survive. Exhausted, she told him that all of her energy was focused on ensuring her son's life was filled with love.

They'd sat at a quiet table near the back of the coffeehouse. Sheila said, "You told me you didn't have news, but there is something, isn't there? Something has come out of this lake search."

"Nothing helpful, I'm afraid. But I wanted you to know that you will hear stories that we've found a body. It's not Britany."

"You're confident?"

"Positive."

"I guess as long as you haven't found her body, I'm supposed to hang on to hope that she's missing and not dead. I'm not sure I can continue to do that."

"I wanted you to know," Wendell said, "that I'm trying to make use of this. To rattle Evans and get him to talk."

"I don't understand."

"If he's responsible and believes we have found Britany's body, he'll believe there's a greater likelihood we now have evidence that can convict him. At the very least, he's more likely to talk, even if that is only to other inmates."

"You mean if he brags about what he's done."

"That's one possibility."

Sheila looked away. They remained silent for a long minute. Then she said, "Tom's convinced she's alive. He reads these things on the Internet. Used to be he'd never turn on a computer. Now he's got his nose in my iPad all night. He's obsessed with articles on human trafficking. He talks to me about it, and I don't want to hear it. These days he only listens to the angriest voices in the room."

"What you two have faced is unnatural. He doesn't know where to turn."

"He was supposed to turn to me," Sheila said softly.

* * *

When Wendell returned to the office, among his mail was a card from Tina, Britany's look-alike coworker from Dairy Queen, thanking him for putting her in touch with a counselor at Flathead Valley Community College. Wendell smiled as he slipped the card back inside its envelope.

He grabbed his sports coat off the back of his chair and steeled himself for a long day on the burglaries, but when he stepped into the June sunlight, he found himself wishing, much to his surprise, that he was on the boat. He wondered how far Victoria had advanced the reconstruction, the hard simplicity of bone laid out on the pilothouse table. How had this ancient man come to rest at the bottom of the lake, he wondered, embracing his need for the "narrative" Veronica had warned him against.

His mind flashed to Sheila's countenance at the coffeehouse. How was it possible a single moment could forever change a life? Forcing thoughts of Britany from his mind, he allowed himself to remember the surprise of Veronica's kiss. He stopped walking and closed his eyes against the bright June sun. He recalled the image of Veronica in the moment she'd been spotlighted in his headlights, illuminating her dress and outlining her legs. He pictured her on the boat, her feet raised on the rail, saw the color of the polish on her toenails—red, in nearly the same tone as the bikini top. He saw her among the bones, the precision and economy of her movements, but he saw the bones too, and seeing them now in his mind, it was impossible not to have the two deaths intertwine, for even the narratives had tumbled together, this ancient man and this modern girl. Imagining Britany's corpse, he withdrew the image from his mind and concentrated instead on her face as revealed in the senior portrait he'd examined a thousand times, the face that stared back at him from his work files and his home bathroom mirror. He tried to shake Britany from his mind. He forced himself to see only the bones before them yesterday, the simple alignment of a skeleton that could belong to a diagram in any high school science classroom, inert, reposed, artifacts for an exhibit, saw too the intersection of animal and beast, this other entanglement of interwoven burial, grave partners for a thousand years? Ten thousand? He heard Veronica's voice, the warning, "It is likely as mundane as an accident, the most unglamorous explanation imaginable." But Britany's face flashed before him again. If an accident, then why was there no admission? Had his push for the invasion of privacy charges done the opposite of what he had intended, forced Evans's hand, made him hide the truth because he already faced prison?

Wendell opened his eyes, horrified to think he might have pushed Britany's truth further away. Had he fumbled the investigation as Tom Rodgers insisted, as the newspapers accused, as superiors hinted? The sun blinded him for a moment and made him see spots. He dropped his chin to his chest, averting his eyes, then closed them again and slowly rolled his neck in a circle, hearing the pop and crack of his bones. *Get moving*, he thought.

He put on his sports coat despite the summer warmth and thrust his hands into the coat pockets. His right hand encountered a stiff square of paper, and he removed it to see Tina's thank you card. He pictured her the night he met her at Dairy Queen, saw the cut and color of her hair and the shape of her nose in profile as she scrubbed the drip tray of the soft-serve machine, and he remembered the quickening of his pulse as she turned towards him at the jangle of the bell on the door and he thought briefly that he was seeing Britany. He looked from the card back to the sky, expansive and blue, then he scrambled to transfer the card to his left hand and reached for his cell phone. He thought briefly of Veronica and said aloud, "Different stars, but the same sun."

* * *

Reaching Tina had taken only two calls, the first to her Dairy Queen manager, who released her cell number with a nonchalance that made Wendell worry about the safety of the employees. He raced through Tina's attempt to thank him again and asked her straight away when he could meet her to show her another photograph. "It will only take thirty seconds," he insisted. "Most likely a longshot." They agreed to meet between classes. He waited for her when she emerged from her math class.

"I take all three classes back-to-back to help with the daycare," she said. Shadows under her eyes revealed a single mother who juggled work, parenting, and late-night homework.

"It will all be worth it in the end," Wendell said. "I promise not to take but a minute of your time so you can get on with it."

"I doubt that I can help, but I'll try."

"When we talked," he said, consulting his typed notes, "you said that you worked with Britany on the Friday night before she disappeared, that you closed together."

"I guess. That seems forever ago."

"And you said that a woman had been in before closing. She and Britany hit it off. Britany took a picture with her on her phone."

Tina nodded. "I remember. But only because you and I talked about it."

"Do you think you could identify that woman?"

"That was months ago," Tina said. "I doubt it."

"Let me show you a picture and see if it triggers anything." He removed a close-up photograph of Annie Tomlinson from the file and handed it to Tina.

"Could be. I really don't remember."

"I know it was a long time ago."

"I mean, there's no reason to remember, right? It was just another night. I mean...you know until after...after Britany disappeared."

"I understand." Wendell returned the photo to the file, then flipped back within the printed pages in the binder. "You told me Britany thought the woman's clothes were pretty. She commented on how she wanted to dress like her."

"You write that kind of stuff down," Tina said.

"I write everything down."

"Wow. Maybe I should take lessons."

"My co-workers like to give me a hard time," Wendell laughed. "Back to this woman. Can you remember anything about her? How she was dressed?"

Tina thought for a moment. "I do remember Britany being obsessed with her boots. She went on and on about them. About how her dad would never let her wear hooker boots like that."

"Hooker boots?"

Tina laughed. "I wouldn't call them that, but like tall, you know, almost up to the knee. Leather. You could tell they were expensive. Britany wouldn't shut up about them."

"You also said that the woman was pretty. What do you remember?"

"Not much. Stylish. I don't know. I mean, I guess it could be that woman you showed me. I'm trying to think back to that night, but it's not like there was anything special about it." Tina frowned. "Wait. I do remember that their conversation started because of her tattoo. She had this huge tattoo on her arm. Britany said that when she left home, she should get a tattoo just to make her parents mad."

Wendell reached for his phone and opened his browser. "Hang on a second, Tina. I want to show you something." Wendell selected an image and then magnified it. "Does this look familiar?" He showed her a picture of an intricate gold snake tattoo curling up a woman's arm.

"Oh, my gosh, yes."

Wendell returned the image to its full scale. "And does this look like the woman who came in that night?"

Tina breathed in a small but audible gasp. "Oh, wow. That's the woman whose picture you showed me."

"It is."

"Does she have something to do with Britany?"

"I don't know. But I'm about to find out."

Chapter Thirty-Three

"Pestering me on my day off," was Knudson's response to Wendell's call.

"I'll bribe you with baked goods, promises of Scotch, undying devotion."

"People will talk," she said.

"What are you doing?"

"Laundry," she said. "Burglary lead?"

"No. Bring your appetite for a murder investigation."

"You've got something from the search?"

"Something else. Maybe nothing, but I'd like to see how it plays."

"Give me half an hour. And make it something chocolate."

* * *

He briefed Herberts on the search findings and gained his approval to leak a story that might shake the grass around Evans. Herberts wasn't in love with the idea but agreed. "Undisclosed source," Herberts said. "I don't mind putting the press to work for us, but let's not burn any bridges."

Wendell nodded.

Wendell scrubbed his desk surface from a bottle of spray cleaner he kept in his bottom drawer. He laid the thick binder from Britany Rodgers's case on the clean surface. He settled on a reporter he didn't care for from Missoula, the two-hour remove perhaps enough to placate valley journalists once the truth about the remains was revealed. Potential murder remains trumped any ancient artifact story, which would get pushed to the fringes as a human-interest piece. He'd already made calls to old probation and parole buddies, some corrections officer friends, and to Martin White Crow.

His next call was to Kristen Schneider. He reached her on the first ring. He dispensed with pleasantries almost immediately and asked, "Do you still smoke?"

"Pardon?"

"Do you still smoke?"

"No," she said defensively. "I barely ever did."

"How'd you hide it from your mom?"

"What?"

"You heard me the first time."

"I do my own laundry. Mom never goes through my things."

"Plus, there wasn't much to hide, now was there? You only smoked when you were with Britany."

"Yeah."

"How'd she hide it from her parents?"

"Mints, perfume. Made her friends carry her smokes."

"Among the things she hid from her parents, does she have a tattoo?"

"No. But she said the day she moved out, she was getting one. Somewhere they would never see."

"Did Britany write things down on her hand?"

"Not her hand. Her arm. You know, on her forearm, where she could read it. All the time. Homework assignments. Phone numbers. She could have a piece of paper in front of her, and she'd write it on her arm."

Ever since he had spoken with Tina, an old oft-repeated line of his father's circled around his head: "There's more than one way to skin a cat." Usually, his father stared down a piece of broken farm machinery when he uttered the phrase. He called Heidi Tomlinson. Perhaps he'd use this bottom of the lake discovery to plant more than one seed.

She answered on the second ring, out of breath, and picturing her slim physique, Wendell imagined her stepping off a piece of exercise equipment. She voiced complaints about the leniency of Evan's sentence. Wendell told her that they might get lucky and see real punishment; he shared news of the body found in Flathead Lake. "I'm hopeful this discovery provides evidence we need to see a prosecution," Wendell said.

"I should know better," Heidi Tomlinson replied, "but I've held out hope that this girl had run away. I guess that's a Pollyanna for you."

"Entirely natural," Wendell said. "You should let Annie know about this development. She's told me how much she wants to stay informed about the case."

"I'm sure she will hope, as much as I do, that this helps you lock Evans away for the rest of his life."

"You might also tell her that I recently bumped into an attorney who would really like to see her press a civil suit against Evans. I would eagerly agree to serve as a witness if she were to decide to pursue such a case. I'd call her myself, but she seems so busy and so difficult to get ahold of."

"I'll call her just as soon as we hang up, detective. I know she's extremely interested in this poor girl. I think she feels they are connected in some way. I guess they are," she said. "I don't like to think about it. I guess this is evidence of how close Annie may have come to something far worse."

"That's why I called," Wendell said.

***

Knudson arrived moments later. She sat on a corner of his desk. She said, "I had the radio on in the car."

"Um-hmm."

"A body found in Flathead. A reminder of a certain missing seventeen-year-old. Hard not to leap to assumptions," she said, smirking. "And you said you weren't a fisherman."

"Midlife hobby reallocation."

"What do you need from me?"

"A fishing buddy."

***

Annie Tomlinson's call came within the hour. "My mother called. She said you found the girl's body."

"We have retrieved remains from Flathead Lake." Wendell walked a verbal tightrope.

"Her family must be so relieved."

"It provides closure. It doesn't bring their daughter back."

"But it does help you, right? Doesn't her body give you the evidence you need?"

"We certainly hope that the forensic evidence can offer an explanation for what happened."

"Evans killed her. This gives you proof."

"I'm afraid there's not many specifics I can share at this point. But this is a vital development." Wendell allowed a purposeful pause. He held Knudson's eyes as he spoke. "However, there remain questions we need to clear up. I'm hoping you can help."

"Questions? About Evans?"

"Follow up, yes. And there's still more we'd like to know about your New York friends—Frank and Johnny. Something that may be delicate."

"Frank and Johnny? That doesn't make sense."

"Well, perhaps you can corroborate statements. Fill in some gaps. I'd really like to speak with you."

"Fine, fire away."

"It would be so helpful if you could come here, if we could talk at the house where we can interact with the setting, refresh my knowledge of that night. Would it be possible to get you here?"

"To Montana?"

"I know you're busy. I can come there if that's easier. But I think your presence here could expedite matters. Then we can be put it to bed. Put the new forensic evidence to work."

Annie remained silent for a long moment. At last, she said, "It's not at all convenient."

"I'd be ever so grateful," Wendell said.

"I'll have to cancel other commitments."

"Come help us cement this case. Put it behind you." When he ended the call, Wendell turned to Knudson, who had rolled her office chair next to him and listened on speakerphone. "Well, how'd I do?"

"Intriguing choice of bait. A nice, delicate presentation that barely rippled the surface. You should offer your services as a guide."

"We'll see about that."

"Are we really looking at her for this?"

Wendell shrugged. "With Evans, we have a history that seems to suggest a possible motive. But we've either got an escalation of behavior that we don't have a clear explanation for or something happenchance. We'll still listen to see if he reacts to news of a body. Don't forget that." He brushed away a piece of lint that did not exist from his pants leg.

"With Annie," he continued, "we've got no motive at all. No history. No logical connections. We have this new evidence that Britany had met her." He tapped his pen against the desk in a rapid, syncopated beat. "Even with Evans, we operate on the assumption of a happenchance encounter. How often have we investigated crimes—assaults, traffic altercations, bar fights—where it's a case of two people in two moods who happen to clash?"

"All the time. But not for murder," she said.

"No, not for murder."

"Unless," Knudson said, "one of the happenchance participants is a murderer."

"There's that," he agreed. He returned his pen to his pocket. "We looked into Annie's background, assuming only that she was a victim."

"Say she's a suspect. When she learns about your lake buddy's identity, doesn't she turn tail and run? I mean, even if the story is only picked up locally, she'll be watching it."

"If she runs, then I think we'll have reason to chase. I think she's playing poker instead of billiards now. We've got to watch if she shows her hand. If we get lucky and she flies in, then there's an important tell we have to watch for."

"What's that?"

"She offers new evidence to put us back on Evans."

"And I thought we were on a nice lazy fishing trip. You've got a whole expedition planned."

"The fish still have to bite, Stacey. But the bait is in the water."

Chapter Thirty-Four

The day appeared bright and clear, the kind of weather that made Northwest Montana summers appear possible only in travel brochures. The pickups and their empty boat trailers had already begun to fill the lot in Sommers and spill out along the highway.

Like the foyer where Heidi Tomlinson greeted the two detectives, she appeared part of a catalog, dressed for summer in harem pants and a tight-fitting sleeveless top. Wendell felt out of place in his sportscoat.

Stepping onto the stone patio, the beauty and enormity of the lake opened before them. The last of the snow still lit the tops of the Swan Range across the lake and the Missions to the south. The lake itself glittered in the full sun, the water a nearly tropical blue-green. Heidi walked with them across the patio, around a rock fireplace, and down curving rock steps that divided planters loaded with colorful flowers.

They stepped onto a smaller patio where they found Annie Tomlinson sunbathing atop a chaise lounge. Clad only in a bikini, Annie made no attempt to cover up. She turned sideways to them as an acknowledgement of their presence, and the three embarked on an awkward process of moving heavy chairs in order to sit near her. Her mother looked annoyed and placed a towel within Annie's reach. It had been just under forty-eight hours since Wendell had spoken to Annie on the phone, and so far, news outlets speculated on the body's identity with headlines such as, "Officials Await Forensics on Flathead Body."

"You're not dressed for the season," Annie said.

"I never get taken seriously when I wear my Speedo," Wendell said. If the joke registered, she showed no indication, while her mother laughed louder than his humor deserved.

Annie wore large-framed sunglasses so dark he could not see her eyes—a thing of great frustration for any cop. It annoyed him that the glasses, like her refusal to move her chaise lounge or cover the skimpy swimsuit, gave her a kind of territorial advantage. A different cop would have wanted the interview to take place on his own turf, but as much as she annoyed him, Wendell was willing to afford her a false sense of control. He was determined to feed that security. "We appreciate you taking the time to fly in. Your testimony is a tremendous asset to this case."

"You said you have questions about Frank and Johnny."

"We need to clarify statements from a number of different witnesses. Solidify the timeline. Establish a window for when Britany Rodgers might have been present on the property. Eliminate people from the inquiry."

"You couldn't do that over the phone?"

"I thought it would be useful to be on the property where we can put times and places and various assertions by witnesses together. Help us see what we've missed."

"You've waited eight months to see what you've missed?" Annie said snidely.

"New evidence has come to light," Wendell said.

"Because you've found the girl's body."

Wendell ignored her. "I wonder if you wouldn't walk us through that night again. Show us where you were when you encountered Evans."

"If you've got new evidence, why not talk to Evans instead of me?"

"I know this seems redundant," he said. "We have to be. We have to go through every possible detail again and again. We can't move from investigation to prosecution any other way. You only get one shot at prosecution."

"How does this involve Frank and Johnny?"

"Actually, their statements have been remarkably consistent. Strikingly so."

"Then I don't get it."

"In this business, you come to expect little inconsistencies. It's part of human nature."

"You don't trust them because they're too consistent. That's seriously whacked, detective."

"We have Frank, Johnny, Greg Evans, and you present, and we have evidence Britany Rodgers was on this property. We have to ferret out a sequence of events from within the differing accounts. Unfortunately, none of the statements from you or your two friends have any clear time markers. It's not like the three of you ordered pizza delivery. All of this is complicated by the fact that Frank, Johnny, and you all acknowledge that you were quite drunk, which naturally only fogs things. If we could physically walk through what you remember, it will help us piece some things together and might trigger more memory for you."

"I can't believe I dropped what I was doing to attend your show and tell."

Wendell wondered how many opponents and tournament officials had suffered Annie's cutting words. He refused to react. He had little doubt that she viewed herself as superior to him. He would not dispel that notion. He only wondered how much of her attitude was calculated and how much was instinctual. "Humor me," he said, "acknowledging that I'm not likely as quick on the uptake."

"Is this really the best use of your time?" Annie asked. She rose to a seated position and slipped her feet into a pair of open-toed sandals.

"They need your help, Annie," her mother said. "He's just doing his job."

"Poorly," Annie hissed. She stood and reached for a cover-up draped over the back of the chair. "Let's get your charade over with."

"I appreciate the cooperation. Did you spend time at the fire pit before or after the hot tub?"

"Before."

"Let's start there."

"Don't I need to bring props? Gather the materials for S'mores?"

"Ann," her mother scolded. "There's no need to be rude."

"It's fine," Wendell said, playing the part. "I know it seems silly, but I'm a visual thinker. It drives my colleagues crazy. Isn't that right, Detective

Knudson?"

"You'll do well if you get away without him making you draw a map," Knudson said. She smiled for Annie's benefit.

The group trouped down another set of steps and a long, curving stone path that descended a landscaped slope. Where the path met the lake edge, a small peninsula jutted into the water next to a groomed beach. The peninsula hosted a circular seating area surrounding a stone fireplace where they stopped. "My husband designed all the stonework," Heidi said. "He loved natural materials. Most of this stone came from Oklahoma."

"Daddy and his rocks," Annie said with venom.

"My father used to work with stone," Wendell said. "He built a good part of my childhood home from rock he quarried from his own property. It's still there," he said, "but it wouldn't exactly make *Architectural Digest*. Any idea what time you might have come here?" Wendell asked.

She shook her head.

"After dinner?"

"Sure."

"Do you remember what you had for dinner?"

"Are you kidding me?"

"This is after dark?"

"Of course."

"You'd been drinking already by this time."

"We'd been drinking all afternoon. These are ridiculous questions. I couldn't give you a timeline from two nights ago. I don't even remember when this was—what was it October, November? So no, I don't know what time we decided it would be a good idea to roast marshmallows. What's more, I don't know why the fuck any of these mind-numbing details matter."

"Annie," her mother scolded.

"What, mom? This is idiotic. Don't scold me for saying so, and don't treat me like I'm ten."

Wendell ignored her. "When did you go out on the water?"

"Pardon?"

"You said you dared Frank and Johnny into swimming."

"I know what I told you."

"When did you swim?"

"After. We'd been in the hot tub for a while."

"How much later?"

"I don't know. A couple of hours."

"And you continued to drink?"

"Is that a crime?"

"No, ma'am. You swam from there?" he asked. He pointed below them to the beach.

"No, from the dock. That way they couldn't pussy out and wade in until their heels touched. Full immersion."

"Show me." He walked ahead.

"Are you serious?"

Wendell did not answer but continued to walk. Knudson and Heidi Tomlinson dutifully followed. Annie steamed for a moment before she too followed. Halfway down the path, Wendell turned to her. "I assume you went to the boathouse, to the bathroom."

"What?"

"You stopped at the boathouse?"

"I wasn't in the boathouse."

"So, did you bring towels from the house then? Do those match the ones you store here?" he asked as they approached the boathouse.

"What? No. I guess you're right. We must have stopped and got towels," she said. "I don't remember."

"Can you show me, please?"

"Show you?"

"Where you keep the towels."

A look of exasperation overtook Annie's face, and she exhaled loudly. "This is a farce. You know perfectly well where we keep the towels."

"Visual thinker." Wendell tapped a finger beside his right eye.

He followed her into the bottom floor of the boathouse. Rolled towels filled a wooden rack beside a double vanity. "Good," Wendell said, without directing the exclamation to anyone. He turned to Annie. "You get towels and change here and then go for a chilly dip."

"I opted for skinny-dipping. Kind of a lake tradition as I see it."

"I see. Can you show me?"

"Are you asking me to strip, detective?"

Wendell marveled at how she juxtaposed outrage and edgy flirtation, annoyance, and humor. "Show me where on the dock," he said.

Annie smirked and led them outside. "Probably about here," she said. They were halfway out to the boat slips along the wooden dock. "You have to get out this far to get enough depth."

"Somehow, I doubt those towels felt warm enough to make much difference once you were wet."

"It was freezing. But that was kind of the point."

Wendell looked around in a circle. Then he asked, "Prior to that night, when was the last time you took the boats out?"

"The boats?"

"Yes."

"Probably the month before. I think I'd been home in September."

"You were," her mother said. "Lisa and the kids, all of us were here for Labor Day."

"Were the boats still in their slips when you were here in October?"

"I don't remember," she said. She looked down into the water. "You would have to ask Evans."

"But you used the boats this summer?"

She nodded. "I like to get out on the lake. It's something my father and I did." As she spoke, a boat rounded the point and passed a few hundred yards off the end of the dock. A child and a woman waved at the group on the dock as they roared past. Heidi and Stacey waved back. Wendell and Annie did not.

"So, that would explain why your fingerprints appeared on the boat cover."

Annie was momentarily taken aback and then said bitterly, "They're our boats, now aren't they?"

"You've spent a lot of time on the lake. You know it well."

"I'm not here often."

"You fish?"

"Not anymore. Dad used to. Mostly I'd go along for the ride."

"Water ski, wakeboard? That sort of thing?"

"Sometimes. If friends or family are around. Mostly we cruise or sunbathe. We'd do barbeques on the pontoon boat. Watch the fireworks on the fourth of July."

"Sounds nice," Wendell said. He turned to Knudson. "Your family does that, don't they? Watch the fireworks from your boat."

"We do. Every year."

"I'm surprised you didn't wear the towels back up to the pool," Wendell said abruptly as he turned to Annie. "Given how cold you must have been. Or is that part of the thrill?"

"Pardon?"

"Evans found wet towels on the dock."

"Oh, well, I think we used several."

"What's the routine? You run back up the hill as fast as you can and jump right into the hot water? Hope you don't have a heart attack."

"Yeah."

"Why don't you take me up there now."

Annie complied without comment. Wendell let her lead and watched her back as she walked up the hill. Something in her had shifted. Her stride had grown nearly as practiced as her mother's. Tension, he wondered? Annoyance? About halfway up the hill, Annie turned and looked at Wendell. "You know, I've been thinking," she said, "about Evans."

Wendell held her eyes but was aware of Knudson in his periphery, walking slightly ahead of him. "What's that?"

"Just that he's a real pro with the boats. He maintained them. I remember he and my dad talked about fishing all the time. He said he could be a guide if my dad ever wanted. He really knows the lake."

"Are you aware if he ever took a boat out on his own?"

She shrugged.

Turning to Heidi, he asked, "Is that a privilege you extended to him?" As he turned to her, he made eye contact with Knudson momentarily.

"We never discussed it. I really don't think he's the sort who would do such a thing without asking, or I mean, I would have believed that before... " Her voice trailed away.

"But he definitely had full access to them?"

"Oh, yes. He's responsible for the maintenance."

"Do others have access to the keys?"

"All the adults in the family know where we keep them," Heidi said. "They're free to use either boat."

"Did you take Frank and Johnny boating that weekend, Annie?"

"No."

"Did you hear a boat that night?"

"I've told you. I pretty much passed out at the end of the night."

The group climbed more stairs and crossed three patios before arriving at a space mostly hidden among tall pines where the spa was molded into the contours of the stone. A half-circle formed one edge of the spa. The gentle curve placed so that it afforded another remarkable view, this one oriented to the southeast into the peaks of the Mission Mountains. "Breathtaking," Wendell said. He walked to the edge of the spa.

"Too bad you didn't pack that Speedo," Annie said. Wendell wanted to reply, 'Welcome back' but said nothing. Instead, he addressed her mother. "You did an amazing job of planning for views. Like a photograph."

"I can't take any credit. That was all my husband."

Wendell turned to Annie. "One of you told me that it was your dad who introduced you to billiards."

Annie nodded.

"He must have been so proud of your success."

Annie did not respond, but her mother did. "A father was never so proud. These two were cut from the same cloth." She gave her daughter a one-armed sideways hug. Annie's did not reciprocate.

Wendell moved and sat down on the edge of a stone planter. "Tell me, Annie, the three of you run up the hill from the lake. You jump back in. How long did you remain here?"

"I don't know. Probably an hour or more."

"You continued the party?"

She shrugged.

"Who's bartender? Who runs back and forth to the house?"

"I don't know. I guess we all were. I'd gone in and put on a swimsuit. Brought us some food. I think the boys opened a bottle of wine."

"Where was it that you broke a glass?"

"I didn't break a glass."

"Evans found a broken glass the next morning. Someone suffered an injury that produced enough blood to require towels to either stop it or clean up after. That seems like something you'd remember."

"That's news to me. You'll have to talk to Frank and Johnny."

"That's one of the things I'm trying to clear up. They both claim neither one of them cut themselves. Yet Esmerelda found bloody towels, and Evans is specific about broken glass."

"Look, I don't claim to be a rocket scientist," Annie said, "but if Evans killed this girl, then surely he's not beyond lying about finding broken glass."

"That's a fair point," Wendell said, "but still, it's an odd detail, isn't it? An odd thing to tell the cops if he's trying to hide?"

"I'd be more interested in what other lies Evans told you," Annie said.

"Was it here at the spa that you saw him?"

"Excuse me?"

"You told us that Evans spoke to you that night. You said it made you wonder if he'd been spying on you. Where were you when you spoke to him?"

"Oh, yeah, that's right. We were here."

"What did he say?"

"Just that he was going to bed."

"Were Frank and Johnny still here then?"

"Yes."

"And did you all go inside at the same time?"

"Yes."

"Yet they say differently. They claim they went to bed first."

"That's not how I remember. I've told you. I was really drunk. I wanted to sleep. I'm sure my memory isn't good."

"It's just that they have an advantage over you," Wendell said.

"An advantage?"

"There are two of them. They have the benefit of accounting for one another."

"What is it I am supposed to account for?"

Wendell ignored her. "You have no memory of what time you went inside?"

"I've told you before, repeatedly. No."

"You've said you passed out. Yet you had the wherewithal to make it all the way to your room."

"Is that so surprising?"

"It's such a big house. Quite a journey for someone ready to pass out."

"A figure of speech. I was drunk and tired."

"There's an odd irony here," Wendell said. He patted the stone beside him and shifted his position so that he could look at Annie head-on. "The video we captured from the camera Evans hid doesn't show you ever being in your room that night. Not at any time after 6:30 in the evening, when you changed into your swimsuit."

"You told me that you recovered only bits and fragments."

"Bits and fragments, yes. But bits and fragments across time, including across the hours of that Saturday night."

"Maybe I fell asleep in the theater. I like to watch movies when I go to sleep. I don't remember."

"Maybe so," Wendell agreed. "Tell me though, Annie, why did Britany Rodgers have the address to this house written on her forearm?"

Wendell had watched criminals, even those accustomed to being questioned by police and who passed regular portions of their lives lying, react to hearing something for which they were unprepared. There was a flicker, often more than that, but always a flicker. Their eyes shifted focus or darted to a new object. In Annie, it lasted only a split-second, but then her face morphed, became almost expressionless. "What?" she asked. Expression returned but looked staged. "I don't know what you're talking about."

"Annie!" her mother said sharply. She took a step away from her daughter. Wendell feared she would fall into the spa.

"Why would *your* address appear on Britany Rodgers's body?"

Annie chose outrage as the expression on which her face settled. "I don't know what kind of game you're playing."

"She wrote it there the night before," Wendell said. "When you met her while she was at work. When you went for ice cream. When you gave her your address."

"Annie, what's going on?" her mother begged. "You knew this girl? Why haven't you told the police?"

"I didn't know her, mom." Annie sounded, Wendell guessed, as she must have regularly throughout her teen years—exasperated, superior.

"You invited her," Wendell said, monotone. His voice, perhaps because he could empty it of emotion, could be calming, the sort of voice to lull one to sleep even if he'd never soothed a restless child too tired for bed. "Were you drunk that night too, Annie? Stoned? Had to have ice cream," he intoned smoothly, softly. "It was a passing invitation, something you'd not given any thought. A pretty girl interested in you. Something offered and forgotten. Have I got that right, Annie?"

"Stop it," she said, without force.

"Why would you ever think she'd take you up on it? Just conversation, right?"

Annie took a step backwards. Her mother's lips moved without words. Knudson took one step closer to Annie. "Stop," Annie mumbled.

"Did you even recognize her when she showed up? She was intrigued, wasn't she, Annie?"

"I don't know," Annie stammered.

"You were here in the spa? Is that right? It was cold. Dark. There must have been a cloud of steam. Like fog."

Annie nodded ever so slightly. Her bottom lip trembled. She brushed at it with her hand as if frustrated her body had betrayed her.

"You were alone?"

She nodded again. Then, nearly whispering, she said, "The boys had gone to bed. I was all alone." Her voice weakened even more. "I'm always alone."

"And then she just appeared," Wendell said, a quiet statement and not a question.

"Out of nowhere," Annie said. "I looked up, and she was there."

Heidi moved abruptly, and Wendell merely raised a finger to her as if the gesture alone held the power to stop her. Knudson placed a hand gently on her arm. Wendell's eyes never left Annie, who looked in a trance. "Tell me, Annie."

Annie did not respond.

"Were you in the water?"

Annie nodded.

"Did she join you?"

Annie's facial expression did not change. "Not at first. She sat down, about where you are. It was dark. Just the spa lights. They glowed inside the steam. It was like talking to someone in a dream."

"What did you talk about?"

"Meaningless things. The designer of my swimsuit. About my tattoos," she said, absently running her hand down the length of the snake tattoo on her left arm.

"Did she join you?"

"She took her shoes off and rolled up her pants legs. I offered her wine. She drank from one of the boy's glasses. We sat with our feet in the water. I was so drunk I thought I might pass out if I stayed in the water." She paused.

"Go on."

"We shared a joint. She was shivering from the cold air. I told her she should get in the water. She said she didn't have a swimming suit." Her voice trailed away. She closed her eyes, but they moved behind the closed lids like someone dreaming.

"I took off my top and told her she could wear it. She looked shocked, but she kept looking. She stepped away into the shadows to change. I remember thinking that was sweet. Shy. It's been a long time since I was around anyone who doesn't pretend they are something they're not. She got in the water in her panties and my bikini top. She started laughing. Said that my top was too big for her and it kept floating up." Annie fell silent.

Wendell feared that this cooperative, complacent Annie would disappear, and the combative Annie would return. He concentrated on keeping his voice unobtrusive, attempted to help sustain the memory, the night, the cold, the steam, the quiet, the clouded drunkenness, tried to keep the bright June sun at bay. "Then what happened, Annie?"

"We started kissing. She said she had never kissed a girl before." Annie's eyes remained closed. "It was nice," she said. "Soft. I felt her relax. We kissed and kissed. I haven't done that in so long. No pressure to escalate." She opened her eyes. Wendell saw resignation in her eyes.

"The two of you are kissing."

"I should have stopped there. But I touched her breasts. I moved slow. I felt her tense, then relax, then tense again when I reached her nipples. She said she was too hot, and she moved up onto the side, there," she said and pointed down towards the spa as if Britany would reappear where her finger indicated. She frowned.

"Annie," he said simply. "It okay to tell us. We need you to."

"I…I should have enjoyed it. It was so nice. She was just a girl experimenting. I should have remembered that."

"You are in the water. She is on the side…"

"I wanted to live in that moment. The tenderness. The exploration. The absence of expectation. That's not quite right. What I really wanted was to trade places with her. To have the world be new. Exciting. I ran my hands up her legs. I felt her tremble. I heard her exhale. I slipped my finger under her panties…and…I…I didn't stop. I heard her say no. She said it again, and I totally ignored her. What the fuck was wrong with me? I forced her legs open. She freaked out. Scrambled away like she was stepping on ants, trying to get to her feet. She hit the wine glass, and it went flying." Annie stopped abruptly, then said, "I'd forgotten about the glass."

Annie looked at her mother, who was staring at her daughter like she was a stranger.

"Annie, what happened next?" Wendell asked softly.

"She fell. She must have slipped on the wet cement. I heard her hit the planter. Like a thud. Right on that corner, there." She pointed. "All that damn rock my dad was so obsessed with. Then she kind of slid down into the shadow of the wall."

"Oh, Annie," her mother said.

Annie continued. "It was dark where she was. I tried to get her to talk. She wouldn't respond. Then she started shaking all over. Like a seizure, I guess. I didn't know what I was supposed to do. I thought she would puke. I tried to roll her on her side, and then I saw all the blood. It was everywhere. I tried to hold her head still, and the blood was in her hair and got on my hands. I didn't know how to help. I used towels to try and stop the bleeding. Then she stopped moving."

Wendell met Knudson's eyes. Knudson stepped to the side, and Heidi reached for her daughter and gathered her in a hug. Annie melted into her mother and started crying. She buried her face in her mother's chest and sobbed. Tears streamed from her mother's eyes as well, and she stroked her daughter's hair.

Wendell gave them time. He remained seated on the planter edge and felt the hardness of the stone under him. He and Knudson looked at one another again, and then Knudson turned away. He followed her gaze to the lake.

After several minutes, he said Annie's name. He said it again, louder, and she turned away from her mother. Long streaks of mascara made her face look bruised. Her mother's blouse was wet and stained with her daughter's tears.

"Annie," he said. "we need you to tell us what you did with her body." He saw Heidi flinch. She took a step backwards. Knudson reached out for her as if she might fall, touched her at the elbow, and helped her sit down on the planter opposite Wendell. Then Heidi looked down at the low wall where she sat and suddenly sprang away. Knudson guided her to a chair. Annie watched her mother, and a visible chill passed over her body.

Annie wiped her nose with the swimsuit cover-up.

"How could I do that?" she said. "The very first guy I was ever with did that to me. Didn't listen when I said no. Jammed his fingers inside of me like my body wasn't mine."

"Tell us what happened next."

Annie shifted her attention from the spa to her mother, then made eye contact with Wendell. "I knew she was dead. Her eyes were open, but they were…they had changed. She wasn't breathing." Annie paused and then restarted, almost whispering. "I was so cold. I couldn't stop shivering. I was all alone. I didn't know what I was supposed to do."

"But you made a decision, didn't you?"

"No. Not really. I didn't know her. I didn't know why she was there. But… but she was there, and she was dead, and she was wearing my swimsuit, and…I freaked out. I tried to shout for help, but it was like the woods swallowed my voice. I ran to that window," she said and pointed to the only first-story window in the closest wing of the house. "I climbed through those bushes to the window and started banging on it. I don't know what I was thinking. That's my dad's study. No one would ever be in that part of the house. I looked through the window and saw my dad's things—his fishing rod on the wall, his trout mounts, the model of his plane on the corner of his desk, pictures, pictures of him with me—I didn't know what to do. If he were alive, and I could call him…" Her voice trailed away and then recovered. "I ran to the main patio. I…I couldn't make myself go inside. I don't know why.

"Johnny had left his clothes on a patio table. Sweats and a shirt. I put on his clothes. His sandals. It felt like the air was rushing by me, like it feels when you're standing on a platform and a train races by, and you can feel the wind it makes. Then I realized that there was no noise at all. The air wasn't moving. I was standing still, and the night was cold and clear, and the only light was from the moon, and it was quiet, so quiet, and I could hear a breeze in the leaves and the water bumping against the shore. Peaceful, you know, if…if what happened hadn't happened." Annie turned and stared out into the lake.

"Why didn't you call 911, Annie?" her mother asked. Her hands were in her lap, but they trembled as if she inhabited the cold night her daughter described. "Why didn't you get help?"

Annie did not look at her mother. She answered in a robotic voice. "I knew she was dead. I knew there would be so many questions. I didn't know why she was here. People would blame me."

"What did you do next, Annie?" Wendell asked.

"I saw the boats. I wanted to make it all go away." She paused, then said. "I just didn't think…about all the people who would be looking for her, the people who would miss her. I didn't think."

"I need to interrupt you there, Annie, and read you your rights."

When he asked if she understood her rights, she nodded.

"Do you wish to waive these rights?"

She nodded again.

"You realize you can reassert these rights at any time, Annie."

"Okay," she said in a whisper.

Wendell motioned for Annie to sit down and drew another chair close. At his prompting, she told how she rolled Britany's body onto one of the big bath towels, how she tied another around her head so that she could not see her face, how she dragged her across the lawn to the docks. She told of lowering the boat on its shore station so that it was level with the dock and she could get Britany's body on board. Annie's voice was flat, dispassionate. She told of going to get the boat key in the cabinet from the boathouse and seeing there, on the wall nearby, a length of heavy chain her father had found when they first started clearing the property. A rusted logging chain. She had no idea why her father had kept it. She said, "He was unpredictable that way, the things he placed significance in and the things he did not. All my life, people have compared me to him." She had taken the chain, along with a pair of gloves she had found on top of the cabinet where they kept the keys. She stopped for more towels. She told how she used only the trolling motor until she was well offshore and then about a light on the far shore she employed as her guide. "Somehow, in my mind, I thought that if only I could make it to the other side, everything would be different. That became my only goal. Like I could cross the lake and walk away from it all. I tried not to think about what I was about to do. I concentrated on driving the boat.

"I knew I needed to go where it was deep. I used to watch the fish finder for my dad. A life on the lake was the one he cherished, even if he rarely lived it. We'd fish offshore in the heat of the day out where it was deep, and there were big lake trout near the bottom. Then we'd fish closer in, up in the coves and bays in the evening, for whitefish and cutthroat. Lunch in Wood's Bay. The same meal every time." Wendell could see the nostalgia in her eyes and gave her the space for it, thinking the complex layers of her memories might be the only path to the information he needed from her.

"I always wondered who my dad would be if he were that man all the time," Annie said dreamily. And when she returned, she said, "Instead, I became someone he would despise."

"Take me there, Annie. I have to know."

"It was so dark. I could just see the bow cut through the water. When I got closer to the far shore, I used the fish finder. When I saw 180', I knew I needed to turn south. But part of me wanted to hit the throttle instead, head for the rocks off the point of Wood's Bay at full speed, like a cue ball into a break.

"I turned south, and l followed the fish finder until there were almost no lights along the shore. Then I turned east again for a little while until the fish finder read 240." She paused. "It's funny how your mind works," she said. "What you remember and what you forget. What you focus on. Like how I could navigate a boat in the dark. But then I looked down at her on the floor, and it all came back. I kept thinking that I had to get my swimsuit off of her. I don't know why. Did I think that if you found her my swimsuit would bring you to me? It looked so odd, my swimsuit on someone else. I wished we could trade places. She could dump me over the side because I really wouldn't care. I deserved it.

"I put the gloves on so I didn't have to touch her. I rolled her on her stomach and untied the bikini. Rolled her off of it. I tied the chain around her feet. I lifted her so that her head was outside the boat. She was face down. I took the towels off her head and tied them into the chain. Then, just before I lifted her legs over the side, I thought, what if I tied that chain around my leg as well? She would drag me down with her. We'd be tied together forever, the way we are now because of what happened, because of what I did. That's what I should have done."

Wendell felt like he was on the boat with her in the dark, the blackness of the water darker than the blackness of the night sky. He closed his eyes. In Annie's voice, he experienced the motion of the boat. He heard the splash as Britany's body met the water, heard the suction of it envelop her, felt the insistent tug of the chain. He felt the water close in and constrict his throat, the darkness flood his eyes. He fought to hold the picture of Britany he'd looked at every day for nine months before his eyes. If Annie would try and hide her face from her vision, he would not. He clung to the image and forced himself to open his eyes. He saw Annie's face. She bent forward in the chair. Her body swayed as if underwater.

Annie whispered. A confessional. "The lake took her. The last thing I saw was her hair, loose, flowing out across the top of the water. I watched the water for a long time. She was gone. Like she'd never existed."

"You scrubbed the boat."

She nodded.

"The gloves? The bikini?"

"I was going to try and burn them. But then I found the bloody towels by the spa. The ones I used to try and stop the bleeding. I used water from the spa to clean, used the chemicals to treat it and the rock around it. I found her clothes. I knew the towels were too wet to burn, and it would be daylight soon. I was going to put them in a bag and take them away, but I thought I heard something moving through the trees. I panicked and ran them to the trash in the garage. I wrapped the gloves and my top and her clothes in them. Then I ran inside. I was so tired. I fell asleep in the theater."

When I woke up, I saw Evans cleaning up after us at the fireplace. I woke the boys, called the pilot, and we bolted within an hour."

Wendell sighed.

Annie looked at him. "It happened fast. Once I decided…to get rid of her. Once I decided, and I took the first step, then I took the next. It's like lying. Once you start, then there's another lie and another."

Wendell nodded and stood. His head felt waterlogged, like part of him had been left behind in Annie's story, left underwater with Britany.

* * *

He and Knudson stepped away to a lower patio out of earshot.

"It could all be a lie," Knudson said. "She's lied this whole time."

"It could," he agreed.

"But you believe her. I can see it in your eyes," she said. "You believe this rich little twat who would do anything to save her skin."

"I do," he said. "For whatever reason." He paused. "Obviously, you don't."

"I don't know anymore," she said. "If it was an accident, then why the elaborate cover-up?"

"You think like a rational person. We've never had that on our side. What would her motive be for killing her?" he asked. "Because Britany spurned her advances? That seems slim. Even for her."

"Say she is telling the truth, then what? She walks away. Another millionaire who doesn't bear any responsibility for her actions? What's that give Britany's family?"

"Answers and justice don't always align," he said.

"The Stone Princess," Knudson said. "We didn't film the confession. We have to do it all over again. What if she stops talking?"

"However you look at it," he said, "what exactly will we prosecute? We've got obstruction of justice, tampering with evidence? That might be all we have. How would we prove intent?"

"She can't walk, Wendell. Not after what she's done. This damn case." Knudson exhaled loudly.

Wendell looked at the lake. "We're looking too far north."

"If we find her," Knudson said, "we might not have a whole lot more than your Indian. We might not have evidence to know if there was a struggle."

"We'll have details we can match up," he said. "The chain. Remnants from the towels. We would know the nature of the wound that killed her. See if it is consistent with the rock."

"True. If everything pans out as she's told us, we still wouldn't know if it was an accident or something else."

"Maybe finding her is enough," he said.

"You could let go?"

"Out there on the water," he said, eying the lake. "Part of Annie never came back."

"And that's what you're going to tell the Rodgers?"

"If you're her mother, is an accident easier to make your peace with than murder? Either way, you don't get her back."

The two stood together for a time in silence. Then without looking at him, Knudson said, "When she told you about disposing of her body, you two were huddled so close, I really couldn't quite hear her, but you disappeared for a minute there. Where'd you go?"

Wendell looked at her, then looked away, his eyes still focused on the lake. "She took me underwater."

Chapter Thirty-Five

At the end of August, a week before Veronica Moore was scheduled to return to Australia, Wendell promised her one more weekend together and another home-cooked dinner. He had coordinated a day when Joel Estes was off, telling him, "I need to borrow you and your boat."

"Can't get enough of the water now that you've had a taste," Joel said.

"Something like that."

In reality, Wendell struggled to shake off the personal memories that had been summoned forth as Annie told how she had disposed of Britany's body. He declined an invitation to go back out with the search and rescue crew. Although a stranger to the water, he had held a fascination with maps since boyhood, appreciating their intersection of art and science. Framed versions of historic maps dominated the scant artwork that decorated the walls of his home. He might not know this lake as someone who frequented it, but by observing the contour lines that swirled like fingerprint rings on Marston's map, Wendell allowed himself to be transported inside Annie's story once more, and he traced his finger in a line from Pleasant Bay across the map to Wood's Bay, and then followed contours at 180' and 190' southward in an eastward arc; when he intersected a cashew shaped depression that dropped to 240', he tapped the map and said, "There. You're going to find her there."

Marston looked at him askance. "It's a big friggin' lake," and then placed an overlay of their prior search coordinates atop the map. If Wendell was correct, their search had ended less than a mile north and remained in water 50' too shallow. "I've got nothing to lose but time," he said. "Right now, your boss is still footin' the bill."

When the search and rescue team had discovered the body the very next day after Wendell had tapped his finger on Marston's map, every aspect of how Marston interacted with him changed. Wendell met the team at the dock. What awaited him in the body bag bore little resemblance to a body, let alone to the photograph he removed from his bathroom mirror later that evening. This time, Wendell was so confident in a DNA match that he took several days off and went climbing with an old college friend from Seattle.

When he provided the Rodgers family with the news, he found the family in shambles. Still, Sheila hugged Wendell and thanked him for never giving up on Britany.

He had done what the job always required: moved on to new cases. There never was a shortage. Most were mundane. Always there were individuals who thought it appropriate to steal benefit from the work of others or who, in fits of emotion, took actions they either regretted or could not explain. Whether premeditated or spontaneous, never was there a shortage of individuals willing to cause harm to others. "Job security" had been the tired joke Wendell heard from before he entered the academy.

Had the first body they discovered in the depths of Flathead Lake arrived there because he had been a victim of another's intolerance or greed or jealousy, perhaps he might have remained in the headlines longer. The media dubbed him "Elk Man," quickly presenting as fact the speculation that the elk remains may have factored in his demise. Had the dead man's story been more tantalizing than an accident, or had he been substantially older or offered some characteristic that allowed him stature or significance in the public's eye, perhaps his story would have lingered in their imagination. Radiocarbon dating placed him at about six hundred years old, an age that offered him "little anthropological significance." "There will be archeologists who will have some minor interest since he predates horse culture," Veronica told Wendell, "but there's nothing substantive from a forensic perspective and no meaningful data for evolutionists." The remains were quickly and quietly provided to the Confederated Salish, Pend d'Oreille, and Kootenai

Tribe for reburial.

Of course, the story of "Elk Man" was knocked to the basement of the news cycle with the discovery of Britany's body, and in turn, her story likely would have lingered in the public imagination longer had the cause of death been determined as murder. As a result, her death quickly faded among the eighteen traffic fatalities and two drowning deaths in Flathead County over the course of the previous year, forgotten by all but those who knew her—another instance of someone dying at too young an age. People shook their heads at the tragedy and offered secret prayers that the ones they loved had been spared.

The Rodgers held a memorial service at the high school, scheduled to afford Britany's fellow seniors the opportunity to attend before many departed for college. The service was well-attended but there was an identifiable sensation that many of her peers already had one foot out the door and could recognize a time when recent memory would resemble a faded yearbook photograph. Sheila was the model of stoic resolve. She invited Wendell to accompany the immediate family that evening when they planned to scatter Britany's ashes back in Flathead Lake. He respectfully declined. "This is a time for your family, Sheila."

* * *

Yet Wendell felt he owed Britany something more than the thought he gave her each time he crested the first high point in his daily run and he saw the lake open below him. Would he one day view every location in this valley only as a previous crime scene?

He wanted Veronica to meet Joel and Christina. That desire, in itself, was novel to him, to share his friendship with this woman who would shortly pass out of his life. He and Veronica had spent two long weekends together over a summer that found her travelling nearly continuously. She had come his way in late June, and he had taken her into Glacier National Park. A month later, they had stayed at Chico Hot Springs and made daily trips into Yellowstone. It was a relationship that felt easy and natural, and Wendell could not decide if he could explain its nature by Veronica's personality or because they both knew it was finite, banded by a firm date of departure to the other side of the planet.

* * *

Wendell had asked Marston for the exact GPS coordinates for where they had found Britany's body. Joel hadn't asked any questions when he said he'd like to go there before the day was done. Over the course of the day, both Joel and Veronica had challenged one another to see who could stay aboard an inflatable tube towed behind the boat. Christina and Wendell declined to join in, Christina because of a bad back, Wendell without offering an explanation. At lunchtime, they tied up on Wild Horse Island for a picnic and then hiked for several hours. Late in the afternoon, Wendell provided Joel the coordinates Marston had given him.

As Joel slowed the boat and then allowed it to coast to a stop in the open water, he said to Wendell, "These are the coordinates."

"Thanks, Joel." The boat drifted on open water without another in sight—such was the benefit of so large a lake. Nearly 240' below their hull stretched the glacial remnant of the Rocky Mountain Trench. An entire second world lay below them, a place as foreign and as inhospitable to humans as ocean depths.

Christina asked, "Everything okay?"

Joel said, "Everything's fine."

"Is this where we get out?" she laughed.

Joel frowned.

Christina looked at Wendell and flushed with embarrassment. "Oh," she said, "I'm sorry, Steve."

Wendell rose from the bench seat in the bow where he sat between the two women. His face held an expression of uncertainty. He turned a slow circle. He could have told the tiny assemblage so many facts about Britany Rodgers's life that he would have filled hours, facts significant and meaningless alike, from the subject of her fourth-grade Montana history report to the contents of a diary she had abandoned when she was fourteen. Despite never meeting her, he knew the sound of her laugh and of her voice as captured in home videos and, as a young woman, from a voicemail she had left her mother during her sophomore year which contained an apology after the two had an argument. He knew her friends and her teachers and the contents of her school locker, knew her favorite foods and the frustrations with chemistry she'd aired in the margins of her textbook. The closest he had come to her was through the lyrics to songs she had written. There, he heard pieces of the woman she was becoming, yet she mainly seemed a girl still trying to define herself.

Beyond these collections of facts and gathered digital data and handwritten lyrics, he knew nothing. He had never met her. He could not know the tilt of her head when she felt embarrassed or the fragrance of her hair when she departed in the morning for school, could not know the thoughts she held within when thinking about the future she desired or understand the motivation that placed her beside a spa at a lakefront mansion occupied by strangers. How was it possible to know intimate details of another's life and have that person remain a stranger?

He looked across the water and then around the boat, looking at his two friends and at Veronica, herself practically a stranger to him. She made eye contact with him and asked, "Is this where they found her?"

Wendell nodded. "I…I thought I should stop. I don't know exactly why, but it feels like I owe her something." Veronica reached up and grasped his hand. "It's probably stupid," he said.

"It's not," Veronica and Christina said simultaneously.

"I felt, I don't know, compelled…" he said, then paused. "She was alone out here. She, she…this is silly."

Veronica stood and gathered Wendell in a hug. "It's not," she said.

"I didn't even know her."

"All the more reason," she said. She dipped under his arm, held her head against his chest.

"I brought flowers," he said. "In my pack."

"I'll get them," Christina said. She retrieved his pack from the stern and brought it to him.

"They're probably a mess," he said. He took the pack from Christina. "Crammed in here like this. I wasn't thinking." He retrieved a cellophane bundle of pink roses, battered but still pretty. "Her mother said she liked pink."

"They're perfect," Veronica said.

He removed the flowers from their package and then, leaning far over the bow, placed them on the lake's surface as if a gentle touch could make up for the absence of ceremony demonstrated on a dark October night the previous year. No one spoke. The movement of the water slowly pulled the flowers away from the boat. Wendell watched as the individual stems of the loose bouquet drifted apart.

Wendell turned away and looked at Joel, who stood behind the wheel. Wendell said, "Get me on solid ground, would you? I've had my fill of this lake."

A late afternoon summer thunderstorm brewed in the south. Dark clouds swirled above the lake and stacked against the mountains. As they sped westward toward the safe harbor of Joel and Christina's dock and the cozy comfort of their cottage, the wind rose, and the lake surface began to turn choppy as if the approaching storm and the lake warned them to hasten their passage to the other side.

Acknowledgements

My wife and I moved to Montana's Flathead Valley seven years ago. Those early days in a new place meant a lot of time exploring life at a lower elevation (having lived in Wyoming and Colorado) and amidst more cloudy days than we'd been accustomed. We found a charming place that leaned a bit Pacific Northwest even as it remained Rocky Mountain West with a few more old loggers and a few less old cowboys, the best chai tea I've ever tasted, and the most breathtaking lake I've ever seen. I have lived in the Mountain West all my life, so I am accustomed to friendly people, expansive vistas, and the homecoming scent of pine. But each place has its own flavor, and this one was filled with new faces, some new rhythms, and lots of new country to explore. That meant a lot of walking, sometimes in the back alleys of the valley's villages and working towns, but more often on trails in thick woods. In Montana, if you walk regularly, you walk in all kinds of weather and under all kinds of skies. It was on those walks amid the tugging appeal of new place that the I found the origins of what became *The Other Side*. Part of the inspiration was simply what my friend Al calls "moody weather". The book emerged in a time when my children, now grown, began to start their own families, which created a lot of backwards glances, including thankfulness for the good, safe fortunes of their youth but also thoughts on times when real crime crossed the path of my own youth. And part of the book was found watching yet another achingly beautiful Western place try to find its balance as new faces seek it out, and in doing so bring new ideas, new money, and new pressures to a state that has struggled to diversify its economy. One result that has echoed among so many desirable mountain towns is that those who keep a place safe, vibrant, and open-minded—its cops, nurses, teachers, and artists—can no longer afford to live in them.

Moving also meant meeting new people, so many of whom have been instrumental in my ability to write this novel. I am particularly indebted to Al Czarnowski, whose weekly conversations fuel my creative soul and whose early reading of the manuscript gave me belief in it. Jana Felt was not only a helpful reader on sections of the book, her baking prowess has fueled me in other ways, and the community hub she is building with a business that feeds the bellies and the spirits of our little village made Lake Baked/Riverview Bar the logical place to launch this book. Among other Montanans who read and commented on parts of the book, I am thankful to Marsha Sultz, Carol Vincent, Marion Foley, Tom Jones, and Pauline Puuri. Special thanks go to Lynne Reddig for sharing with me her story of a mother's heartache; my characters cannot live up to her grace but I hope they cast an authentic shadow of it.

A Montanan who proved indispensable to writing a crime novel set in the Flathead Valley was Travis Bruyer. Travis not only read an early draft of the manuscript, as a retired Sheriff's Detective, he patiently guided me through questions on police investigative procedures, witness/suspect interview approaches, and law enforcement culture. Any failures, fictions, or fallacies regarding law enforcement are of my own making, and I hope Travis and others will be forgiving. Encountering Travis was one of those serendipitous events; when he substituted for a colleague at a community policing event, I discovered not only an experienced, caring cop but a filmmaker who intuitively understood the balancing act between accuracy and art.

There are many friends, resources, readers, and confidants far from Montana as well, and this book, like the others, would not exist without them. Room does not permit me to name all here. I am humbled by their support. The first reader and critic I always turn to is my youngest daughter, Sydney; she is capable of the candor to ask her dad tough questions, not something always present in daughters who love their fathers; she is an insightful, intuitive reader—so much so she will remain stuck with seeing many more books in their roughest stages.

I count myself as blessed to have a number of people who indulged my requests to read early versions of manuscripts; their patience and guidance is far greater than any simple thanks can convey; chief among my regulars are Tim Sandlin are Susan Yandell. On the best writing days, their voices are in my head. Tim has been a tireless champion and is one of the most generous people I've ever met; thanks to Tim, my work has been fueled by fellow Jackson Hole Writers Conference faculty members, the friends I have made there, and by the enthusiasm of its students. Catherine Mackenzie, without hesitation, found time she surely didn't have and provided a reading of a book that still needed more work than her kind heart might confess, one that bolstered my confidence when I needed it.

The "Dames of Detection" at Level Best Books are gracious ladies with a dedication to authors that is difficult to find in the publishing world. My humble thanks to Harriette Sackler for taking a chance on me and to Shawn Simmons for so ably wearing all the many hats required of her.

This book is dedicated to my late father. Both he and my mother never once flinched when their son, the first family to complete a college degree, decided it was a wise move to try and earn a living by words. I hope I have made them both proud.

Thank you for the unwavering support of my three daughters—Jennifer, Abbey, and Sydney, who not only steadfastly believed in me but who are quick to ask, "How's the writing going, Dad" and to indulge in long conversations about books, writing, and big ideas. They are extraordinary women.

There are not words that can express all that I owe to my wife and life partner Patti. She's never once stopped believing in me and has long been diligent in reminding me to write the stories I need to write. She manages the uncanny and unnatural position of hearing a story even while it is still formulating in my head with grace and enthusiasm. She regularly sacrifices in order that I might pursue the books, characters, and ideas that wake me in the middle of the night and follow me through my days. This book, and all the others, would not exist without her.

About the Author

The Other Side, a contemporary mystery novel, is the crime fiction debut from Mark Leichliter. Writing as Mark Hummel, he is the author of the contemporary literary novel *In the Chameleon's Shadow* and the short story collection *Lost & Found.* His fiction, poetry, and essays have regularly appeared in a variety of literary journals including such publications as *The Bloomsbury Review, Dogwood, Fugue, Talking River Review, Weber: The Contemporary West,* and *Zone 3.*

A former college professor and writing program director, he has also served as a teacher in an independent high school, directed a writers' conference, worked as a librarian, and taught on the faculty of several writers' conferences. He is the founding editor of the nonfiction magazine *bioStories.*

A native of Wyoming, Leichliter lives in Montana's Flathead Valley.

Author website: http://markleichliter.com/

Twitter: https://twitter.com/LeichliterMark

CPSIA information can be obtained
at www.ICGtesting.com
Printed in the USA
JSHW050823250222
23323JS00003B/5

9 781953 789525